I0719127

Vigilant

Vigilant

The Night Guardians Series

By

Sara Davison

Vigilant
Published by Mountain Brook Ink
White Salmon, WA U.S.A.

The website addresses shown in this book are not intended in any way to be or imply an endorsement on the part of Mountain Brook Ink, nor do we vouch for their content.

This story is a work of fiction. All characters and events are the product of the author's imagination. Any resemblance to any person, living or dead, is coincidental.

Scripture taken from the Holy Bible, NEW INTERNATIONAL VERSION®, NIV® Copyright © 1973, 1978, 1984, 2011 by Biblica, Inc.® Used by permission. All rights reserved worldwide.

The Author is represented by and this book is published in association with the literary agency of WordServe Literary Group, Ltd, www.wordserveliterary.com.

The Team: Miralee Ferrell, Nikki Wright, Cindy Jackson
Cover Design: Indie Cover Design, Lynnette Bonner Designer

Mountain Brook Ink is an inspirational publisher offering fiction you can believe in.
Printed in the United States of America

Dedication

To my dad, who claims to love all my stories (and who assures everyone he meets, including perfect strangers, that they will love them too). I am blessed to have such a wonderful, godly father.

To first responders and child support workers who witness the worst of humanity on a daily basis. You wield the torch that beats back the darkness, if only a little, for us all. Thank you.

And always and above all, to the One who gives the stories, and who is always near to the broken-hearted. It is all from you and for you.

Acknowledgments

It is my daily joy to share life with my husband Michael and our three (almost adult) kids, Luke, Julia, and Seth. I could not do what I do without the support and encouragement of all of you.

Thank you to early readers who offered the constructive criticism and advice that helped to shape and strengthen this book. Special thanks to Jordan Hageman, whose honest feedback and invaluable insights helped make this story better in more ways than I can say. I owe you a great deal. And to Ramona Maynard, friend and former police officer, who read the manuscript for procedural accuracy. Any mistakes in that regard are entirely my own.

To my agent Sarah Joy Freese, and to Greg Johnson and the amazing team at WordServe Literary – thank you for your unwavering support and encouragement. It means so much to have you standing behind me.

And to Miralee Ferrell, Nikki Wright, and the rest of the team at Mountain Brook Ink, thank you for believing in me and in my stories. I'm thrilled to be part of the family!

Defend the weak and the fatherless;
uphold the cause of the poor and the oppressed.
Rescue the weak and the needy;
deliver them from the hand of the wicked.
(Psalm 82:3-4 NIV)

Chapter One

Luke's eyes widened at the sight of the knife.

"Hold out your hand, like this." His older brother Ben held up his palm.

Luke's breath came in short gasps as he lifted a pale, shaking hand into the air over his crossed legs.

"Ready?" Sliding one hand under Luke's to hold it still, Ben moved the knife until it hovered over the soft flesh of Luke's palm.

He swallowed hard and nodded, his eyes locked on the sharp tip of the jackknife.

"Look at me."

Tilting his head up to meet his brother's stare, Luke sucked in a breath as the knife

pierced his skin.

"All done. See?"

Luke looked down at the drops of blood rising to the surface of his skin and trickling into his palm. The movement of the knife caught his eye and he watched, fascinated, as Ben sliced a small cut into his own hand and snapped the blade shut before dropping it onto the floor. In the glimmer of light from their bedroom that shafted through the slight crack in the closet door, Ben's forehead was wrinkled in concentration. Luke suppressed a nervous giggle.

Ben held out his hand.

Luke pressed his palm to his brother's, the blood a damp and sticky warmth mingling between their clasped hands.

"Now repeat after me. I, Luke ..."

The grim tone of his brother's voice squelched any desire to laugh. "I, Luke ..."

"Do solemnly swear ..."

"Do solemnly swear ..."

"To lay down my life for my brother."

Luke looked up, his eyes narrowing in confusion.

"It means you have to be willing to die for me," Ben explained.

Luke hesitated.

"I'd do it for you in a minute, Luke. We have to take care of each other."

He nodded. That much he understood. Even though his brother was just ten, three years older than Luke, Ben was the only one who'd ever taken care of him. "To lay down my life for my brother."

"And to always be there for him, no matter what."

Luke repeated the words, a powerful feeling growing inside him, like a balloon expanding in his chest. He wasn't sure what it was, but he knew the words they were saying to each other carried a special magic. When Ben repeated the words, the feeling grew so strong that tears welled in his eyes. Turning his head, he wiped them away quickly with the worn-thin sleeve of his train-covered pajama top.

Ben squeezed his fingers. "Now we're not just brothers, we're blood brothers. That's even better, stronger. It means we'll always be together, and we'll always keep each other safe, okay?"

"Okay."

The front door slammed. Panic swept over Ben's face, but he pushed back his shoulders, trying, like Luke knew he always did, to look brave.

"Ron ... no!"

Ben's grip on Luke's hand tightened as their mother cried out from downstairs.

"Out of my way!" The sound of a fist smacking flesh hurt Luke's ears, as if he had taken the blow himself. He winced. A kitchen chair crashed to the floor.

Their mother didn't make another sound.

Ben pushed onto his knees. He didn't look scared now, he

looked mad.

Luke's heart sank. "Ben, don't go. You can't help Mom. When you try, it makes things worse."

His brother's breaths came out in short, angry gasps, but he didn't leave, only peered through the small crack in the closet door.

Luke tugged on his hand. "Maybe someone will come and help us," he whispered.

Ben whipped around to face him. Closing the fingers of his free hand around Luke's upper arm, he shook him. "Stop saying that. No one's coming to help us. You know that. No one ever comes. It's just you and me."

Heavy boots tromped up the stairs.

Ben let go of Luke's arm and raised a finger to his lips. Luke nodded. If they were really quiet, their dad might not find them. Maybe he wouldn't come into their room tonight. Sometimes he left them alone and went into his own room. Luke slid the hand not clutching Ben's behind his back and crossed his fingers tightly.

The bedroom door flew open. Luke's stomach tightened. A cry rose in his throat, and he bit his bottom lip hard to keep the sound inside.

"Where are you!"

Objects clattered off the walls. Luke jumped as something heavy thudded against the door of the closet. Still holding his brother's hand, he pressed against the wall behind him. He and Ben didn't have a lot of clothes, and what they had they usually tossed over a wooden chair in the corner of their room, so only bare hangers hung from the rod above their heads. *Make us invisible. Make us invisible.* He held his hand in front of his face. Blood dripped down his wrist. His throat tightened. No one ever answered his plea, or prayer, or whatever it was. Ben was right. They were on their own.

Their father flung open the closet door so hard it crashed against the wall. "There you are."

The smell of whiskey filled the air, so strong Luke's eyes

stung.

Ben shrank back beside him as his dad's arm clawed through the air.

"Get out here!"

"Ben!" Luke cried out in desperation as his dad grasped his brother's arm and yanked hard. Luke held onto Ben's hand as tightly as he could, but his dad was too strong, and Ben's fingers slid from his. Luke doubled over and buried his face in the stained, threadbare carpet. The musty smell clogged his nostrils. His thin shoulders shook with sobs.

"You come when I call, do ya hear me, boy?"

Luke squeezed his eyes shut at the sharp smack of a hand against bare skin.

His brother cried out.

Luke pushed himself upright. Something cold and hard pressed into his stinging palm. His hand closed over it. The jackknife. He stared at it for a moment then swiped the tears off his cheeks with the knuckles of his trembling hand.

His fingers tightened around the handle of the knife as he fumbled with the blade. *We're blood brothers now. It means we'll always be together, and we'll always keep each other safe.*

Luke pushed back his own shoulders, trying to make himself feel brave. The knife helped a little. Gritting his teeth, he struggled to his feet.

Across the room, his dad swung a clenched fist and smashed it hard into Ben's face. Ben staggered backward, and his head cracked against the metal footboard of the small cot. He fell to the floor with a hard thud and lay still.

The knot in Luke's stomach grew tighter as blood seeped slowly into the carpet beneath his brother's head.

"That'll teach ya."

Ben moaned and tried to roll over.

Their father aimed a boot at his face.

"No!" Luke sprinted across the room and raised the knife. Before his father could react, he swiped the blade as hard as he could across his dad's arm.

"What the ...?" Curse words filled the air.

Luke skidded to a stop. A line of blood crawled across his father's forearm. He didn't see his dad's other hand shoot out until strong fingers gripped his small wrist. Pain slithered up and down his arm like a writhing snake. The knife fell from his hand, taking with it the small amount of courage he had mustered. He stared into his father's dark, wild eyes.

"I'll kill you, you little ..."

Letting go of Luke's wrist, his father wrapped large, calloused hands around his neck.Luke struggled to breathe but couldn't draw in air. His father increased the pressure until black spots shimmered in front of Luke's eyes. His hands raked empty air. The room spun around him.

Suddenly, his father's grip loosened. Luke dropped to the floor, coughing and gasping for breath. Holding his throbbing throat, he looked up. His father had grabbed his neck with one hand. His bloodshot eyes bulged. The bright red on his cheeks and nose faded to white.

Luke pushed against the carpet with both feet and scrambled out of the way as his dad crashed to the floor. He stared at the jackknife protruding from his dad's neck. Slowly, Luke lifted his head. Ben was on his knees at their dad's feet. Blood trailed across the carpet.

"Ben ...?"

Pain-filled eyes met his. "Luke," Ben whispered, his voice ragged. "You okay?"

Luke nodded then leaped toward his brother as Ben started to topple forward. He was too heavy for Luke to hold, and he struggled to lower Ben to the floor and over onto his side.

"Ben! Wake up." Luke shook him by the shoulder.

Ben didn't open his eyes.

Luke sank to the floor beside him. Grasping his brother's hand, he pressed it against his own blood-stained palm, rocking back and forth. Tears slid down his cheeks, dripping onto their clasped fingers.

His brother was gone and so was the magic. He was completely alone.

Chapter Two

Nicole Hunter nudged the vase of pink plastic daisies in the middle of the table aside and swiped at a pile of crumbs with a damp cloth. The diner was quiet tonight. The last of the customers in her section had finished their burgers and fries and gone ten minutes earlier, although the aroma of hot grease still hung in the air above their table. The tip they'd left her wasn't worth much more than the crumbs she'd gathered in the cloth. She sighed. Given the nasty February blizzard that had swooped in and ground life in the city to a halt, it wasn't likely there'd be many more people in tonight. She'd have to grab an extra shift on the weekend if she wanted to indulge in anything frivolous in the next few weeks. *Like eating.*

A wry grin crossed Nicole's face as she palmed the two quarters and slipped them into her apron pocket, then leaned across the table to take care of a puddle of spilled milk. No matter what, she wouldn't go hungry. She worked hard to earn enough to make ends meet, refusing to rely on the money her parents sent her every month. That would mean admitting the payment was a fair trade for their actual presence in her life. So the money sat in her account, drawing interest from the bank, if not from her.

A movement outside caught her eye. Nicole straightened with a groan and pushed a hand into her lower back. She caught her reflection and wrinkled her nose at the freckles sprinkled across it. Would she ever outgrow those? She tucked a strand of blonde hair that had come loose from her ponytail behind one ear as she peered out through the lacework of frost etched across the large front window of Joe's Diner. Wet, heavy snow fell from the sky, covering Toronto in a thick blanket of white that faded to soot-gray almost as soon as it landed on the streets and sidewalks. Nicole frowned. "Connie." She twisted her head to call out over her shoulder. "Your friends are on their way."

Joe's wife, her short gray hair neatly covered in a net, pushed through the swinging kitchen doors and out into the diner, wiping her hands on a towel. "The boys coming, sweetie?"

Nicole's lips twitched. Although it was a bit tricky assessing the ages of the men trooping over from the homeless shelter, most of them had to be about Connie's age or not much younger than her seventy years. Still, she always called them *the boys* with such affection in her voice it was clearly a term of endearment to her. Respect, even. Nicole turned back and narrowed her eyes, trying to distinguish between the snow-covered shapes huddled together as they passed beneath the dim glow of the streetlight on the corner. "Yep. Looks like four or five of them."

Connie tossed her towel below the cash register and glanced at the clock above the door. "Almost eight. Right on time." She pulled a pot from the coffee maker on the counter. "They'll be looking for this, with all that snow coming down." She lifted the pot in Nicole's direction. "Sure you don't want to help them tonight?"

Nicole bit her lip. It wouldn't kill her to take a turn waiting on the group of men that wound up at Joe's most nights looking for hot coffee and a warm smile. Connie served both as naturally as she breathed. As good as Nicole had become at pouring coffee, though, she'd never been able to master the other, not for the unkempt people that trudged in sporting several layers of clothes and several more layers of grime.

Do it Nicole. Don't be such a coward.

Nicole sighed as she grabbed the pile of dirty dishes from her table and swung around to face Connie. "Do you think you can handle them tonight? I'll take these dishes to the kitchen and see if Joe needs any help."

Connie's bright blue eyes didn't lose their sparkle, although her shoulders drooped a little. "Maybe next time?"

"Sure." Nicole leaned in to press a kiss to the soft, papery cheek of the woman who had all but adopted her after she started working at the diner. "Next time."

Connie tugged the pencil she always teased Nicole for carrying around with her, old-school style, loose from behind Nicole's ear and held it out to her. "Joe can handle the kitchen, Nic. Why don't you go home? Your shift was supposed to end a couple of hours ago."

Nicole shook her head as she took the pencil from her friend. "I'm okay. I can stick around as long as you need me."

"We'll be fine. With this weather, no one else is likely to come in. Go home, get some rest."

"Well, if you're sure …" It *had* been a long day, since she'd started at seven that morning.

"I'm sure."

"All right then." Nicole saluted her friend with the pencil before turning to head to the kitchen. "I'll see you tomorrow."

The jangle of bells stopped her short.

As the men she'd seen coming down the sidewalk spilled into the diner, Nicole jumped back between two tables. She clutched the dishes tightly as the men swept by.

The last man through the door stopped long enough to remove a rumpled fedora from his head and dip his chin. "Ma'am."

Nicole nodded and watched him as he made his way toward the rear of the diner where Connie poured steaming coffee into mugs. With her eyes still on the corner table, Nicole stepped into the aisle and right into a tall man dressed in a long black coat, damp from the falling snow. When his hands instinctively cupped her shoulders, she jerked away, sending the mug on top of the pile she carried crashing to the floor.

"I'm sorry." The man crouched down to retrieve the broken dish. His dark, tousled hair brushed the collar of his wool coat.

Warmth crept up her neck as Nicole set the rest of the dishes on a table and dropped to her knees, reaching underneath a chair for a piece that had skittered across the black and white tiles. "My fault. I didn't see you come in."

The man straightened and held out his free hand to help her stand. Nicole hesitated before placing her hand in his. His strong fingers closed over hers and he pulled her to her feet. After eight years of working in the diner, she'd come up with three hard-and-fast rules to discourage unwanted male attention. Third on her list was to not hold anyone's gaze longer than necessary. Still, she found herself staring into dark, almost black, eyes, unable to look away. Maybe because he still had her fingers clasped in his, which, incidentally, fell under rule number two—avoid physical contact at all costs.

Nicole blinked rapidly and pulled her hand away. She spun around and grabbed the pile of dishes she'd set on the table and held it toward him. "Here. I'll take them."

The man tipped his hand and the pieces of ceramic clinked softly onto the top plate.

She nodded in the direction of the nearly empty dining area. "Sit wherever you like. Connie will be right with you." When he didn't move, Nicole maneuvered around him and strode toward the swinging doors.

Joe glanced over at her from his place at the grill as she came into the kitchen. "You all right, sweetheart?"

"Yes. Sure. Fine. Of course." She dropped the dishes onto the counter with a thud. "I … broke a mug."

His forehead wrinkled. "Nothing to get upset about. It's not the first dish to break in this diner, and it won't be the last, I'm sure."

"I'm not upset. Only a little tired. Connie suggested I call it an early night and head home." She reached behind her but paused midway through untying the strings of her apron. "Unless you need my help here?"

Joe waved his spatula through the air. "No, go. Everything's pretty much done."

The doors swung open and Connie flew into the kitchen. "Checks came today, Joe. The boys'd like burgers with their coffee."

"Gotcha." Joe winked at Nicole as he returned to his grill.

Connie tucked a loose curl beneath her hair net. "Nic, I'm sorry. I know I told you to go, but if you're really okay to stay, you could take that table of two for me."

"Two?"

"That man who came in behind the boys says he's waiting for someone. I seated him, but if you could take care of them, that would be great."

"Connie, I know what you're—"

Connie's smile deepened the laugh lines around her eyes. "I'm not match-making, honest. Not this time. I really need your help, please."

Nicole's shoulders slumped. She could never refuse Connie anything. Not that she minded helping, but she knew her friend had an ulterior motive and that, by staying, Nicole was playing right into her hands. With an exaggerated sigh that only served to widen Connie's smile, she re-tied her apron and headed for the doors.

"Although …"

Groaning, Nicole turned to face her friend and raised an eyebrow.

"… it wouldn't hurt you to keep an open mind. He seems like a very nice man—with no ring on his finger."

With a quick glance toward the doorway, Nicole moved closer to Connie and lowered her voice. "I'm sure he is nice, but I really don't think he's my type."

"You always say that. I'm beginning to wonder if you even know what your type is." Connie laid a comforting hand, rough and worn from years of washing dishes and waiting tables, on her arm. "Not everyone leaves, Nic."

Nicole swallowed hard. "I know. But it's better this way. For now." She patted her friend's hand before taking a deep breath and pushing through the kitchen doors.

Chapter Three

Bells jangled loudly as the diner door swung open again. Nicole pulled her pale green sweater closer as a blast of frigid air blew inside. A man bundled in a red Columbia ski-jacket and scarf stepped into the restaurant and pushed the door shut behind him. He yanked off his gloves and tucked them under one arm so he could blow on his clasped hands.

When he raised his head, a grin appeared beneath round, fogged glasses. Nicole smiled as he pulled them off. He wasn't quite as tall as the man she'd bumped into, and his dark hair was shorter, curling just over his ears, but the intense black eyes scanning the restaurant were the same. They had to be brothers. When he lifted a hand and started across the room, Nicole grabbed the coffee pot and followed him.

"Holden!" The first man jumped to his feet and pulled him into an embrace, slapping him on the back.

"Hey, Gage."

The two men slid into opposite sides of the red vinyl booth.

Nicole raised the pot. "Coffee?"

"That'd be great." Holden pushed his mug toward her before pulling off his coat.

Nicole filled both cups. She felt Gage's eyes on her but focused her attention on the steaming liquid. Clutching the handle tightly, she looked at Holden. "Do you need a minute?"

He glanced from her to his brother before closing the menu. "No. That's okay. I'll have a cheeseburger deluxe with fries."

"I'll have the same." Gage picked up both menus and smiled as he handed them to her.

Joe passed the plates of food to Nicole through the kitchen window a few minutes later, and she set them in front of the men and left quickly. Before she pushed through the kitchen doors, she glanced at the booth. Gage's hands were folded and both he and his brother had bowed their heads over their food. Nicole leaned a shoulder against the doorframe and watched them, absently reaching for the small gold cross she wore on a chain around her neck and rubbing it between her thumb and forefinger. *Interesting.* She dropped the cross and pushed away from the frame and through the swinging doors.

After grabbing a cloth from the basin on the kitchen shelf, she headed back into the diner and started scrubbing the tops of tables and polishing napkin holders, trying to keep busy. When there was nothing else to do, she returned to the counter and gathered the scattered sections of a newspaper. In spite of her efforts not to notice them, her gaze slid over to the brothers several times, lingering a few seconds when Gage's voice rose, his hands gesturing wildly as he told a story.

Holden burst out laughing.

A grin crossed Nicole's lips just as Gage glanced her way. He broke off the story mid-sentence, an uncertain smile breaking across his face as he slowly lowered his arms. She dropped her gaze quickly to the front page of the paper she clutched in both hands. Another child abducted. Chills rippled through her. That was the second child to have gone missing in Toronto in the last month, and no trace of either had been found. Nicole stuffed the other sections inside that one and tossed the paper into the blue recycle bin beneath the counter.

Her gaze flicked from one corner booth, where the boys chatted away noisily as they slurped their coffees, to the other. *Coward. Stop avoiding your customers. The sooner you serve them, the sooner they will finish and leave.* She walked over to the counter and grabbed the coffee pot.

Holden lifted his hand before she could fill his mug again. "No thanks, I need to get going."

He reached for his wallet, but Gage shook his head. "I've got it."

"Thanks."

A burst of laughter from the boys in the corner rolled across the room. Nicole glanced over. Connie held a coffee pot in one hand and had rested a hand on the shoulder of the man with the rumpled fedora. Nicole swallowed and shifted her attention to her own table, stepping out of the way as Holden stood and pulled on his coat and hat. He held out a hand toward his brother. Gage grasped it tightly.

Nicole waited until the diner door shut behind Holden before turning to Gage. He was studying her intently, and she swallowed hard.

"That's a beautiful necklace."

Nicole closed one hand around the delicate cross. "Thank you."

His eyes held hers for a few seconds. "Would you … have a cup of coffee with me sometime?"

Her throat tightened. "Oh, I don't think—"

"No time like the present." Connie came up behind Nicole and took the coffee pot from her hand, gesturing toward the table with her other.

"Connie, I don't think he meant now. Besides, I need to …" She glanced around the empty diner. Every surface gleamed, and she mentally kicked herself for finishing all her work. She absolutely could not break her number one rule, which was—

"Go ahead, honey. It's quiet tonight. Sit down and relax for a few minutes."

—to never, ever sit down at a table with a customer. Nicole bit her lip as her friend grasped her elbow and guided her to the seat across from Gage. The rich aroma of coffee curled up around the pot in her hand and wafted on the steam. Connie grabbed a clean mug from the table behind her and filled a cup for both of them before returning to the boys.

Nicole shot a frustrated look at her retreating friend. *So much for not match-making.*

When she looked at Gage, he had a sheepish look on his face. "Sorry about that. As flattering as it is that you literally have to be pushed into having coffee with me, if you have other things you need to do, please don't feel you have to stay."

Grab the out he's giving you. She leaned against the bench with a sigh. "No, it's okay. It feels good to get off my feet. Even involuntarily."

Gage grinned. "On the plus side, you've saved me."

"From?"

He lifted his mug. "Drinking alone. Apparently, that's a bad sign or something."

"I'm pretty sure that's alcohol, not coffee." She pressed her lips together to suppress a smile.

"Still, better to err on the side of caution, I always say." Gage sipped from his cup before setting it down. "So, Nicole." He nodded at her nametag.

She was used to strangers calling her by name but hearing it from this man sent her heart racing. Her jaw tightened. This was ridiculous. She was a reasonably high-functioning adult, most days. Chances were good that she could carry on a coherent conversation for a few minutes without dire consequences. Nicole drew in a deep breath and met his gaze. A lock of dark hair had fallen over his eye. A sudden, inane urge to reach out and brush it back struck her, but she pushed the thought away.

"Will your boyfriend mind you having coffee with me?"

Her fingers tightened around the mug.

Gage winced. "I'm sorry. That wasn't very subtle, was it? I'm usually a little smoother than that. Not that I'm in the habit of picking up women I've recently met." His cheeks flushed. "Not that I'm trying to pick you up ... oh man." He lifted his cup of coffee and sniffed it. "Are you sure this is coffee and not alcohol?"

Nicole gave in with a small laugh. "So, Gage."

His mouth turned up in a half-smile.

"That's an unusual name. Let me guess, your mother is a big fan of romance novels?"

The smile disappeared. "Actually, no. I was named after my grandfather, Gage Kelly the first. He died the night I was born, in the same hospital. My father, Gage Kelly the second, rushed me to his room when I was barely a few minutes old and placed me in his arms. My grandfather took one look at me, smiled, closed his eyes, and he was gone."

Nicole pressed two fingers to her mouth. "I'm so sorry. I had no …"

His lips twitched.

He wouldn't. She dropped her hand. "You totally made that up, didn't you?"

"Yep. My grandfather's name is Raymond, and he's still alive, as far as I know. I haven't seen him in years."

"And the name Gage?"

"You're probably right, and it was the romance novel thing. My mother died when I was young, and I don't remember what she liked to read, if anything."

Nicole's eyes narrowed. She wasn't about to fall for that one again.

He met her gaze. "That one's true, actually."

"Oh." Her stomach tightened slightly, but she forced herself to relax. She'd known the man for five minutes. Why should she care whether or not he'd grown up without a mother? Like she had. "That's really sad."

Gage shrugged. "Them's the breaks." He rubbed his forehead with the side of his hand. "Wow. No idea where that came from. I don't think I've ever used that expression in my life. Sounded like something out of *Goodfellas*." He laughed and lifted his mug to his lips.

Her eyebrows rose. "Why are you laughing? Am I funny? Do I amuse you?"

Gage snorted and nearly spewed his mouthful of coffee across the table. He set down his mug so he could reach for a napkin and press it to his mouth. When he had composed himself, he lowered the napkin and looked at her. "You know *Goodfellas*?"

"Way too well." She rolled her eyes. "The brother of a friend of mine in high school loved it so it was often on at her place when I was hanging out there."

"Did your parents know that? It wasn't exactly wholesome teenage viewing."

Nicole ran a finger around the rim of her mug. "My parents weren't around much. They really didn't know what was going on in my life."

"I'm sorry to hear that."

She lifted her shoulders. "Them's the breaks."

The compassion in his dark eyes stirred something deep inside her. Something she would rather not have to deal with tonight. Or ever. She shifted in her seat. "So your dad raised you and Holden on his own?"

A shadow crossed his face. "Actually no. He died when we were young too. Holden and I are all that's left of the Kelly clan."

"I'm sorry."

"Don't be." Gage crumpled the napkin he'd used to wipe his face and tossed it onto an empty plate. "It's been the two of us for a long time. At least we have each other."

The stab of pain that shot through her must have reflected on her face. He tilted his head. "What is it?"

"It's nothing. I just …"

"You don't have any family?"

Nicole had no idea how to answer that. Technically family members existed. That didn't mean she wasn't alone. Except for Connie and Joe, of course, who were more like her parents than her own parents had ever … She straightened on the bench abruptly. That thought was like eye contact with her male customers, lingering too long could only bring trouble. "Not really." She let out a short laugh. "This has to be the most depressing first-date conversation ever."

Heat flared in her cheeks. "Not that this is a date." She tipped her nearly-empty mug toward her and gazed into it. "You might be right. I think Connie may have slipped something into this before she filled our cups."

Gage chuckled. "Yeah, we kind of skipped the ice-breaker stage, didn't we?"

"We definitely did. I'm not sure, but I think it was the fake dead grandfather story that set the tone for the evening."

"That was mean, I admit. Let me make it up to you. Have dinner with me next week."

Say yes. For once in your life, take a chance. "I can't. I work long hours, and when I'm not here, I'm doing research for my thesis. I … don't have time. I'm sorry."

He contemplated her in silence. Nicole bit her lip. Had anyone ever looked at her that way? *He's reading me.* She was used to men looking at the cover she hid behind. She didn't love it, but the sensation was familiar and almost comfortable. Few, however, made any attempt to search deeper, to find out her story, who she really was. Which was exactly how she wanted it.

Wasn't it?

I can't do this. "I should get to work." She slid to the end of the bench and stood.

"Are you sure? It seems pretty—"

"I'm sure. Besides, we're … we're closing."

Gage glanced over at the corner table where the boys appeared to have settled in for the night. When he turned to face her, Nicole crossed her arms. For a few seconds, Gage didn't move then he grabbed his coat and pushed to his feet. She stepped back as he slung it over his shoulders and thrust an arm into the sleeve.

"For interest's sake …" His voice was low and soft.

She looked up. His dark eyes still studied her, as though trying to figure her out. *Good luck with that.* She'd been trying to do the same thing for twenty-nine years and hadn't gotten very far. The tingling in her stomach intensified as she waited for him to finish his sentence.

"If we'd gone the ice-breaker route, discussed something a little more neutral, like the terrible weather we've been having, or last night's hockey game …?"

"We'd still be closing."

Gage nodded slowly. "All right then." He pulled his wallet out of the pocket of his jeans.

Nicole reached out to straighten the glass vinegar bottle and the beige and black plastic salt and pepper shakers on the table. A small tremor worked its way through her fingers, and she pulled her hand away quickly and stuck it into her apron pocket.

Gage dropped some bills on the table and smiled. "Thanks, Nicole. Everything was … great." He took a step toward the door then turned around. "Maybe I'll stop in again sometime. We could talk about how the Leafs are doing."

She shook her head. "It's usually a lot busier in here. I don't make a habit of sitting down with customers."

"Ah." He pulled on his gloves. "It was nice to meet you then."

"You too," she mumbled, pressing her palm against the speckled Formica tabletop and forcing herself not to turn and watch as he crossed the diner. When she was sure he was gone, she grabbed the mugs from the table and headed to the kitchen, Connie's words still echoing in her head.

Nicole did know that not everyone left. They just left *her*.

Chapter Four

"Hey, Mom." Detective Daniel Grey crouched down and ran his gloved hand over the top of the smooth, brown headstone, brushing away the snow. "It's me."

She wasn't there, but even now, two years after her sudden, unexpected death from complications after what should have been routine surgery, it helped Daniel to have a place to come and talk to her, to focus his grief. "I'm sorry I haven't been here in a while. Life's been a little crazy the last few weeks, since Sharleen and I got assigned that child abduction case at work."

He pulled off one glove and ran his fingers over the letters engraved in the stone. *Cara Elizabeth Grey. Beloved wife and mother*. His chest squeezed. *Yes, she was.* He tugged his glove on and sank back on his haunches. "And no, since it's the first thing you'd ask me if you were still here, I'm not seeing anyone." Snow drifted down from a steel-tinged sky. Daniel brushed a few flakes from his knees. "You'll be happy to know Becca has picked up the torch from you and bugs me about that every time I see her." He sighed. "I haven't met the right woman yet, I guess. Although, even if I did I'm not sure it would work out. It's not easy being married to a cop." He let out a short laugh. "Look who I'm talking to. I don't have to tell you that, do I? Somehow you did it, but it was tough some days, wasn't it?"

It had to have been, but his mom never complained. Just prayed every day that his dad would come home to them and then left him in God's hands. Something Daniel prayed too, for himself, every time he headed out for a shift. *Maybe, if I could meet a woman with a faith like that ...*

He shook his head and pushed to his feet with a groan. He didn't have any interest in starting a relationship right now. He had to focus on his job if he wanted to prove that he and his partner could handle this case, their biggest one yet. Two missing kids were more than enough to think about. He stood for a moment, head bowed. Footsteps crunching across the snow pulled him from his reverie, and he looked over.

"Hi, Son." His dad stopped on the other side of the engraved stone and rested his cane against it. He tucked a red and black plaid scarf more securely down the front of his coat—a barrier against the icy breeze that swept through the rows of headstones—and zipped the coat to his chin.

"Hey, Pop. I didn't know you were coming here today."

"Yep. Your sister brought me. She dropped me off and went to park the car." He waved a hand toward Daniel's younger sister Becca. Her long brown hair hung over the shoulders of a multi-colored wool coat as she picked her way carefully through the cemetery toward them.

When she reached them, Daniel pulled her in for a hug. "Hey, Bec."

"Hey, yourself." She scrutinized him. "I haven't seen you in weeks. What's new? Seeing anyone these days?"

A smirk crossed Daniel's face as he glanced at his mother's grave. "See?"

Becca nudged his arm. "Well?"

He blew out a breath. "Could we talk about my love life—or lack thereof—somewhere else?"

"We could, if I ever saw you anywhere else. You haven't been over for ages."

Daniel slid an arm around his younger sister's shoulders. "Sorry about that. Work's been crazy. Tell you what, if you promise to make that fried chicken I like, I'll come by one night next week. I'm dying for a home-cooked meal. TV dinners get old pretty fast."

"I'll bet." She wrinkled her nose. "Unfortunately, I can't promise you fried chicken. My stomach does not appreciate the aroma of hot grease these days."

"What are you talking about? That's your favorite smell in

the ..." *Wait.* Was she saying what he thought? Daniel cocked his head to one side. "Something you want to tell us?"

A sheepish grin crossed her face. "I waited until we came today so I could give Mom and Dad the news together, but I'm glad you're here too. Austin and I are having a baby."

Daniel pulled his sister to him again. "Becca. Congratulations. That's the best news ever."

When he let her go, she brushed hair away from both cheeks with red-mittened hands. "Thanks. We think so too. Although ..." Tears sparkled in her eyes as she rested a hand on their mother's gravestone.

Joy and sorrow mingled in Daniel's chest. His sister and brother-in-law had been trying to get pregnant for a couple of years. As thrilled as he was for them, though, aching loss assaulted him again. Mom would have loved being a grandmother, and she would have made an amazing one.

Pop cleared his throat. "Come on now. This is a time for celebration. Mom wouldn't have wanted you to be sad. Not today." He took Becca's hands in his and kissed her cheek. "Finally. I was starting to think I would never be a grandfather." He shot a pointed look in Daniel's direction.

A conspiracy. Daniel shook his head as Becca laughed.

In spite of his dad's own admonition, a shadow crossed his face as he let go of Becca's hands. Daniel's chest squeezed. His father had married later in life, when he was almost forty. His wife had been fifteen years younger—a beautiful, vivacious twenty-five-year-old when they met, with the dark hair and bright blue eyes Daniel and Becca had inherited. The story, which both their parents loved to tell, was that they had reached for the same loaf of bread in a bakery downtown and that was all it took. A few weeks later, she confessed she'd fallen as in love with him as he had with her. As far as Daniel could tell, his dad had never quite gotten over the wonder of that. Just like it seemed he would never get over the shock of losing her.

Time to give him a moment with Mom. Daniel held out his arm. "Come on, Bec, let's go for a walk."

"Good idea. I can fill you in on all the wonderful symptoms I've been experiencing the last four months."

"Great." Daniel rolled his eyes. "We'll be back soon, Pop."

Their dad nodded, but his gaze had fallen to the stone slab at his feet.

Daniel led his sister to the shoveled-off cement walkway that wended its way around the cemetery.

They walked in silence for a couple of minutes, until one of her tan, faux-fur-rimmed boots slipped on a small patch of ice. Daniel clutched her arm tighter to keep her upright. "Watch it. We don't want anything to happen to that little one."

She patted his elbow. "Look at you, Uncle Daniel. Taking care of your niece or nephew already."

He grinned. "Uncle Daniel. I could get used to the sound of that."

"It doesn't have quite the ring of *daddy,* but I guess it will have to do, for now."

"Becca." Daniel sent his sister an exasperated look.

"All right, all right. I'll back off." She squeezed his arm. "I just want you to be happy."

"I know. But what you ecstatically married people never seem to be able to grasp is that it is possible to be happy *and* single. I have my family, my church, lots of good friends, and a job I love, most days. My life is full."

"Is it exciting?"

"What, my life?"

"Your job. Is being a detective as challenging and glamorous as it looks on TV?"

"Glamorous, no, but it's definitely challenging. I've barely been home the last few weeks. Sharleen and I have been working night and day, trying to figure out who is taking these kids so we can prevent any more from disappearing. There's a lot of pressure, believe me." He stopped and turned to face her. "And now that I'm going to have a little niece or nephew growing up in the city, I am more motivated than ever to nail this guy."

Becca slid a hand through his elbow as they started walking

again. "I hope your DS knows how lucky he is to have you and Sharleen working for him."

Daniel snorted. "There's no way DS Lector will ever consider himself lucky to have us. He is the toughest guy I've ever met. He looks at me like I'm some kind of bug crawling across the floor that he'd like nothing better than to stomp on with his boot and be done with. My only consolation is he looks at everyone else the same way." He repressed a shudder. "When I first started, I thought I'd be taking every opportunity to impress him with my superior skills and intellect, but instead I spend most of my time trying to stay out of sight. Even the veterans are terrified of him."

"Why does he still have a job?"

"Because he's the best Detective Sergeant in the city. It's not only the other cops who are scared of him, it's the criminals. The police chief loves him for that, and the Police Services Board loves the chief for appointing him, so the DS isn't going anywhere."

"Speaking of Sharleen"—Becca stepped around another icy patch in her path—"are you going to her place for dinner next Saturday night?"

His eyes narrowed. "She asked me, but I haven't said whether I'm coming or not. Why, are you going?"

"Yes, she invited Austin and me too. If you come, we can catch up there. That would be better than me having to cook for you." She flashed him the mischievous grin he was rarely able to say no to.

Daniel made a half-hearted attempt to fortify himself against it. "Since when are you and Sharleen such good friends?"

"Since forever. You know that."

"I know you've met her. I didn't realize the two of you hung out."

"We don't, usually. Mostly we talk on the phone, or text."

A growing suspicion swirled through his gut. "What do you talk about?"

"All kinds of things. Life, work, her kids …"

"So, not me."

Becca appeared to be laser-focused on the walkway in front of her as she made her way carefully across the slick surface.

Daniel let go of her and stopped walking. "Rebecca." He injected as much firmness in his voice as possible.

She faced him. "Don't do that."

"Do what?"

"Use your cop voice with me. I'm not a criminal."

"Then why do you look so guilty?"

Her shoulders slumped. "All right. Your name does come up, occasionally. We're both concerned about you. You're not getting any younger, you know."

He planted both fists on his hips. "I'm thirty-five years old, not quite ready to apply for social security yet."

Her lips twitched. "Maybe not, but you are becoming more cemented in your bachelorhood with every passing day."

Oh brother. "Putting that drama degree to good use, I see."

She ignored the dig. "What happened to that girl you brought to church a couple of months ago?"

"Who, Anna? Nothing happened to her. She was fine, last I heard."

His sister raised an eyebrow.

Daniel blew out a breath. He was tired, suddenly. Visiting his mother's grave had taken quite a bit out of him, and he didn't have it in him to have this discussion with his sister. Again. "Anna is great, but she wasn't the right one for me. And since— as you are fond of reminding me—I'm not sixteen anymore, I have no interest in dating for the sake of dating. If there's no future in it, I'm not going to waste my time. Or hers." He dropped his hands from his hips and started walking.

"Fair enough." Becca fell into step beside him. "So you'll come on Saturday?"

"Will you promise to limit the topics of conversation to work, life in general, and Tom and Sharleen's kids? It shouldn't be hard if that's really all you usually discuss with her."

"Of course."

"You'll keep my personal life off the table?"

"If that's what you want."

Daniel pursed his lips. It wasn't like his sister to capitulate to his requests that easily. "That's what I want."

"Fine." She smiled at him again and, although he tried to hold on to it, his irritation slipped from his grasp.

He sighed. "Okay then, if I can get away from work, I'll come. But enough about me. Weren't you going to tell me about your newly-acquired cravings for pickles and ice cream and all that other fun, pregnancy-related stuff?"

"Much as I'm sure you'd love to hear about all that, I'll hold off until I see you on Saturday. Dad's waiting at the car." She inclined her head toward the parking lot ahead of them. Daniel followed her gaze. Sure enough, their dad had propped his cane against the side of the car and leaned against the passenger door of Becca's white Corolla, rubbing his hands together as icy puffs of air spurted from his mouth. "I better get him back to the retirement home. He's always a bit down after we come here."

Daniel studied their dad. He was a big man, but he seemed small suddenly, shrunken. Coming here obviously took even more out of him than it did Daniel. "Do you bring him here often, then?"

She lifted a shoulder. "Every couple of weeks."

He should have known that. And taken his turn. "I'm sorry, Becca. I haven't been there for you guys lately. I'll try to do better."

"It's all right. We really do understand. And we're proud of you. Especially Dad. He brags about you to his friends all the time."

That didn't help ease the guilt any, but Daniel offered her a small smile as they made their way to her car.

Becca pulled the keys from the pocket of her coat as they approached their father. "Ready to go?"

Pop cast one more glance toward the cemetery. His eyes held sadness, but he managed a grin as he tugged his cap down over his ears. "If you are." He held out his hand to Daniel. "It was good to see you, son."

He grasped the proffered hand and pulled his dad in for a hug, slapping him on the shoulder a couple of times. "You too, Pop."

"Don't be a stranger."

"I won't. I promise." Daniel reached past his dad to open the car door. His dad settled himself on the passenger seat and Daniel closed the door, lifting a hand as the car reversed and headed for the exit. For several long moments he watched the road where the Corolla had disappeared.

He didn't make promises lightly, and he had every intention of keeping the ones he'd just made to his sister and his dad. Even if that meant fielding questions about his non-existent love life.

Ted Stiller pressed against the brick wall of the house. If his luck held, his target would be fast asleep in an upstairs bedroom, oblivious to the fact that her life was about to change forever. Blanketed in shadows, he forced himself to take slow, deep breaths. The frigid air drove icy darts into his skin, even through the black denim of his jeans.

Normally he wouldn't tug the ski mask down over his face until he'd reached the back corner of the house and disappeared from the view of anyone who might happen to drive by, but at minus ten degrees, it was too cold to wait. He grasped the bottom edge of the wool hat and yanked it down over his face. The eye holes limited his vision a little, but the protection the mask offered his cheeks and nose canceled out any potential danger.

He cursed the thinness of his gloves. It was imperative that he be able to use his hands freely, but his range of motion was hampered as his fingers stiffened in the cold, so he might as well have worn the thick leather ones he'd left in his home on Woodmount Avenue. A home he'd give anything to be in right now, sitting in front of the woodstove reading the latest John Grisham novel.

Stiller shoved back his shoulders. That would happen later,

after his job was done, a reward for the risk he was taking to follow the orders he'd received earlier that day. After tugging his gloves up a little higher, he pushed away from the wall and crept toward the rear of the house. His sneaker caught a patch of ice and he nearly lost his footing. A good reminder that even they couldn't predict every eventuality. He steadied himself with a hand pressed to the brick wall until his pulse slowed to a manageable rate.

Before rounding the building, he scanned the small, fenced-in yard. It took every ounce of patience he had not to move as cold crept from the frozen asphalt up through the bottom of his sneakers, penetrating his socks and numbing his feet.

The threat of snow hung in the air. A storm was coming, the second blizzard in two weeks, but the calm before it hit lent the yard—trees and bushes shadowy in the meager light of the ringed moon—an aura of stillness and peace. An aura distinctly at odds with the clamoring in his chest and mind.

The branches swayed slightly in the wind, but nothing else moved behind the house. *Hurry up, they'll be waiting.* He slipped around the corner of the building.

In and out. In and out. He repeated the mantra over and over, reminding himself, not only of his mission, but to breathe. When he reached the back door, he rubbed his hands together to get the blood flowing, then retrieved the tool they had given him, jimmied the lock, and returned the pick to the inside pocket of his jacket. This was one of the trickiest parts. A squeak of the door would echo through the silent neighborhood like the wail of a siren. He turned the knob and pushed the door open slowly, only exhaling when the opening was wide enough to slip through.

If getting to the house without being seen was his first test, he'd just passed the second. Like Hercules fighting the Hydra. He grinned wryly. If *they* were watching him—and he never knew when or how they were—he hoped they were impressed.

Inside, all was silent. Stiller had memorized the layout they had given him of the house, and in seconds he had crossed the main floor and started up the stairs. The house reeked of cigarette smoke and he was grateful for the mask. The child's room was the third one on the right. He started past the washroom and froze. A man lay on his stomach on the cold tile floor, head resting against the base of the toilet. Stiller reached around and gripped the handle of the Glock he'd stuck in the back of his jeans but didn't withdraw it. Should he abort?

For a couple of minutes, he stood without moving, evaluating the situation. Then he leaned forward, far enough to peer through the crack between the door and the frame. The man hadn't moved. The smell of rum and vomit hung thick in the air and Stiller swallowed back the bile that rose in his throat. He knew those smells. How many times had his foster dad passed out on his bed or on the floor somewhere, emitting those same foul odors? His muscles relaxed. He could drive a truck through this house and likely not yank the girl's father out of the unnatural slumber he'd fallen into.

Heart still thudding, Stiller crept past the washroom to the partly opened door of the girl's bedroom and pushed it an inch farther to check for creaks. The hinges moved easily and without a sound, and he nudged the door open with gloved fingers, far enough to slip into the room.

The little girl's breathing was deep and even. In the soft glow of the princess nightlight stuck into an outlet in the wall, he could make out the outline of her body, half-covered by a blanket that had slipped partway off the bed. She didn't stir as he approached, not even when he withdrew the needle from his jacket, released the air, and stabbed the tip into the thin little arm, above a large, yellowing bruise. Two minutes later he scooped her up and retraced his steps. The man was still sprawled out in the same position he'd been in earlier, only now he was snoring loudly. Clutching the girl to his chest, Stiller continued down the stairs and made his way to the back door.

When he rounded the corner of the house, headlights flashed, and a vehicle glided up the street toward him. Wary of losing his footing on the ice again, he picked his way down the driveway.

The dark sedan stopped, and the rear door opened. Stiller released the sleeping child into the arms that reached through the opening. The girl disappeared inside and he closed the door. For a few seconds, he watched as the car continued down the street. When it disappeared, he let out his breath in a rush of white misty air, shoved the ski mask up onto his head, and started for home and his book.

His third mission was complete.

Chapter Five

Nicole clutched the paper bag of groceries to her chest as she trudged along the sidewalk. A bitter north wind swept past her, and she pulled the hood of her powder-blue ski jacket tighter with a gloved hand. As usual, she'd stayed at the diner long after her shift ended. There was no reason to rush home. Her condo had always seemed cold and empty, but lately the silence practically echoed off the earth-toned walls.

What would it be like if Gage Kelly were there? Her head jerked. Gage Kelly? Why on earth was she thinking about him? She'd spent twenty minutes with the man. He was a complete stranger, a serial killer, for all she knew. She grimaced. *Highly unlikely, Nicole.* He'd been warm and friendly with his brother, and with her, for that matter. And she'd seen him praying. Not that that was necessarily a guarantee of anything. Plenty of outwardly pious people committed atrocious acts. Still …

Nicole slammed the door on her wayward thoughts. Coming home to an empty house was a good thing. No one waiting for her with incessant demands or endless stories about their problems at work. No one to take her coat and rub her aching feet or make her dinner and ask about her day. Nicole sighed. Most of all, no worrying that whoever was rubbing her feet was silently making plans to leave. *It's better this way. Easier.*

She rounded the corner and stopped abruptly. Half a block up, the man she'd just banished from her thoughts sat on the wide, curved steps in front of her building, long legs stretched out in front of him, both hands stuck in the pockets of his long black wool coat as he leaned on his elbows on the step above. Nicole glanced behind her. Gage hadn't seen her yet. She could back around the corner and find a café to hang out in until he gave up and went home. *Go now, before it's too late.* She squared her shoulders and marched to the bottom of the stairs.

"Hey." A tentative grin crossed Gage's face as he straightened up on the step.

"Hey. How did you know where I lived?"

"I stopped by the diner yesterday and coerced Connie into telling me."

Nicole shifted the bag of groceries to her other arm and propped one foot on the bottom step. "She shouldn't have done that. You could be a stalker for all she knows."

His grin widened. "I'm not a stalker."

"That's just the sort of thing a stalker would say. And you've shown up at my place of work and now, uninvited, at my home a week later. How do you define stalking?"

His smile faded slightly as a tiny crease appeared between his eyebrows. "Hmm. I guess that does look like suspicious behavior, now that you mention it."

"Well then, I guess you have five minutes until I call the police and have a restraining order issued against you."

"That's about four and a half more than I expected, so I'll take it." Gage patted the concrete step beside him.

Stay where you are, Nicole. Distance is good. Helps you think more clearly.

His face grew serious. "Please."

With a heavy sigh, she climbed the three stairs toward him.

"Here." Gage reached for the bag of groceries and set it on the other side of him as she sank onto the step. "You must be exhausted."

Nicole swiveled her head toward him in surprise. "I am, actually. How did you know?"

"Connie mentioned you would be working the seven to four shift today, and since it's now ..." he stretched out an arm and glanced at his watch, "... 6:45, I'm guessing you pulled a couple of extra hours at the diner."

Nicole frowned. "I do have a life, you know, besides working at the diner and watching over my shoulder for people who might be stalking me. It's possible that I went out for dinner or to a movie with friends or something."

"Did you?"

She stared at him for a long moment before her shoulders sagged. "No."

Gage pressed his lips together.

She straightened up. "But I could have."

"I will concede you the point. You could have gone out with friends. I'm glad you didn't though, because I really wanted to see you tonight."

"Why?"

He shifted on the step until he faced her. The intensity in his dark eyes blew away the last of her resistance like a paper cup in a hurricane. "Look, you made it pretty clear the other night that you're not interested. And normally I would absolutely respect that. The thing is, I can't seem to get our conversation, or you, out of my mind."

Nicole sighed. "Me neither. And, for the record, it wasn't that I wasn't interested. It's just that ..." *Be honest. Tell him you're scared.* "... I wasn't expecting this."

One corner of his mouth turned up. "I wasn't either. I hope you know I don't usually go around trolling the diners of Toronto, looking for amazing women. I'm as surprised that this has happened as you are." His eyes softened with a sadness that tore at her heart. "I'm going to be honest with you. I'm not very good at this. Holden and I come from an extremely messed-up family. All my parents did was fight and hurt each other. I've seen some great relationships, from a distance, but it's not something I experienced growing up."

Gage leaned forward and clasped his hands together between his knees. "In spite of all that, it felt like there was something there the other night, you know? Something real. Which I'm not sure has ever happened to me before." He glanced at his watch again. "I know my five minutes are up, but would you consider extending the time long enough for us to have dinner?"

Nicole hesitated. She'd felt it too, but ... "Maybe I could

hold off making the call for an hour or two."

Gage's eyes glowed with a warmth that drew her in like she'd been outside in the cold and suddenly offered shelter.

She held up a hand before he could speak. "Consider it a trial period. I can't promise I won't kick you out again, though."

"I can't promise I won't drive you to it."

Nicole studied him. *Suggest somewhere public. Somewhere safe.* "I picked up groceries on the way home. Do you want to eat here?"

"Are you sure?"

"No."

His mouth quirked, sending butterflies fluttering through Nicole's stomach. "Then I'll accept before better judgment prevails."

Nicole didn't think it was necessary to inform him that better judgment—like everyone else in her life—had clearly abandoned her the moment he walked into the diner.

Gage rose to his feet with a groan and brushed off the back of his jeans.

Her eyes widened. "You haven't been sitting there since four o'clock, have you?"

He shrugged. "I took the subway straight from work. I wanted to make sure I was here when you got home."

"Gage, you must be freezing."

"It was a little like sitting on a block of ice." He leaned down and grabbed the bag of groceries. "I'm a Canadian. I can take it."

He followed her up the stairs to her condo apartment. Nicole fumbled with the keys for a moment. *This is a bad idea.*

Gage touched her shoulder. "What is it?"

"I was just thinking this might not be the wisest thing I've ever done."

The corners of his eyes crinkled. "What, inviting me in? Or hesitating about spending the evening with a charming, successful, wildly attractive guy like me?"

The key slid into the lock. Nicole shook her head and pushed open the door. "Either way, it's a little late for second thoughts. Come on in. I'll get a fire going so you can thaw out your ... self." Heat rushed into her cheeks.

His lips twitched again. "A fire would be great, thanks."

"Sit down and relax. It won't take long." Nicole shoved paper and kindling into the wood stove and lit a match. In a few minutes bright flames leaped in the stove. She shut the door and turned to him.

Gage reclined on the couch, watching her. The glow of the fire reflected in the eyes that met hers. "This is a great place."

"Thanks. My parents bought it for me. A guilt offering, I believe."

His face softened. "I guess you haven't had the best relationship examples either."

"No, except for Connie and Joe, I really haven't." She shook off the self-pity that threatened to wrap itself around her. She already had enough emotions swirling through her to keep her busy for a while. "Would you like a glass of wine?"

A shadow flickered across his face. "No thanks. I don't drink."

"Tea or coffee, then?"

"Anything's fine, as long as it's hot. Can I help?"

"No, I've got it." Nicole pushed through the French doors and into the kitchen, her hands trembling as she reached for the canister of tea bags on the counter. *What is going on here?* Gage was good-looking, gorgeous even with his long dark hair, and deep, way-too-penetrating eyes. She'd seen attractive men before though, plenty of them, at the diner, without reacting to them like this. Something else was drawing her to Gage so strongly it frightened her. Nicole shook her head. She'd feed the man and get him out of her apartment, which she'd been crazy to invite him to in the first place. One hour, then he definitely had to go.

Nicole filled the kettle with water and set it on the stove, then quickly put together a salad. After heating a pot of minestrone soup, she dished it into two bowls, set everything on a tray, and pushed through the swinging doors into the living room.

Gage jumped to his feet when she walked into the room. "Here, let me." He took the tray from her and set it on the coffee table, then turned back. A smile crossed his lips. "You have some soot, here." He ran his finger over her cheek. Nicole fought to take a breath.

Better judgment chose that moment to return. *Run, Nicole. Get out before it's too late.* Her forehead wrinkled. Was that better judgment? Or was it actually the fear and distrust she'd lived with so long they'd become as comfortable and familiar as a pair of well-worn jeans?

Gage studied her face, as though he could read her thoughts. "Don't run."

The whispered words sent a shiver through her. "I won't."

"Good." He stepped back. "Hungry?"

"Starving." She sank down onto the couch, grateful the intensity of the moment was broken.

Gage handed her a bowl of soup and poured a cup of tea that he set in front of her before settling himself at the other end of the couch with his own bowl. "So tell me about your day. You must have a lot of great stories about things that happen at the diner."

He seemed much more relaxed, now that she had assured him she wasn't going anywhere. Or maybe he was just starting to thaw out. Either way, she took his cue and shifted to lean against the arm of the couch so she could face him while she ate and share with him about the characters that came into the diner every day. To her great surprise, they talked and laughed easily together.

Nicole swirled her spoon through the soup. The smell of oregano drifted from the bowl, and she took a deep, calming breath. "What is it you are so successful at?"

"I'm sorry?"

"At the door, you said something about being … what was it, charming, wildly attractive, and successful, I believe. So what is it you are so successful at doing?"

"Oh." Gage leaned over to set his bowl down on the coffee table. "That part may have been a slight exaggeration. I'm with the Crown Attorney's office."

Nicole's eyes widened. "You're a lawyer?"

"Does that surprise you?"

She pursed her lips and studied him. "I guess you just don't strike me as the lawyer type."

"And what is the lawyer type, exactly?"

"I don't know, a little stuffier maybe, more arrogant, flashier."

He grinned. "You've seen too many of those fancy, big-firm lawyers on TV. Crown attorneys can't afford to be flashy, and we definitely don't have anything to be arrogant about. The stuffy part I guess you'll have to decide for yourself." He reached for his mug and wrapped both hands around it. "How do you like working at the diner?"

"I love it. Connie and Joe are great to me. Like family." She picked up the soft, ivory-colored napkin and ran her fingers across it.

"How long have you been there?"

"Since I finished high school. When I got accepted into university, I didn't want to ask my …" She stopped and cleared her throat. "I wanted to pay for it myself, so one day when I was walking past the diner, I saw the *Help Wanted* sign in the window and went in and applied." A smile touched her lips. "As soon as I met Connie I knew I had come to the right place. It was like I had come …"

"Home?"

The color in her cheeks deepened. "Yeah."

Gage probed tentatively, his voice soft. "Didn't you ever have a real home?"

"You mean like with a mother who meets you after school with a plate of cookies, and a dad who teaches you to ride a bike, and a backyard with swings and a dog? That kind of home?"

"I'm guessing that's a no?"

She laughed. "Apparently you can add incredibly astute to those characteristics you mentioned earlier."

"So, to sum up, you'd say wildly attractive, charming,

successful, and astute make up my list of desirable qualities?"

"*I* didn't say that. *You* said …" Nicole leaned back against the arm of the couch. "Okay, I believe you now."

"I'm glad to hear it. About what?"

"You really are a lawyer, aren't you?"

Gage lifted his shoulders. "Guilty."

"Ah." She pointed a finger at him. "What about Holden? What does he do?"

"He's a social worker."

Nicole winced.

"Yeah, it's a tough job. He's seen some pretty awful things. He loves it though." Gage touched her elbow. "What did you study in university?"

"Business. It took me eight years of working and studying part-time, but I graduated a couple of years ago, and now I'm working on my Master's."

He gave her a skeptical look. "You've been out of high school for ten years?"

"I'm older than I look. Anyway, I'm still at the diner, partly so I can keep financing my schooling, but even more because I can't bring myself to leave."

"You feel like you belong there."

Tingles of fear whispered across her arms. How could he read her so well already? *Don't let him get too close.* Nicole set down her bowl. "I don't mean to be rude, but it's getting late and I still have studying to do tonight."

He glanced at his watch. "You're right. I've overstayed my grace period by at least an hour and a half. Time to go."

She had propped her bare feet up on the couch between them, and he grabbed her big toe and shook her foot lightly. "Hey, can I ask you something before I leave?"

Nicole swallowed. "Sure."

He flicked a finger in the direction of her throat. "That necklace you wear, is it just an accessory to you?"

Nicole touched the piece of jewelry lightly, almost reverently, with the fingertips of her right hand. Her gaze met his.

"No."

Gage's shoulders relaxed slightly, as though he'd been afraid to ask. "Good. It's more than that to me too."

"I gathered that when I saw you and your brother praying before your meal last week."

"Yeah, my faith is important to me."

"Me too."

He smiled and pushed to his feet. As tired as Nicole was, part of her would have liked him to stay longer. A flicker of not-quite-conquered fear niggled in her stomach. *Don't get attached. You'll be sorry.*

Nicole considered that advice as she rose. The problem was that it presupposed she wasn't already at least a little bit attached, and she was no longer sure that was the case. Especially when he gathered up all the dishes and carried them into the kitchen before following her to the door. When she turned to face him, a warm smile spread across his lips and reflected deep in his eyes. "Thank you for not running."

She leaned against the doorframe. "That's the good thing about taking your date to her place for dinner. Makes it hard for her to leave."

Gage slipped on the black wool coat he'd lifted off the stand by the door and tilted his head to one side. "Are you saying this was a date?"

Her cheeks warmed. "Well, I ..."

"I'll take that as a yes." He leaned in and touched his lips to hers, a sweet and gentle kiss she felt all the way to her knees. When he eased away, he did up the buttons on his coat, his eyes not leaving her face. "Get some rest. I'll talk to you soon, okay?"

Nicole nodded and closed the door behind him, bracing herself with both hands against the dark wood. *Not very good at this, yeah right.* If he were any better, she'd be a puddle on the floor right now. Her gaze traveled across her hands, pressed white against the door. One was clenched tightly and the other spread flat against the wood. Which was exactly how she felt inside. Part of her reached out to grasp what was happening between her and Gage and pull it to her. The other part, that reason-slash-fear part that had dictated how she lived so much of her life, demanded that she shove it away.

She took one hand from the door and brushed her fingers lightly across her lips. Heat rose in her chest. Why did he have to do that? Until he had kissed her, she could have walked away, could have pushed him out of her life like she had every other man who had tried to get close to her. Not that she hadn't been kissed before, but she'd always managed to be gone before any of the kisses actually *meant* something.

Gage hadn't given her that luxury.

Chapter Six

Daniel hesitated, his finger hovering over the doorbell. *Not too late to back out.* Except he'd never hear the end of it from his sister or his partner if he failed to show up. *It's just dinner.* Before he could change his mind, he stabbed at the bell. The low bong echoed through the house, immediately followed by the pattering of little feet down the wood-lined hallway. Daniel smiled.

The door swung open. Four-year-old Leticia, tight black braids covering her head, dropped from her tiptoes onto her heels as she let go of the handle.

"Dan-el!" Little Allie toddled up behind her sister, dark eyes sparkling as she raised both hands.

He bent down and scooped one giggling child up under each arm. "How are my two favorite girls?"

"What? I risk my life every single day to protect you, and *they're* your favorites?" Sharleen's voice drifted down the hallway from the kitchen.

Still clutching the girls, Daniel started toward his partner. "Sorry, I meant to say two of my three favorites." He went through the kitchen doorway. Sharleen closed the oven door and turned to face him. He set both girls down on the floor. Allie wrapped her arms around his leg as he leaned in to kiss Sharleen on the cheek. "Where's Tom?"

"He's in the living room with … the others."

Daniel's eyes narrowed at the hesitation. *They wouldn't, would they?* "What others?"

She waved a hand through the air. "You know, Austin and Rebecca. And I also invited Lou and Esther."

"Oh good." He hadn't seen his former partner, Lou, since Daniel had been promoted to detective. Although the idea of spending the evening with three couples as the odd man out didn't exactly thrill him, he'd still be happy to catch up on all the news from his and Sharleen's old precinct. Daniel leaned down and swung little Allie up into his arms. "Come on, beautiful. Want to be my date tonight?"

"Me too." Leticia held up her arms.

Daniel crouched down and picked her up as well.

"Perfect. A gorgeous girl on each arm. Just how I like it."

Sharleen shot him a wry look as he straightened. "Go on in and say hi to everybody." She turned back to the stove.

Daniel shifted both girls more securely in his arms and headed out of the kitchen. When he went into the living room, Tom gave the fire one more shove with the poker, then closed the door of the woodstove and dropped the tool into the metal holder with a clang. He came over to Daniel and took Allie from him. "Hey, Daniel."

"Hi, Tom."

Tom turned and surveyed the room. "I think you know pretty much everyone."

Lou walked over and gave him a brief hug. "Good to see you, man."

"You too." Daniel raised a hand to Lou's wife Esther and to Austin and Becca.

"And this is Elizabeth."

A tall woman with long, shimmering brown hair rose gracefully from her chair in the corner and crossed the room.

Ah. The hesitation. Daniel pasted on a smile as she approached him and Tom.

When she reached them, she held out a slender hand. "Daniel, hi."

He shifted Leticia to his other arm and took her hand. "Nice to meet you, Elizabeth."

"You too."

Her fingers were soft and warm in his. Daniel waited, but the only feeling that ignited in him was a slight irritation that he had been blindsided by his sister and his partner. He let go of her.

Elizabeth's smile faltered slightly, as though she either read the reaction in his eyes or had experienced the same one at his touch. She nodded and returned to her armchair in the corner. Daniel headed over to Becca. As he pulled her into a one-armed hug, Leticia between them, he whispered softly in her ear, "We'll discuss this later."

She offered him one of her patented impish grins as she pulled away and touched her hand to her stomach.

Daniel rolled his eyes. *Oh no, you're not going to start using that against me.* "Later," he mouthed as he turned to greet her husband, who was watching the two of them with an amused smile.

"I warned her," Austin said in a low voice as he shook Daniel's hand, the classical music piping through the room masking their exchange.

"Then my sister deserves what she gets." Daniel clapped his brother-in-law on the shoulder.

Sharleen appeared in the doorway of the living room. "Dinner's ready."

Daniel followed Lou into the dining room and pulled out the chair next to him.

"Here." Sharleen reached for Leticia.

Daniel had been hoping to set the young girl on the seat beside him, but Sharleen took Elizabeth by the elbow and led her over to it before taking her daughter to sit with her. So be it. *There are worse ways to spend an evening than in the company of a beautiful woman.* Daniel held the chair out for her and pushed it in a little when she had settled on it.

The smile she flashed him as he took his seat did send a little rush of warmth through his chest, which was something. Not nearly enough to let his sister or partner off the hook, but something.

"So, how do you know Sharleen?" Daniel held the bowl for Elizabeth as she used the tongs to delicately transfer a helping of salad to her plate.

"We met at the gym. We were beside each other on the bikes

one spin class and started talking. After we'd gotten to know each other better, she told me about her partner and suggested I come to dinner tonight to meet you." She inclined her head toward him a little and lowered her voice. "I gathered from the look on your face when Tom introduced us that she hadn't given you the same amount of information."

"No, she hadn't. You were a total surprise, to be honest. I'm sorry if I reacted poorly."

"Don't be. I wouldn't have appreciated that either. I didn't realize that was the case, or I would have insisted they let you know I would be here." Elizabeth passed the bowl on to Tom on the other side of her. "Tell me about your work."

Daniel filled her in, as much as he could, on the case he and Sharleen were working on. She laughed at the stories he told her about Detective Sergeant Lector. Daniel studied her surreptitiously as he ate. She really was attractive, with eyes— such a deep blue they were almost purple—that widened with every story he told as though she was intensely interested in each word. She was so good at getting him to talk about himself that he'd been doing it for twenty minutes before he realized he hadn't asked her anything about her life. "What do you do?"

"I'm a surgeon at Sick Kids."

"Wow. Impressive."

She lifted one slender shoulder in a self-deprecating gesture he found surprisingly endearing. "It's what I always wanted to do. I think God instilled the desire in me practically from the moment I was born. I 'operated' on all my dolls and quite a few of the animals we had on the farm. In fact, I seriously considered becoming a veterinarian until …" She picked up the linen napkin she'd laid across her lap and pressed it to her lips.

Until what? Daniel gave her a moment.

When she lowered the napkin, her smile was sad. "My younger sister was hit by a car when she was seven and I was nine. We'd been riding our bikes together and laughing and talking and didn't see the vehicle speeding toward us. Apparently, the driver, who had been drinking, didn't see us either. He hit her and almost collided with me, but I managed to swerve out of the way. She was rushed to the hospital and into surgery where they worked on her for eight straight hours. Thankfully, she survived and ended up recovering fully. I'll never forget the look of fear on my parents' faces as we sat in the waiting room that long, agonizing day, or the joy that exploded across them when the doctor came to tell them she was going to be okay, the way they clung to each other in shared relief.

"From that day on, I knew that was what I wanted to do, what I had been born to do, the type of work that could bring terrified patients and their families such hope and joy. Of course," she twisted the napkin around in her hands, "it doesn't always work out that way. Most of the time it does, though, thankfully."

He had to give credit to the two most important women in his life. They did know how to pick them. Elizabeth was remarkable. Someone he would be happy to call a friend. He doubted it would ever be more than that and couldn't detect anything in her eyes or body language that suggested it would be for her either. Not that he believed in love at first sight, but he did think that, when you met the person you were meant to be with, there would be something—some kind of flame that hinted at a potential inferno somewhere down the road. With Elizabeth, as much as he admired her, there was barely a spark. Nothing more than he'd feel for any attractive, intelligent woman.

A low buzzing sound caught his attention. Elizabeth pulled a pager from her pocket and glanced at it. She looked over at him. "It's the hospital. I need to go."

He nodded. "I'll walk you out." Another reason it would be difficult for the two of them to embark on a relationship. His pager hadn't gone off tonight, but that was a rarity. If one or the other of them was always being called away from wherever they were, it would be a trick to spend any amount of time together. A twinge of regret over a lost opportunity worked its way through him, but he didn't question the decision.

After she had said farewell to everyone, Daniel followed her down the hallway and helped her into her coat. She turned and smiled at him as she held out her hand again. "It really was a pleasure to meet you, Daniel."

A goodbye. Daniel held her hand briefly before letting her go. "You too." He waited until she had gone outside and was almost at her vehicle before he closed the door firmly behind her.

When he returned to his seat, ignoring the questioning looks from his sister and Sharleen, Lou nudged him in the shoulder. "How's the new job going? Miss pounding the pavement on our old beat yet?"

Daniel grinned. "Every single day."

"I'm glad to hear it, because I need a favor."

"What's that?"

"I'm supposed to go speak to a group of school kids on my day off in a couple of weeks, and my new partner has decided he'd rather spend the day with his fiancée, if you can imagine. Any chance you'd help me out for an hour or two?"

Daniel thought about it. Could be a nice break from the intensity of the case. "What's the date? I'll see if I can work it out."

"That'd be great." Lou gave him the day and the time and Daniel entered it into his phone. They chatted for a bit over dessert, until Becca yawned for the third time and Austin announced that they were going to head out.

Daniel tossed his napkin down on his plate and excused himself from the table to follow them to the door.

Austin held Becca's coat for her. Her eyes met Daniel's as she slid her arms into the sleeves and did up the buttons. She had the good sense to look contrite, which stemmed the flow of the lecture he'd been about to unleash on her.

Grabbing her knitted hat off the hook, Daniel tugged it down over her ears, then, one hand on each side of her head, he tipped it back so she was looking up at him. "No more set-ups, do you hear?"

She sighed. "All right, but you have to admit Elizabeth is pretty great."

"Yes, she is, but she's not the woman for me. And if and

when I am ready to get involved with someone, I'll find her myself. Clear?"

"Clear."

"Good." Daniel wrapped his arms around her and gave her a hug. "Now go home and get some rest."

She smiled up at him. "I will."

Daniel watched as she and Austin walked out to the car. His brother-in-law held her arm until they reached their vehicle. Then he pulled open the door for her and waited until she got in to close it behind her.

Daniel shut the front door. He couldn't have chosen a better husband for his sister if he had tried. Which he hadn't. Because he'd figured out that she was an adult and perfectly capable of getting her own life together. Something both she and Sharleen could take a lesson from.

He headed down the hallway, a wry grin on his face. He'd wait until everyone else had left the party, then lay down the law with his partner too. As much as he appreciated her and Becca's concern for his happiness and well-being, the two of them were going to have to back off and let him find his own way, even if that meant he was destined to live his life alone.

Chapter Seven

The panic hit Nicole as soon as she hung up the phone. Gage was bringing take-out over for dinner. She should have said no. When he'd kissed her, she had been shaken to the core. Then she hadn't heard from him for over a week. She was almost relieved when he didn't call, although she had also checked the connection on the phone several times, wondering why he hadn't.

Nicole dropped her head into her hands. She couldn't do this. She didn't need the conflict that raged in her over being with him. It would be better to call if off now, before either of them was in too deep. If she waited, it would just be cruel. She lifted her chin. She would tell him tonight.

The doorbell rang, twisting her stomach into knots. Nicole drew in several calming breaths as she crossed the living room and pulled open the door.

The last bit of air she'd taken in dissipated, and she pressed a hand to her stomach. Gage stood in the hallway, holding a paper bag from a Chinese food restaurant and offering her the lopsided grin that did strange things to her insides. Nicole swallowed hard and stepped back.

"Hi." He moved past her into the living room.

She shoved the door shut hard and turned to him. "Hi." Her voice stayed cold and flat.

The warmth in his eyes cooled slightly. "Everything okay?"

Tell him no. He can leave now, and this will all be over. "Sure. Come into the kitchen." Without waiting for him, she walked across the living room and through the French doors at the far end. She reached into the cupboard to grab two plates and set them on the counter. Nicole heard his footsteps on the marble floor, felt his presence in the room even more clearly than that, but didn't look up as she yanked open the silverware drawer and grabbed the knives and forks.

Gage didn't speak as he set the bag down on the island. She refused to look at him, concentrating instead on getting out glasses and filling them with water from the tap. Her hands shook as she carried them to the table and set them down with a thud.

When she turned back, he had leaned a hip against the counter and was watching her. He'd taken off his coat and her breath caught when she saw him. If he didn't look so good, even dressed casually in a long-sleeved black T-shirt and jeans, what she was about to do would require considerably less willpower. It took every ounce of determination she had to walk past him and reach for the food. The combined aromas of ginger, garlic, and sesame seed oil wafted from the paper bag.

"Hey."

Nicole dropped the container into the bag and turned around slowly. Gage had come up behind her and stood inches from her. She couldn't breathe without drawing in the faint scent of his musky aftershave that was making it hard for her to think straight.

"What's wrong?"

She started to turn away. "Nothing."

"Nicole." He touched her arm. "Come on. Something is obviously bothering you."

She faced him. "You don't know me, Gage. Don't pretend you know how I'm feeling."

His hand dropped. "You're right. I don't know you, not nearly as well as I'd like to, anyway. Hence the whole ..." he gestured toward the food on the counter, "... dating thing. But I don't have to know you that well to see that you're upset about something. I know I didn't call you for a few days, but that wasn't because I didn't want to, it was because I didn't want to come on too strong. Is that what you're upset about?"

"Of course not. There's nothing between us. You don't have to report in to me." The words were sharp, and she saw the wounding in his eyes.

His face, though, and his voice, when he spoke, remained carefully controlled. "What, then?"

"Maybe we shouldn't get into it right now. Let's eat first."

"I don't think so."

"Okay, fine." Nicole straightened her shoulders. "I don't want this."

His gaze flicked to the paper bag on the counter. "That's okay. We can order piz—"

Nicole shook her head. "No. I mean, I don't want this." She waved a hand between them. "You and me."

"You don't want this."

The dullness in his tone cut into her. She hadn't meant to hurt him. Better now than later, though. "That's right." Her voice threatened to break, and she bit her lip. "In fact, maybe you should just take your food and leave now."

For a few agonizing seconds neither of them moved, then Gage stepped closer and rested a hand on the counter on either side of her. When he spoke, his voice was low and soft. "I thought you weren't going to run."

Her pulse pounded in her throat. "I'm not. It's just that I don't see this going anywhere, so I think it's best to end it now before either of us has too much invested."

His jaw tightened. "Well, I hate to burst your nice, neat little bubble here, but I already care about you, Nicole, a lot, so it may be a little late for that."

"All the more reason to end it now, before—"

He leaned in and found her mouth. His hands lifted to her face, and he pulled her to him as he crushed his lips to hers.

Heat streaked through her. She held herself rigid for two seconds before her knees weakened and she leaned against him. Her hands rested on his hips, gripping his T-shirt in both fists. She kissed him too, frantically. For a few seconds Nicole filled her senses with the feel and smell and taste of him. Then fear welled up, dousing desire, and she broke away, flushed and breathless.

His dark eyes probed hers. Her chest tightened until it hurt to draw a breath. He saw too much when he looked at her like that. She felt naked and exposed. The anger that slashed through her gave her the strength to pull herself up to her full height, right below his chin, and meet his gaze. "Sex wouldn't change anything."

Gage recoiled, as if she had slapped him across the face. "Sex? Who said anything about sex?" His hands, clenched into fists, dropped to his sides. He took a step backward, his eyes blazing. "Is that what you think all this is about? That I'm trying to get you into bed?"

Nicole closed her eyes and took a deep, shaky breath, trying to compose herself. This conversation was not going at all like she had planned. He was supposed to see the reason in her calmly worded arguments and walk out the door, and out of her life, without either of them getting upset. Nice and easy. She sighed and opened her eyes. "I only meant—"

Gage lifted both hands to stop her, then raked them through his long, dark hair and turned around, clasping them behind his head as he walked toward the window above the sink. "God, help us."

His words cut deeply into her chest. He hadn't spoken them lightly, like a cliché. Gage obviously knew the one he was calling on. This would be a lot easier if he didn't. Nicole's cheeks burned. She pressed her crossed arms tightly against her abdomen, misery thickening her throat.

He stood in front of the glass for a moment, staring up at the sky, before he dropped his arms and turned and strode toward her. She stiffened, but he stopped inches from her and didn't touch her. "Okay, look." Gage was clearly forcing calm into his voice, although a tiny vein throbbed in his forehead. "I'm not going to lie to you and tell you I haven't thought about it. I'm a guy, and you're a beautiful woman. And I have feelings for you. But I won't sleep with you."

Nicole blinked.

Gage drew in a deep breath. "And since it would be really great if at least one of us was being honest here, I'll tell you that

I've made that mistake before. It was a mistake, and I spent hours on my knees repenting over it. I won't go down that road again unless—and I may really make you run here, but I'm going to take my chances—we get married. Which, in spite of your insistence that this isn't going anywhere, I can see happening someday. If you quit pushing me away, that is." His eyes swept over her and he exhaled loudly. "They really messed you up, didn't they?"

Her throat tightened. "Who?"

"Your parents, for starters. And whoever else you feel abandoned you in your life. Maybe your best friend in third grade moved away, or your date in high school left you for the prom queen, or maybe you were the prom queen, I don't know. But I want to know. That and every other little thing about you, like your favorite kind of ice cream and how you spend Saturday mornings, and what types of books you read. Everything. But most of all, what I'd like to know is how any of those people could have ever walked away from you. Because I've only known you for a couple of weeks and I can't do it, and you're shoving me out the door as hard as you can."

"I'm not shoving you." Her voice was strained. "I'm being realistic about our chances. And I don't like you accusing me of not being honest."

Gage moved a step closer. "Okay, you want a chance to show me how honest you're being? And I don't just mean with me, I mean with yourself? Answer one question before you toss me out."

She clasped her hands together to keep them from shaking. "Fine. But then you go." His eyes burned into her, but Nicole refused to look away.

"Do you really not want this, or are you scared of how much you want it?"

Tell him you don't want it. He'll walk out the door and you'll never have to see him again. She opened her mouth then shut it again. A revelation streaked across her consciousness like a flare. The thought of not seeing him again was even more terrifying than the thought of getting close to him. She pressed her eyes shut tightly. "I'm scared."

Gage wrapped his arms around her and pulled her to him. "Good. I can work with scared." He spoke the words softly in her ear. A shiver moved through her and his arms tightened. "I'm not going anywhere, Nicole."

She rested her head on his chest. His heart thudded beneath her cheek, driving away the cold fear that had settled in her stomach. They stood like that for several moments, until he eased back and looked at her. "Okay?"

Nicole managed a weak smile. "Okay."

"Can we eat now?"

Her laugh was shaky. "It'll be cold."

"That's what microwaves are for." Gage took her hand and led her to the table. "Sit down. I'll get the food."

He warmed it up and set a plate in front of her. "You actually do like Chinese food, right? Because that *would* be a deal breaker."

She laughed. "I do, don't worry."

"Good."

Nicole watched him as he went back for one for himself. "The knives and forks are on the counter."

He waved a hand at her. "Knives and forks are for the unadventurous." Gage grabbed chopsticks out of the bag and brought them over to the table. "Which, clearly, we are not."

"Oh, no." Wrinkling her nose, she grabbed a set and made a futile attempt to pick up some rice. "Talk about getting to know someone. This is not going to be pretty."

"It might not be pretty, but it will be worth the effort, I promise."

Nicole looked up and met his gaze. His long, dark eyelashes framed smiling eyes that locked with hers and held them. Her heart rate quickened. Neither moved for a few seconds, until a grin quirked the corners of her mouth. "Shelley Silverstone."

"Who?"

"Shelley Silverstone. She was our prom queen."

Gage leaned back in his chair. "Wow. She must have been some kind of gorgeous to have beaten you out."

Nicole tucked a strand of hair behind her ear. "Gorgeous enough that I'm not going to show you her picture."

His eyebrows rose as he looked around the room. "You have her picture?"

Nicole grinned. "Not in here. I don't keep it on my fridge or anything. And I said I wasn't going to show it to you."

He leaned forward and caught her hand, pressing one finger to his mouth. "Okay, fine. I'll just have to look at you then."

Her heart skipped a beat. "You don't give up easily, do you?"

"Nope." He kissed another finger. "Not when I know it's right. And in spite of what I told you earlier, which we can talk about any time you want, I've never felt this right about a relationship before in my life. I'll fight for us, Nic. And I won't walk away."

Don't make a promise you can't keep, Nicole. She lifted her chin. "Then I won't run."

Chapter Eight

Daniel slapped the light onto the front dash then had to grab it as Sharleen took the next corner on two wheels.

She shot him a sideways glance. "Sorry."

"It's fine." He held on to the light with his left hand and clung to the handle of the door with his right. "We have to get there." Thankfully, since it was the middle of the night, traffic was light and the few drivers who were on the roads had the good sense to pull over to the right to let them pass.

A concerned citizen had called 911 to say he'd seen a man wearing a black wool cap pulled down over his face creeping around the backyard of his neighbor's house. Daniel let go of the door handle long enough to check his watch. 1:11. The call had come in seven minutes earlier, and they were still two minutes out. Would they get there in time? If there was any chance this was their elusive child abductor, Daniel was desperate to arrive at the scene in time to catch him in the act. This was the first real break they'd gotten, the only credible lead they'd come across in this case, and he did not want to blow it.

Sharleen squealed around another corner, and Daniel grabbed the handle again. They'd called for back-up, but had requested no lights or sirens, not wanting to give the guy any warning that they were coming, so he had no idea whether anyone else was close. Sharleen approached the final turn before the street where the man had been seen. Daniel yanked the light from the dash, switched it off, and tossed it into the back seat.

His partner slowed for the final turn and eased up on the gas as she turned onto the street. Daniel leaned forward to peer through the front window, scanning the neighborhood for any signs of life. He stabbed a finger through the air in front of him.

"There!"

In the dim light of a street lamp, he could make out a dark sedan idling at the curb half a block ahead. As they drew closer, a figure strode down the driveway of a house and approached the rear passenger door. "He's carrying something."

Sharleen pressed down on the gas again. Caught in their headlights, the man turned his head in their direction as the door of the waiting vehicle opened. Just as quickly, he looked away and thrust the bundle he'd been carrying into the arms that reached for it then slammed the door shut. The vehicle squealed away from the curb, and the man spun on his heel and sprinted toward the back of the house.

"Let me out. You go after the car." Daniel shoved open the door and jumped out onto the sidewalk before Sharleen had come to a full stop. He barely managed to slam the door shut before she peeled away again in pursuit of the sedan and, quite possibly, their fourth abducted child.

Daniel ran along the side of the house and into the yard. The man had almost reached the fence at the edge of the property. Daniel increased his speed. If the guy got over the fence and into the maze of streets and alleys on the other side, Daniel could easily lose him. A shaft of moonlight sliced through a break in the clouds, and he caught a glimpse of the man, dressed all in black, ski mask still pulled down over his face, leaping toward the fence and grabbing the top of it. Daniel closed the gap between them as the suspect swung a leg up over the top rail. Reaching deep, Daniel surged forward. The man swung his other leg over the fence as Daniel reached it.

One of the man's sleeves got snagged on a nail. Daniel lunged forward and hit the fence with one foot, propelling himself upward. He managed to grasp the man's hat and rip it from his head before grabbing hold of a post to steady himself. For two seconds their eyes locked. In the dim moonlight, he attempted to memorize the man's features. Then the suspect yanked his arm free, drove his elbow up under Daniel's chin, snatched his hat out of Daniel's hand, and dropped out of sight.

Daniel lost his grip on the fence and dropped back into the yard. The sound of a vehicle screeching to a stop sent a new rush of adrenaline coursing through him. Ignoring the throbbing pain in his jaw, he scrambled to his feet, took a running leap, and hauled himself over the fence and into the neighboring yard. No sign of a vehicle, or of the man. Daniel ran to the sidewalk and stopped, scanning the street in both directions. He couldn't see anything moving and, as hard as he strained to listen, couldn't hear anything but the distant hum of an engine rapidly growing fainter.

Daniel grabbed the cell phone from the inside pocket of his jacket and called it in, asking for anyone in the direction of the fading sound to be on the lookout for a speeding vehicle. How could the guy have disappeared so quickly? How did whoever was driving the vehicle know when and where to pick him up? It was as though the man had been plucked from the street and carried to safety like something from the scene of an action movie. Or maybe he had never been there at all. If it weren't for the pain in his jaw and neck, and the vague image of the man's face burned into his brain like the imprint of a sudden, bright light slashing through darkness, Daniel might have wondered if he actually had seen someone, or if his desire to catch the abductor had been strong enough to conjure up the sighting.

Biting back an oath, he jogged around the block, knowing he wouldn't find anything. Whoever this person was, he was good. These child-snatchings were clearly well-planned, or he couldn't have escaped detection this long. At least now they knew the man wasn't acting alone. Someone was driving the getaway car. And a minimum of two people had to have been in the vehicle that took the child, one to drive and the one who took the child from the kidnapper. Maybe Sharleen would have better luck than he'd had and be able to overtake them. And he should be able to give a halfway-decent description of the person he'd been chasing to a police artist. *We're further ahead than we were an hour ago. Except that another child might be gone.* Daniel kicked at an empty pop can in his path. It clattered across the sidewalk and hit a fire hydrant with a dull clank that shattered the pre-dawn silence of the neighborhood. That little fact would not go over well with Detective Sergeant Lector. He winced. *Well, it doesn't go over well with me, either.* One way or another, they had to stop these people.

He rounded the corner onto the street where they'd seen the man hand off the child. Sharleen pulled up in front of the house as he approached. Not a good sign. Obviously, she'd lost the car she'd been chasing. Not that he blamed her. The city frowned on police chases through their streets, and the cops had been warned to avoid them if at all possible. And if the dark sedan was as prepared for escape as the suspect had been, she likely never had a chance anyway. He could only hope she or her dash cam had caught a good look at the plates at some point during the pursuit. She climbed out of the vehicle and glanced over at him. The grimace on her face extinguished the flicker of hope he'd been nurturing.

"I called it in, gave them what I had." Sharleen slammed the car door and rounded the front of the vehicle to meet him on the sidewalk. "No luck?"

"Not really. I got close enough to him to rip off his mask and catch a quick glimpse of his face before he knocked me back off the fence. By the time I got over, he was gone."

"Do you still have the hat? We should be able to get a DNA—"

Daniel shook his head. "He grabbed it from me before he disappeared."

His partner exhaled. "Can you give the artist a description?"

"I'm sure going to try."

A second police car pulled up to the curb. Daniel quickly filled in the two female officers, Fernandez and Penner, who had joined them on the sidewalk. When he finished, he inclined his head in the direction of the back yard. "Why don't you two look around behind the house, see if he happened to drop something on his way in or out. We'll go talk to whoever's inside. I'm guessing from the silence that they're still asleep and have no idea their child has been taken."

Fernandez winced. "I don't envy you that conversation."

Daniel got that. Being the bearer of bad news to horrified family members was the part of his job he hated the most. And what news could be worse than this? He trudged to the front door after Sharleen. When they reached it, she pressed the doorbell. The low bonging sound echoed through the silent house.

Daniel gritted his teeth. They'd come so close. His fingers curled into a ball and he smacked the brick wall of the house with the side of his fist. Not nearly close enough. And now that they knew how well-organized this operation was, chances were good that they would never come this close again.

Sharleen rang the bell two more times before Daniel caught the faint sound of shuffling feet on the other side of the door. They waited through a pause, likely while whoever was on the other side looked out the peephole, before the door was yanked open. A woman with tousled, shoulder-length brown hair and crooked teeth, yellow in the dim porch light, clutched a pink robe to her throat as she stared at them. "What is it?" Her voice was deep and raspy—clearly a career smoker.

"Ma'am, I'm Detective Grey and this is Detective Roberts from Toronto Police Services." He flashed his badge and nodded toward the house. "May we come inside?"

The woman closed the door a little. "Not until I know what this is about."

Daniel drew in a deep breath. Every second counted, and they were ticking away far faster than he would like as they stood there on the porch. "Do you have a child living here with you?"

"She's not mine, she's my husband's girl, but yes, she lives here."

"Is your husband at home?"

The woman snorted. "The only home he belongs in. Cirrhosis got him last year, like I told him it would."

"So you are the girl's guardian?"

"Apparently." The woman's eyes narrowed. "Why? Did CAS send you here again? That girl is fine. The only ones harming her are those social workers that keep poking their noses into our business." She uttered a few choice words that made her opinion on Children's Aid workers abundantly clear. Daniel's jaw tightened. "Ma'am, is the child at home?"

She frowned. "Of course she's home. It's one o'clock in the morning, and she's five years old."

"Would you mind checking to make sure?"

Her features hardened and for a moment he thought she'd refuse. Then she rolled her eyes. "Whatever." The door slammed in their faces and the sound of shuffling feet receded.

Daniel looked at Sharleen. "Wow."

"No kidding. Not exactly mother-of-the-year material, is she?"

"Not my initial impression, no. She sounds more than a little resentful that her dearly departed husband's child has been thrust upon her."

Even through the closed door, they could hear the woman stomping around upstairs, calling out the girl's name, Mia.

Sharleen inclined her head in the direction of the sounds. "Not that we're here to investigate her, but it's worth noting that she's obviously had some run-ins with CAS, like the parents of the other kids who have disappeared, which confirms that's relevant, as we'd suspected."

"It definitely looks like it."

The tromping of footsteps grew louder, and the door swung open. Even in the dim light of the cobweb-encrusted bulb on the porch, the woman's face was ashen. "Mia's not in her bed. What's going on?"

Sharleen pressed a palm to the doorframe and leaned in a little closer. "I'm sorry to have to tell you this, but we believe she may have been taken."

"Taken?" The woman's voice was approaching hysteria, and Daniel shot a glance down the quiet street. "Did those CAS—"

He held up a hand before she could launch into a full-blown

tirade. "No ma'am. CAS doesn't break in and sneak children out of their homes in the night. We think Mia might have been abducted by the same person, or persons, who have recently taken three other children in the city."

The woman swayed on her feet. "I think you better come inside." She spun around and headed into the living room.

Daniel held out a hand for Sharleen to go ahead, then followed her in and shut the door. The smell of second-hand smoke assaulted his nostrils.

"Have a seat." The woman flapped a hand in the direction of the couch. "You think she's been kidnapped? Why? Who would take her? I don't have any enemies, or any money for ransom. Why would they bother with her?"

Interesting choice of words. Daniel sat down beside Sharleen on the couch. The acrid smell of cat urine rose from the cushions to compete with the smoke. He tried to ignore it—and the thick layer of animal hair that coated every visible surface—as he pulled a notebook from his shirt pocket. "That's what we're trying to find out, ma'am."

She flapped a hand again. "Enough with the ma'am stuff. It's Darlene."

He clicked open his pen. "Last name?"

"White."

Sharleen cleared her throat. "Is Mia's mother in the picture?"

Darlene sank onto a chair and retied the belt on her robe. "Not really. I mean, she's alive. Doesn't have much to do with her daughter though. She comes by to see her every few months, whenever she gets herself straight."

"Any siblings?"

"Nah. She's an only child. Thank—" She pressed her lips together as though she'd realized she might be saying too much.

"Can you tell us what she was wearing?"

"Her Little Kitty pajamas, I think. White with pink letters on the front."

"She appeared to be wrapped up in something. Does she have a blanket?"

"Yeah. She always slept with an old, worn out knitted blanket her mother gave her one time. Light blue, although pretty faded now."

Daniel scribbled down that detail. "Do you have a picture?"

The woman frowned. "I think she brought one home from school a while ago. I'll see if I can find it." She stood and crossed the room to a sideboard covered in books and papers.

Daniel glanced around the room. Two small running shoes lay on their sides near the door, a hole in the bottom of each. Not a lot of protection from the snow. No boots? He couldn't see any from where he sat.

After a moment of rummaging through piles, the woman pulled out a plastic bag. "Here." She carried it back and thrust it at Sharleen.

His partner tugged out a proof photo, turned it in his direction, then, when he nodded, shoved it back in the bag. "Is it all right if we take this with us?"

The woman shrugged. "Sure."

Sharleen set the bag down on the coffee table in front of them. "So you didn't hear any noises in the house in the last twenty or thirty minutes?"

"No. I was asleep. I go to bed at eleven and don't wake up until it's time to get the kid off to school."

The kid? Daniel studied her. Just what kind of relationship did the two of them have, anyway? Obviously not a terribly warm and fuzzy one.

She shifted under his intense gaze. "Mia, I mean. Look, I'll do whatever I can to help. I worry about her, always falling and hurting herself so I have to take her to the hospital. She's real clumsy, you know? I have to keep an eye on her all the time."

A five-year-old that falls and hurts herself so badly that she repeatedly has to go to the hospital? *That doesn't sound suspicious at all.* Daniel frowned. It was tough not to get cynical in his line of work, but sometimes that was a good thing, made him pay closer attention to body language, and to what a suspect *wasn't* saying, as much or more than the words they were spewing. Not that this woman was a suspect, as Sharleen had reminded him. "Do you mind if we go upstairs and take a look around?"

Her face darkened a little. "I guess not. Mia's room is the second one on the left."

"When we come back, we'll need to get contact information for her mother, if you have it." He headed for the stairs without waiting for a response.

Sharleen followed him up to the little girl's room. Daniel flipped on the light switch. Several worn Barbies, one missing a leg and another a head, and two dolls, both naked with short, jagged hair, as though they'd been shorn with dull child's scissors, were scattered across the floor. Whoever the intruder was, if he hadn't used a light, Daniel was surprised he hadn't tripped or made any sound while making his way over to the bed. Several candy wrappers, an empty juice box, and other bits of garbage littered the floor around the bed. The sheets were rumpled and looked like they hadn't been washed in a while. Otherwise, the room appeared to be a fairly ordinary little girl's room, the mess a result of playtime, not a struggle. "Why wouldn't she have cried out?"

Sharleen had been examining the window, which was closed. She turned when he asked the question. "What?"

"Wouldn't she have woken up when he wrapped the blanket around her and picked her up? I'm surprised she didn't scream or call out for Darlene or something."

Sharleen lifted her shoulders. "Maybe she did, and her stepmother is a really deep sleeper."

"Maybe." His phone vibrated, and Daniel pulled it from his shirt pocket and glanced at the screen. "Forensics is here. Hopefully they'll be able to find evidence we can't see, because nothing looks out of the ordinary to me."

Sharleen sighed. "Me neither. Let's go get that contact information and see if the mother can offer any insight into who might have taken Mia."

"Yeah. And I'd like to look into the fact that CAS has been

involved with all four kids, see if we can connect those dots to find out what that means."

Daniel trailed after his partner as she headed out into the hall. In the doorway, he turned for one last look at the room. A Barbie in a long golden gown and glittering crown, the only new-looking thing in the room, lay beside the pillow. Probably Mia's favorite. Was she asking for it, even now? She had to be terrified, although she hadn't appeared to be moving when the abductor handed her off to the person in the back seat. Daniel's chest squeezed. Had the man killed her? He scanned the room again, looking for a hint of blood or anything else that might indicate violence, but saw nothing. Maybe she was a really deep sleeper too. Or the abductor had drugged her. That thought jogged a memory. On a hunch, Daniel walked back across the room, his gaze fixed on the floor. As he approached the bed, a tiny object on the wooden floor, almost hidden beneath a doll's dress, caught his eye. Daniel took the pen out of his pocket, crouched down, and poked the dress aside.

Sharleen came up behind him. "What is it?"

"I got to thinking that, since she didn't make any noise, maybe the girl had been drugged. Then I remembered seeing a tiny piece of plastic on the floor with the other garbage. What do you think, does it look like the right size to cover the tip of a needle?"

"Possibly. Make sure you mention it to forensics. Maybe they can get something off of it."

"Here's hoping." Since he'd lost the chance to provide a DNA sample to them when the suspect grabbed back his ski mask, Daniel would be very happy if he could supply it to them some other way. The suspect had been wearing gloves when he saw him, but it was possible he'd left prints earlier, when preparing the needle. He straightened up, and he and Sharleen picked their way carefully to the hallway.

Darlene was waiting for them at the bottom of the stairs. "Here." She held out a crumpled piece of paper. "Mia's mother's name and the last number I had for her. Can't guarantee it's still good, though."

"Thanks." Daniel took it and stuck it into his jacket pocket. "Is she in Toronto?"

"Last I heard."

A knock sounded on the door. Darlene turned toward it, a scowl twisting across her face. "Now what?"

"That's the forensics team." Daniel gave her an apologetic look as Sharleen went to open the door and let them in. "They'll be going all over Mia's bedroom, and anywhere else in the house the intruder might have been, hoping to find evidence." He reached into his shirt pocket and pulled out a card. "Here's my contact information. If you think of anything else that might be helpful, please give me a call."

"I will." She stuck the card into the pocket of her robe then grabbed his arm. "Do you … will you be able to find her, do you think?" Her voice wavered, and for the first time, Daniel saw fear in her eyes. Maybe she cared about the girl a little more than it had seemed, at first. Or maybe it had occurred to her that she could lose her monthly child allowance check.

He patted her hand, which was ice cold. "I promise you we'll do everything we possibly can to bring her home safe."

Darlene slid her fingers out from under his. "Thank you."

Daniel spoke briefly with the forensics team, filling them in on what little he and his partner knew as he took them upstairs and showed them the piece of plastic beside the bed. When he came back down, he and Sharleen headed out to the porch.

He contemplated what he'd said to the woman as he pulled the door shut behind them. He had every intention of doing everything in his power to keep his promise to her and bring Mia home.

The problem was, based on the disappearing acts he'd witnessed tonight, the possibility of finding Mia safe and sound felt terrifyingly slim.

Chapter Nine

"His hair was medium brown and cut slightly above his ears." Daniel drew a line along the side of his head with one finger to demonstrate to the artist.

With his guidance, the woman penciled a sketch that Daniel really hoped captured the look of the alleged child abductor. It had been fairly dark in the backyard, and he'd only had a couple of seconds to take in the guy's face, but what he saw on the paper seemed a decent likeness. It was the best the two of them could do, anyway. "That's all I can remember. Looks good." He stood up and stretched his arms above his head before crossing over to open the door of the room they'd commandeered down at police headquarters.

The woman started gathering up her supplies. "We'll run this through our facial recognition software and get it out on the Internet as quickly as possible." She closed the lid on her box of pencils. "With the amber alert still on, the public should be paying attention." The artist zipped her bag closed and slung it over her shoulder before walking to the door. "Someone has to know who this guy is. Hopefully we'll get some solid tips in the next few hours."

"I hope so. Thanks."

The sketch artist nodded and brushed past him. Raised voices in the room next door caught Daniel's attention, and he propped a shoulder against the doorframe to listen, in case someone needed assistance.

"So, you understand that if you post bail, he will be able to come home, right? At least until we decide whether or not this will go to trial."

Through the six-inch opening, Daniel caught a glimpse of a

dark-haired man, a lawyer, from the sounds of it, sitting at a table, hands clasped tightly in front of him.

Daniel shifted slightly so he could see the woman, a bottle-blonde in a tight blue tank top, perched on the chair across from him. Two little girls, doll-like with strawberry curls and big blue eyes, shared the chair beside her and silently watched the man across from them.

"You'd be wasting your time if you dragged this into court. I over-reacted, that's all. It was no big deal. I want him to come home." Her eyes, rimmed with heavy dark make-up, traveled down the length of the man across from her and slowly back up. "That is, unless you'd like to come home with me. I could do with an upgrade right about now." Her bag slid from her lap and several items spilled out across the floor. Letting loose with a string of curse words, she hopped off her chair and crouched down to shove everything back into the bag.

"Godzilla would be an upgrade, lady." The man muttered the words, too quietly for the woman to hear him, but Daniel caught them. He pressed his lips together to keep from laughing. Whoever the guy was, Daniel liked him already.

The woman settled back onto her seat and looked him over again. "Well?"

He didn't bother to respond this time, just leveled a cool stare in her direction.

After a few seconds she let out a harsh laugh. "Guess not, huh. Well, your loss." She flipped her long, stringy hair back over her shoulder. "So, can we go or what?"

The lawyer pulled a piece of paper out of his briefcase and slid it across the table to her. "Sign this."

"Umm, a pen would be helpful."

The lawyer's jaw tightened, but he pulled a pen from his shirt pocket and handed it to her.

Daniel admired his composure. His gaze drifted to the little girls. The red welt on the cheek of the youngest one sent anger twisting through him. Was that what this was about? Was the woman refusing to press charges against her husband or boyfriend or whatever he was after he'd clearly pounded on this innocent child? His hands clenched into fists. Nothing should surprise him anymore, but the willingness of a parent to allow her child to be abused by another adult while she did nothing still always did. The lawyer managed a smile for the two little girls, but they only stared at him, eyes wide.

The woman scribbled something at the bottom of the page, then shoved the chair away from the table and grabbed her black bag from the floor. "See ya, sexy."

Taking the hand of her little sister, the older girl pulled her toward the door after their mother.

The man jumped to his feet. Striding past the girls, he slapped a palm against the doorframe. The woman whirled toward him, eyes flashing.

Alarm bells went off in Daniel's head. He took a step forward then stopped, waiting to see what would happen.

Leaning in, the lawyer locked his gaze on the woman's. "You have one main job in life, to take care of your girls. That's it."

"My girls are my business." She spat the words at him.

"If I see you in here again, maybe they won't be."

A flash of fear darted through her eyes before they turned insolent again. The lawyer stepped to the side as she stormed out of the room.

Daniel ducked into the space he'd been in with the artist. He watched the woman cross the lobby, her daughters on her heels. That tiny flicker of fear was a good sign. Maybe the lawyer had actually gotten through to her, and she would think about what he had said. Probably not, but maybe. Daniel stepped forward and peered into the other room. Rolling one shoulder and then the other as if to relieve the tension of the meeting, the man turned to grab his briefcase.

A disturbance at the front desk outside the rooms caught Daniel's attention, and he turned to see what was going on. A man in a white undershirt, beer belly hanging out underneath, stood at the counter, clutching the arm of the girl's mother. "I told you I didn't do anything. I'm gonna talk to my lawyer."

"You do that, sir." The officer at the desk spoke mildly.

The man was in no mood to be placated. He tossed a few choice words at the cop who didn't flinch.

The lawyer had walked to the doorway of his room, observing the scene like Daniel was.

"Let's go, *sweetheart.*" The man shoved the door open with one foot and yanked the woman outside. The girls slipped out behind them, like wraiths. The door slammed shut.

The lawyer's eyes met Daniel's. "Ain't love grand?"

Daniel offered him a wry grin. "You handled that well."

The man sighed. "Best I could do. I know I got a little out of line at the end there," he shot Daniel a sheepish look, "but at that point I really didn't care."

"I don't blame you." Daniel stuck out his hand. "Detective Daniel Grey."

The man took his hand in a firm grip and shook it. "Gage Kelly."

"Crown attorney?"

"Yep." Gage walked back to the table and began stuffing papers into his briefcase.

"Frustrating job, I'm sure."

"It definitely can be. Nights like this are the real perks. I get to drive all the way down here to facilitate the process of sending an animal back home to his two defenceless little girls. And now I'll be stuck in the office half the night filling out the paperwork. And so will my brother Holden. He's the social worker who got called to go to that home this afternoon." He snapped the briefcase shut and picked it up. He rounded the table and came back to stand in the doorway. "He couldn't get the woman to agree to press charges either, and neither he nor his partner could convince either of the girls to admit to being hit. They made up some story about how they were playing tag when the little one tripped and hit her face on the coffee table." He nodded at the door where the family had disappeared. "It's rough, seeing kids in situations like that and often not being able to do a lot about it." Anger darkened his eyes, but his voice remained even. "I'm sure you can relate, with everything you see in your line of work."

Daniel stuck both hands in the pockets of his dress pants. "Yes, unfortunately I can."

"Well," Gage clapped a hand on his shoulder, "back to the trenches. Good to meet you, Detective."

"You too." Daniel watched him as he strode across the lobby and went out the door, pulling it shut behind him a little harder than necessary. Daniel didn't blame him. Their jobs *were* frustrating sometimes. It certainly hadn't taken long for the idealism—the belief that he could actually have a big enough impact through his work to make the world a better place—to fade away. He *was* able to help some people, to make a difference in a life or in a family once in a while, which he clung to when days like this had him questioning whether or not it was all worth it.

Gage clearly struggled with the same thoughts, and his brother likely did too. Still, they all had to keep trying. Someone had to do something about all the evil in the world; beat it back, at least, like a pack of ravenous wolves kept at bay by a tiny torch. If not, they'd all soon be lost in the darkness.

With a heavy sigh, Daniel tugged the door closed behind him and headed for the exit. The lawyer's words about heading back into the trenches echoed in his head. The expression was apt. This was war, and all any of them could do was fight one small battle at a time.

Fighting back nausea, the woman finished reading the boy's account of what had happened that night then forced herself to read every word of the police report that followed before snapping the folder shut and tossing it across her desk. Prickles of disgust and horror crawled across her skin, and she rubbed her hands hard up and down both arms. No matter how many times she read the stories, how often the frightened little faces flashed, unbidden, across her mind, they never failed to sicken her.

For ten seconds. That's how long she allowed herself to

wallow before she shoved what she had seen or heard back into a compartment deep inside her mind and slammed the door shut. She flipped her long gleaming black hair over one shoulder.

Twisting her arm, the woman checked the silver watch clasped around her slender wrist. Twenty seconds. She exhaled loudly and reached across the desk for the folder again. Well, this story had been worse than most. She was entitled to a few extra seconds of grieving for the losses those two boys had suffered; loss of childhood, of innocence, of a normal, carefree existence. It was a terrible, terrible shame.

And it was exactly what she needed.

Clutching the file in her right hand, she stared down at it, absently pushing away a tall pile of similar, cream-colored folders with the back of her left hand. In her fingers she held the last piece of the puzzle. The final member of the team the board of their organization had assembled to carry out their rescue missions in the city. Now, after their recent setback, they could continue their work. All she had to do was convince him to join them. The image of two terrified boys pressed against the back of a closet wall, hands clasped together, dark eyes wide with terror, jolted through her mind. Dropping the folder, she yanked open the top right drawer of her desk and reached for her pack of cigarettes.

Only after drawing in several deep, nicotine-laden breaths, did the fury that had gripped her body begin to ease. She blew out a puff of smoke and tapped the perfectly manicured fingers of her free hand on top of the folder.

With a curt nod, she stubbed out the cigarette in the small glass bowl that she'd washed clean after the last time she'd indulged in one. Other than the pile of folders, the only items on the dark cherry surface were the bowl, a small black phone, a laptop computer, and a ceramic vase that held several blue and red pens. She believed in order. Clutter detracted from the control she held over herself, her circumstances, and, as often as possible, the circumstances of others.

Which was where he would come in. Picking up the file

again, the woman tapped it slowly on the desk. It would cost him, of course, everything he had and more. But he would agree. One of her greatest assets was her ability to make people see things her way. She flipped open the folder and focused her intense gaze on the boy's haunted eyes, steeling herself for the task ahead. She'd spent years meticulously building up an arsenal of tactics she could use to bring someone over to her way of thinking, and the tiny spark of fire that still burned down deep in those dark eyes suggested that she might need every one of them to convince him he was the only one who could help them.

With the sigh of resignation she could never quite repress when she was about to change the course of another human being's life, she reached for the phone to let the rest of her team know they had found the one they'd been looking for.

Desperate to get home after a long, infuriating day, he pounded on the computer keyboard, trying to finish his paperwork. When the phone rang, he grabbed it and pressed it between his chin and shoulder, continuing to type. "Kelly."

"Frustrating, isn't it?"

"What's that?" He didn't recognize the woman's voice. A little lower and smoother than any of his female friends or colleagues, with the slightest hint of a foreign accent he couldn't quite place. He tabbed ahead to the next question on the form. Only a few more sentences and he could leave.

"The inability of the system to save everyone."

He stopped typing. "Who is this?"

"Someone who cares about helping those kids as much as you do."

"What kids?"

"All the kids whose parents think it's okay to ease their own frustrations by taking them out on their children. Starting with those two adorable girls you saw today."

His head shot up, and he looked around the room as though he might see the lens of a camera sticking through the window blinds. "How do you know who I saw today? And what did you say your name was?"

"My name doesn't matter. All that matters is that I know how you feel. I understand that you are angry, and you feel helpless to do anything about it. But you're not. There is something you can do."

He swung his chair around and toed the door shut. "What do you mean?"

"I can't tell you any more over the phone. We need to meet face to face. There's a café on the corner of Yonge and Davenport. Annie's. Do you know it?"

He paused. He did know Annie's. Whether or not he was ready to meet some sultry-voiced stranger there to hear about something that sounded a little cloak and dagger to him was another matter.

Two pairs of blue eyes peering out of serious little faces flashed through his mind. He sighed. "Yes, I know it. When do you want to meet?"

Chapter Ten

She looked like her voice sounded. Dark. Beautiful. Slightly exotic. The man knew it was her as soon as he saw her. Her ebony hair was pulled back in a sleek ponytail, emphasizing a high-cheek-boned, porcelain face that appeared almost fragile until his eyes locked with her steel-gray ones from across the room, and the illusion was shattered. Long, graceful fingers resting on the table, she exuded a calm strength that seemed out of place somehow in the middle of the buzzing downtown coffee shop.

He slid onto the bench across from her, drawing in deep breaths of air rich with the scent of brewing coffee to calm himself.

For a long moment she looked at the man without speaking. It took every ounce of willpower he had not to shift in his seat under the intense scrutiny. Finally, the corners of her full, red lips turned up slightly. "You came."

Although he knew it was rude, he glanced down at his watch, hoping to give himself an out if this conversation was as bizarre as he expected it to be. "I don't have a lot of time. It's been a long day."

The sadness in her smile didn't soften the steel in her gaze. "It must have been difficult for you, walking away from those two little girls."

It had been, more than she knew. He looked deep into the eyes that continued to watch him intently. *Maybe she does know.* He shrugged. "Just part of the job."

Her mouth evened to a straight line. "How would you feel if someone had said the same thing about you and your brother?"

His head jerked. "How do you ...?" Narrowing his eyes, he

studied her, a cold sense of foreboding settling in his stomach. "You've seen my file."

"It was necessary, unfortunately. Does that bother you?"

"Of course not. I love the feeling of being stripped naked in front of strangers."

A glimmer of humor twitched the corners of her lips. "I suppose that might have been another way to go. Reviewing your file seemed more efficient, if less ..." Her gaze flicked over him, "... pleasant."

Her levity did nothing to ease his trepidation. "I think it's time you tell me who you are and what you want from me."

She laced her fingers together. "I'd be happy to discuss what we want with you."

"We?"

"Yes. There are others who want to help these children, like you do. Many others. And we are fully prepared."

"Prepared for what?"

"To rescue the children, like the sweet girls you met today. As you are aware, sometimes Children's Aid is not able to pull these little ones out of their situations for one reason or another. The system is good and helps many, but it has limitations. That is where we come in."

"What does all of this have to do with me?"

"We have a network in place to take the children and place them with families who will care for them and give them the safe and loving home they deserve. All we need now is the person to go into the homes and get the children out."

His first instinct was to laugh. The sound died in his throat though, when he met her eyes. "Is this some kind of a joke?" He clenched his hands together tightly in front of him.

"I assure you I am dead serious."

He stared at her then slid to the end of the bench.

Long, graceful fingers closed over his arm in a surprisingly strong grip. "Hear me out. Please. That's all I ask."

He didn't move for several seconds until, with a heavy sigh, he shifted back to his seat.

Her hand dropped from his arm. "Thank you. As I was saying, the children—"

Leaning forward, he lowered his voice. "Are you sure Annie's is the place to have this conversation?"

Amusement flitted across her face. "What did you have in mind? A covert meeting down at the docks, perhaps? An abandoned warehouse at midnight?"

His jaw tightened.

The amusement faded. "I'm not laughing at you, I promise. Experience has taught me, however, that those types of meetings only tend to be more conspicuous and elicit more suspicion than meeting in the open. Here, in the busiest section of the biggest city in the country, no one will pay any attention to us. We can say or do anything we like, and no one will give us a second glance."

He hesitated, battling with himself, until curiosity narrowly edged out wariness and he leaned back in his seat, keeping his voice low. "All right then. So you're looking for someone to help you get these children out?"

"We're not looking. We've found the man we want."

He struggled to find his footing, to not be swept away as confusion—and, down deep, a flicker of excitement—swirled around him. "And you think it's me."

She rested both her hands, soft and warm, on his. "I know it is."

The breath that had made it halfway down his throat stuck there.

She was drawing him in, like a spider into the web she was slowly spinning in front of his eyes. He could see her setting up the trap for him but, although his mind yelled at him to run from the danger, his feet refused to move.

A light, heady perfume drifted in the air around her, mingling with the coffee. The enticing combination made his head spin. He struggled to keep the emotional turmoil off his face as he studied her. Eastern European, he decided, although time and distance had softened the accent to an alluring trace. A thousand questions flared across his mind, but he was having trouble latching on to any one of them. The scent of her, and the feel of her hands on his, wasn't helping. He settled for a simple, "Why?"

She pulled her hands back and intertwined her fingers again.

He drew in a quivering breath and pulled his hands out of her reach, pressing both palms against the cool leather seat on either side of him. If she was about to make some crazy proposal, he was determined to stay clear-headed long enough to hear it.

"You understand what those children are going through. You care about people, or you wouldn't be doing the job you are doing. You're smart and resourceful, and full of courage, or you would never have survived your own childhood. And you have access to the information we need."

"Information?"

"About the children. You can get into the files, tell us who needs us the most so that the team can plan out the missions."

The quiet words extinguished the excitement that had sparked, against his will and reason, deep inside him. "You want me to get confidential information for you? You know that's illegal."

She met his gaze steadily but didn't speak.

Everything she's proposing to me is illegal. Passing along information appeared to be the least of the offences. A revelation struck him. "Did you have something to do with those four recent child abductions in Toronto?"

She hesitated then straightened her shoulders. "Those *rescues* were the work of my organization, yes."

His forehead wrinkled. "Then you already have someone to do this job."

"We did, yes. Unfortunately, he was compromised on his last mission and has been transported from the city to a safe location. He will no longer be able to work for us, not in Canada, anyway."

His shoulders slumped. "So the same thing could happen to me. What makes you think I would risk everything to help you?"

As an answer, she pulled several file folders out of her briefcase and set them in front of him. He kept his eyes on her for a moment more before dropping them to the pile. Slowly, he reached for the first one and lifted the cover. His eyes scanned the page. When he came across one particularly heart-wrenching story, he swore softly and slammed the file shut. He flipped quickly through the other ones.

The fingers of her right hand twitched. If she wasn't a smoker, she had been, and she clearly wanted a cigarette now. *Maybe not as in control as she pretends to be.*

When he finished looking at each file, he lifted his head. His stomach churned. This was insane, but if there was any chance she wasn't a psychopath and there really was something that could be done ... "I'd go in alone?"

Her fingers stilled. "Yes. Every extra person that goes in increases the risk of discovery exponentially. One man can move much more quickly and discreetly."

"How would I handle more than one child?"

"We choose our cases very carefully. These would all be only children, with no siblings to comfort or help protect them. And they all live with just one parent, in order to decrease the chances of someone detecting your presence, or you being accosted by more than one adult at a time."

"Even so, how would I get the child out without him screaming and alerting his parent?"

"There is a lot of money behind our operation. You should know that. A lot of planning and research has gone into preparing, and you will have many resources at your disposal. We have found the best drug to give to the children so they stay asleep until they arrive at their destination. It does them no harm, I assure you."

"And if I am confronted by an angry parent anyway?"

"You will have everything you need to handle any situation."

He tilted his head. "You mean ...?"

"You will have everything you need."

He chewed on his lower lip. "What would I do with the child when I bring him out?"

"A car will be waiting to take him from you. You simply

hand him over and then disappear. In the past we have used a getaway car for that, but with our recent close call, we have decided it would be better for you to make your own way home, less conspicuous."

Transportation was the least of his concerns. "Where do the kids go from there?"

She contemplated him.

He met her gaze steadily. No way he would even consider getting involved in something this crazy if she wouldn't tell him what happened to the kids after he handed them over. *I almost hope she doesn't.* That would make walking away that much easier.

The woman nodded, as though she had made up her mind about something. "For six months they will be held at our facility, a type of protective custody if you will. During this time, they will receive counseling to help them through their period of transition. After that they will be placed with a family who has agreed to move to a new city, begin a new life with a child they will introduce as their own."

He shook his head. "I don't see how that would work. Kids whose parents treat them like garbage still have an innate desire to protect those parents, even feel a kind of love for them. It seems like drugging them, ripping them away from their homes, and handing them over to strangers would only add to the trauma they already have to deal with."

She reached into the bag she had set on the floor and pulled out another cream-colored folder. Silently, she set it down on the table and slid it across to him.

A muscle in his cheek twitched. The cover of the folder shook slightly as he lifted it. "What are these?"

She waved a hand toward the stack of photographs. "Look closely."

He leaned in to look at the first photo. A young boy holding an ice cream cone rode on the shoulders of a tall, athletic-looking man. Both the man and the boy were laughing as a woman with long red hair and kind, smiling eyes, wiped ice cream from the boy's chin with a napkin.

He lifted the photo to get a better look, then pulled the first pile of folders closer and flipped through them until he found the one he was looking for. He laid the new picture beside the one in the folder. His forehead wrinkled as he looked up. "This is the same kid?"

She nodded. "All those photos match up to the ones you viewed earlier. Each shot was taken one to two years after the children were rescued. You will find that in every case the children are happier, healthier, and more self-confident than they ever were in their old lives. I'm not saying it is easy, Mr. Kelly, but as you can see, it *is* possible. Children are amazingly resilient, and our counselors are among the best in North America. They have never failed to get through to a child and convince him that he or she really can have a better life."

"What about paperwork? They wouldn't have birth certificates or anything."

She didn't respond, simply scrutinized him as if waiting for the light to go on. It didn't take long.

He shook his head. "I guess anything's possible if there's as much money as you say."

A smile played at the corners of her mouth.

"Where does all that money come from anyway?"

"We have spent years cultivating an extensive group of investors. Each of them has been chosen based on his or her personal power and financial resources as well as past history."

"Past history?"

"Yes. Every one of them grew up in similar circumstances as you and your brother. I'm sure it won't surprise you to learn that, when we approach them, very few of them turn down the opportunity to help children whose pain they understand all too well."

He slumped against his seat. "This is a lot to take in. Can I have some time to think about it?"

"We can give you forty-eight hours. I realize this is a big decision, but ..." She stared down at her fingers for a moment before looking up. "As I said, everything is ready. The children we are trying to help are all in extreme situations. Their lives are in danger, which is why we are willing to risk everything to help them. And every day that we delay is another day that these children wait, alone and terrified, for someone to come and help them."

He bent forward slightly, the words hitting him like an elbow to his ribs. "I understand."

"I know you do. Eight p.m. the day after tomorrow then. We will meet down at dock number five."

He managed a shaky grin.

"All right, at the Starbucks one block west of here. And you understand that you cannot tell anyone about this."

"Of course not."

"Not even your brother."

His muscles tightened again. "If you read my file then you know my brother has had to live his whole life with the fact that he killed our father. I'd never add to that burden by asking him to keep another secret."

"I trust you. That's the biggest reason I want you for this. I sincerely hope you will agree to help us. I believe with all my heart that you are the one to save these children."

He slid off the end of the bench and got to his feet.

The woman reached up and rested a hand on his arm. "Whatever you decide, Kelly, it was a pleasure to meet you. You are an exceptional man."

He nodded and, when she pulled back her hand, turned and headed for the door. *I'm not an exceptional man, I'm an exceptional fool.*

Because only a fool would even consider getting involved in a scheme like the one that woman had described to him.

Chapter Eleven

The hours of darkness stretched on. He'd known he wouldn't sleep, but it was more than restlessness that kept him tossing and turning in his bed until the sheets, damp with sweat, hung off the side of the bed. Agony twisted his insides, and with a low moan, he clasped both arms tightly across his abdomen, trying to ease the pain.

When the thick blackness outside gave way to a cold mist that pressed against his bedroom window, he gave up and swung his legs over the side of the bed. Elbows digging into his knees, he dropped his head into his hands.

Lord, I have no idea what to do. Show me. The anguished plea ripped through him as he lifted his gaze to the ceiling. *What if she's lying? What if she is really part of a child pornography ring or the sex trade or...* He couldn't think of anything more heinous than either of those things. A picture of the woman he'd met at the coffee shop flashed through his mind. Although she was the most guarded person he had ever met, he'd seen something there, deep in those gray eyes—an intense dedication to a cause she believed to be just. There was nothing shifty in her gaze, nothing to hint that she felt guilty or uncertain about what she was doing. Whether or not it was right, she was completely committed to what her organization was doing and was willing to risk a great deal for it. Not exactly the profile of someone involved in something sordid and illicit.

And what about all those people who'd invested in the organization? Personal power. What did that mean? Business people? Politicians? How high up did this thing go anyway? He rubbed his face with both hands. It wasn't likely she would tell him if he asked. *She's probably already told me a lot more than she wanted to. Or was supposed to.*

He glanced back at the rumpled bed. Maybe this had all been a bad dream, a remnant of the take-out Mexican food he'd indulged in at the office.

The sick feeling in his stomach at the idea that this might not be real told him a lot.

His eyebrows drew together. So, the thought of last night's encounter being nothing more than a bizarre kind of nightmare disappointed him. Maybe he simply wanted to keep his options open. To cling to the idea for a couple of days at least that he actually *had* options when it came to helping suffering kids. That didn't mean he was going to blindly jump, like some desperate hobo, on board whatever crazy train these people were riding.

Exhaling loudly, he untangled the navy sheets from around his legs and tossed them onto the bed so he could stand up. *Time to go to work.* Back to the real world where everyone went quietly about their own business, no one typing on their computer keyboards or gossiping around the water cooler while secretly plotting to take the law into their own hands. The same law that he had a deep respect for, and other than the odd speeding ticket, had always operated within the confines of. *An attitude that has served me well so far in life.*

He stumbled into the washroom and twisted on the tap in the sink. Grabbing his toothbrush, he squeezed on some paste and began vigorously brushing his teeth. *Has it? Has it served me— or anyone else—well?*

His head whipped up, and he glanced around the tiny room as though whoever had thrown that question out was hiding in the shower or crouched behind the clothes hamper. With a grimace, he dropped his toothbrush into the holder, stripped off his boxers and T-shirt, and shoved open the shower curtain, hoping to gain a little perspective under a stream of hot water.

Although somehow he knew it would take a lot more than that.

Chapter Twelve

The red light was flashing on line two. Daniel's heart rate picked up. A couple of other cops had been handling most of the calls coming in with potential tips after the suspect's picture had been released three hours earlier. If this one was being passed along to him, it was either because they were overwhelmed by all the responses or, more likely, it sounded like it actually might have merit.

Daniel snatched up the receiver and hit the button to open line two. "Detective Grey."

"Uh, yeah, I'm calling about the picture I saw on the news, of the man who might be kidnapping those kids?"

"Great. Do you think you know who he is?"

"Yeah. I went to school with the guy. Name's Ted Stiller."

Daniel's chair snapped into place as he straightened up. "Can you tell me where he lives?"

"He grew up in East York. Still there, from what I hear."

He was already clicking away on his laptop keyboard, looking up Stiller in the East York Toronto neighborhood. There were three in that area, but only one T. Stiller. "Woodmount Avenue?"

"Yeah, that's it. Used to be his foster parents' place, but they're both in a retirement home now, so he lives there alone."

"And you're sure he's the same man as the one in the picture?"

"Positive. I mean, I haven't seen him in, like, ten years so he looks a little older, but I'd know him anywhere. And, to be honest, I wasn't that surprised to hear he was in trouble."

"Why is that?"

"He had a rough upbringing. His dad was gone before he

was born, and his mom was an addict. He came to East York to live with his foster parents when he was ten or eleven. From what I gathered, his foster dad wasn't a good guy. Ted would try to hide them when we changed for gym class, but I often saw bruises on him. And while he came to my house quite a bit, I was never invited to go there. I suggested it a couple of times, but he got all weird about it. Anyway, after high school we went to different colleges and kind of drifted apart. I always wondered what happened to him, and now I guess I know. He obviously went down a bad road, which I'm sorry to hear."

Daniel asked for the caller's name and number then jotted it down on a notepad on his desk. "Thanks for calling in. I really appreciate it. I'll be in touch if I have any other questions for you, okay?"

"Sure. I hate to rat the guy out, but I have kids of my own, you know? I don't know what I'd do if anyone took them from me."

"I understand. Thanks again." Daniel hung up the phone and leaped to his feet. He crossed the hall to his partner's cubicle. "Shar, I think we've got something."

She spun her desk chair around. "What is it?"

"Someone just called in and ID'd our guy. Sounds legit. He said he went to school with him and was positive he was someone named Ted Stiller over in East York."

She grabbed her jacket off the hook by the door. "Let's go."

They made their way to Daniel's car in the parking lot. When they reached it, he tossed her the keys. "You drive. I need to call for a warrant."

A thought occurred to him as he dialed. If Ted Stiller had been in the system, CAS would have information on him that might give them insight into his motivation, maybe even his plans for the children he'd taken. While Sharleen drove, Daniel put in a request for a warrant to search the suspect's home, and another one to gain access to his CAS file. Traffic was heavy, and Daniel tapped his hand on the car door handle until Sharleen shot him a look and he realized he was doing it.

"I'm getting there as fast as I can."

"I know. I just want to make sure we get to this guy before he skips town, if he hasn't already. And if he happens to be holding the kids at his place, every second counts." It wasn't likely, given that Stiller and the latest abducted kid—Mia—had headed in opposite directions, but at this point anything was possible.

Sharleen didn't answer, but she did step a little harder on the gas, which he appreciated. To take his mind off the traffic, Daniel pulled out his phone and logged into his account. He did a search for Ted Stiller, but nothing came up. So the guy didn't have a police record—that didn't mean he hadn't committed any crimes without getting caught, or that he hadn't recently gone bad.

"Here we are."

Sharleen turned into the driveway of a well-kept, middle-class home. A silver Camry sat in the driveway. Daniel ran the plates. "It's registered to a Theodore John Stiller. Hopefully that means the guy is home or that he hasn't gone far." He quickly called up his messages then looked over at his partner. "No warrants yet."

She shrugged. "If there's any chance the kids have been brought here, that justifies a search under exigent circumstances. Let's go."

That was good enough for him. He wasn't about to sit around waiting for permission, not when children could be in danger. "Right behind you." He shoved open the car door and jumped out.

No one answered when he rang the doorbell. The mailbox had been propped open by a bunch of fliers and several pieces of mail. Three newspapers had been tossed onto the porch. Looked like Stiller hadn't left the premises in a few days. Or hadn't returned to it. Daniel's stomach tightened. They waited a couple of minutes, ringing the bell, knocking on the door, and peering through the front window. There were no signs of life in the place. Daniel tried the handle. Locked.

Sharleen jerked her head toward the side of the house. "Let's check the back door."

Daniel followed her around the building to the yard. The back door was locked too, but older and wooden. Should be easier to break through than the front door. Sharleen nodded at him. Daniel shoved a shoulder against the door three or four times before it crashed open and they stepped inside. "Toronto Police Services." Daniel called out the warning and listened for any noise or movement in response.

Nothing.

"I'll check upstairs."

She nodded. "I'll do a walk around the main floor then go down to the basement."

Daniel headed for the stairs. He kept one hand on the butt of the Glock 27 in the holster on his belt as he edged up, his back to the wall. The first room on the left appeared to be largely unused, possibly a guest room. A double bed in the corner was neatly made up, but a thin layer of dust covered the surface of the dresser lining the wall. Daniel checked the closet and lifted the bedspread to look under the bed, but there were no signs of life.

The washroom was clean and the shower empty. He proceeded to a larger bedroom, likely the main one. Again, everything was neat and tidy and sparsely furnished, although this room appeared to have been recently used. A pair of pajama bottoms had been tossed over a wooden chair in the corner, and a glass of water sat on the bedside table on top of a folded newspaper. Daniel leaned in to check the date on the paper. March 8th. Mia had been abducted in the early morning hours of the 9th. Today was the 11th. As he'd feared when he saw the papers on the porch, it looked like Ted Stiller had been away from his home since the evening of the latest abduction.

Which meant there was a good chance that the man had fled the city, possibly even the country, by now.

He quickly finished his check of the last room, clearly an office. Shelves of books lined the walls and a laptop sat on a large oak desk that took up much of the room. As soon as they had a warrant in hand, they could seize that and do a more thorough search for any other items that might provide them with information about Ted Stiller and what he was up to.

Daniel went back down the stairs and met Sharleen in the kitchen. She lifted both hands. "Nothing. There's no one on the main floor or in the basement. And no signs that anyone has been held here against their will. Everything is tidy."

"Upstairs too. He does have a computer that we should grab, and there was a newspaper beside his bed dated the 8th. I'm guessing we'll find papers from the 9th to the 11th on the porch, which would indicate he hasn't been home since the latest kidnapping."

"Which does make him look like a prime suspect, at least."

"That's true. Let's get a team down here to go over the place more thoroughly, and we should report to the Detective Sergeant, update him on what's going on."

Sharleen tugged a phone from her pocket. "I'm on it."

While she called in, Daniel headed out to the porch. He confirmed the dates on the newspapers but left them where they were.

Leaning a shoulder against the post at the top of the porch stairs, Daniel ran a mental checklist of everything they knew so far. Sharleen was right. The guy really did look like a viable suspect. His heart pounded in his chest. This could actually be the big break they'd been working toward. If they could bring Ted Stiller in and put him behind bars, they might have made the city a safer place for all the kids who lived there.

Now all they had to do was find him.

Chapter Thirteen

They were crying. Even from far away—where they always seemed to be, no matter how hard he tried to get to them—the fear and desperation in the children's voices swept through the frigid air between them like a moaning wind. Branches whipped across his face as he stumbled through the woods, frantic to find them. Both arms in front of him, he swiped at the low-hanging branches and crashed his way through the thick underbrush.

It loomed in front of him so suddenly he barely managed to skid to a stop and avoid thudding up against it—a stone wall so tall it swallowed up the thin light of the sun and cast a shadow onto him as thick and heavy as a net.

"No!" He pounded the unyielding rock with his fists until blood dripped down his arms. Shaking fingers dug frantically for a hold, but the stone was smooth, seamless. Planting both throbbing palms against the wall, he rested his forehead on the cold face of it. *I've been here before. Many times.* The pungent odors of moss and decaying leaves hung in the air, clinging to his shallow, gasping breaths and choking him as they flooded his throat.

More heart-wrenching pleas shattered the damp stillness. He lifted his head. They were close this time, closer than they had ever been. He strained to hear.

"Help us."

His heart sank. They were on the other side of the wall.

Look up.

Tipping back his head, he scanned the impenetrable rock in front of him. His breath caught. Above him, a dark shadow appeared, a small chink in the stone. He reached for it, sliding his fingers into the opening and pulling himself a few inches off the ground. Another dark hole gaped above the first one, and he flung his free arm up and grabbed hold of it with trembling fingers. His sneaker caught a tiny lip of rock, and he stepped on it and pushed up onto his toes. Hole after hole appeared in the stone. He made his way, slowly and excruciatingly, up the cold rock face, the voices growing louder as he neared the top. At last he threw a scratched, aching arm over the top of the wall and hauled himself up to sprawl across it, panting for breath. He glanced down. A sea of tiny hands reached for him, the frantic cries crashing over him like raging water.

"Help us."

His eyes flew open.

Trembling violently, he bolted upright in bed. He tossed back the blanket and flung his legs over the side. His heart skipped and hammered against his ribs. The liquid that had dripped from the broken skin of his hands in the dream slid down his arms, and he lifted them up to examine them. In the rose-tinted light of the rising sun filtering through his window, the sweat covering his skin glowed red.

He slid off the edge of the mattress and down onto the thick carpet, the sheet wrapped around him like a dark blue shroud. For several minutes he sat with his knees pulled to his chest, his eyes tightly shut as he concentrated on drawing in one painful breath after another. Gradually the tremors gripping his body eased, and his heart slowed enough that he could no longer hear it thudding in his ears.

He dropped his head onto his arms, his hands clasped together in supplication. "Lord." The word came out in a stifled groan followed by silence. He had no words to ask the question haunting him. He didn't even know what the question was. How could he frame his request to the God who knew all, who saw all, whose gaze penetrated deep into the heart that had broken so many times at the sight of helpless and hurting children?

"Help me," he whispered. That was it. The one thing he could ask, the only words that could be grasped hold of and torn out of the fear and confusion swirling through him.

He had no idea how much time passed as he sat there, crying out the words over and over, a hundred times, a thousand. *Help me. Help me.* Gradually, like an object coming into focus as it drew nearer, he realized that warmth was seeping through him. He lifted his head and squinted in the bright sunlight that poured through the window, passing around the wooden frame that split the glass into four sections to cast a cross-shaped shadow onto the blue carpet. A shudder moved through him.

Was that a sign? A warning? A blessing?

His gaze locked on the unwavering shadow. Pressing his fingers to his forehead, he massaged his temples, trying to ease a throbbing headache. The opportunity the woman had presented him with had resonated with an intense need deep inside. A need that he'd known was there, but that he hadn't realized was so strong. The need to do something, anything, to offer hope to the little innocent ones who had so little of it left.

But is that enough to risk everything for? My career, my freedom, maybe even my life? How can I? A tormented groan escaped him.

How can I not?

He dropped his hands as the thought brought his head up sharply. Now that he knew there was something that could be done, that the situations he faced everyday were not as achingly hopeless as he'd always believed, could he go back to living the way he had been?

The answer crashed through him on a wave of panic. Even as he struggled to keep his head above the swirling emotion, he knew it was right. The excitement and relief that flowed through him in its wake confirmed it.

He glanced at the carpet again as a cloud drifted across the face of the sun. The sudden coolness shivered across his skin. The shadow faded until it was barely discernible on the carpet. Reaching over, he ran his fingers over the place, gathering strength.

Then, with a deep sigh, he pulled his hand from the faint outline and rose to his feet.

She didn't speak when he sank onto the seat across from her. In spite of the urgency of her organization's mission, she appeared to be capable of limitless patience. Probably why she always got what she wanted. Like she had gotten him.

Or, to be more accurate, *they* had gotten him. Whoever they were. He suspected he would never know.

Drawing in a deep, mind-clearing breath, he met her intense gaze with the calmness that had settled in his core after the initial flood of emotion had drained. "When do I start?"

The flicker of relief in her eyes, the strongest reaction he'd seen in their depths yet, came and went quickly. The full red lips curved upwards. "Immediately. Your instructions will be delivered to you within the next twenty-four hours. Your code name is Rogue." After a brief hesitation, she held out a hand toward him. "And my name is Natalya."

Chapter Fourteen

The warrant to obtain access to Ted Stiller's file in his pocket, Daniel headed down to the CAS office on Isabella Street. The search of the suspect's home had turned up nothing that could help track him down. He and Sharleen had attempted to talk to the foster parents, but Stiller's father was in a nursing home with advanced dementia, and his mother had passed away six months earlier. More dead ends.

Since Daniel hadn't seen the vehicle he'd disappeared in, and Stiller's own car was still in his driveway, they couldn't track him down that way, and the licence plate of the sedan that had whisked the child away had been covered with enough mud to be unreadable. There hadn't been any record of the man attempting to purchase a ticket for a bus, train, or plane, or using a credit card to rent a vehicle, although they continued to monitor all of those possibilities closely. Information had been supplied to border patrols at every crossing into the States, but for all intents and purposes, Ted Stiller had disappeared from the face of the earth as quickly and easily as he had disappeared from the scene of the crime.

Daniel yanked open the front door of the CAS building. A young woman in a pink sweater and black skirt sat at the desk in the front lobby. Daniel approached her and flipped open his ID. "Detective Daniel Grey, Toronto Police Services. I need to speak to someone about opening the file of a man who was in the system as a child."

The woman looked up at him and her eyes widened. "Of course, Detective." Her cheeks flushed pink.

Daniel smiled at her. He wasn't proud of exploiting his looks to get someone to cooperate with his investigation, but in this case, he was desperate enough to use any tool at his disposal to move things along quickly. "Thank you. I really appreciate it. I have a warrant with me." He held it up for her to see.

The woman swallowed. "I can let you speak with one of our social workers who would have access to those files." She picked up the phone.

He lifted a hand. "Wait." His mind raced. What was the name of the lawyer he'd met down at police headquarters? Kennedy? Kelly. That was it. "Do you have a worker here with the last name Kelly?"

"There's a Holden Kelly."

"That's him. Is there any chance he's available?"

"I'll check and see." She dialed a number and spoke quietly into the phone. After a moment, she set down the receiver and motioned toward the waiting area. "Mr. Kelly is finishing up with a client. He said he would come and get you in ten minutes."

"Great, thanks." Daniel headed over to a bank of chairs and settled onto one to wait. Thankfully, it didn't take long. In under ten minutes, a man strode into the waiting area. Daniel knew at once he had to be Gage Kelly's brother. The two of them looked remarkably alike, except Holden was a little younger, his hair was shorter, and he wore trendy round glasses. His smile was genuine and welcoming as he held out his hand. "Detective?"

Daniel rose and grasped his hand. Like his brother's, Holden's grip was firm. "That's right. Daniel Grey. Thank you for seeing me."

"No problem." Holden gestured toward the hallway. "We can talk in my office."

Daniel followed him to a small office halfway down the hall. Holden held the door until Daniel had gone into the room, then he closed it behind them. "Make yourself comfortable."

Daniel went around to the far side of the desk and settled onto one of two hard white plastic seats. Comfortable might be a stretch, but he wasn't here to socialize anyway. The sooner he could get the information and get back to work, the better.

Holden dropped onto a wheeled desk chair across from him.

"You have a warrant for me to open a file?"

"Yes." Daniel passed it over to the social worker.

Holden scanned it before handing it back and turning to his computer. He clicked a few keys.

Out of habit, Daniel surreptitiously watched Holden's fingers, able to pick up on the password he entered as he clicked it in. Not that he'd ever use it.

"Everything's filed electronically now, but I can print this off so you can take it with you if you'd like."

"That would be perfect, thanks."

Holden clicked a few more keys then closed his laptop. "I'll go down the hall and retrieve those pages. Be right back."

Daniel nodded. While the worker was gone, he pulled out his phone and checked for messages. Nothing new on the case. He quickly read over his other texts and emails, then sighed in frustration and stuck the device back into his shirt pocket as Holden came in.

"Here you go." Holden passed him a file folder and sat again. "May I ask what this is about?"

Daniel hesitated. He probably shouldn't get into it, but given all the kids this guy must have worked with, maybe he could provide him with a little insight into the mind of a child who had been through the system, especially under less than ideal circumstances. Having been raised in a loving, stable home, Daniel really had no concept of what that would do to a person, although he witnessed the effects of it every day. He set the folder down on the desk. "Confidentially?"

Holden nodded. "Of course."

"This guy is a possible suspect in the four recent child abductions in the city."

The worker's eyebrows rose. "Really."

"Yes. We're trying to locate him. During the course of our investigation, we discovered that he had come up through the system. A friend of his from high school suggested that the foster father might have been a bit abusive."

Holden's face darkened. "Unfortunately, as much as we try

to vet them, that does happen sometimes."

"Interestingly, all of the kids who have been abducted have files with CAS as well."

"Yeah, I knew that. I'm familiar with two of the children. Nasty cases."

"In what way?"

Holden lifted the lid of his laptop and clicked on the keys again. "This first one, Nadine Parker. We made ..." he ran his finger down the screen, "... seven visits there in two years. She was taken to the hospital four times in that period."

"But she wasn't removed from the home?"

"She was, several times, but she was returned each time." Holden keyed in a second entry and winced.

"Another kid getting beat up?"

"Yeah. Charlie Edwards, four years old. Nine visits in eighteen months."

"And again, not taken out of the home?" Heat rose from Daniel's belly to his chest.

"Not permanently. I never met the most recent victim, Mia Sumner, personally, but from what I hear, her situation was similar."

Daniel leaned forward in his seat. "So they all have the same story. Kids in some kind of desperate domestic situation that your office wasn't doing anything about."

The worker's jaw tightened. "I didn't say we weren't doing anything, Detective. All four of them have a file with us. We obviously went into the homes, likely quite a few times, and did what we could. It's not always possible to remove kids, even when we'd really like to. One of the more frustrating aspects of my job." Although his voice remained carefully neutral, Holden's dark eyes had gone almost black, as though he was struggling with barely-controlled rage.

At me or the system? Daniel pushed back his own rising anger. "Mine too. It's maddening to get called to someone's home and see evidence that abuse is going on, arrest them, and hear later that they were let go and allowed to return home, or that the kids who had been taken away were now back in the same circumstances. I've often wondered why you are not able to permanently remove kids from homes where one or both parents are clearly abusing them."

"Usually it's not as clear as you might think. There are lots of reasons why we can't, or don't, remove kids from their homes. Parents lie. Kids lie. Families try to protect each other, even when they're being abused. It's a bizarre phenomenon, but we see it over and over. If another adult in the home won't press charges and makes up a plausible story to explain the injuries, it's difficult to obtain the court order to have the children taken out. And policy has shifted over the last decade too. The top choice is always to try and keep families together, to teach parents to deal with anger, or get help for addictions. The basic belief is that kids are usually better off with their parents than in the system, if we can help those parents learn how to raise them without resorting to violence."

"From what I've seen, that's a big if." Daniel wasn't sure he approved of the new *shift in policy*. Not when it left kids undefended and vulnerable to attack in their own homes.

Holden's features remained calm, but his hands closed into fists on the desk.

Daniel blew out a breath. "Look, I'm sorry. I know this isn't your fault. I really do understand that you guys do the best you can, same as we do. Unfortunately, the law doesn't always work on our side, and there's no way to get around that."

"No, of course there isn't."

Daniel's eyes narrowed slightly. Holden didn't seem as certain about that as he would have expected.

A soft knock sounded on the door before it opened slightly. "Holden?" A woman with long reddish hair and hazel eyes stuck her head into the room. "Oh, I apologize. I didn't realize you were with someone."

"Yeah, sorry Chris. I forgot we were going to get coffee. I'll be done in a few minutes."

"No problem. Come by my office when you're free." The

woman flashed Daniel an apologetic grin. "Sorry to disturb."

"No worries."

With a last glance at Holden, the woman disappeared into the hallway.

Holden studied the computer screen intently.

Daniel almost smiled. Chris was obviously more than a co-worker. Not that it was any of his business.

"Sorry about that." Holden finally glanced over at him.

"Not a problem. I know this was last minute, and I appreciate you seeing me. And again, I apologize if I was out of line. I know we're on the same side here, trying to help these kids."

"Forget about it. I understand your frustration, believe me."

"I'm sure you do." Daniel picked the folder up off the desk. "Can I ask you one more thing?"

"Sure." Holden crossed his arms over his chest. In spite of Daniel's apology, clearly his guard was still up a little.

"Do you think it's feasible that growing up in that kind of environment could motivate someone to harm other children as an adult?"

Holden blinked. "I suppose it could. Hurt people do hurt people, as they say. Is that what you think he's doing?"

Daniel frowned. "Well, he's taking them from their homes in the night. And there have been no demands for ransom or any follow-up threats. That suggests that he's not planning to return them, so I have to believe he has some kind of malicious intent. Don't you agree?"

"I suppose so."

You suppose so? Daniel studied the man for a moment. He'd had extensive training in analyzing body language. Holden's was tricky to interpret. His jaw was still slightly tight and his posture closed. Even so, when his eyes met Daniel's, the anger was gone, and they were now warm and friendly. Clearly his hostility was directed at the situations they'd been discussing, not at Daniel.

The social worker uncrossed his arms. "Was there anything else? Because if not, I should probably ..." He jerked a thumb in the direction of the door.

"Of course." Holden had an appointment with someone he'd clearly rather be with at the moment than him. Daniel pushed back his chair and rose. Tugging a card from his pocket, he set it on the desk. "If you think of anything else that might be helpful, I'd appreciate it if you'd contact me."

The worker left the card on the desk but nodded. "I will."

Daniel walked out of the office, feeling the other man's gaze on him as he left. *Interesting.* Holden had given him a lot to think about. And he'd agreed that a person who had grown up in a violent home, as Ted Stiller clearly had, could conceivably turn on others later in life and cause them harm.

Although it hadn't seemed as though Holden fully believed that was what was happening in this case. Daniel's brow furrowed. What other possible explanation could there be? It seemed fairly obvious that …

Electricity jolted through him. Probably because of some of the terrible things he'd seen happen to kids over the years, Holden had jumped to a conclusion that hadn't even occurred to Daniel until this moment.

Maybe whoever was taking these kids wasn't doing it for evil or self-serving purposes at all. Maybe Ted Stiller and his accomplices were stealing children for an entirely different purpose.

To save them.

Chapter Fifteen

"This breakfast better be as good as you say. I'm starving." Daniel punched his former partner lightly on the shoulder as they walked toward the diner.

"It is, trust me. And it's on me." Bells jangled as Lou grasped the door handle and pulled it open. "I appreciate you coming with me to talk to the kids."

"No problem. There's nothing I enjoy more after a twelve-hour shift than driving to the other side of the city in rush hour traffic to tell a bunch of fifth-graders to make sure they wear a helmet when they go biking."

"I'll make it up to you. Joe's serves the best bacon and eggs around."

Daniel laughed. "I'm kidding. There's nothing to make up for. I had a good time actually. Those kids were great." He ran his fingers through his hair in an attempt to straighten his short, slightly spiky hair as he followed Lou across the crowded room. "Felt good to be back in a school again, actually. It's been a while."

"Yeah, I thought it would be good for you to get out of that office and slum it with us beat cops for a few hours." Lou elbowed him in the ribs. "Help you remember what real work is like." He slid into a red vinyl booth along the back wall and Daniel sat across from him.

The man in the booth next to them smiled and nodded at him. Daniel started. Gage Kelly. What were the chances of that? Daniel lifted a hand in greeting before picking up the menu and studying it. If the tantalizing smells of fried eggs and bacon hanging in the air were any indication, it had been worth the drive to get here.

"Can I get you a cup of coffee?" The rich aroma wafting from the pot in the server's hand had Daniel reaching for the mug in front of him.

"Sure." He looked up as he lifted his mug in her direction, and a tiny jolt of shock zipped through him. The woman was tall and slim, and her blonde hair was pulled back in a loose ponytail that made her look far younger than she was. The freckles sprinkled across her nose contributed to the illusion. His eyes riveted on hers—jade-green with tiny gold flecks—as she poured the steaming liquid into his cup. Something deep inside them that didn't look young at all—some kind of hurt from the past, maybe—clutched at his chest. With a small shake of his head, Daniel tore his gaze from hers and concentrated on getting his mug back down on the table without spilling any of the contents on his fingers.

He was vaguely aware of his partner ordering across the table from him and used the opportunity to draw in several deep breaths, praying Lou hadn't noticed his loss of composure.

"What can I get you?" Her voice was calm and friendly.

Daniel closed the menu. "Just the coffee for now, thanks." He glanced at her name tag, careful not to make eye contact this time. Nicole. She closed her notebook and slipped it into the pocket of her apron before picking up the pot of coffee she'd set on the table. He didn't look up at her again, but the moment she moved away he let out the breath he'd been holding. For the first time, he understood why people called it a *spark*–his entire body tingled as though he'd grabbed hold of an electric fence.

Lou smacked Daniel's arm lightly with the back of his hand. "Not eating? I said breakfast was on me."

"I know." Daniel's voice rasped, and he cleared his throat. "I guess I'm not as hungry as I thought." He sipped from his mug and leaned against the back of the bench, trying to pass off the shock to his system as fatigue.

"Everything set for your birthday dinner next week?"

Daniel's head jerked. Gage was smiling up at the server as she re-filled his mug. She leaned down and spoke softly to him in response, and they laughed. When she straightened, she ran her fingers lightly over his cheek. He grabbed her hand and pressed the palm to his mouth.

Ah. That's that, then. A white-hot flash of longing slashed through Daniel's gut. Not for her, he tried to convince himself, but for that closeness, the ability to make it seem like they were the only two people in a crowded room. What was the matter with him? Why couldn't he have had this reaction to the lovely doctor that night at Sharleen's? That would have been much more convenient. From what he'd gathered from his own experience and other people's stories, however, love and convenience rarely went hand in hand.

You're staring. He blinked. What was he doing, intruding on such an intimate moment? His cheeks, already warm, flared to over-heated. He dropped his gaze to the coffee mug he gripped in his hands. *What is going on?* He never reacted this way to a woman. Never. And he had absolutely no interest in a relationship with anyone right now. Not to mention that she was clearly involved with someone else, someone who, from all appearances, was a decent guy. Daniel must be more exhausted than he'd thought for his defences to be torn down so easily.

"You okay, Grey?" Lou's brow furrowed as he studied him.

"Yeah, fine. I'll be right back." Daniel stumbled off the end of the bench and made his way around several tables to a hallway leading to the restrooms.

When the door had closed behind him, he gripped the sides of a porcelain sink and stared into the mirror. *What are you doing? Don't you think you have enough to deal with right now with this case?* He let go of the sink and turned on the cold-water tap. Cupping his hands, he filled them with the water and splashed it on his face. Time to go home. And back to reality.

Drawing in a deep breath, he yanked open the door and made his way to the table. When he reached it, he clapped his former partner on the shoulder. "Look man, I'm sorry. I'm exhausted. I think I'm going to jump on the subway and head home. Talk to you later?"

Lou's forehead wrinkled but he shrugged. "All right." He

nodded toward a booth in the corner where three uniformed cops were deep into breakfast. Daniel only knew one of their names, but all of them looked familiar, cops from one of the east side precincts. They'd give Lou a hard time for being out of his territory, but they'd also welcome him to join them, the whole big blue wall thing. "I'll go eat with those guys. Thanks again for coming with me."

"No problem." Daniel spun on his heel and made his way toward the door.

"Leaving already?"

His stomach clenched. Nicole stood in his path, holding two plates of steaming eggs and ham. He allowed himself one more look into those green eyes and forced a grin. "Yeah, sorry. My friend will cover the coffee for me."

"No problem." She lifted the plates in her hand. "Nothing appeal to you?"

"Just my bed." Prickles of heat scrabbled along his skin as he realized how that sounded. "I mean, I'm coming off a twelve-hour shift, and I realized I need sleep more than food at the moment."

Her smile widened. The effect went straight to his knees. A few days ago he'd stared down a guy, crazy high on meth and waving a gun in his face. Somehow that had been easier than standing here in front of her. He reached for a chair to steady himself.

"Well, if you're sure. Come back soon. We serve the best breakfast in town."

"So I've heard. I will." Except that he wouldn't. One thing about him, he rarely made the same mistake twice. Stepping back, he let her pass. A light, floral scent drifted in the air behind her.

Daniel pushed through the door and out onto the sidewalk, swallowing mouthfuls of relatively fresh air in an attempt to slow the rapid beating in his chest. Giving his head a shake to clear it of the aroma—and the memory of green eyes, freckles, and shimmering gold hair bouncing in a ponytail—he headed for the nearest subway station and the safety of home.

Chapter Sixteen

Nicole reached for the *Open* sign on the door and stopped. A man strode down the street toward the diner, long black coat flapping behind him in the wind. Nicole smiled and pushed open the door. "Hey, you."

Gage bounded up the stairs and came inside. "Wow. You're beautiful."

Nicole busied herself with turning the sign around and closing and locking the door. "I don't know about that."

A big band song drifted from a speaker in the corner of the room. Gage grabbed her hand and spun her around, then wrapped an arm around her waist and they danced until she was breathless and laughing. The pale green sheath-dress she'd purchased for the occasion, the one the saleslady promised brought out the green in her eyes, swirled around her calves.

As the music came to a crashing crescendo, he twirled her again, until her back was pressed against his chest, then leaned down to whisper in her ear, "You *are* beautiful."

A tiny smile flitted across her lips as she turned to face him. "Okay."

"Okay." He touched his lips to hers. "Happy birthday."

Warmth suffused her cheeks. "Thank you."

"I'm looking forward to celebrating with you."

"I'm glad you could." Her smile faltered as she stepped back, out of his arms. "Otherwise it would have been a pretty small dinner party."

His eyes narrowed. "Did you get hold of your parents?"

Nicole swallowed. "Yeah, I talked to them a couple of days ago. They're in Britain somewhere."

"So, not coming for your thirtieth birthday."

"Not unless they hijack the Concorde or something." Her mouth twisted. "Although that would require more effort than they have ever expended trying to see me."

"I'd do it."

Nicole studied him. "You would, wouldn't you?"

He nodded. "Nothing could have kept me from being with you today. Not even an ocean."

"Well, I'm glad you weren't that far away." She lifted one shoulder. "Anyway, enough about them. They did try to get away but got delayed. I'm sure they would have come if they could have."

"I'm sure."

Nicole tilted her head. *Is that bitterness in his voice?* Her chest squeezed. It was nice to have someone care that much about how other people treated her. "They're still coming, but not until next weekend, they said. And they want to meet you."

His eyebrows rose. "You told them about me?"

Nicole grinned. "My father is always warning me about stalkers following me home from the diner, so I told him about mine."

"Oh, that's great. Set it up so they don't like me even before they meet me." He tapped her nose gently. "I could have gotten them to that point on my own, you know."

"I've no doubt."

Gage wrapped his arms around her waist and pulled her close. When he pressed his lips to hers, she rose up on her toes, responding with an eagerness that shocked her. After a moment, he stepped back and rested his hands on her shoulders. "As long as you like me, that's all I care about."

"Well, it's hard not to like a guy who swears he'd cross an ocean to be with you on your birthday."

He ran his fingers lightly over her hair before dropping his hand. "Are Connie and Joe here?"

"Yes, they're in the kitchen putting the finishing touches on dinner." Nicole let out a short laugh. "Just a heads up. They tend to go a little overboard on my birthday."

"They're proud of you. As much as if they were your parents."

"I know."

"And we all want to celebrate you getting old."

Nicole smacked him on the shoulder.

Gage laughed and caught her hand. "What? You're not fooling anyone with those freckles, you know. As someone once told me, you're a lot older than you look."

"Well, that someone is allowed to say that. You are not." She tried to pull her hand away, but he held it tight.

"I'm sorry. I didn't realize that someone was so sensitive about her age. She needs to realize that every day that passes makes her lovelier and more desirable, not less."

"That is very sweet, thank you. My favorite birthday present ... so far."

One side of Gage's mouth turned up. "You weren't expecting more than that, were you?"

Her eyes locked with his. "No, actually. That, all of this in fact,"—she rested the back of her hand lightly on his cheek—"is a lot more than I ever expected."

"Me too." Gage turned his head and brushed his lips across the tips of her fingers. The swinging doors leading to the kitchen creaked open behind him, and he winked as he let go of her.

Joe pushed through the wooden doors leading to the kitchen, a large covered dish in each hand. Connie bustled into the diner behind him, clutching a tray loaded down with plates of food. "Hi, Gage."

"Hello, beautiful." Gage kissed her on the cheek before taking the tray from her.

Connie's blue eyes twinkled. "Now that's what I call a greeting." She nudged Joe in the ribs with her elbow.

"Darlin', if I called you beautiful every time I thought it, you'd be well sick of hearing it by now."

Pink tinged her wrinkled cheeks as she pushed her grey curls away from her face with one hand. "Oh, Joe, go on now."

Nicole's eyes met Gage's and he grinned. Was he wondering

if that's how the two of them would be with each other in forty years, like she was? Her own cheeks went warm as she looked away. He read her too easily, and that thought was one she needed to keep to herself.

As always, Joe rescued her. "Why don't we eat while it's hot?" He inclined his head toward the back corner. A black tablecloth adorned a table in one of the booths. A vase of carnations and two glowing candles created an elegant feel that, while it definitely wasn't typically Joe's Diner, absolutely suited the occasion.

Gage held out his arm. "Shall we?"

Feeling a little overwhelmed by how special the night had been already, even without the presence of her parents, Nicole slid a hand into the crook of his elbow and followed him across the room.

"To Nicole." Joe lifted his glass of water into the air.

Nicole clinked her glass against Gage's, which he'd filled with ginger ale, as he winked at her and echoed Joe's words, "To Nicole."

Connie reached across the table to touch her glass to Nicole's. "To finding your type. Finally."

She'd said the words quietly, so only the two of them could hear. Still, Nicole shot her a warning look. The twinkle in Connie's blue eyes didn't dim. Nicole pressed a hand to her stomach. Joe had outdone himself, as usual, with a three-course meal that included salad, Chicken Alfredo, and birthday cake. She wouldn't need to eat again for days.

"Joe?"

Gage's voice was thick with concern. Nicole looked at Joe. His face had gone sheet-white, and he gripped the edges of the table with both hands. Her stomach clenched. "Joe? What is it?"

Gage started to get up, but Joe lifted a hand, and he sank back down.

"I'm okay." Joe drew in a slow, shaky breath. "Overdid it a

bit today, that's all. Give me … a minute."

Connie fumbled in her purse, her cheeks almost as pale as Joe's. She pulled out a pill bottle, nearly dropping it as she struggled to remove the lid. "He needs a nitro pill."

Nicole took the bottle from her. Her fingers weren't much steadier than Connie's, but she managed to wedge her thumb under the lid and push it off. "How many?"

"One." Connie held out her hand.

Nicole knocked a capsule filled with tiny white beads onto Connie's palm.

Joe took it from his wife and slid it under his tongue. Gradually color began to return to his cheeks. Nicole realized she'd been holding her breath, and she let it out slowly. The painful knots in her stomach refused to loosen. What was wrong?

Gage's fingers tightened around hers, but she couldn't take her eyes from Joe. *What if something happens to him?*

"I'm okay, honey." Joe managed a slight grin as he reached across the table and patted her arm. "Not as young as I used to be. I'm past seventy-five, you know. I kind of forgot that today, I was so excited about your special day."

Nicole smiled weakly as she snapped the lid back onto the pill bottle and handed it to Connie. "Are you sure you're all right?"

"A good night's rest and I'll be all set."

"Why don't you and Connie go upstairs? I'll clean up here and lock the doors."

Gage nodded. "I'll help her." He clasped Joe's shoulder. "Sure you shouldn't go to the hospital, though? I'd be happy to take you."

Joe shook his head. "Nope. The doctor gave me some medication, and a dose of that and my own bed will do me a lot more good than sitting in an emergency room for hours."

Nicole bit her lip to keep from arguing. After all, he was probably right. "Are you okay to get upstairs?"

"We'll manage." Joe slid down the bench. "Don't worry, honey, I'm fine. Sorry to end your celebration dinner so abruptly though."

"It's okay, Joe. Please just take care of yourself."

Joe stood up, bracing himself on the table with one hand. Connie, lines of concern etched across her forehead, grasped his arm. "Will do. See you tomorrow."

In spite of Joe's admonition, Nicole's worried gaze followed the couple until they disappeared through the back door.

Gage slid an arm around her shoulders and pulled her to him. "You all right?"

"I guess so. I ..." Her voice broke. "I've never really thought about something happening to Joe or Connie. I assumed they'd live forever, I guess, and always be here for me."

"He'll be okay."

"I know. This time. But he's right. He's not young anymore, and obviously he has health problems. What if ..."

Nicole shuddered and pressed her forehead to his shoulder. Gage wrapped his other arm around her, holding her close. One hand stroked her hair as they sat for several minutes without speaking.

Finally, she summoned the strength to move. "Let's clean up. I really want to get home."

"Okay." He kissed her forehead before standing up and starting to stack the dirty dishes.

Nicole followed him into the kitchen and turned on the water in the sink. Gage set the dishes down on the counter and moved to stand behind her, wrapping his arms around her waist. "I'm sorry your birthday dinner got ruined."

She shook her head and squirted dish soap into the sink before reaching for a plate. "It didn't. I mean, I'm worried about Joe, of course, but dinner was great. It was exactly what I wanted, an evening with the people I ... care about the most in the world."

She swallowed. Had she almost told him that she loved him? That was ridiculous, wasn't it? She'd only known him for a few weeks.

Gage pulled his arms from her waist and took her by the

shoulders to turn her around. His dark eyes glowed and her breath caught. "I … care about you too."

He lowered his head and pressed his lips to hers. Nicole lifted her hands to his face as he pulled her close. The warmth that coursed through her pushed away the fear that still hovered at the edges of her consciousness, and the ache in her stomach finally eased.

Gage lifted his head. Nicole looked up at him and pressed her lips together.

He tilted his head. "What?"

Still in his arms, she half-turned to grab a towel off the island. "You have soap all over your face."

"Oh yeah?" He moved back when she tried to wipe it off with the towel, and instead used his hands to remove the white bubbles from his cheeks. Before she could move, he swiped his fingers across her nose and chin.

"Hey." Nicole pursed her lips and blew, sending a cloud of bubbles into the air.

Gage snorted, and suddenly they were both laughing. The heaviness of the last few minutes dissipated like the soap into the air. When her laughter died down to the occasional giggle, Gage, still grinning, tugged the towel from her hand and gently wiped her face before cleaning the last of the soap off of his.

When they'd finished loading the dishwasher, Nicole dried her hands and rested them on his chest. "Thanks, Gage."

"For what?"

"Being here. Making me laugh. Celebrating my birthday with me."

"There's nowhere else I'd rather be." Gage slipped a hand into his pocket and pulled out a small, square package. "I was going to give you this at dinner, but …"

Her eyes widened. "You did get me a gift."

He laughed. "Unfortunately, I didn't know at the time I could have gotten away with only giving you a compliment."

She took the box from his hand. "You couldn't have."

"I didn't think so."

Nicole tore the light blue paper off the gift. It dropped to the floor as she lifted out a small box with the words Peoples Jewellers scrawled across the top. Her eyebrows rose as she looked up at Gage.

He offered her a lopsided grin. "Just open it."

Her heart thudding against her ribs, Nicole lifted the lid of the box. A pair of pearl studs were nestled in the black velvet lining of the box. She drew in a quick breath. "Gage. They're beautiful."

He lifted a shoulder. "Pearls are the symbol for thirty years, apparently. That's what the saleslady said, anyway."

She set the box down on the island, slipped off the small silver hoops she always wore, and dropped them onto the counter. One at a time, she tugged the pearl earrings loose and put them on. Holding her hair back with both hands, she tilted her head. "What do you think?"

"Gorgeous." He wasn't looking at the earrings.

Nicole let her hair drop. She struggled to pull air into her lungs.

Gage lowered his head.

Time to go. If he kissed her now, she wouldn't have the strength to stop whatever happened next. She pressed a hand to his chest and drew in a shuddering breath. "I love them. Thank you."

"You're welcome." He pulled back and studied her for a moment. As always, she felt far too exposed under his intense gaze. He didn't comment on the change in climate, however, as he held out his arm to her. "Shall we?"

She slid her hand through the crook of his elbow. "I think we should."

They walked to his car in silence. When they reached it, Gage pulled open her door and rested his hand on top of it as she climbed in. Then, his hand still on the top of the door, he leaned down closer to her. "Nic, remember what I told you that night I brought Chinese food to your place, about the mistake I'd made in the past, and wouldn't make with you?"

Her stomach clenched as she looked up at him. "Yes."

"Well, that still stands."

The tense muscles across her shoulders relaxed. "Good to know. Thanks."

He nodded and closed the door.

Nicole twirled one of the earrings in her ear. Once again, she'd pushed Gage away, and once again, he hadn't gone. Could she trust that, then? Trust him?

He climbed behind the wheel and flashed her a smile before starting the car.

If she could, then of all the gifts he'd given her tonight, that one would be the greatest of them all.

Chapter Seventeen

You have to admire them. Everything they had told him was right so far, down to the sensor light attached to the back wall of the house. The bulb would have come on if he had walked anywhere within a fifteen-foot radius of that corner, thrusting him onto center stage beneath a glaring spotlight. In the dim glow of the quarter moon, Rogue could barely make out the shape of it, set back in the bricks so that, if he hadn't known it was there, he would have tripped it for sure.

Skirting it carefully, he made his way to the brick wall and pressed his back against it. Somewhere down the street, a dog barked, and he jumped then forced himself to take several deep breaths. This would go a lot smoother if his nerves were under control.

Moving slowly, he pulled a slim tool out of his jacket pocket and held it in his gloved hand. He glanced through the glass and positioned himself in front of the door, blocking the view of what he was doing from anyone who might look out a neighboring window. Not that anyone was likely to see him in the watery light of the thin moon. Even *that* they had factored into the equation when they chose this particular night. Rogue slid the tool into the lock and turned it to the right and then the left, exactly as they had shown him. A soft click brought a grim smile of satisfaction to his face. He straightened. Grasping the handle, he turned it slowly and pushed the door open, one careful inch at a time, listening for any sound inside the house after each movement.

He opened the door just enough to slip through, then pushed it against the frame without latching it. Drawing in another deep breath, he turned and made his way through the living room. The only light came from the flashing green numbers on the Blue-Ray player. *Perfect.*

Rogue felt along the hardwood floor with the toe of his running shoe, checking for any loose boards. He tested each step for creaks before putting his full weight on it. At the top of the stairs he sidled along the wall, past the small circle of light that fell onto the hall floor from the nightlight left on in the upstairs bathroom.

When he reached the little girl's room, he paused for several seconds to slow his breathing before reaching into his pocket to grip the thin needle he'd stuck there. He'd have to proceed carefully. It was impossible to predict what might be lying on the floor of a child's room. His next few steps, taken in near-darkness, would be crucial. If he stepped on a roller-skate and slipped, or his foot came down on a rubber squeaky toy, or he tripped over a book or blanket lying in his path, he risked waking up the mother sleeping in the next room and losing his opportunity to grab the girl. Or worse.

He pulled the needle out of his pocket, plucked off the protective top and shoved it into the pocket of his jeans, then depressed the plunger far enough to expel the air. Gripping it tightly, he moved one foot ahead gingerly, then the other, pausing after each step. After what seemed like hours, the edge of the mattress lying on the floor pressed against his shin and he stopped. Straining into the darkness, Rogue listened for a sound, any sign that the woman next door had heard him. Except for the soft exhalation of deep breaths coming from the child at his feet, the house remained blanketed in silence.

He lowered himself into a crouch beside her. A weak shaft of moonlight struggled its way through the leaves outside her window and fell, dappled, across a thin arm resting on top of the blankets. His hand hovered over her skin for a moment as he braced himself for the most dangerous part of the mission—the few seconds after contact with her arm, and before the contents of the needle took effect. She appeared to be in a deep enough sleep that the tiny prick shouldn't wake her, but he wouldn't breathe until enough time had passed to know that he was safe. He bit his lip in concentration, slid the sharp tip of the needle under her skin, and pushed down the lever. His heart stopped when she yanked her arm away and the point slipped out. Thankfully, the slender tube was empty.

He froze as she turned over onto her back, long, tangled hair spilling across the pillow, but her breathing deepened again almost immediately. For several more seconds he held his position, until his legs began to ache. Then, inhaling deeply, he peeled back the blanket and slipped his arms beneath the child's back and knees, shifting her to the edge of the mattress. He paused again, but she lay still, and he lifted her to his chest. Although she was nearly seven, the child weighed next to nothing, and he pushed to his feet easily.

Holding the tiny body close to his, Rogue retraced his steps, making his way down the stairs and back across the main floor of the house. The door remained closed but unlatched, the way he had left it. He shifted the girl in his arms and reached for the knob to pull it open and step out into the backyard.

Almost done. Adrenaline shot through him, and for a second his focus wavered. He jerked to a stop. He'd almost wandered straight into the path of the sensor light. Heart pounding, he recalculated his route, widening his path to give himself enough room to safely round the corner of the house.

As he edged his way toward the front of the property, headlights came on down the block and a vehicle rolled toward him. He increased his pace slightly, taking care to avoid the drain spout sticking out into the driveway. The dark-colored car slowed to a stop and the back door opened. Breathing a prayer for the child in his arms, that the people he was giving her to were all they claimed to be, and that they would find her a safe and loving home, he placed her gently into the arms that reached for her.

The face of the person inside remained in shadow. *Just how I want it.* He had to deal with Natalya, and with a young man at the office where the organization had set up temporary headquarters who showed him how to use all the tools and electronic equipment they supplied him, but those were the only ones he wanted to have contact with. The young man hadn't offered his name and he hadn't asked. If he were ever put on a stand, the less he knew the better.

The car pulled slowly away from the curb, and Rogue stood and watched it until it turned at the next corner and disappeared from sight. Then he slipped off his black ski mask and gloves, shoved them into the pocket of his jacket, and headed for the subway.

Chapter Eighteen

Daniel smashed a fist down on the boardroom table. "Are you kidding me? How did Stiller manage to grab another child? I thought he was long gone from the city."

Sharleen grabbed his mug of coffee as it started to tip over and wiped up the few drops that had spilled onto the table with a napkin.

"He is." Steve Simons, one of their IT guys, set a laptop down in front of him and his partner. He clicked a few buttons and an image appeared, grainy, but clearly their suspect. "This footage came from a security camera located outside a store on a street in Copenhagen."

Daniel checked the time stamp. It was dated the day before, April 12th at 11:44 pm EST. An hour before the latest child, another girl, had been reported missing in Toronto. No way he could have gotten from Denmark to Canada in time to abduct the child. Had they made a mistake then? Were they on the trail of the wrong guy? Or had Stiller taken the other kids and then disappeared after Daniel had seen his face?

"That doesn't mean he didn't take the first four."

As usual, his partner was reading his mind. "I know. But it does mean that, if he was the original kidnapper, someone else has picked up where he left off."

"Looks like it." Sharleen looked up at Steve. "Good work getting your hands on that. Were the Copenhagen police able to pick him up?"

"No. Although they were in the neighborhood within minutes of this shot being captured, the guy was gone, and they haven't been able to pick up his trail since. This Stiller's as elusive as Sasquatch. I'll stay on him, though, let you know if he's spotted again." He picked up the laptop and started for the door.

"Thanks." Daniel turned to his partner as Steve closed the door behind him. "Are we back to square one?"

"Looks like it."

"What do you think this latest abduction is then, some kind of copycat crime?"

Sharleen pursed her lips. "I don't think so. The MO is exactly the same, and all those details weren't released to the public. Feels more like the new guy's a replacement on the team."

"Team?"

"Yeah. There are obviously several people involved in these operations. At least two drivers, plus the person in the backseat who takes the children. Who knows how many more there are behind the scenes? These abductions are too well planned out, and carried out far too professionally and efficiently, for this to be a group of small-time criminals."

"Hmm." Daniel propped his elbows on the table and pressed his fingertips together.

"What?"

"I was thinking about something the social worker I talked to hinted at."

Sharleen moved his coffee mug into the center of the table. "What's that?"

"He didn't come right out and say it, but I got the impression he didn't think that whoever is taking these kids means them any harm."

Her forehead wrinkled. "Why else would they take them?" Her face cleared immediately. "He thinks they're trying to help them, doesn't he?"

"That's what I gathered. All the kids, including the one that was taken last night, were only children living in abusive situations. That's too much of a pattern to be a coincidence. As crazy as it sounds, I think we have to at least consider the possibility that these aren't heartless criminals we're dealing with, but members of some kind of group that believes they're actually rescuing these kids."

Her features hardened.

Daniel's eyes narrowed. "What?"

"I was thinking that, if whoever is doing this was caught up in one of those situations we see kids in all the time himself as a kid, I would actually kind of understand why he's doing what he's doing."

"What he's doing is breaking the law."

"I understand that, I'm just saying—"

"There's no room for vigilante justice in this country, Shar. Whatever the motivation."

"I suppose you're right."

"I am. You make a good point, though. We know Stiller was abused as a kid. Good chance his replacement was too, which would explain why they both might be willing to risk everything to help other kids in that situation."

Sharleen picked up a spoon and absently stirred her cup of tea. "How do they know which kids those are?"

"Good question. They'd pretty much have to have access to CAS files to figure that out."

"That would be the fastest and simplest way. Who would have that kind of access?"

"Besides the social workers themselves?" Daniel contemplated the recent meeting he'd had with Holden Kelly. Given the level of frustration and anger the man hadn't quite been able to keep hidden, it wasn't a stretch to think a social worker could be persuaded to work outside the confines of the law to try and help kids he or she couldn't otherwise do anything about.

"Yeah. Police officers, I suppose. At least, we do know who a lot of these kids are." She shot Daniel a look.

A tight fist squeezed his gut. There was nothing he'd rather do less than investigate a fellow cop. They did get called to those types of situations though, as he well knew, so they had to be on the list of possibilities. He racked his brain to come up with alternatives to that scenario. "Since these cases often go through the courts, we have to look at lawyers too, and judges. Maybe this is a *Star Chamber* kind of deal." The old Michael Douglas movie about a group of judges who, after being forced to set accused people free on technicalities, decided to take justice into their own hands, was one of his favorites.

She grinned wryly. "Unlikely, but let's not dismiss any possibilities at this point. Anyone else who might know about these kids? What did Stiller do?"

"Good question." Daniel reached for the file Nate Black, another detective in the office he'd asked to do research on their suspect, had compiled. He flipped it open and scanned the first page. "He's a paramedic. He was a first responder in Toronto for six years before disappearing the night I saw him."

Sharleen clasped her hands in front of her face and tapped a finger against her chin. "Then we have to consider any and all first responders. That does make sense, since they'd be the initial ones on the scene if someone called in a domestic. Anyone working in the ER. And what about teachers? They see these kids every day and would know, or at least suspect, which ones had difficult home lives." She dropped her hands onto the table. "Daniel, there are thousands of doctors and teachers in this city. How are we going to look into all of them, as well as the social workers and cops and ambulance drivers? It will take us years."

"I know. Let's rule out teachers for now, though. They would only know about kids in a fairly small geographical area, and they'd all be from the same school, which would start to look suspicious pretty quickly. Since the last guy was a paramedic, let's assume they're going a different direction this time to arouse less suspicion." He glanced at the closed door and lowered his voice. "That leaves cops, lawyers, and social workers as the most likely possibilities."

Sharleen swallowed. "I don't like it, but if you want, I can dig around on the cops in the city, find out about any that might have had a difficult childhood. Social workers make the most sense, so hopefully I'll be ruling out any possibilities."

"I'm sure you will be." Daniel pushed his chair away from the table. "But we will both have to keep an open mind.

Basically, we're looking for any cop, lawyer, or worker who might have a file of their own, or who were foster kids themselves, to make up our short list."

"Should we get a warrant to access the CAS files?"

"Let's hold off on that for now. Since we don't know who, if anyone, at CAS might be involved, I'd rather not tip them off too early. We should be able to get a list of social workers online then we can cross reference the names to police records. If cops were called to any of their homes in the last twenty or thirty years, it should be in the electronic files. We can narrow down the search that way anyway, and only check out CAS files if and when it becomes absolutely necessary."

"Makes sense." Sharleen stood and picked up her cup of tea.

Daniel stood too and leaned across the table to grab his mug of coffee. "Shar?"

His partner had reached the door, but she turned back, one hand on the knob. "Yeah?"

"Let's go through these people as fast as possible. If this is the same group and they're as well-organized as they seem, they may ramp up operations now that the new front man is in place. Given the look on the DS's face when he announced another kidnapping this morning, the last thing I want is for him to catch us sitting in front of a computer sifting through names when another child disappears."

Chapter Nineteen

Nicole dumped her coat on the chair inside the door of her condo, and dug through her bag, trying to find her buzzing phone. Hopefully the call wouldn't take long. Gage was picking her up in a couple of hours to take her to the airport to pick up her parents. Since she hadn't seen them for several years, she wanted to shower and make sure she looked her best. When she felt the cool metal object in the bottom of her purse, she tugged it loose, hit the connect button, and pressed the device to her ear. "Hello?"

"Nicole?"

"Mom?" That couldn't be right. Her parents should be in the air right now. How could her mother phone her? "What is it? Did your flight get delayed?"

"No, we didn't actually end up taking the flight."

The connection was poor, and Nicole strained to make out the words through heavy static. "Did you miss it? Can you get a later one?" She pressed a hand to her abdomen where a hard ball had formed. *No. They aren't going to do this to me again, are they?*

Even through the bad reception, Nicole heard her mother's sigh. She could almost hear her saying the words that had been a constant refrain throughout her childhood, whenever Nicole had protested the fact that her parents were leaving, again. Abandoning her to the care of one of a long string of nannies, each worse than the one before. *Don't be difficult, darling. This is something your father and I have to do.* "I'm sorry, darling. Something came up last minute. An engineering conference in Cairo."

"But can't Dad tell them no? Couldn't you tell them you already had plans?"

Her mother sighed again, more audibly this time. "Don't be difficult, darling. This is something we have to do. We have no choice."

You always have a choice. You just never choose me. Bitterness rose from the cold, hard ball in her stomach up into her chest. Nicole swallowed back the stinging bile. "I understand." She almost choked on the lie. "Can you come after the conference?"

"We'll have to see. I'll be in touch."

The fingers clutching her phone had gone numb. "All right. Just let me know when—" She was speaking into dead air. Her mother was already gone. Nicole pulled the phone away from her ear and stared at it in disbelief. *This isn't happening.* She pressed her eyes shut. How could she not believe it? The truly unbelievable thing would have been if her parents had actually shown up to see her. Her grip on the phone tightened. Why did she do this to herself? How could she allow herself to keep getting her hopes up, when they had let her down so many times?

Nicole sank down onto the couch and pulled her knees up to her chest. She rocked back and forth, willing the tightness in her stomach and chest to ease. This was it. Never again would she believe anything they had to say to her. Never again would she trust that they would do something when they told her they would. She was done hoping. Done believing that somewhere, deep down, they actually cared about her, that someday they would come back and the three of them could be a family. They had let her down for the last time; she was letting go of that dream forever.

Except that she couldn't.

"Nicole?" Gage's voice, calling out her name, keys jangling as he pulled them from the front door lock, yanked her from the fog she'd lost herself in after her mother had ended their phone call. Still, she couldn't summon the strength to move as his footsteps sounded across the living room floor.

"Are you ready to go?" Gage rounded the couch, clutching a bouquet of flowers in one hand. "We should—" He stopped abruptly. "Nic? What is it? What's wrong?"

When she didn't answer, he sank onto the coffee table in front of her and set the flowers down. "Are you sick? Maybe we should call your mom and dad and tell ..."

Her gaze locked with his and his dark eyes went hard. "They're not coming, are they?"

She shook her head slightly.

Rage flashed across his face and he swore.

Nicole blinked but didn't speak.

He exhaled loudly. "Sorry." Gage reached for the phone that she'd forgotten she still gripped in one hand. "Here." Gently he pried it from her and set it behind him, then took both her cold hands in his. "When did they call?"

"I don't know. Around three, maybe?"

Gage glanced down at his watch. "It's 5:10. Have you been sitting here the whole time?" He was clearly forcing calm into his voice, as though talking her down off a window ledge.

Her head barely moved as she nodded. His jaw worked but he didn't speak, just massaged her hands in his. Nicole rested her head against the back of the couch. She wouldn't cry. She'd shed enough tears over her parents to do her for a lifetime. More than enough.

"Do you want me to make you a cup of tea? Or something to eat?"

She lifted her head. "No." Her voice cracked. "Unless you're hungry."

"I'm okay. I grabbed a bite before I left work because I thought we'd be going straight to the airport."

She didn't respond.

"Nic?" He waited for her to look up at him. "Why aren't they coming?"

She squeezed her eyes shut. "I don't know. Something about an engineering conference in Egypt, I think. I kind of faded out after my mother told me their plans had changed."

"I'm really sorry."

Nicole swallowed. "Why does it still bother me so much? They've been doing this to me my whole life. Am I ever going to get over how much it hurts?"

"I don't think you ever get over the people who are supposed to love you the most hurting you so badly." The anger in his eyes had morphed to grief. For her or for himself?

"Is that what happened to you?"

He shrugged that off. "It happens to a lot of people. I cannot grasp your parents not wanting to see you though. They have this amazing daughter and they've thrown away any chance to be with her, to see her grow up. How can parents be so blind, so selfish? Why did they bother having children at all?"

"Child."

"What?"

"They only had one child. I've always wished they had more, so at least I'd have someone in the world."

He tightened his grip on her fingers. "You have someone."

Nicole slumped against the cushions. "Why are you here?"

His forehead wrinkled. "What do you mean? I came to take you to the airport."

"No, I mean, why are you here, with me? I tried to warn you what a disaster I am. I gave you plenty of chances to leave, plenty of reasons. Why are you still here?"

Gage studied her, as if trying to figure out the driving force behind her words. His face softened. "Because I love you."

Her eyes widened. "What?" He'd never said those words to her before. Did he mean them or was he trying to make her feel better?

He leaned forward. "I love you, Nicole." Gage pressed the backs of her hands to his lips.

"You don't have to say that."

"I do have to. Not because I'm trying to make you feel better, although I'd do anything for that to happen, but because I feel it so deeply and strongly I think I might explode if I don't say it."

Nicole studied him, her eyelids flickering in confusion. Could it be true? Could someone actually love her? *Joe and Connie love you.* That was true. They were the first people in her life to really and truly love her unconditionally, so maybe it was possible that … A small smile played at the corners of her mouth. "Really?"

Gage smiled too. "Yes, really."

Joy rushed through her. "I love you too."

He let go of her hands and scooped her up in one quick movement, then turned and settled himself on the couch, cradling her in his lap.

Nicole trailed her fingers lightly over his cheek.

Gage leaned down and brushed his lips across hers.

Nicole slid her hand behind his neck and pulled him closer, deepening their kiss. After a moment, she let him go and gazed up at him. "Did you bring me flowers?"

He glanced over at the bouquet on the coffee table. "Yes. Daisies."

Nicole pushed back the hair from his forehead. "That was sweet."

"I know." He grinned.

"I should put them in water." She didn't move. Her eyelids were heavy, and she felt as though she could drift right off to sleep.

"Yes, you should."

"I don't appear to be getting up."

"Good." His arms tightened around her. "You're right where I want you. The flowers will be fine. Why don't you rest? You look exhausted."

Nicole sighed. "It has been a long day."

"Sounds like it. Close your eyes. I'm not going anywhere."

She stifled a yawn. "Maybe for a few minutes."

He shifted on the couch so he was leaning against the arm.

Nicole rested her head on his chest. She felt his eyes on her, his gaze warm against her skin, but couldn't find the strength to open her eyes. Although he hadn't answered her question, about whether or not the people he loved the most had hurt him, she knew they had. Deeply. The two of them were a couple of lost souls. Except that, somehow, through the grace of God, they had found each other.

Gage lowered his head until his mouth hovered right above her hair. "I'll be your family, Nic." He whispered the words and pressed his lips to her forehead.

Peace flooded through her. Gage loved her. He would never leave her. Her stomach tightened again. Could he make that kind of commitment to her? If her parents had taught her anything, it was that promises weren't always kept, and that sometimes the people you loved the most were ripped from you, no matter how tightly you tried to hold on to them.

He pulled her closer, as though he could sense her thoughts and was trying to convince her. Nicole forced herself to relax. Now, in this moment, Gage was with her.

That was all she could think about today.

Chapter Twenty

Daniel slid into the pew beside his sister. Although the service didn't start until eleven, he'd been up half the night thinking about the abductions and had slept through his alarm. Thankfully, a fire truck had driven past his building half an hour ago, alarms blaring, or he'd have missed the whole thing. "Where's Austin?"

Becca wrinkled her nose. "Working." She held out her hymnbook. Austin was a firefighter and, although he tried to avoid Sunday shifts, he wasn't always able to accompany her to church.

Daniel took hold of his side of the hymnal to share it with her. The slightly musty smell of old, yellowed paper drifted from the book, bringing back fond memories of being in church with his family—his mom, dressed in her Sunday best, at his side.

When the singing ended, he sat down on the pew beside Becca. Thoughts whirled through his head and he struggled to focus as the pastor began to speak, but soon he was caught up in the powerful story and its lessons. The Good Samaritan. Radical love for the ones others turned away from. Selfless, sacrificial love for the poor, the broken, the vulnerable, the disenfranchised. Did he have that? *God, show me if I don't. And give me a deeper love for those I see every day who need it so much.*

Becca shifted beside him. At nearly six months pregnant, she was often uncomfortable, and the hard pew likely didn't help.

Daniel shot her a sympathetic look before turning back to the front. When the service ended, he took her arm and helped her to her feet. "Can I take you to lunch?"

"That would be great." She slid a hand through the crook of his elbow as they started down the aisle. "Every meal I don't have to cook these days is a win, as far as I'm concerned."

They left her car in the parking lot and Daniel drove to a restaurant in the neighborhood. Becca sighed as she wriggled into her seat. "Next time I'm going to have to sit at a table. This booth ain't big enough for the two of us."

Daniel laughed as he slid onto the bench across from her. "Are you quoting an old western or *Toy Story*?"

"I guess it better be *Toy Story*. I'm going to have to brush up on all my children's movies soon." She cocked her head. "How do you know lines from that movie?"

"Are you kidding? *Toy Story*'s a classic. It's one of my favorites."

Becca grinned. "Just a big kid, aren't you? You're going to be a great uncle."

"I hope so. It will help boost my ego if I can excel in one area of my life, at least."

Her forehead wrinkled. "What does that mean? What areas aren't you excelling in? Other than your love life, of course, which I'm not going to bring up."

"Thank you. I appreciate your self-control." Daniel picked up his menu and perused it in an attempt to avoid meeting his sister's eyes.

"What are you doing?"

He repressed a sigh. "I'm looking at the menu. Typically what one does before one orders a meal in a restaurant."

She reached over and pushed his menu down. "No, you're not. You've avoiding looking at me. Why?" He winced at her quick intake of breath. "You met someone, didn't you?"

Daniel set the menu on the table. "No, I didn't. And I wasn't talking about my love life earlier. I was referring to my job."

"Who is she?"

Like a dog with a bone. "I told you I didn't meet anyone. And the server is coming. Do you know what you want?"

He leaned back when the woman stopped at the end of their table and filled his mug with coffee. Becca shook her head when the middle-aged woman in a mustard-yellow uniform held the pot up to her. "I'll have water, thanks." The woman took their order and left. Becca bent forward a little and inhaled, waving one hand toward her to direct the steam rising from his mug over to her. "Mmm. That smells so good. I think I miss coffee most of all."

"Sorry." Daniel grimaced. "I forgot you weren't drinking it these days. I shouldn't have it either."

"No, it's fine. Smelling it is the next best thing." She settled back on the bench. "So?"

"So I'm a little frustrated with the way the investigation is going, that's all."

"Why?"

"I can't really go into specifics, except to say that we keep hitting one roadblock after another. Sometimes it feels as though Sharleen and I are in way over our heads with this one."

"I doubt that."

Daniel smiled affectionately at his sister. They'd had their battles over the years, like all siblings, but no one stood up for him against the rest of the world like she did. Or saw more potential greatness in him than anyone else did, including him. She got that from their mom, who had always made both of them feel like there was nothing they couldn't do. A twinge of sadness worked its way across his chest, but Daniel pushed it back. "I appreciate the vote of confidence. I wish I could share your sentiments, but it seems like for every step forward, we've lost two. And if we don't come up with something concrete soon, more kids could be taken. It's a little overwhelming, to be honest."

"I know you will."

"I hope you're right. We are following up on a new idea, so hopefully that will pan out. This case is going to take up a lot of my time for the next few weeks, at least. I know I promised to be there for you and Dad more, but—"

She reached across the table and gripped his arm. "Don't worry about it. I understand completely, and so will Dad. You have to do your job, especially if it means protecting the children of the city. I'll be praying for you."

"I'd appreciate it. We'll need all the help we can get."

Becca squeezed his arm before pulling her hand away and resting it on her stomach. "I do know what you mean about feeling overwhelmed. Now that this impending parenthood thing has gotten so real, I'm starting to get a little panicky. Am I ready to be completely and utterly responsible for another human being? What if I can't do it? What if I turn out to be a horrible mother?"

"Becca. There's no way you are going to be a horrible mother. You are one of the most loving, caring, fiercely protective people I know. And you had an amazing role model. You've totally got this. And Austin will be there for you, and so will I, as much as I can." He nodded at her stomach. "This little one is going to be well taken care of, I promise."

Her shoulders relaxed. "I know. Thanks."

"You're welcome. I mean it. And so you know, I'm praying for you and Austin, as you launch into this new adventure."

"Please do. We'll need all the help we can get too."

The server appeared at their table again and set a plate with a BLT sandwich and fries in front of each of them. "Anything else I can get you?"

Daniel shook his head. "I think we're good for now, thanks."

She nodded and left.

His sister picked up half of her sandwich. "I know you and Sharleen will catch this guy soon. And how great would that be?" She rubbed her stomach with her free hand. "In a way, you'll be making the world a safer place for this little girl to come into."

Daniel almost choked on the bite he'd taken. "Girl?" He reached for his mug and gulped his coffee.

Becca grinned. "Yep. We found out last week. I think that's what's made this all so real for me."

He set the mug on the table. "Becca, that's amazing."

"I think so. And Austin does too."

"I'll bet. She'll have him wrapped around her little finger in no time."

Becca laughed. "I'm sure she will." She reached for her glass and took a sip of water. "Now tell me about this woman."

Daniel let out an exasperated sigh. "Have you ever let go of anything in your life?"

"Not when I know there's something to hold on to."

He rubbed his hands together to brush off the toast crumbs. Why did he even bother to try and keep anything to himself? "All right. I did see someone, our server, actually, a couple of weeks ago at the diner Lou took me to after we did that safety talk at the school. I admit I kind of shocked myself with the strong reaction I had to her, but then she started talking to her boyfriend, or husband for all I know. And that was that." Daniel dipped a few fries in ketchup and shoved them into his mouth.

"Well, was it a boyfriend or a husband? There's a big difference."

He took his time chewing and swallowing the fries. "I don't know, and I'm not about to go back there and ask her, so you're going to have to let this one go. There really is nothing to hold on to."

Becca contemplated him for a moment. "All right, fine. At least you opened your mind to the possibility, if only for a minute or two. That gives me hope."

"And buys me some time, right?" Daniel wiped his mouth and tossed the paper napkin on his plate.

"I suppose. Sounds like you're going to be too busy to think about anything but work for a while anyway."

"Yes, definitely." Daniel nodded at the server as she set the bill and two peppermints on the table and walked away. "I'll come see you and Dad when I can, but otherwise, if Sharleen and I are going to have any chance of solving this case, I will have to be completely focused. No thinking about women or dating or anything else but work until this investigation is wrapped up."

Chapter Twenty-One

Nicole took her last bite of scrambled eggs and bacon and set down her fork. She usually went to church with Joe and Connie, but that morning she'd decided to join Gage and Holden at their small Baptist church not far from the diner. Afterwards, she'd invited the two of them back to her place for brunch.

"That was great, Nicole. Thanks." Holden grabbed her empty plate and slid it on top of his to carry into the kitchen. "Here, Gage. I'll take yours too."

Gage's eyes were on Nicole and he didn't look up when his brother took his plate. "Thanks, Luke."

Nicole raised her eyebrows. "Who's Luke?"

Gage's face paled. He didn't answer her, just lifted his gaze to meet his brother's. Holden stood for a few seconds, frozen, the plate Gage had handed him suspended above the table, then he cleared his throat and added the plate to the pile with a clatter. "You know what? I think I'm going to head out. I have an early meeting tomorrow that I need to prepare for." He pushed through the kitchen door.

Nicole watched Gage carefully, but he appeared fixated on folding his napkin carefully and precisely before setting it back on the table. The dishes Holden had carried into the kitchen thudded onto the counter before he came back out through the door.

"Thanks again, Nicole." He leaned down and kissed her on the cheek before punching Gage lightly on the shoulder. "I'll call you later, bro."

Gage nodded and waited until the front door closed behind his brother before looking up.

Nicole clasped her hands together in her lap. What was

going on? She'd never seen such a strange look on his face.

He drew in a shaky breath.

"So?"

"So what?"

Her head tilted to one side. "Come on, Gage. What was that all about? You called your brother Luke. I would have thought it was a slip of the tongue, except you both got so weird all of a sudden. Who is Luke?"

Gage let out a deep breath and pushed back his chair. He stood up and grabbed the back of it as though he needed the support. He reached for her. "Come here."

Nicole slid her hand into his and followed him across the room. Gage sat down on the brown leather couch, and she sank down beside him, still clutching his hand.

"Okay, now you're starting to freak me out," she said, her voice trembling slightly. "What's the big deal?"

His laugh sounded forced. "It's not a big deal, actually. When Holden and I were kids, we used to play *Star Wars*. We were crazy about those movies and liked to pretend we were characters from the early ones."

The tension slowly leached from her body, like air from a tire. A smile played across her lips and he traced it with one finger. Her breath quickened and she pushed his hand away. "No distracting me. So Holden was Luke Skywalker. Who were you, Yoda?"

Gage laughed, freely this time, as he dropped his hand into his lap. "No. If my little brother was going to be a Jedi in training, I had to one-up him, of course, and be a Jedi Master. Yoda wasn't quite tall enough for me, and I couldn't get into rearranging the order of my words in every sentence, so I was Obi Wan 'Ben' Kenobi. Holden called me Ben."

How crazy is that? "Wait here a second." She let go of his hand and sprang up from the couch to head down the hall to her bedroom. After rummaging around on the shelf in her closet, she pulled down a shoebox and carried it out to the living room.

"What's that?"

"I have to show you something." Nicole sat on the couch and pulled the lid off the box. It was filled with photographs. "It's in here somewhere, I'm sure. I saw it not that long ago."

Gage looked over her shoulder as she rifled through the pictures. Most of them were of her parents, some as old as twenty-five or thirty years. They'd looked so young back then. She paused with one in her hand. Her father was tall with a beard and neatly-trimmed, sandy-brown hair and green eyes. Her mother had short blonde hair and her head barely reached his shoulder. She knew they'd changed, but since it had been a while since she'd seen them, she really had no idea how they looked now. A twinge of sadness niggled through her.

Gage nudged her shoulder with his. "Are those your parents?"

She nodded and dropped it into the box. "Yes."

"Hey."

She stopped flipping through the photos and looked up at him.

"Someday we're going to have to talk about them, you know."

Nicole shrugged. "Maybe. Someday. There's not much to say." Her head lowered again, and she tugged at the corner of a photo, freeing it from the rest. "Here it is!" She held it up, triumphant.

Gage tore his gaze from her face and looked down at the picture in her hand. A wide grin spread across his face. "I don't believe it."

The photo was of an eight or nine-year-old Nicole, looking very much like Leia Organa, down to the flowing gown and long braids coiled on either side of her head. "I loved those movies. I watched them all the time. I wanted to be Leia so badly." She looked up at him and smiled.

Gage brushed his fingers across her cheek. "I guess that makes you Princess."

"That sounds about right." A mischievous grin quirked the corners of her mouth before she dropped her gaze back to the photo. "I made my nanny do my hair like that every day for a year. She always tried to talk me into something else, but I only wanted to be Leia. I think because she was so beautiful, and so strong, even though she didn't have any parents either." She swallowed hard. A tear started to trickle down one cheek, but she brushed it away quickly.

Gage caught her hand. "Don't do that."

"Don't do what?"

"Don't hide what you're feeling from me. It's okay to cry."

Nicole dropped the photo into the box and set it on the coffee table. She shifted to face him on the couch and rested a hand on his knee. "I'm not hiding anything from you, I promise. The thing is, I've shed so many tears over my parents, I can't do it anymore."

"All right, as long as you know you can talk to me about anything."

"I do know that." Nicole bit down on her thumbnail of her free hand as she studied him.

"What?"

"You and Holden must have played that game a lot."

"Why do you say that?" His leg muscles tightened beneath her hand.

They'd tiptoed around the subject of their pasts ever since that night in the restaurant. Nicole rarely mentioned hers, and she had never asked Gage about his again. Clearly he was apprehensive about the idea that she might be reaching out tentative fingers to probe deep, likely still-gaping wounds. She searched his face. "Wow. I can actually feel you withdrawing. And see it in your eyes."

"See what?" His voice was strained.

Was that panic? "Nothing, actually. I can't read them at all. I don't usually have to work too hard to see what you're feeling, but now—"

Gage stood up abruptly. "I'm thirsty. Do you want a drink?"

"No thanks."

She got up too and followed him as he strode across the

room and into the kitchen. When she walked into the room, he had pressed both palms hard against the counter and dropped his chin to his chest and was drawing in one deep breath after another.

Nicole shoved back the panic that was beginning to grip her now. *What is going on?* She crossed over to the refrigerator. "What do you feel like? Cranberry juice? 7-Up?"

"Got anything harder?" His laugh sounded strange, like a rusty gate squeaking open.

Nicole peered around the fridge door at him. "Okay, now I'm really worried. You never drink. I've often wondered ..." She leaned back into the fridge and pulled out two cans of soda. After pushing the door shut with one foot, she set the cans down on the counter and opened a cupboard door.

For a moment he didn't ask, as if he was afraid that, if he did, he'd be forced to have the conversation he very clearly did not want to have.

His shoulders sagged. "You've often wondered what?"

Nicole popped the tab on one of the cans and poured the contents into a glass. The swirling bubbles rose to the surface and popped in the air. She handed him the glass and he took it, his fingers brushing against hers. Neither of them moved as their eyes met. "If maybe your father or mother drank. A lot." She pulled her hand away and moved to the other side of the counter. What was she afraid of, that her words might spark a reaction she'd need to protect herself from? Gage would never hurt her. Would he? That thought had never crossed her mind, but she'd never seen him struggling with such angst either. The wildness in his eyes was new, and she pressed a hand to her stomach.

Gage lifted the glass to his lips and took a sip before setting the glass down on the counter with a clink.

Nicole watched him as she poured her own glass and sipped from it. "Do you want to sit down?"

"I should go."

She closed her eyes for a few seconds. When she opened them, she sent him a pleading look. "Please don't."

He held her gaze for a long moment. If she looked away, he'd win. He'd be free to walk away, and she would never be able to bring up the subject again. But they would both lose that way.

She couldn't look away.

Finally, Gage nodded. She crossed the kitchen and held the door open for him. His feet appeared leaden as he dragged them across the thick beige living room carpet.

Nicole set her glass on the coffee table and opened the door to the wood stove. She poked through the ashes and added wood pieces until a bright flame flickered through the glass when she closed the door. Then she tossed a couple of pillows onto the floor in front of the couch and sank down before the warm blaze.

Gage set his glass down on the table beside hers and lowered himself to the carpet. In spite of the warmth flowing from the fire, he shivered.

"Gage?" She spoke as gently as she could.

A deep shudder moved through him, and she wrapped her arms around him and pulled him close. He pressed his face into her shoulder. After a moment, he drew in a quivering breath and sat up. "You're right."

"About the drinking?"

"Yes. It was my dad. He ..." His gaze dropped to his hands. "He did drink a lot. In fact, he got drunk pretty much every night. And when he did ..."

Gage lifted his head. Her breath caught in her throat at the look of pain in his eyes. "He'd get violent. Hit us. Me and Holden and our mom."

Nicole let go of one hand and gently brushed the hair from his forehead. Her fingers ran lightly over a tiny scar at the hairline. "Is that how you got this?"

He nodded. "I have a much bigger one on the back of my head."

Nicole winced.

"How could he have done that?"

"I don't know," she murmured.

"I've been asking myself that for years. I mean, the thought of smacking defenceless little kids around like that ..." Gage pulled his other hand from hers and pressed both palms against his forehead, his fingers gripping clumps of hair. "I see it all the time at work and it rips me apart. I want to grab those parents and shove them up against the wall and tell them to lay off their kids or I'll ..."

"You'll what?"

"That's the thing. More often than not there is nothing I can do, nothing that will stop them from hurting their kids over and over and over." Gage clenched his fists, pounding them against his knees. "All I can do is stand there and watch them walk out of the courtroom, heading home to take out their frustrations on the little ones they're supposed to be protecting."

Nicole was silent for a few seconds then she covered one fist with her fingers, waiting until he unclenched it and turned his hand over to grip hers. "How did you ever find God in all that mess?"

His shoulders relaxed. "Actually, that's the one thing my dad did do for us. He forced my mom to take Holden and me to church every week so the house would be quiet and he could sleep off the night before. We had to pretend for years that we hated it so he'd let us keep going, when really it was the lifeline we all clung to just to survive."

"What happened? Did Children's Aid finally take you out of there?"

Gage swallowed hard. "No. They came to the house sometimes. I think they wanted to take us. But my mom, she'd tell them we had fallen, that we were clumsy and hurt ourselves all the time. She always protected him for some reason. Although, so did Holden and I. When they asked us, we made up stories about how we had gotten our cuts and bruises." His voice broke. "I should have told them, Nic. If I had, I could have protected Holden, could have gotten him out of there before ..."

"Before what?"

"Before the night my dad came home and punched my mother so hard she hit her head on the kitchen counter and died."

"Oh Gage." His eyes had filled with tears and she wiped away one that had started down his cheek with her finger. "Why did you say you should have gotten Holden out? Did your dad hurt him that night too?"

Gage shook his head. "You're a real sucker for punishment, you know that?" They both laughed, shakily. "Do you really want to hear the rest?"

"Want to? No. But I need to. I need to know what happened to you."

"Fine. But remember, you asked for this." He drew in a deep breath. "After my dad hit my mom, he came upstairs looking for us."

She stroked the backs of his hands with her thumbs, trying to draw out some of the horror of the memory. "Holden and I ... we'd been in our make-believe *Star Wars* world again. And you're right, we were there often. It was so much better than our real world. We were strong there, and brave, like real heroes. Not that it helped us any when he came after us, but it helped to pretend. And it helped to escape, even if it was only for a little while." His eyes searched hers. Nicole nodded encouragement.

"We were in the closet, hiding. But he found us, of course. He always found us. And he grabbed my arm and pulled me out. He was worse that night than I'd ever seen him. I think he wanted to kill us, that he came home meaning to." The words came out in a rush, as though he had to finish, had to get out everything before he couldn't go on anymore. "All I could think about was my mother, downstairs, and Holden, and that I had to save them. I had to stop him, somehow."

Gage shook so hard that his teeth chattered. Nicole moved her hand to his back and rubbed up and down in a desperate attempt to ward off the cold that seemed to be freezing him from the inside out. "Then he punched me. Hard. I fell backward and my head slammed against the footboard of the bed."

He lifted his glass with trembling fingers and sipped. He studied the clear liquid for a moment, then set the glass on the table and reached for her again. His hand felt like ice as she wrapped her fingers around his. "This black cloud was swirling around me, but I opened my eyes for a few seconds and my dad was going after Holden. He was choking him, Nic, killing him, right before my eyes. I couldn't let him do that. I had to do something."

He turned his hand over in hers. "We'd had a jackknife in the closet. Holden and I had used it to cut ourselves, to become blood brothers."

She gently traced the small white scar in his palm with her thumb.

His eyes met hers again. Horror swirled in them. "I saw it on the floor near Holden. I knew if I could crawl over there somehow, get hold of that knife …"

Oh God, no. He killed him. He killed his own father. Gage shook violently now. *It's too much. Don't make him say the words.* Nicole cupped his face in her hands. "It's okay," she whispered. "That's enough. For tonight, that's enough."

His shoulders slumped, and he nodded and rested his forehead against hers.

Nicole rubbed her hand in circles around his back. That was enough for now.

But someday, for his sake, he'd have to tell her the rest.

Chapter Twenty-Two

Daniel stared at the computer screen like he'd been doing for hours, his mind racing. He picked up a pen and twirled it around in his fingers. Who would want to save these kids badly enough to risk going to prison for years—or worse? Every time they went into a home in the night they risked waking up a potentially violent person who likely wouldn't hesitate to use whatever means necessary to keep them from taking their kids. Even if they did beat up on those kids themselves regularly.

Since he and Sharleen had started going through the lists on Friday, he hadn't found anything promising, and he was already almost halfway through. Maybe this was going to be a dead end after all, and they'd have to start in on the cops. He tightened his grip on the pen. After going through a couple more names without success, Daniel massaged the back of his neck with one hand and rose to his feet with a groan. Grabbing his mug from the desk, he started down the hall, stopping outside Sharleen's door. "Any luck?"

"Nothing yet." She shifted in her chair until she faced him.

"Me neither. Keep looking, okay?"

Sharleen turned back to the computer. "I'll let you know if anything looks promising."

"Thanks." Daniel walked to the end of the hall and grabbed the pot from under the coffeemaker. His mind raced as he filled up the mug and replaced the pot.

After sinking onto his desk chair, he took a sip and made a face. Definitely not Starbucks. He set the mug down and pulled up the list again. A quick Google search of the next few names, Lewis, Lyman, Kane, revealed nothing. Holden Kelly was next. After meeting him, Daniel doubted he was their man, although he hadn't sounded as emphatic as Daniel would have expected him to be when Daniel made the comment about there being no way to get around the law. Hmm. His finger hovered over the name. Better not to discount anyone at this point.

What about Nicole? Daniel dropped his hand down on the desk. If she was seeing Holden's brother, and Holden turned out to be the kidnapper, she would no doubt be devastated. Could he do that to her?

Daniel closed his eyes and rubbed them with his thumb and finger. Could he do that to her? Where had that come from? Nicole whose last name he didn't even know was nothing to him. He certainly wasn't about to let one moment of insanity in that diner interfere with a criminal investigation. *Get a grip, Grey.* Opening his eyes, he typed Holden's name into the police files search bar and perused the screen. His eyes widened. Leaning forward in his chair, he read the entire file again, slowly this time. Could it be? It *was* uncanny, how often one or the other of the Kelly brothers had crossed his path lately. *Is that some kind of sign?*

Daniel pushed to his feet and walked across the hall. "Shar, you have to come see this."

"Did you find something?"

"Maybe. Come and tell me what you think."

She followed him to his office and pulled the chair up to the desk. His fingers shook as he pulled up the file, adrenaline pumping through his system.

Sharleen read everything on the screen as he drummed his fingers on the desk. When she finished, she raised troubled eyes to meet his.

"What do you think?"

"It does seem to fit. We still have a lot of names to check out though. Why don't I keep going through my list while you see if you can get any more information on this guy?"

Daniel nodded. "Good idea. I'll let you know what I find out, and you tell me if you come across anyone else that sounds like a possibility."

Before she had left his office, he was typing away again. Over the next hour, he managed to find quite a lot of information. Everything he found increased his level of excitement, although he tried to stem the rising tide. The last thing he wanted was to let emotion cloud his judgment, to try and force someone to fit the theory he'd come up with, and end up accusing the wrong person. He'd have to proceed with extreme caution. Especially since Gage was a lawyer for the Crown Attorney's office and could also have access to confidential information. Either of them—or both—could be involved. Daniel thumped his hands on the desk as if he were playing a drum, releasing some of the excess energy flowing through him as he considered the possibilities. *Should I see if he has a file with CAS?*

Daniel glanced around his cubicle as though someone might have overheard the thought. Using Holden Kelly's secret password, which he didn't have permission to do, was bad enough, but using it against the man himself was extremely unethical at best. Doing so without a warrant was borderline illegal. Unless this constituted a time-sensitive emergency. Daniel pursed his lips. Could he make a case for that, if needed? After a moment, he nodded, slammed the front legs of his plastic chair onto the floor, and began typing again.

In thirty seconds he had the files of both Holden and Gage Kelly on his computer. Daniel turned the laptop so no one coming through the doorway could see the screen before starting to read. He winced as he perused the files. Between the two Kelly brothers, there had been eleven trips to the hospital in three years. None after 1993 though, when the oldest was ten. Daniel pursed his lips. Why was that? They were too young for Children's Aid to write them off. He scanned the file. Each hospital visit was followed by a notation laying out the mother's explanation of their injuries. According to her, they'd fallen out of a tree, or down the stairs, or hurt themselves while wrestling with each other. Daniel's jaw clenched. How could a mother lie to the authorities and allow her own children to continue to be beaten? He shook his head in disgust. And why were there no notes after

1993?

He scrolled to the next page. Different forms this time. His eyes narrowed. It looked like the boys had been taken into care at that point. He pursed his lips as he read on. Both parents deceased, November 11th, 1993. He sucked in a quick breath. Deceased? Both of them? How had that happened?

Dropping his hands to the keyboard again, he opened up the police department files and entered his own password. Typing in the boys' names, he held his breath as a report showed up on the screen. He read it over quickly, his stomach churning. The end of the report contained the results of an investigation into a double domestic homicide. The boys' father and mother had both been killed on the same night. A chill shivered through him as he read the details.

Daniel slumped against the back of his desk chair, completely drained. He clicked back on the Children's Aid file, and photographs of the two boys filled the screen. The deep brown eyes that stared back at him were empty and old way beyond their years. His mouth opened and he whispered one word, completely void of the triumph he thought he would feel at this moment.

"Gotcha."

"Sir?" Daniel knocked softly on the door and drew in a deep breath before sticking his head tentatively around the partially open door of his boss's office. "Do you have a minute?"

Detective Sergeant Lector didn't look up from the pile of papers he was signing, but he did wave a hand in the direction of the empty chairs in front of his desk.

Daniel stepped back and gestured for Sharleen to go in ahead of him. She shot him a dark look but complied. The two of them had decided the best recourse was to let the DS know what they had come up with so far, and request that a surveillance team be sent out to monitor the activities of both Holden and Gage Kelly, beginning as soon as possible.

Daniel slipped into the room and shut the door quietly behind them. For several minutes he sat on the hard leather chair, shifting periodically in a vain effort to get comfortable. His partner appeared equally uncomfortable beside him. Their uneasiness stemmed less from the hard seats than the presence of their superior. Even buried in paperwork, the tough, no-nonsense aura the man was famous for radiated out from him in cold, discomfiting waves. Like most of his colleagues, Daniel had never entered this room without being summoned. It had taken every ounce of nerve and several strong cups of coffee to propel him, with Sharleen trudging along behind, down the hallway and into the inner sanctum of the station that morning. Unfortunately for Daniel, both his nerve and the caffeine were dissipating rapidly.

Finally, the detective sergeant scribbled across the last page on his desk, lifted the paper, and smacked it down on the pile. Yanking open his top drawer, he capped the pen, tossed it in, and slammed the drawer shut. Daniel jumped. The grim smile that flitted briefly across the DS's lips did nothing to lower his blood pressure.

"Well?" His boss leaned back in his chair and crossed both arms over his thick chest. The man could easily have been a marine in his younger days. Still probably could be, as far as that went. The muscles in both arms clenched. The effect was knee-weakening, as it was no doubt calculated to be. "What is it, Grey, Roberts?"

For a few, terrible seconds, Daniel couldn't remember what they were doing there. Then Sharleen nudged him in the arm with her elbow. Daniel cleared his throat. "We wanted to bring you up to date on the child abduction investigation, sir."

Thick eyebrows rose above emotionless eyes. "Good. What have you got for me?"

"We've been following up on a few leads and think we may have come across a person of interest. Possibly two."

"Ah." The eyebrows lowered. "Who are they?" He turned his glare on Sharleen.

She cleared her throat. "Two brothers, Holden and Gage Kelly. Holden is a children's aid worker and Gage a crown attorney. We got to thinking that, since whoever is taking these kids appears to be targeting those who have a file with CAS, it makes sense that the abductor would be someone with access to those files so he would know who was in need of …"

The detective sergeant glowered at her. "In need of what?"

Daniel leaned forward. His partner had been about to say *rescue*, he knew, which did not seem like the right word to use in front of the DS. "In need of someone to watch out for them, sir. Without that, those kids make easy targets for a kidnapper."

"Ah." The DS uncrossed his arms. "Do you have enough to bring either of them in for questioning?"

"No sir. It's basically a hunch at this point, although everything seems to fit."

"A hunch."

"That's right. We're hoping to get surveillance on them, catch them in the act."

The DS tented his fingers in front of him and tapped them on his chin, studying Daniel. "Let me get this straight. You want me to commit money and personnel to stake out a couple of men who may or may not be remotely involved in this case because the two of you have a hunch."

It did sound ridiculous, when he put it that way. Heat crept up Daniel's neck. "Yes, sir."

The detective sergeant pursed his lips. "Sorry, detectives. I can't do it."

If anyone had ever apologized with less remorse in his voice, Daniel hadn't heard it.

"Look, it's been months since the first kid was taken and, hunches aside, we're no closer to figuring out who's behind the latest disappearance, especially now that this Stiller has slipped through our fingers. The public is in an uproar over this, and of course that means politicians and media." The detective sergeant grimaced as he said the words, as though they left a sour taste on his tongue. "They're watching us too closely. We can't afford to take any missteps. And wasting money and resources is a major misstep. Having said that, if you can get me something more on either of these guys, solidify your case a little, I will re-think that decision." He gestured toward the door and swung his gaze to his computer. They'd been dismissed.

Without a word, they both rose and headed for the door, then froze at their boss's parting words. "I want this case wrapped up yesterday, if not before. Do *not* let me down."

Neither of them spoke as they headed down the hall. Sharleen grabbed Daniel's elbow when they reached his cubicle. "Well? What do we do now?"

Daniel exhaled loudly. There was no way around it that he could see. "How do you feel about heading out on a solo stakeout?"

Chapter Twenty-Three

Daniel tipped back his head to swig the last of the now-cold coffee. Grimacing, he crumpled up the paper cup and tossed it onto the floor in the backseat, where it joined the three others he'd already shot back there. Four cups of coffee were no substitute for sleep, but they'd have to do for tonight.

He blinked to clear his vision and bring the door of Gage Kelly's apartment building back into focus. Three straight nights of surveillance, followed by a couple of hours of sleep before reporting into the station, were starting to take a toll on him. He pressed the button to light up the screen on his phone. 2 a.m. Already later than any of the abductions had taken place, and there was no activity around the building. Or anywhere in the quiet neighborhood, for that matter.

Daniel ran a hand over his face. This was getting ridiculous. His partner hadn't spotted anything unusual over at Holden's place either. How many nights were the two of them going to have to spend out here? Sharleen should be home with her husband and kids. Tom was pretty patient, but his patience had to be wearing thin, especially since this wasn't technically official police business.

His phone vibrated and he glanced down. A text from Sharleen. *Nothing here. I'm calling it.*

He punched in his reply. *Go for it. I'm heading home too. Talk to you in the morning.* Daniel sent the text and then tossed his phone onto the passenger seat. There was one other thing he could try. Pulling his seatbelt down over his chest, he locked it in place. Then he started the engine and headed downtown.

"I take it you didn't see anything either?"

Daniel swung his chair around. Sharleen stood in the door of the cubicle, a steaming cup in her hand. She preferred tea to coffee. Herbal tea. How on earth did she manage to look so perky when she'd been keeping the same lousy schedule as he had without the bolstering effects of caffeine to keep her going?

"Not at Gage's place, no."

Her eyes narrowed. "Did you go somewhere else?"

"Actually yes. After you told me you were going home, I drove past the diner downtown where Gage Kelly's girlfriend works. Obviously she wasn't there, but I wanted to remember where the place was exactly so I could go back there today."

She planted her free hand on her hip. "How on earth do you know where his girlfriend works? Or even that he has a girlfriend?"

"I saw them there together a few weeks ago, when Lou and I went for breakfast at the diner. Well, he had breakfast anyway."

"And you didn't?"

This conversation was heading into dangerous territory fast. Daniel shifted in his chair. "No. Lou offered to take me out, but when we got there I realized I was more tired than hungry, and I ended up leaving."

She tilted her head to the side. "Did something else happen?"

"I was only there for five minutes."

"Which doesn't answer my question."

Daniel worked to keep his face composed under Sharleen's intense scrutiny. Having a partner who knew him so well was a big advantage on the street, but it was a definite liability when he was trying to keep something from her.

"Are you planning to start watching her now too?"

Daniel moved the mouse around on his desk, not meeting her gaze. "I thought I might go talk to her, actually. See if I can speed things up a bit."

"Do you think she'll tell you anything that might get her

boyfriend or his brother in trouble?"

"Maybe, if I can convince her they could be in danger, which, if we catch them abducting another child, they definitely would be."

Sharleen managed to take a sip of tea without looking away from him. "Do you want me to come with you to see this woman?"

"No, that's okay." He injected as much casual as possible into his voice. "I can handle this. I don't want you being away from home any more than you already are." Would taking an altruistic tact work with her?

Sharleen glanced down the hallway before coming into his office and dropping down onto the black plastic chair beside him. Apparently not. Daniel's heart sank.

"You know her, don't you?"

"Who?"

"Don't mess with me Grey. You know who. Gage Kelly's girlfriend."

"I wouldn't say I know her. I did see her there that day, but that's it."

"And then you left without eating. That's a major red flag. I've never known you to put sleep ahead of food. Did something happen between the two of you?"

"What could have happened in five minutes?"

"That's what I'm trying to find out."

To save time, he gave up and submitted to the inevitable. "All right, fine. She was our server that day. I thought she was really attractive, but then I realized she was with someone else, Gage Kelly, to be exact, so I left. End of story. I haven't thought about her since."

"Sure you haven't. That's why you still can't look me in the eye when you're talking about her."

Daniel forced himself to meet her gaze. "Shar ..."

His partner raised both hands. "Okay, I'll drop it. As long as you promise me you can be professional when you meet with her."

"I can. As far as I'm concerned, she's someone of interest who might be able to give us information to help solve a criminal investigation."

Sharleen pressed her tongue into her cheek, clearly trying to decide if he was telling the truth. Daniel held his breath.

After a moment she exhaled loudly. "Okay fine. I'll keep working here while you go see her. But I want your word that you'll tell me if you don't think you can stay objective."

"You have it."

She started to leave his office then stopped. "Oh, and Grey?"

"Bring you tea."

"Peppermint. Thanks." She pointed a finger at him. "Professional."

"Have you ever known me to be anything but?" He shook his head as she opened her mouth to speak. "Don't answer that."

Sharleen grinned and walked away.

Daniel shifted back around to his desk. Seeing Nicole again would be a good thing. It would show him that whatever had hit him over the head that day was a fluke, a moment of weakness brought on by lack of sleep, or maybe by his sister planting the thought in his head that he really needed a woman. When they met again he was sure he would feel nothing more for her than he would feel for any other person of interest. Of interest to the force, that is, not to him personally.

Jumping to his feet, he pulled on his jacket and headed for the parking lot. Only one way to find out.

Chapter Twenty-Four

The sun was warm for mid-May. Daniel flapped the sides of his suit jacket before leaning against the outside wall of a building, soaking up the coolness of the stone against his shoulders. The stench of warm garbage from farther down the alley drifted on the air and he grimaced as he peered cautiously around the corner. Nicole should be coming by soon. He'd used his two days off this week to follow her, and she seemed to keep a pretty regular schedule. She'd worked at the diner both days from seven in the morning until five at night. After work, she'd stopped at the market to pick up a few groceries. Then she had crossed the street and walked home through the park near her building.

If she stuck to her regular routine, she should be passing by him in the next few minutes. He was hoping to make contact with her today, try to feel her out a bit to see if she knew anything about the children that had gone missing.

He scanned the crowds of people making their way down the sidewalk in both directions and zeroed in on one woman in a pale pink jacket, blonde hair caught up in a ponytail. She was coming. Daniel edged closer to the corner of the building. After she'd passed by, he'd fall into step behind her and follow her to the market. Maybe he'd have an opportunity to engage her in casual conversation there, ask her if she knew where he could find something, anything to make that initial connection with her. He'd have to be discreet though, or she'd—

"Hey!"

His head whipped in her direction. A kid in a black sweatshirt, hood pulled over his head, had grabbed her purse. Nicole wrestled with him for a few seconds, until the guy wrenched it from her hands and sprinted away, heading toward

Daniel.

So much for being discreet.

He waited until the little thief had almost reached him, then he jumped out and planted a hand on the kid's chest, driving him up against the wall and holding him there with his forearm. "Give it back."

The guy's eyes were hard as flint. "I don't think so." He shoved against Daniel's arm, but Daniel held him firmly in place.

With his free hand, he pushed back his jacket, far enough so the kid could see both his badge and the gun strapped across his chest, but no one else could. "Want to re-think that?"

If possible, the kid's eyes grew harder. "Whatever." He shoved the bag against Daniel's stomach.

Daniel contemplated him as he took the bag. If the little criminal had seemed even the tiniest bit remorseful, he'd let him go without a qualm. Since he didn't appear to be, Daniel would like nothing better than to arrest him and let him spend a night behind bars to cool off. Unfortunately, if he slapped cuffs on the guy in front of Nicole, the game would be up. It went against everything in him, but if he had to let a petty thief go in order to capture a much bigger prey, so be it.

"Stop taking things that don't belong to you." He pressed a little deeper into the guy's chest, driving home his point. "Next time you might not be so lucky." He dropped his arm and stepped back, clutching the bag in one hand.

The kid took off, weaving in and around the other pedestrians until he was gone from view.

"That was amazing." Nicole sounded breathless as she jogged up behind him.

Daniel turned around. Exactly like he'd hoped it wouldn't, the sight of her smile, the freckles sprinkled across her nose, hit him full force. For a moment, he struggled to draw in a breath.

An uncertain look crossed her face. "May I?"

Daniel glanced down. How long had she stood there, holding her hand out to him? His cheeks warmed. "Sorry." He offered her the bag.

She clutched it to her. "I don't know how to thank you. My whole life is in this bag."

"It was nothing." His voice had gone all Sam Elliot on him and he cleared his throat.

"It wasn't nothing." She held out her free hand, her gaze locked on his. "Thank you."

Was that a glimmer of recognition in her eyes? Daniel sincerely hoped not. He hesitated before reaching for her hand. "You're welcome."

Nicole nodded and, after a few seconds, slowly extricated her fingers from his. "I need to …" she pointed down the street.

"Of course." Daniel stepped away.

With a slight nod, she turned and continued down the sidewalk, heading in the direction of the market. Daniel watched her until she disappeared from view, lost in the crowd of people scurrying along the Toronto sidewalk.

Now what?

Nicole stepped into the market. Her heart still pounded, and she leaned against a freezer and took several deep breaths to slow it down. Did that just happen? She was always careful to hold onto her bag tightly when walking down a crowded sidewalk, but that kid had come out of nowhere. And so had her rescuer. What was he, some kind of superhero? *I mean, who does that? Risk their life for a complete stranger.* Not that he'd seemed in danger at any point. He'd appeared in complete control of the situation the entire time. And those eyes …

Nicole shook her head and pushed away from the freezer. All right, enough about him, whoever he was. She'd thanked him and that was that. She grabbed a basket and filled it with the dinner she planned to make for Gage that night. *Remember him?* She winced and attempted to force all thoughts of the heroic stranger from her mind.

After paying for her groceries, Nicole crossed the street and headed into the park. Now that the long, cold winter had finally ended, she welcomed the spring sun that warmed her neck and shoulders. It was almost hot today. The man who'd chased her would-be thief had to be uncomfortable in his suit jacket. Her forehead wrinkled. Had she met him before? At the diner, maybe? He'd looked familiar. Of course, that dark hair and blue eyes combination was difficult to forget. He mustn't have come often, or she definitely would have remembered him.

I thought you weren't thinking about him anymore. Nicole hiked the paper grocery bag up higher in her arms. She wasn't, of course. She was thinking about dinner, and what she could make for her boyfriend. A stir-fry, maybe. She'd picked up a bunch of vegetables at the market, and had chicken at home, so that would be an easy …

"Excuse me?"

Startled by a man's voice close behind her, Nicole whirled around. The paper bag in her arms ripped, sending groceries scattering across the pathway. Heat rushed into her cheeks as she crouched down and grabbed for a tomato.

The man—or superhero, or whatever he was—crouched down beside her. "Sorry, I didn't mean to startle you. I just … wanted to ask you something."

She scrutinized him for a moment before setting what was left of the bag down on the ground and reaching for a head of lettuce. "It's fine. I'm a little jumpy from before, I think."

"Can I give you a hand?"

"That's okay. You've done more than enough for me today. I've got it."

"I don't mind." He picked up a bag of apples.

Nicole straightened up, her arms filled with the rest of the items from the bag. Two red peppers and a yellow one slipped from her grasp and fell to the sidewalk. "Okay, I guess I don't have it."

His blue eyes danced when he laughed. Which was neither here nor there. Still, she watched him as he stooped down and grabbed the peppers. "Do you have far to go?"

"No, I live …" She started to wave a hand in the direction of her building, then stopped and wrinkled her nose. "I guess I shouldn't be giving out that information to a perfect stranger, even if he is the Good Samaritan type."

"Probably wise." He nodded. "I could wait here until you take those things home and come back, if you'd prefer."

Nicole hesitated, studying his face carefully. Could she trust him? Of course she couldn't. He was a stranger in the city, and he had appeared out of nowhere. Twice. It was quite possible that *he* was the stalker her dad was always warning her about. *Be smart, Nicole. Tell him you can manage on your own.* "No, that's silly. If you don't mind walking there with me, I'd appreciate it."

"Sure." The man fell into step beside her. When they reached her building, a large limestone edifice a block from the park, Nicole stopped.

Her hero—or stalker—inclined his head toward the condo building. "Nice place."

"Thanks." She paused. "I don't mean to be rude, but—"

"I'll wait out here until you come back for the rest of your groceries," he offered quickly.

Her shoulders relaxed. "Okay, thanks. I'll be right back."

Nicole hurried up to her condo and set the groceries down on the island in the kitchen. He did look hot. From the sun, that is. Should she offer him a drink? *Absolutely not.* Nicole tugged open the refrigerator door and took out two cans of lemonade. It really was the least she could do after he'd rescued her. Even Gage would see that, when she told him about everything that had happened to her today. Which she would.

When Nicole came out into the warm sunshine, the man was standing with his back to her, attempting to juggle the three peppers. She stopped at the top of the stairs and watched him for a moment, biting her lip to keep from laughing. Then one of the peppers slipped from his grasp and the other two quickly followed, the last one bouncing off the side of his head before dropping onto the cement. She did laugh then.

He turned toward her, his face red. "Sorry." He bent down and picked up the peppers, brushing them off on his shirt before placing them carefully on the step beside the apples.

"It's fine." Nicole came over to join him, setting the cans of lemonade down so she could pick up the peppers. "I used to be good at this myself, although it's been a while." She tossed one up in the air, but it landed in her waiting hand before she could throw either of the others up after it. On her second attempt, she managed to get all three items up and keep them there for about three seconds before they hit the sidewalk hard enough to crack one open.

She looked over at the man, her grin sheepish. He chuckled. "Good form. A couple more … years of practice and you should have it."

She sat down on the step behind her and picked up one of the cans. "I don't want to hold you up, but I thought I could at least offer you a drink." She held the can out to him.

For a moment, he seemed to hesitate. Would he do that if his intentions weren't honorable? "Yeah, sure. Thanks." He lowered himself onto the step beside her.

"So what did you want to ask me?"

"Excuse me?"

"Before, in the park, you said you wanted to ask me something."

"Oh, yeah." He pulled back the tab of the can and it popped open with a hiss. "I don't know this side of the city very well, so I wondered if you could recommend a good place to eat."

Really? That's why he had stopped her in the park? It seemed a bit contrived. Maybe he really was a stalker. "Oh." She bit the inside of her lip as she studied him.

He met her gaze steadily and she relaxed. Or maybe he was just hungry. "It depends what you're looking for. You can find a restaurant featuring pretty much any kind of ethnic food around here and most of them are great. Otherwise, there's a good diner, Joe's, at the corner of Bathurst and Queen, a few blocks from here."

"That sounds like what I'm looking for. I'll check it out."

Nicole rested her elbows on the step above and leaned back,

lifting her face to the sun. "I love spring. Especially days like today, all this sunshine and warmth."

The man leaned on the stair behind him too and tipped back his head to take a drink of the lemonade. "It is a gorgeous day," he agreed, after setting the can on the step beside him. "I love spring as well. It's like my third favorite season."

Nicole rolled her head sideways to smile at him. "That's not exactly a ringing endorsement. What's number four on your list?"

"Fall, definitely. I hate watching all the leaves come down, and everything looking bare and stark and gray until winter when the snow comes."

"Then it looks brown and dirty as the cars drive over it and turn it into a slushy mess so your feet get wet and cold every time you step out the door."

"Hmm. That's true. Okay, I'll bump spring up to second place after summer. How's that? Do you have anything against summer?"

"Not really. Other than the relentless heat, the mosquitoes, and the suffocating smog, of course."

The man chuckled. "Fine. You made your case. Spring is now officially my favorite season."

The corners of her mouth twitched. "Not a man to hold tightly to his convictions, are you?"

"Normally I am. Must be the blow to the head."

Nicole feigned a contrite look as she tipped her can in his direction. "I'm sorry. I didn't even ask if you were okay. Should I take you to emergency?"

"Uh no. I really don't want to have to explain that one to a doctor. I'll take my chances that it's just a twenty-four-hour head injury thing and that my convictions will be back tomorrow, stronger than ever."

She laughed again, not taking her eyes from his. They really were the most incredible shade of blue she'd ever seen. She could look into them all ... Nicole straightened up so suddenly a few drops of her drink splashed onto the step in front of her. *He needs to go. Now.*

As though he'd read the thought in her eyes, the man's smile disappeared. He lowered his gaze and the moment was gone.

A shutter dropped down over the emerald eyes that had been open and laughing seconds before. It was as though Nicole had forgotten herself in the sunshine, and in the warmth of what she assumed were his random acts of kindness—guilt prickled over his skin—suddenly realized she was being far too open with a total stranger. If Daniel hadn't felt the disintegration of the fragile bridge their lighthearted conversation had built between them so keenly, he would have been fascinated, watching her maneuver her defences back into place.

Watching Nicole was like looking through a View-master—a blank screen when she pulled the blinds over her eyes, followed by a sudden, breath-taking picture. Her voice, when she spoke again, had dropped several degrees. "I'm sure this is the last thing you are thinking of, but to be clear, I am seeing someone."

Yeah, I got that. His grip on the can tightened, but he managed a small grin. "Hey, no worries. I happen to be familiar with the story of the Good Samaritan, and I'm pretty sure there isn't anything about romance in it."

"You're right. There isn't." Nicole studied the drink in her hand. "Only help from a stranger. Which I'm sure the traveler was very grateful for, like I am." She set down the can and stood up. "So thank you." She rubbed her palm against her black dress pants to brush off the dirt from the step and held out her hand.

Daniel took her cue and rose. Reaching out, he grasped the hand she offered and held it in his. Her skin was soft and warm, and for a moment he couldn't draw air into his lungs.

She bit her lip as she pulled her hand from his. "I should go. My boyfriend is coming for dinner, and I need to see what I can salvage from my collection of bruised vegetables."

"Personally, I always chop up the ones I smash while juggling and make soup out of them. That way no one ever has to know."

Her smile didn't soften the gaze that had settled somewhere around his shoulders. "Good tip. I may do that."

"I'll see you around then."

She nodded, the curt movement, and the rigid way she held herself, sending the clear message that it wasn't likely.

Daniel bent down and picked up the vegetables and handed them to her. Resisting the urge to watch her until she had climbed the stairs and gone into her building, he headed through the park to the car he'd left on the other side. His mind sifted through the information he had been able to gather from the time he'd spent with Nicole that might be useful in their investigation.

It didn't take long.

Daniel reached his car and yanked the remote from his jeans pocket. He went over the exchange on the steps of her building again in his mind as he pulled open the door and slid behind the wheel. Her abrupt withdrawal from the conversation was not a good sign. Whatever Nicole's past, it had obviously made her wary of opening herself up too much, especially to someone she didn't know. *Too bad.* He really could have used someone close to his persons of interest who had *more* than the usual level of trust in people, not less.

Daniel smacked the steering wheel with his left hand as he pulled away from the curb. He should have gone as soon as she had returned for her groceries. Those extra few minutes had cost him any ground he'd gained by helping her carry them.

A small smile turned up the corners of his mouth. It had been amazing though, for those brief moments, to catch a glimpse of her being as open and friendly as she had been that day in the diner. He'd give anything to spend a few hours, or days, in the presence of *that* Nicole.

Unfortunately—his smile faded—given the circumstances under which he would be seeing her from now on, it was highly unlikely he'd see that side of her again.

Chapter Twenty-Five

A light breeze rustled the leaves of the huge oak tree in the middle of the yard, partially masking any sound and movement Rogue made as he crept from the shadows of the bushes in the backyard. With hours to go before the sun's rays would begin to streak across the early-morning sky, the soft swish of his shoes on the wet grass was swallowed by the thick mist that hung heavy over the yard.

He scanned the building in front of him. No lights gleamed through the windows of the second story. Creeping across the yard, he moved from tree to bush until he reached the house. The soft hoot of an owl broke the silence as he pressed against the brick wall. Rogue pulled the black mask down over his face and stood still for a moment, drawing in calm with the night air.

When his heart rate evened out and his hands felt steady, he pushed himself away from the wall and moved stealthily to the sliding doors that opened on to the back patio. Through the glass, he could make out a coffee maker and toaster sitting on the kitchen counter in the dim glow of the digital clock on the stove. He pulled a small tool out of his pocket and inserted it into the lock. *Slowly. Slowly.* A soft click sounded, and he slid the door open, barely enough for him to ease through.

As soon as he set his foot through the opening, the shrill wail of an alarm shattered the silence. His heart hurtled into his throat. For two seconds, he thought wildly about racing up the stairs, grabbing the little girl, and taking his chances on trying to get away with half the neighborhood alerted to his presence. Muttering a curse, he yanked his foot out, spun around, and sprinted for the fence. He stuck one running shoe on the lowest board and hurled himself over.

As Rogue darted through the narrow opening between two houses, he heard it, the desperate cry of the little girl he'd been sent to rescue. His chest clenched so tightly he could barely draw a breath as he ducked into the nearest subway stop and took the stairs three at a time to the bottom. He slipped through the doors of the train right before they closed. He had ripped off his hat and gloves and stuck them into his jacket pocket as he ran through the yards, and no one in the nearly empty car spared him a glance as he dropped onto a seat.

He clenched his fists tightly. Everything in him desperately wanted to lash out at someone or something. Instead, he bit his lip until he tasted blood to hold back a scream of frustration and pressed his crossed arms hard against his stomach as he slumped down in the corner of his seat.

Weeks of research and planning had gone down the drain, he'd nearly been caught, and—worst of all—a five-year-old girl was still at the mercy of her violent father, more terrified and in danger than ever. Rogue pounded his fists on his knees. What could have gone wrong? They had assured him the house had no alarm system, and the information they passed along had never been wrong before.

He straightened in his seat. He wanted answers. Yanking his phone from his pocket, he sent a message, in the code they'd given him, demanding a meeting. The second she told him when and where, he would go and see Natalya. Although he knew from past experience it was almost impossible to get information out of her that she didn't feel he needed to have, he wouldn't leave her presence without it.

Before the elevator doors had fully opened, Rogue had stormed out and down the hall. He stopped in front of the organization's temporary headquarters, set up to look like a high-end business in a skyscraper downtown. He scanned the words on the door: Worldwide Investment Strategies – By appointment only. He snorted. *Good luck getting one of those appointments.* Not bothering to knock in the manner they'd described to him, he shoved through the door. The secretary jumped up from behind her desk and moved to stand in front of a closed office door. Rogue ignored her as he stormed across the room. When he reached her, she held out one arm. "Sir, you can't just go—"

He reached around her and turned the knob, flinging open the door so hard it slammed against the wall behind it.

Seated on the far side of a large dark cherry wood desk, Natalya looked up from a laptop. Her face was calm and her eyes steel cold when they met his.

"I'm sorry, ma'am. I tried to tell him ..."

She raised a hand. "It's all right, Lydia. Give us a few minutes, please."

Lydia shot Rogue a reproachful glare as he moved past her. He had to step forward to avoid being hit as she grasped the handle and pulled the door shut behind him with an indignant click.

Natalya propped her elbows on the armrests and clasped her hands under her chin.

Her silence threw fuel on his already blazing fury, and he strode toward the desk and slammed both palms down on the smooth wooden surface. She didn't flinch.

"What happened?" He spat the words out between clenched teeth.

"Why don't you sit down?" Her controlled voice mirrored her expression.

His eyes narrowed as he mentally ran through a list of possible actions that might elicit a reaction, any reaction, from her. Nothing that wouldn't get him arrested came to mind. "I don't want to sit. I want you to answer my question."

Natalya didn't speak, just continued to meet his gaze with a cool stare. Finally, with a deep exhalation of breath, he straightened and dropped onto the leather chair behind him. "Well?"

She lowered her clasped hands to the desk. "We do our best to prepare for every mission. An entire team of people investigates every possible problem, contemplates every eventuality. In spite of our best efforts, we cannot always know everything going in. In this case, we had no way of knowing that an alarm system, not connected to any known service provider, had been installed in the home." She leaned toward him. "It is unreasonable of you to assume that everything will go perfectly every time. Part of your responsibility is to deal with the unexpected the best way you can. Which, in our opinion, you did in this instance."

"Leaving a child in a home with a parent who sent her to the hospital three times last month was the best possible thing I could do?" Bitterness clogged his throat so thickly he had to work to get out the words.

She nodded. "In this instance, yes." The gray eyes studied him for a moment. When she spoke, her voice was low and soft. "You have to let it go, Kelly."

Heat rose in his chest. "I can't. We were so close to getting her out of there. We just—"

"I'm not talking about her."

Her words were like an ice-cold blast that sucked the air from his lungs, quenching the fire inside him. Rogue stared at her, his jaw tight. "This isn't about me. Or my past."

"Isn't it?" She tilted her head to one side.

Neither of them moved for several seconds, until he slid to the edge of his seat and rested his arms on her desk. "Let me go back for her."

"No."

Rage ripped through him again. "She's completely alone in that house, with no brothers or sisters to protect her. The last time I saw her she had her arm in a sling for the third time. Seriously, what four-year-old breaks her arm three times playing T-ball?" His hands closed into fists. "When she glanced at her father in court, she looked terrified, although unfortunately, the judge didn't see it. Horrific things are going on in that house. If we don't go back and get her, he will kill her. I promise you that."

Nothing flickered in the slate-gray eyes that locked with his.

"I will only give you this warning once, Kelly. If you ever go in on your own and take out a child, we will not recognize her. We will not take her into the system. And you will be out."

Every muscle in his body vibrated with anger and frustration. She was the only person in the world he could talk to about what had happened last night. He desperately needed her to be as worked up as he was. Or at least—he studied her calm, controlled features—worked up to any appreciable degree at all. He bit his lip to keep from screaming, or leaping across the desk, grabbing handfuls of that dark shimmering hair and yanking a response out of her. "You have no idea what it's like to be in a situation like that. You sit up here in your nice neat office with your nice neat life and your nice neat desk ..." He flung out his arm and knocked over a pile of papers beside the computer. The ceramic vase filled with pens crashed onto its side and shattered into pieces. "Do you ever feel anything at all?"

The door opened behind him. Natalya raised her gaze slightly to look over his shoulder. "Everything's fine, Lydia. It was an accident. I'll take care of it." After three or four seconds, the door clicked shut.

Natalya reached out calmly and started to pick up the pieces of the vase.

He exhaled. "I'll get it."

"No, it's all right. I've—"

He jerked his head up at her quick intake of breath. Blood pooled in the palm of her hand.

He jumped to his feet and strode around the desk to stand beside her. "Let me see." Circling her wrist, he lifted her hand to inspect the wound.

"It's nothing." She tugged on her hand, but he didn't let go. "I need a bandage. Here." Abandoning her efforts to free herself, she pulled open the top drawer of the desk with her other hand.

He felt sick. It didn't look to be a deep cut, but blood was already trickling down her arm. "Do you have a tissue or something, it's—" Rogue pushed back the sleeve of her white blouse slightly so it wouldn't get stained. He stiffened. Angry red marks, and criss-crossed, puckered skin, marred her arm.

She glanced over at her injured hand and yanked free of his grasp. This time he didn't resist. Natalya grabbed a box of Band-Aids before sliding the drawer shut and getting to her feet. She strode into the washroom, her high heels clicking on the marble floor before the door closed softly behind her.

He pressed his eyes shut for several seconds, listening to the water running in the sink. When it stopped, he walked around to the other side of the desk and gathered up the fragments of the broken vase. The washroom door opened. He dumped the pieces of ceramic into the empty garbage can with a clatter as she sat at her desk, smoothing her short black skirt beneath her with her good hand as she did.

He caught a glimpse of a square brown bandage before she folded her hands in front of her on the desk. The sleeves of her white shirt and suit jacket were pulled down past her wrists. Rogue pressed his palms to the top of her desk and leaned closer to her. Her eyes, when they lifted to meet his, were colder than he had ever seen them. He suppressed a shudder. "Your father?" The question came out in a hoarse whisper and he cleared his throat.

Natalya shook her head slightly. "My father was gone before I was born. It was my mother. She suffered from some kind of mental illness. According to her, both my older brother and I were possessed by evil spirits that needed to be burned out of us. She hung herself in the basement when I was twelve. My brother found her which, presumably, snapped the fragile grasp he had on his sanity, so he decided to join her. That left me to find both of them." Her chin lifted. "So no, Kelly, I don't feel. Not often, anyway, and never for very long. I just act."

"Natalya." He waited until her gaze locked with his again. "I'm sorry."

Her eyes softened. The change was so slight that someone who wasn't searching wildly for a hint of emotion might not have noticed. She sighed. "I know you went the other way after what happened to you and your brother. Frankly, between the two of us, I'm not sure who is luckier."

His shoulders sagged, and he pushed himself away from the desk. "I'll wait to hear from you about what I'm supposed to do next."

She gave him a brief nod and began typing on her keyboard.

Rogue watched her for several more seconds before stumbling for the door.

"Kelly."

One hand on the knob, he stopped and looked back.

"You've done good work, you know. Five children from this city are safe and being cared for and loved already, thanks to you and your predecessor. Do not dwell on the things you cannot change."

He swallowed hard and nodded before turning and pulling open the door. Stepping into the elevator, he pressed a hand against the wall and gulped in several deep breaths to quell the waves of nausea. When his stomach settled enough that he was pretty sure he wasn't about to lose its contents, he slumped against the metal railing, completely drained. The numbers flashed over the top of the door and he watched himself descend. All the way down to the ground floor he went over and over her statement in his head, about which of them was luckier, trying to decide if he had an answer.

When the heavy doors slid open and he stepped out into the lobby, he still had absolutely no idea.

Chapter Twenty-Six

Nicole knocked on the door of Gage's apartment. No response. Same as yesterday. And the day before. Like there'd been no answer any of the times she had called or texted him over the last forty-eight hours. He'd been a little withdrawn since the Sunday after church when he'd called his brother Luke by mistake. She hadn't seen him until the Friday after, the day she'd dropped all her groceries in the park. He'd been quiet that night, and only picked at his dinner. She'd called him Monday evening to see if he was coming over, but he'd been curt, telling her that he couldn't talk because he was heading in to work for the evening. Then nothing for the next three days, despite her repeated attempts to get a hold of him. What was going on? Was he hurt? Sick? Maybe she'd pushed him too hard, and he was trying to tell her to back off. Since he wasn't talking, she could only guess.

In any case, she wasn't leaving this time until he came to the door and gave her a reasonable explanation for dropping off the face of the planet. Closing her hand into a fist, she pounded on the wood. "Gage?"

A door down the hall opened and an elderly woman stuck her head out. "Is everything all right?"

Nicole lifted her hand. "Yes, sorry. This is my boyfriend's apartment and I haven't heard from him for a while, so I'm making sure he's all right." She stepped away from the door. "You haven't seen him around, have you?"

The woman frowned, creating more wrinkles in her already heavily-wrinkled face. "Mr. Kelly? No, come to think of it, I haven't. I hope he's all right. Should I call 911?"

"That's okay. I'm sure he's fine." Nicole tugged her phone from her pocket and held it up. "If he doesn't answer soon, I'll call them. Thanks, though."

"All right, then. Let me know if there is anything I can do to help." The woman disappeared into her apartment.

Nicole waited until the door closed behind her before taking a deep breath and typing a message into her phone. *Gage Kelly, you have ten seconds to open your door before I call the police.*

She pressed an ear to the wooden door. For eight seconds, she couldn't hear a sound on the other side. She was about to type the number for emergency services into her phone when a sound stopped her. Heavy footsteps tromping across the floor.

The dead bolt slid open with a clang, but instead of the door opening, she heard the same heavy footsteps retreating. Seriously?

Nicole turned the knob and pushed open the door.

Surrounded by an empty pizza box and crumpled soda cans, Gage sat slumped on the couch, both feet propped on the coffee table in front of him. Blue light from the television flickered off the walls. He stared at the set and didn't look at her as she picked her way around a couple of takeout bags that had been crumpled up and tossed onto the floor. What in the world?

"Gage?" Nicole shoved a fist against her hip as she stared down at him. His eyes didn't leave the flickering screen. His hair was disheveled, and he looked like he hadn't shaved since she had seen him last. Panic and fury tangled in her belly like a pair of wild cats. "What is going on?"

"I'm on a retreat."

Fury won the battle. "A retreat." The chill in her voice must have finally gotten through to him because he raised his head. Instead of the contrition she'd expected, anger flashed in his dark eyes.

"That's right. I needed to get away from it all for a few days."

Nicole's jaw tightened. "Did it occur to you to mention these plans to me?"

"I don't need your input about the way I live my life. Or your permission."

"What do you need, Gage?"

"To be left alone."

"It doesn't look to me like that's working for you." The smells of stale fast food and body odor hung in the air and she kept her breaths as shallow as possible. *What is going on here?*

Gage crossed his arms over a filthy sweatshirt. "What do you think I need?"

"A shower would be a good start." She turned her head and stared at the television screen for a minute. Some guy with slicked-back hair was gesturing wildly, extolling the virtues of a food chopper they were practically giving away for the next twenty-three minutes.

Slowly she swiveled to face him.

Gage lifted his chin.

"Why are you watching this?"

"Why not?"

Nicole shoved aside an empty cola can with her tan leather boot as she moved toward the couch. "Why don't you turn it off so we can talk?" She reached for the remote.

Gage grabbed her wrist and squeezed. "Don't do that."

Her eyes narrowed to glittering slits. "Don't do what?"

"Don't try to fix me, princess." His fingers tightened. "I've got God and my shrink for that, and last time I looked you weren't either of those."

Nicole spoke through gritted teeth. "You are hurting me."

He dropped her wrist and lifted both hands in the air. "I'm sorry."

She stepped away from him and spun toward the door.

"Nic, wait." His foot crushed an empty bag as he strode toward her.

She gripped the handle but didn't turn it. When he reached her, he touched her arm. Nicole whirled around.

"I said I was sorry. I didn't mean that the way it sounded."

She pushed back trembling shoulders. "I think you did. You don't need me. Got it."

"That's not what I said."

Nicole reached behind her for the knob.

Gage pressed a hand against the door. "Don't go, please. I want—"

Her furious expletive cut him off. His eyes widened.

Her shoulders sagged. "I don't really care what you want at the moment." Her voice dragged with exhaustion. "I'm tired, Gage. I can't do this anymore."

Gage let go of the door and Nicole pulled it open. Brushing past him, she slipped through the opening and pulled the door shut behind her. Hard.

Chapter Twenty-Seven

Daniel pulled into an empty spot in the parking lot across the street from Gage's building and settled into his seat, prepared for a long wait. Not that he expected anything to happen. A few nights ago there'd been another attempted child-snatching, thwarted by an alarm going off. The report had come in shortly after three a.m., later than any of the other abductions, and an hour after he'd left his post. Had Gage or Holden figured out they were being watched and waited until the coast was clear to head out? In any case, since there were usually at least a couple of weeks between attempts, nothing was likely to happen tonight. Still, he couldn't take the chance that it might.

Ten minutes later, at quarter after eleven, the door swung open and he straightened up so quickly he nearly spilled coffee onto his lap. Dropping the paper cup into the holder between the two front seats, Daniel leaned over his steering wheel to peer out the front window. *Nicole.*

In the glow of the parking lot lights, he watched as she stalked toward a red car parked in the corner. What was wrong? His eyes narrowed. Did she and Gage have a fight? Nicole jumped into the car, slammed it into gear, and spun toward the parking lot exit.

Daniel grabbed for his seatbelt, locked it into place, and started his vehicle. By the time he pulled out of the lot, her vehicle had nearly disappeared around the next corner. He followed her at a safe distance for fifteen minutes, until she pulled to the curb across from Joe's and jumped out. He parked a couple of blocks away, gave her five minutes, then undid his seatbelt and climbed out of the car.

A light rain misted the air around him as he strode toward the building, dampening his jacket. He hitched the collar up higher around his neck. What reason could he give Nicole for showing up at the diner at this time of night? He shrugged. He'd think of something. Daniel climbed the stairs and stopped in front of the glass door.

For a few seconds he peered over the *Closed* sign to watch her at the table in the far corner, her back to him as she scrubbed hard at the surface. Every muscle in her body was tense. Good. It didn't appear as though her anger had dissipated any. He didn't enjoy seeing her go through that, but trouble with Gage could only be good for him. For the investigation, that is.

Nicole straightened and pressed a hand into the small of her back. For a moment she stared out the window. *What is she looking at?* Then she must have seen his reflection in the glass because she spun around. The fear that flitted across her face disappeared when recognition replaced it, which he was happy to see. He lifted a hand.

Nicole wove her way through the tables until she reached the door. He smiled at her. While she didn't return the smile, she did turn the lock and open the door a few inches.

"Am I too late to get a cup of coffee?" Daniel spoke quietly, hoping the fear wouldn't reappear. Not that she'd so far shown herself to be the nervous type.

He searched her eyes and found, to his relief, only mild curiosity. *Please let me in.*

"We're closed." She propped a shoulder against the doorframe. "Typically that means all the customers have to leave."

"What about the friends?" He bit his lip, ninety percent sure she wouldn't consider placing him in that category, and one-hundred percent sure he shouldn't ask her to.

"I already have all the friends I need."

"Not here." He glanced over her shoulder at the empty diner. "And from the way you were scrubbing the top of that table down to the wood, it looks like you could use one. Do you want to talk about it?"

"Not particularly."

He searched her face. She appeared to be open again, like she'd been that day in the park, before she'd told him she was seeing someone. Except that tonight, nothing about her was relaxed. If Daniel had to guess, the anger that radiated off her in waves was fully directed at Gage, which was taking all the energy she might otherwise have used to keep her guard up against him. That and the fact that she clearly needed to vent, and if she was willing to let loose on him, he was more than happy to offer her the opportunity.

The other possibility, one that he was scared to even allow himself to entertain, was that she'd felt the connection between them that day in the park, as strongly as he had. Or at least strongly enough for her to lower her defences. Temporarily, anyway. If there was any chance of her closing up as quickly as she had the last time, he needed to move fast, although with extreme caution.

"We Good Samaritans are known for being excellent listeners, you know."

Her lips twitched slightly. "You'd have a hard time proving that from the Bible. The man the Good Samaritan rescued was unconscious throughout the entire story. I don't believe two words were exchanged between them."

She had him there. "Well, they spoke more in the original Greek version. It lost something in translation."

"I see. And you always read your Bible in the original Greek, do you, Mister ...?"

"Grey. Daniel Grey. And not the whole Bible, no, only the New Testament."

Her lips twitched again. "Of course, it would be tricky to read the Old Testament in the original Greek, since it was written in ..."

"Hebrew," he finished with her.

Nicole contemplated him. The fire in her eyes had definitely died down. A little too much. He needed her at least a little angry, so she'd be more willing to talk about Gage. Time to stoke the flames a little.

"Look, you've obviously had a rough night. If you'd rather be alone …" Daniel moved down a step.

Nicole's green eyes darkened as she pushed away from the doorframe and opened the door wider. "No, it's all right. You can come in. For a few minutes."

Setting the boundaries. *Fair enough.* Daniel walked into the diner. The sounds of silverware clattering into drawers, dishes clinking together, and people calling out to one another, came through the swinging doors from the kitchen.

Nicole waved a hand toward the thoroughly sanitized table in the corner. "So you know, the staff is still in the kitchen cleaning up. In case you were contemplating doing anything *unfriendly,* that is."

Daniel nodded. "I wasn't, but I am glad that you don't let strangers into the diner when you're here alone." He paused briefly as he passed the cash register. A white sheet with a list of names, dates, and times—some type of work schedule, from the looks of it—had been taped onto the counter. He scanned it quickly as Nicole rounded the counter, heading for the coffee pot on the ledge attached to the back wall. Nicole Hunter was the fourth name down, and the only Nicole on the list. Good. He had a last name. Daniel crossed the diner to the table she'd indicated and pulled out a chair. He sat, his back to the door. That went against every instinct he had, but maybe being able to keep an eye on her escape route would help her relax a little. Open up to him faster.

At this point, he'd take any advantage he could get.

Nicole grabbed the coffee pot from the machine on the counter. *What are you doing?* Inviting someone she barely knew, especially given that he was someone she was far too drawn to, was definitely not the smartest thing she'd ever done. Of course, very little she'd done around this man was smart, or typical for her. She wouldn't have let him in if there weren't still people working in the kitchen. Even so, they'd have a quick coffee and then she'd send him on his way. She made her way to his table. When she reached him, she turned over two mugs and filled them expertly before setting the pot on the table and dropping onto the chair across from him.

"How did you know where I worked?"

"I was driving past the park where we met the other day, and that reminded me that you'd recommended Joe's, so I thought I'd scout it out, in case I wanted to try it sometime. When I saw you through the window, I decided to press my luck and stop by." He wrapped his fingers around the warm mug and pulled it closer. "You looked upset when I came in. Is everything okay?"

She pursed her lips and contemplated him. He looked tired. His eyes were as bright blue as she remembered, but now shadows were smudged beneath them. She leaned forward and rested both arms on the table. "Not really. But I'm sure you didn't come in here to listen to some waitress you barely know dumping her tales of woe on you."

"Actually, I did."

Don't do it. Do not talk to this man about Gage. Nicole hesitated. *I need to talk to someone.* She laced her fingers tightly and stared down at her hands. "All right then. But remember, you asked for this." She let out a soft sigh. "It's my boyfriend."

"Man trouble? Really?"

"What, you didn't think I had a man in my life? I told you I was seeing someone."

"No, it's not that. I'd be a lot more surprised if you didn't. I just can't imagine one foolish enough to treat you badly."

"He's not a fool. Not really. Unfortunately, he forgets that himself sometimes."

"Ah. A common affliction. Not usually fatal."

Nicole's throat tightened. "Well, in this case," her voice lowered and he leaned in closer, "I think it might be."

Her hand was inches away from his on the table. For a moment neither of them moved, then the man slid his hand across the space between them and lightly covered her fingers with his.

Nicole drew comfort from the strong warmth of them for a few seconds. *What are you doing?* She stared at their hands before slowly pulling hers away. She rose and stood facing the window, arms crossed over her chest.

"The thing is, I thought I knew him, you know? But tonight I saw another side of him, and it scared me."

Her voice caught, and he got up and moved to stand behind her.

Nicole faced him. "I shouldn't be talking to you about this. I barely know you." Why was she opening up to him? There was something about the man in front of her. Something that invited trust, that promised empathy and compassion. Precisely what she needed at the moment. A tear slid down her cheek.

He reached out and wiped it away with his thumb. Their eyes met, and Nicole's heart thudded wildly in her chest. He had to go now, before she did something she would regret forever. "You should …" A movement at the front door caught her eye and her gaze slid from his over to the door. Gage. At the sight of him, everything that had happened that night came flooding back. Guilt and anger coursed through her, and rational thought fled. Before he could react, Nicole lifted her hand to the back of Daniel's head and pulled him down so she could press her mouth to his.

His senses exploded. He'd caught Gage's reflection about the same time she'd seen him, but about half a second in, Daniel stopped caring that she was only doing this to prove something to another man. The light scent of apple blossoms wafting from the hair that brushed against his cheek, the soft lips against his, for a few seconds there was nothing else in the world but her. And then she pulled away, flushed and breathless.

Nicole shot another brief glance toward the door and her shoulders sagged. Gage must have gone. Daniel didn't turn to look in case Gage recognized him. One of Nicole's hands was still pressed against Daniel's shirt. Her eyes met his briefly before she looked at his chest and stiffened. He followed her gaze and his heart sank. His jacket was hanging open slightly and his police badge, clipped to his shirt pocket, was clearly visible.

Nicole moved away, her forehead wrinkling in confusion. "You're a cop?"

"Yes, I …" His head was spinning, and he was having a hard time coming up with his own name, let alone a plausible reason for keeping that fact from her for so long.

"But that kid on the street, he committed a crime right in front of you and you let him go. Were you … off-duty?"

Here we go. His chest tightened. "No."

Her eyelids flickered, as though she was trying to comprehend what he was saying. "Are you off-duty now?"

Daniel didn't answer.

"So the street, the park, here … you didn't *happen* to bump into me, did you? You were, what, watching me? Following me?"

"No. Yes. I mean … could we maybe start over here?" He pulled out his ID and flipped open the case. "Detective Daniel Grey, Toronto Police Services."

Nicole didn't look at it.

Daniel slid the badge into his pocket.

"Why are you here?" she demanded.

He gestured toward the table. "Could we sit?"

Nicole hesitated, then walked over and lowered herself onto her chair, back rigid and hands clasped tightly in her lap.

He sat down across from her. "Okay, here it is. I *have* been watching you."

"For how long? And why?"

"For a few days now. I wanted to talk to you about a case I'm working on and I was waiting for the right time." He hesitated, but she only lifted her shoulders. Daniel pressed on. "I don't know if you're aware of this, but we've had a string of unsolved kidnappings in this city."

"I read about them in the paper. And about how the police don't have a clue how to stop those guys."

Daniel let the dig pass.

Nicole shifted in her seat. "What does all this have to do with me?"

"We've been working on the case for months without really getting anywhere. The odd tip and a few clues here and there but, until recently, not enough to add up to anything substantial. For example, a few weeks ago a single parent reported that her daughter had been taken from the home in the night. Several hours later a neighbor brought in a digital camera and showed us a picture he'd taken of a man carrying a child out of the home around one in the morning."

"Could you tell who he was?"

"No. He wore a mask. The neighbor did get a picture of a car that pulled up to the curb and took the girl away, though. We got a partial from the plate, although we were never able to track down the vehicle."

"Sounds like you don't have much."

"We didn't, until a few days ago. Then we stumbled across a new angle that might be the break we've been hoping for."

The light from the lamp hanging above them glinted off the hair she'd pulled into a ponytail, picking up strands of gold.

"So you think you're getting close to finding out who is doing this?"

Daniel dropped his gaze to her face.

Nicole was watching him intently.

His face warmed. "We feel like we're making progress. In fact, we have the names of a couple of persons of interest."

"You have suspects?"

If his words were making her nervous, or guilty, it didn't reflect in her eyes. Daniel shook his head. "No, not yet. They're persons of interest, not suspects. People we believe may know something about the kidnappings, whether or not they were actually involved."

"Why did you come to me? It sounds like you have a lot more information than I do. All I know is what I've read. I don't see how I can help you."

"I wanted to talk to you because you know the people we're

interested in."

Her forehead wrinkled. "I find that hard to believe. Who are they?"

"Gage and Holden Kelly."

Her green eyes widened in shock. As Daniel watched, they deepened to dark, glittering emerald.

"You are on the wrong trail, Detective. I can assure you that Gage and Holden are decent, law-abiding citizens." She pushed the words out through clenched teeth.

"I'm not accusing them of being otherwise." Daniel pulled out the calm, reassuring voice that made him one of the best negotiators on the force. "I'm merely gathering information at this point."

Nicole Hunter was not in the mood to negotiate. She jumped to her feet. Flattening both hands against the top of the table, she leaned toward him. "Then you should talk to them, not me. And you had no right to talk to me without telling me who you were." The gold flecks in her eyes flashed like sparks of fire. "Do I have some sign across my forehead that says 'Keep Things from Me'? Because that seems to be everyone's favorite pastime lately. That and lying."

"Look, I didn't mean to lie to you. I—"

She flung both hands up in front of her. "Of course you meant to. What is it with men? You can't help yourselves, can you?"

His jaw tightened.

"You pretended to be this big hero the other day, showing up out of the blue to save the day. Then tonight, you came in here *intending* to lie to me, asking casual questions like you were simply making conversation, calling yourself my friend, when the whole time you were trying to get information about the man I ..." her cheeks flushed, "... about Gage. Which means that you weren't only lying to me, you were using me too."

Heat rose in his chest. "And you weren't using me? I saw Gage in the doorway right before you kissed me."

The rush of crimson deepened across her cheeks, but she

moved in closer. "That's very interesting, *Detective*. If you knew why I was kissing you, then why did you kiss me back?"

Daniel bit his tongue to keep from blurting out the answer. *Because I wanted to. Because I've wanted to since the first time I saw you in this diner. And in spite of everything you've said to me in the last five minutes, and the fact that you are clearly still in love with Gage, everything in me wants to grab you and kiss you again.*

He might as well have said the words out loud. He saw it in her eyes, in the way she dropped her gaze and took a faltering step backward, that she heard them as clearly as if he had.

"You need to go." Nicole pointed toward the door.

Daniel's eyes narrowed as he pushed to his feet and grabbed her hand.

"What are you doing?" She tried to pull away from his grasp, but he didn't let go.

"Looking at these." He turned her arm slightly until the dark red marks on her wrist, already deepening to bruises, were visible. He sought out her eyes as fire blazed across his chest. "He's even more of a fool than I thought."

Nicole yanked hard and he let her go. "Gage didn't do that. I did it to myself. At the gym."

"The gym."

"Yes."

"Because if Gage did do that to you, that's a crime. You can press charges."

She let out a cold laugh. "You'd like that, wouldn't you? If I did your job for you and handed you a possible suspect, nice and neat, and made him look guilty by charging him with a completely unrelated crime. Well, forget it. If you want to take Gage down so badly, you're going to have to do the work yourself. And you'll be the one who looks like a fool when he's proven innocent."

Daniel drew in a long, slow breath. "I don't, you know."

"You don't what?"

"I don't necessarily *want* to take Gage down. Especially

since it would hurt … a lot of people." He pushed back his shoulders. "But I will do whatever I have to do to protect the children of this city and to prevent more of them from being taken."

"Gage would never hurt me, and he would never hurt anyone else either. He's a good man."

"I'm sure he is. But a lot of good people have made bad choices over the years. Some of them even for the right reasons. Unfortunately, they're still bad choices. And lives can still be devastated by them." Daniel took a step closer to her. "Think about this. If a man could hurt a woman he cared about, would it be such a stretch to believe that he could also commit another crime in a misguided attempt to save children?"

"I told you Gage didn't hurt me, and he would never hurt a child either. And you need to leave. Now." She turned and strode across the diner. Bells jangled a discordant noise as she yanked open the door.

Daniel closed his eyes for a few seconds before bending to pick up her chair then follow her across the room. He walked out the door she held for him, but stopped on the first step and pressed a palm to the glass beside her head. She swallowed hard but met his gaze.

"I'll be in touch, Ms. Hunter. Soon. And if you know anything about these kidnappings, if you even suspect that Gage might be involved, you need to tell me."

"And if I don't?"

"Then I will take you down to the station and we can talk there. It's your choice. Obstruction of justice is every bit as much a crime as taking children out of their beds at night."

"What about deception, Detective? How do you justify that in your mind?"

Daniel let out his breath. "I don't. You're right. I should have told you who I was and why I was here right from the beginning."

"Yes, you should have."

He nodded. "I'll make you a deal. No more keeping things

from you. And no more lying. I'll be completely honest, and in return you tell me everything you know, or suspect, about what Gage is doing. If you cooperate, I'll do everything I can to keep you from going down with him."

Her jaw clenched. "Gage is not involved with this, and if I *do* decide to talk to you, it will be to give you information that proves he's not."

"Don't wait too long to decide. This is a temporary offer. If I think you know something you aren't telling me, I *will* take you in for questioning."

The door started to move toward him. "Good night, Detective."

He moved down another step to avoid being hit and pulled a card out of his pocket. "Here is my cell number and the address of my station. I'll expect to hear from you soon."

Nicole snatched the card from his outstretched hand. "Stop watching me. You have no right to invade my privacy when I have nothing to do with any of this. If I see you following me again, I will talk to a lawyer." She slammed the door in his face. The lock slid into place with a loud click.

He stood on the step a moment longer, watching through the glass as she strode past the counter and slammed through the kitchen doors, her blonde ponytail bouncing between her shoulder blades. The doors swung wildly behind her.

Daniel touched a knuckle to his lips briefly, before shoving both hands into his pockets. "Yeah. That went well." Shaking his head, he stepped onto the sidewalk. He was glad he'd parked a couple of blocks away. A walk through the chilly night air was exactly what he needed at the moment.

Chapter Twenty-Eight

Nicole rang through her last customers and thanked them when they left a five-dollar bill on the counter for her. After they'd gone out the door, she tugged her phone from her pocket. 6:40. Her shift had technically ended at 5, but the diner had been busy at that time so she'd stayed a little longer to help. She hit the button for her inbox. No messages. She'd been checking every ten minutes all day, but she hadn't heard from Gage since he'd seen her at the diner with Daniel Grey the night before. Did he go home after that? Should she go over?

Nicole dropped down onto a stool, propped her elbow on the counter, and lowered her forehead onto the palm of one hand as the events of the evening before flashed through her mind. First Gage, then the detective. A real red-letter night. And what Daniel Grey had said about Gage and Holden. That was ridiculous. How could the police be that far off? They really must be desperate, to go after innocent people like that. Gage sure didn't need them harassing him after everything he'd been through.

She lifted her head. He had been through a lot. A ton of garbage. And he was still going through it. At the moment, he was wading ankle-deep in it, literally and figuratively, and whose fault was that? Guilt pricked her chest. She was the one who'd pushed him to open up to her. What did she think she was, some kind of expert? She wasn't God or his psychiatrist, as he'd rightly—if somewhat cruelly—pointed out last night. What made her think she'd be able to help him? She'd only made things worse by confronting him. And then kissing another man in front of him … Nicole groaned and buried her face in both hands. As if he wasn't dealing with enough.

Her head jerked up. *Was* he dealing with it? He'd appeared to be right on the edge when she was at his place. What if seeing her with the detective had pushed him over? Her stomach roiled, and she pressed a hand to it. He wouldn't have done anything crazy, would he?

Sam, one of the dishwashers, pushed through the swinging doors carrying a gray bin of clean silverware and stuck it under the counter. "Nic? Everything okay?"

Umm no, absolutely nothing is okay. Nicole forced a smile and twisted the stool around to face him. "Yes, fine. Could you do me a favor? Table thirty-four just left. Would you mind clearing it for me? I need to go see a friend who isn't feeling well."

"Sure. No problem. You go." Sam jutted his chin toward the kitchen.

"Thanks, Sam." Nicole was already untying her apron as she hurried into the back. She slipped it over her head, hung it by the door, and grabbed her coat. Joe and Connie had gone upstairs, and the evening shift had taken over the kitchen. "Good night, everyone." She offered a quick wave before heading out the back door.

The ride up the elevator to Gage's apartment seemed to take forever. *God, help him. Don't let him do anything foolish. Please, please help him.* When the doors opened, she bolted from the elevator and down the hall. He'd given her a key to get into the building, and to the lock in the door knob, but not to the dead bolt, which he rarely turned. Last night she could see that it had been slid across, and it was again today. Everything in her screamed out to pound her fists on the door again, but with a quick glance toward the neighbor's apartment, she rapped quietly. She'd bang if she had to, but hopefully she could get his attention without alerting the entire floor.

Immediately she heard movement from inside the apartment, the clanking sound of the remote being tossed onto the coffee table, the creaking of the couch. Relief poured through her. When the lock slid across and the door opened to reveal Gage on the other side, Nicole couldn't decide whether to throw herself into his arms or burst into tears. She did neither.

Instead, the two of them stared at each other for a moment. Then Gage stepped out of the way and gestured for her to come in. When she did, he closed the door behind her.

"You came back."

"Yes."

"Why?"

"I needed to make sure you were all right." Although he hadn't shaved, he'd showered since she'd seen him last, and the smell of soap wafted from him. What did that mean, that he was okay? Nicole crossed her arms. "What is going on with you?"

"Nothing you want to be anywhere near." His dark eyes, slightly hooded, met hers. The wildness was gone. All she could see in them now was utter exhaustion. And sadness. Because of her? Her throat tightened as he drew in a ragged breath. "I mean it Nic. You should—"

"No."

The corner of his mouth quirked slightly. "No what?"

"I'm not leaving. Not this time."

"If you knew what was best for you, you would." He inclined his head toward the door.

"I'm not going anywhere."

"What if I ordered you to go?"

"Then I would."

Both eyebrows rose as he contemplated her.

"But you would never see me again."

He held her gaze steadily, his face unreadable for several seconds. Then his shoulders sagged. "Well. You're throwing your cards on the table with a lot of confidence considering everything that's happened, aren't you, princess?"

"Is it unwarranted?"

He braced himself against the wall with one hand. The fingers supporting him trembled slightly. "No, actually. Your hand definitely trumps mine." He spoke slowly, as if forming words took more energy than he had in him. "I want you to stay far more than I want you to go, especially if there's the slightest chance you won't return this time."

She stepped closer. "Tell me."

"Tell you what?"

Nicole waved a hand around the room. "What was all this? What was going on with you earlier?"

He blew out a breath. "It was the black hole, as Holden and I affectionately call it."

"The what?"

"Here." He took her hand, gently this time. "I need to sit down. I'll tell you about it, if you're sure you want to know."

"I'm sure. I think."

He dropped onto the couch and tugged her down beside him. A half-filled garbage bag sat on the floor beside the coffee table, as though he'd been able to throw all the trash in it but then run out of steam. "It happens sometimes, to both Holden and me. Not very often, maybe once every year or two, but if something triggers a memory of when I was a child, it can set me off. It's a kind of PTSD." He rested his head against the back of the couch.

"Why did you feel the need to keep it from me?"

His eyelids drooped. "I don't know. I guess I didn't want to suck you into the hole with me."

"Maybe I could have kept you from being sucked in, if you had trusted me enough to share what you were going through."

"You probably could have. And I do trust you. More than I've ever trusted anyone other than Holden. I just got lost there for a bit."

"I shouldn't have pushed you."

He squeezed her hand. "No, you should have. I'm glad you did. It was the first time I've ever told anyone but my doctor about my past. As much as it dredged up a lot of garbage, it was remarkably healing too." He rolled his head to the side until he was looking at her. "And seeing you last night, even though it all went terribly wrong, brought me out of it. Made me realize that I needed to get my act together before I blew the best thing that had ever happened to me, if I hadn't already. Which is amazing, because often the darkness lasts for days, sometimes weeks."

He rubbed the side of his hand across his forehead. "Holden can help, usually, but when I felt myself starting to fall a couple of days ago, I went to see him, and he was in a bad way too. I'm not sure why, maybe me calling him Luke the other day triggered him as well. I don't know if it's ever hit both of us at the same time before. I could barely help myself. There wasn't anything much I could do for him, so I called his doctor, handed Holden the phone, and told him to talk. I hope it helped. I need to go over there again to check on him."

"Do you want to go now?"

"No. I shouldn't drive like this. I can barely keep my eyes open. I took a cab to the diner last night and still barely made it home. Then I crashed on the couch for sixteen hours." He blinked a few times, as though having trouble focusing. "I'll go tomorrow. All I want right now is to be here with you. To try and somehow make things right." He turned her hand over and glanced at the bruises before pressing his eyes shut. "Nic, I am so sorry. It won't happen again. Ever."

"No, it won't. It can't." She tugged her arm from his grasp and forced steel into her voice. "If it ever does, I will walk out that door and it will be over."

His eyes opened halfway. "And I wouldn't blame you. But it won't. I swear I will never hurt you again. Not physically, anyway. I can't promise I won't hurt you any other way. I can be a bit of a mess."

Nicole sighed. "Well, I can't really hold that against you. We're both a bit of a mess."

"So you forgive me?"

"Yes."

Gage slid a hand behind her head and pulled her to him. He kissed her, a slow, deep kiss that drove away the last of the cold that had been shivering through her body since she had stopped by the night before. He rested his forehead against hers. "Thank you for coming back."

This man, this beautiful, broken, remorseful man, he could never do the things that detective suspects him of. Never. Nicole's chest ached at the thought. "Don't ever shut me out like that again."

"I won't." He lifted his head and she brushed away the long, dark hair that had fallen over one eye. "Nic ..." he swallowed hard. "I don't know how much right I have to ask you this after the way I treated you last night, but—"

"He's no one."

He searched her face, as though trying to read the truth there.

"He's a customer who's been in the diner a couple of times and who happened to be in the wrong place at the wrong time. I'm not proud of using him like that, but I was really confused and angry when I left here earlier. When I saw you, I acted without thinking. I was trying to get back at you, I guess. Hurt you a little."

"It hurt more than a little."

"I'm sorry." She rested her fingers on his cheek. "Can you forgive me?"

He nodded slightly. Dark stubble rasped against her palm.

"Good. I'm glad all is forgiven. But if you think you're ever going to kiss me again, we're going to have to do something about that scruff on your face."

His eyelids had dropped closed, but he managed a wan smile as he mumbled, "It'll be gone first thing."

"Here." Nicole grabbed a pillow and set it on her lap. Gage stretched out and rested his head on it. In a couple of minutes his breathing had evened out and deepened. Even though he'd fallen asleep, Nicole ran her fingers lightly through his hair, trying in some small way to offer comfort, to remind him that she was there.

Still, it wasn't until sometime in the middle of the night that the trembling that had gripped his entire body eased, and the deep lines of sorrow and weariness gave way to a look of peace.

Chapter Twenty-Nine

Daniel wasn't a big fan of cursing, but several choice words flitted through his head as he sat in the meeting and listened to his boss rant. Another child, a three-year-old boy, had been taken in the night, ten days after the last one. The organization was clearly stepping up its operations, like he'd been afraid they would. He and Sharleen had been at the scene most of the night, trying without success to get something out of the single father, who hadn't seen or heard anything. Both beyond exhausted, he and his partner had taken the night off, betting on the odds that nothing would happen if they missed one stakeout.

They'd lost. Would it have made a difference if they'd been there, or had Gage or Holden figured out they were being watched somehow and waited until the night that no one showed up to carry out the latest kidnapping?

Or maybe it wasn't Gage or Holden at all but someone else entirely, and they'd been wasting their time sitting there every night. Daniel rubbed his closed eyelids with his thumb and forefinger and blew out a breath. He really had no idea what to think anymore, and the fact that he'd missed the only good night's sleep he'd been about to have in weeks because he'd gotten called to the scene of the crime wasn't helping.

The bottom line at the moment was that Detective Sergeant Lector was not happy, which meant that no one in the station was happy, least of all he and his partner. She shifted in the seat beside him, clearly as uncomfortable as he was.

He had taken his time in establishing a relationship with Nicole Hunter, not wanting to move too quickly and make a mistake that could cost them. Unfortunately, the slow and steady approach *had* cost them. They'd lost valuable time. Even more devastating, another parent had lost his child. His fists clenched. It had been a week since she'd kicked him out of the diner. He'd go and see Nicole again today, ramp up the pressure. They needed to find whoever was taking these children, and they needed to do it now.

Dragging his feet, Daniel followed Sharleen down the hall and into her office. She collapsed onto her desk chair, and he pulled up the plastic one from the corner and sank down beside her.

She swiveled in her seat to face him. "Now what?"

"Now we take a deep breath. I know this is bad, and the last thing we wanted to happen, but I don't want it to push us into doing something rash and blowing this investigation completely."

Sharleen nodded. "Okay. Deep breath. Got it. Now what?"

Daniel grinned. Only his partner could joke at a time like this. The tension that had gripped his chest loosened slightly. "I still think we're on the right track here. Let's find out where Holden and Gage Kelly were last night. I know we can't watch them both every minute, but let's play the odds and see if we can increase surveillance on Holden, at least."

"We can't keep doing it on our own. I'm going to try submitting another request to the DS. Maybe he'll reconsider now that a sixth child has been taken."

"Hopefully." It would be nice to sleep for more than a couple of hours at a time.

"What about Nicole Hunter? Did you get anything from her when you saw her?"

Nothing that I want you to know about. Heat crept up Daniel's neck. "Not yet. I've talked to her a couple of times, but she is extremely guarded. The last time she got pretty worked up. She told me to stop watching her."

Sharleen began rifling through the papers on her desk.

Daniel's eyes narrowed. "What are you doing?"

"I'm looking for the memo that says that suspects will now be telling us how to do our job. I must have missed it."

He shot her a dark look. "That's very cute. And she's not a

suspect. But she did threaten to lawyer up, so I want to tread carefully here."

"Lawyer up? That sounds a little fishy. Maybe she's more involved than you believe."

"I don't think so. I watched her face when I mentioned the kidnappings and she didn't react at all. I honestly don't think she knows anything about them. Not yet, anyway, but she is in the best position to help us, as long as we can get her to trust us."

Sharleen sat back in her chair and studied him intently.

"Now what?"

"I've been watching your face when you talk about her. And you do react. A lot." She frowned, still scrutinizing him. "What's going on here, Grey?"

"Nothing. But she is our only link to these guys. I don't want to have to go through a lawyer to talk to her, or we'll never get anything we can use."

"Did you at least get a sense that that's a possibility?"

"Definitely. If we can plant the idea in her head that helping us would be the best way to keep whoever is doing this safe, I really believe she will watch for anything unusual and report it to us."

"What's her previous relationship with the law, any reason she might have to distrust us?"

"Actually, that's a good point. I haven't done a lot of research into her background. I'll start there this morning."

A smirk crossed his partner's face. "I don't know. That doesn't sound like something she would approve of at all." Sharleen spun in her chair and grabbed the phone. "Do you want to call and check with her, just in case?" She held out the receiver.

Daniel batted it away. "You're a real comedian, you know that? Any chance you could save that routine for open mic night so we can get some work done here?"

She laughed and replaced the receiver. "Okay, so I'm going to submit a formal request for surveillance to the DS, in writing this time, and you're going to check into Nicole Hunter's background. Time to figure this thing out. I do not want to sit through another meeting like this morning's."

"Me neither." Daniel pushed to his feet. "I'll check in with you later and we'll see what we've got, okay?" Sharleen nodded as she swung around to her computer. He stared at the back of her head, briefly contemplating whether or not to tell his partner he was going to pay another call on Nicole that afternoon. He turned and headed for the door. For the first time since they'd started working together, he decided the best recourse might be to keep information from her. Sharleen was already suspicious of him and his feelings for Nicole. He didn't want her to insist on coming with him. After his last visit to the diner, Daniel knew that would only increase the chances that Nicole would go to a lawyer. He'd tell Sharleen after he went, apologize if he needed to, but hopefully also have some information, or a lead of some sort, to give her by way of a peace offering.

Daniel crossed the hall to his office and settled himself in front of his computer. An hour later, he tapped a fist to his mouth. Very interesting. Nicole was an only child, and her parents currently resided in London, England where her father was project manager for an international engineering firm. He couldn't find a record of them having returned to Canada in at least five years. Unless Nicole traveled occasionally to see them, she appeared to have been essentially cut off and left on her own here.

He shook his head. What kind of parents would do that to their only daughter? Given her father's job, money couldn't be the issue, so why wouldn't they make an effort to see her once in a while?

Daniel snatched his mouse. His chest was actually aching for her. *What is wrong with you?* Children were disappearing, and he was letting himself become emotionally involved with the one person who might be able to help them stop the abductions. He had to pull himself together, steel himself against allowing any feelings he might have for Nicole Hunter to grow.

He clicked on a few more buttons and drew in a quick breath

as a picture flashed across the screen. A little blonde child smiled back at him. She looked to be around two or three and could easily have been Nicole as a toddler. Quickly he scanned the story, shock sending cold prickles across his skin. It wasn't Nicole, it was her twin sister, Ella. According to the news article he'd pulled up, she had disappeared from a park a couple of months before her third birthday and was presumed dead. Before *their* third birthday.

Did Nicole even know she'd had a sister? Should he tell her? Daniel clasped his hands behind his head. No. More than likely she knew. Her parents couldn't have been cruel enough to abandon her without any explanation, could they? And if they had, and she didn't know, the last thing she needed at the moment was another traumatic revelation that something else in her life was not as she had always believed it to be. Maybe sometime, after all of this was over, he could talk to her, make sure she knew the truth.

It did help him to understand why her parents couldn't bring themselves to see her. The memories her appearance would stir had to be unbelievably painful. Maybe, if she had distracted them somehow in the park that day, they even blamed Nicole for her sister's disappearance. Which was crazy, since the two of them would have been toddlers at the time. Of course, in his work, he'd seen people doing crazier, more damaging things to each other, but when it happened to someone he cared about … Daniel dropped his arms to his sides. Whatever their motivation, it was still an incredible cowardly thing to do. Did they have no idea how leaving her on her own had affected Nicole's life?

He pushed to his feet and grabbed his jacket. *Enough of this.* Even given this new information, he couldn't let himself feel anything more for her. It was time—past time actually—for him to rid his mind of any distractions and focus on doing his job.

Chapter Thirty

"Ms. Hunter?"

As Daniel watched, every muscle in her body contracted. Nicole set the pile of dirty dishes into the gray bin on the cart behind the counter with a loud clatter and turned around slowly. "Detective."

"I need to speak with you for a moment."

"I'm working."

"So am I." A good reminder for both of them.

A shadow flickered across her face. She glanced around the diner, obviously hoping to be able to claim she was too busy to meet with him. The restaurant was empty, like he'd figured it would be at this time of the afternoon. Her shoulders slumped. "You'll have to be brief. We're getting ready for the dinner crowd."

Daniel nodded and followed her to the table they had sat at before, in a quiet corner. No coffee this time. He wasn't surprised. The social had gone out of his call pretty abruptly when he'd stopped by here a week ago, and Nicole was clearly not interested in re-establishing it.

Daniel slid into the booth across from her and pulled a notebook from the inside pocket of his jacket. He flipped it open and drew a pen from his shirt pocket. "I'm sorry to bother you at work again. As you have probably heard, another child was taken last night, and I need to ask you a few questions."

She stiffened at the sight of the notebook. "I really have nothing to say to you."

He narrowed his eyes and studied her for a moment. Then he set the pen down, flipped the notebook closed, and clasped his hands together on top of it. "Here's the thing, Ms. Hunter. I think you probably do know something about these cases, more than you told me the last time, maybe even more than you realize. For example, I'm sure you know where Gage Kelly was last night and what he might have been doing. I'd like to keep this relaxed, but if you push me we will have to move this down to the station for formal questioning."

The green eyes hardened. He had a pretty good stare, one that usually managed to intimidate, but Nicole Hunter didn't back down one bit as she met it. Neither of them moved for a few seconds. When she spoke, her voice was as cold as ice. "Fine. I'll answer your questions. But Gage is innocent, and I will not allow you to twist anything I say to make it look otherwise. If I think that's what you are doing, I will tell him that you are investigating him without his knowledge and using me to get information. He's a lawyer. He'll know how to handle this."

Great. He'd managed to infuriate her and alienate her in less than thirty seconds this time. Either he was losing his touch, or this case was affecting him like no other case had in his fifteen years on the force. He had no desire for things to turn nasty, and he wasn't ready for Gage or Holden to find out they were under suspicion. Better go back to his original plan of treading very carefully where she was concerned. Somehow he'd managed to veer away from that the first time he'd opened his mouth.

"That's all I ask. And I would advise you against telling Gage anything at this point. If he is the one taking the children, you'll only drive his operation further underground, and greatly lower the chances that we can stop him before someone, likely him, gets hurt. Or worse. If he is innocent, and he very well may be, then anything you can do to help me with this case can only move us toward clearing his name."

"And Holden's."

"And Holden's, of course." He almost smiled. She wasn't about to give him an inch. No problem. He'd take a lot less than that at this point. "Do you mind?" He pointed to the notebook.

Nicole shrugged. "I guess not."

Daniel flipped it open again and checked the notes he'd

written on the first page. "So, do you know where Gage was last night?"

"He was working late, but he called me at ten o'clock to say good night."

"Land line or cell?"

"His cell. He sounded the same as always, a little tired, maybe, but he's been working a lot lately. Then he came into the diner for breakfast this morning. We talked for quite a while and nothing struck me as different or unusual about the way he was acting."

Daniel decided to switch gears. "Are you aware of Gage's home situation when he was a child?"

Her eyes grew wary. "If you are referring to the fact that his father was a drunk and beat him and Holden up continually, then yes, he told me about that. What is your point?"

"It has to do with motivation. All the kids that have been taken were living in violent, abusive situations." He was giving her way more information than he should, but he was desperate to put a crack, however small, in the shield she'd wrapped around herself.

"What does that have to do with Holden and Gage?"

"It makes sense that the person willing to risk everything to save these kids would have had a similar childhood."

Something flickered in her eyes. *Is that anger or fear?* Hopefully fear. If he could place even the smallest amount of doubt in her mind, she might be of some use to him.

Nicole drew herself up in her seat.

Anger, then. His heart sank.

"Let me get this straight, Detective. Your entire case is built on a theory, quite possibly faulty, that you came up with one day while sitting in a little cubicle. And that theory has led you to the conclusion that of the three million people in this city, the only possible perpetrators are two good, hard-working men who go to church every Sunday and spend the rest of the week trying to make an honest living?"

His glance flicked over her shaking hands, and the way she

clenched them to keep them steady. He raised his eyes to meet hers. She was clearly angry, but something else churned in their depths too. Something he couldn't quite put a finger on. The woman had more safeguards in place against possible losses than a Vegas casino. It wouldn't be easy to break through them to reach the real Nicole. Somehow Gage had done it. If he were a betting man though, Daniel would wager a lot of money that it hadn't been easy. "Why do you think the theory is faulty?"

"Maybe narrow would be a better word. You've latched on to the idea that the person responsible for these kidnappings has purely selfless motives. Isn't it more likely that anyone who would steal someone else's children would do so for personal gain? What about human trafficking? Selling children to wealthy, infertile couples? Or some kind of child pornography ring? Have you even considered these possibilities, or did you reject them off-hand because it was so much easier to go with the theory that left you with a nice, neat list of two possible suspects?"

Heat rose in his chest. Daniel counted to ten slowly in his head as he slid the notebook back into his shirt pocket and leaned forward. "I assure you, Ms. Hunter, that over the last several months every single possibility has been put forth and thoroughly investigated, including all of those you mentioned. This *faulty theory* of mine is the only one that has given us any concrete, plausible explanation for the disappearance of these children."

"And yet here you are," Nicole countered, "scrambling for information from someone who has already told you she knows nothing. That shows me that your explanation and, more importantly, your evidence, are considerably less concrete and plausible than you would have me believe."

Daniel closed his eyes and rubbed his forehead with his fingers, trying to calm himself. The woman was impossible. In all his years of police work he had rarely come across anyone who raised his ire so quickly and so thoroughly. *Of course, you did stop just short of accusing the man she loves of kidnapping two children.* The heat in his chest cooled a couple of degrees.

Bells jangled above the diner door. Daniel dropped his hand.

"Look, do one thing for me. Keep an eye on Gage's activities. If he does anything unusual, or if he says anything to arouse suspicion, let me know. If you help me, we might be able to eliminate him as a suspect."

"And if I refuse to spy on him for you?"

"Think of it as helping me clear his name." The weight of working so hard to stay focused and speak firmly when the ground that had always been solid beneath his feet quaked and bucked, pressed down on him. Daniel reached for his pen, suddenly desperate to end this conversation. The side of his hand inadvertently brushed against hers, still clasped together on the table. He froze, her skin like silk against his. Her hand jerked, as though she felt the current that had jolted up his arm, but she didn't pull away.

Slowly, she raised her eyes to meet his. The doubt and fear he'd been hoping to see in their green and gold depths swirled through them now, but the sight didn't bring him comfort, like it would have earlier. Instead, it sent a hot flush of guilt and confusion pouring through him. *What are you doing? Go. Leave. Get away from her.* He didn't move.

"Nic? Is everything okay?"

Nicole yanked her hands into her lap as an older woman walked toward their table, her soft blue eyes clouded with concern.

Daniel mentally kicked himself for having this conversation in such a public place, surrounded by people who knew Nicole. He'd hoped that she'd be more comfortable, maybe even cooperative, in familiar territory. *Another faulty theory.* He suppressed a grim smile.

"Everything's fine, Connie," Nicole said, her voice strained. "Mr. Grey was about to leave."

He'd been dismissed. Daniel stood.

Connie didn't look convinced, but she nodded in his direction. "Come again soon."

His eyes met Nicole's over Connie's head. "Oh, I will. The coffee here is very good. Apparently."

A pink flush crossed her cheeks, and he immediately regretted taking the jab. So much for treading carefully around her.

"I'll see you again, Ms. Hunter."

She didn't respond, only inclined her head slightly.

Daniel made his way through the diner which had begun to fill up with customers looking for an early dinner.

He could only hope, for their sakes, they were able to leave the restaurant considerably more satisfied than he was.

Chapter Thirty-One

Daniel stopped in the doorway of Sharleen's cubicle and shoved both hands into the pockets of his black dress pants. "I talked to Nicole Hunter this afternoon. She said Gage Kelly worked late last night, until ten or eleven. No verification since he called her from a cell phone to say goodnight. Were you able to submit the surveillance request to the DS?"

His partner crossed her arms. "Could we back up a couple of sentences? You went to see her again? Were you planning to mention that to me at some point?"

He repressed a sigh. "I just did."

"That wasn't mentioning, that was trying to slip by. Last time I checked we were still partners, Grey. Are you planning to start acting like it anytime soon?"

Daniel crossed the room and sat down beside her. "I had a feeling she would open up more if I came alone, not with someone she didn't know."

"And did she?"

He bit his lip, scrambling for an answer that would melt the ice in his partner's eyes. "Some. Like I said, she did tell me that Gage said he was working late last night. It would be better if we had a surveillance team out there that could verify when he goes out since, as you said, the two of us can't keep doing it." Diversionary tactics had never, to the best of his recollection, worked on his partner, but he was willing to try anything at this point.

Sharleen didn't answer.

Daniel held out under her intense gaze as long as he could. "I'm sorry, all right? I know we're supposed to be doing this together, and we are. But with Nicole Hunter being one of the few people we can talk to that might be able to give us something we can use, I want to make sure we handle her properly."

"I'm terrified to ask what you mean by 'handle her,' Grey. I'm not even sure I want to know. What I do want to know is whether you are going to keep going off on your own without letting me know what you're doing. Either we're in this together, or we're not."

"We are, honest. I'll let you know what I'm doing next time, okay?"

"*Before* you do it?"

"Yes. Now, did you request surveillance or not?"

She uncrossed her arms and Daniel relaxed slightly. "Yes, I did. The detective sergeant must be getting fed up with this case, because he agreed to a few hours at night. From 8 pm until 2 am for Holden, since he is the most likely suspect, and from 10 pm until 1 am for Gage."

Daniel shrugged. "That's a lot better than nothing. Good work."

"So, did this woman tell you *anything* today that we can use?"

"Not really, although I did ask her to let me know if Gage says or does anything unusual, and I think she will."

Sharleen waved a hand in the air. "Well, I guess that's something. Let me know if you hear from her. I'm going to meet with the surveillance teams to update them on the case."

"Okay. I'll look into any security camera footage that might have caught Gage coming out of his office so we confirm that he was there. Maybe we can see if he went anywhere other than home afterwards. I'll check around Holden's neighborhood as well."

"Good idea."

Daniel headed to his office and settled in front of the computer, trying to let go of his frustration so he could think clearly. Carrying out an investigation with so few leads and fewer witnesses was agonizing, one tiny, snail-paced step at a time. At least they did appear to be inching forward at this point. What they needed now was one good tip to make all the little, seemingly random pieces fit together to make one big clear picture. If Nicole came through for them, or the security footage showed anything helpful, or if he could start acting like the trained professional he was, they might be able to figure this thing out yet.

As long as nothing else went wrong.

Chapter Thirty-Two

"What can I get you?" Nicole scribbled the order on the notepad and headed for the kitchen. "Okay Joe, four burgers with the works, four fries, four colas, nice and easy." When he didn't answer, she pushed through the swinging doors. "Joe? Did you get—?"

The words caught in her throat. Extending past the far side of the island, a pale hand was splayed on the floor, unmoving. "Joe!" Nicole scrambled around the counter. Joe was sprawled on his back, his lips tinged blue, eyes open, staring up at the ceiling. "Connie!"

Rubber-soled shoes squeaked across the kitchen floor. "Nic? What is it? What's wr—" Connie gasped. "Joe! Is he ...?"

Nicole turned and met her eyes. "Stay with him, Connie. I'll call 911." She sprinted for the phone beside the till. After giving the information to the dispatcher, she grabbed the defibrillator from the wall and rushed back to the kitchen.

Connie had dropped to her knees beside her husband and taken his hand in hers. She turned tear-filled eyes to Nicole. "I think he's gone."

Nicole fumbled with the electrodes, her fingers numb and trembling. Before she could attach them to Joe's chest, a siren wailed outside and then died down. Seconds later, paramedics circled Joe, attempting to revive him. Connie and Nicole moved out of the way. Nicole slid an arm around Connie's waist and held her tight. *God, don't take him. Please don't take him.* Her friend pressed both hands to her mouth. After a couple of minutes, the paramedics lifted Joe onto a stretcher, raised it, and pushed it toward the swinging doors. Nicole followed them out into the diner. "Where is he going?"

"East General."

Nicole nodded. "We'll follow you." She guided Connie to a stool at the counter. Connie's thin shoulders trembled beneath her fingers. "Sit here for a minute, sweetie. I'll tell everyone we're closing."

Her friend nodded, a dazed look on her face. The few customers paid and left quickly, and Nicole held out a shaking hand. "Come on. Let's go to the hospital."

Connie grasped her fingers and stood with a groan. "What am I going to do, Nic?"

All Nicole wanted to do was drop to the floor and weep, but she pushed back the desire. She had to be there for Connie. Joe would have wanted her to take care of his sweetheart. She squeezed her hand. "Don't worry about that right now. I'm here—we'll get through this together." The words caught in her throat. Joe was like a father to her. His death would rip a huge hole in the heart that had been pieced together gradually after she had met him and Connie. The pain in her chest was real, and she struggled to take a breath as they climbed into the back of a cab.

"Come with me." A nurse in a pale blue uniform and long red hair pulled back in a braid spoke quietly. Nicole followed her down the hallway, Connie clinging to her arm. "Wait here a moment." The nurse pointed to a small waiting room. "I'll see if they're ready for you." She touched Connie's shoulder, compassion etched across her face.

Connie slumped against Nicole on the couch as they waited. She straightened when a young man in green scrubs came into the room. "Mrs. Murphy?"

"Yes." Her voice was hoarse, and she cleared her throat.

The doctor sat down in a chair across from them. "I'm very sorry. Your husband was already gone when he arrived at the hospital. There was nothing we could do."

The tears that had been pressing against Nicole's eyelids spilled over and streamed down her cheeks. She'd known it, but hearing the official pronouncement still sent ripples of shock through her body. "Do you know what happened?" she asked, her voice quivering.

"It was a heart attack. Massive. It would have happened very quickly."

Connie released a long breath. "May I see him?"

"Of course. I'll take you." The doctor rose.

Nicole stood too and reached for Connie's hand to help her to her feet. "Do you want me to go with you?"

She patted Nicole's hand. "Give me a few minutes alone with him, sweetie. I'll come and get you when I'm ready."

Nicole nodded and watched her friend walk beside the doctor down the hallway, supporting herself with a hand on the wall as she went. Nicole fumbled in her pocket for her phone and pushed the keypad button. The face of Detective Daniel Grey flashed through her mind. She backed up against the wall and leaned against it for support, horror flowing through her. Why was she thinking of him? She didn't want him anywhere near her. The man had turned her life upside down. Every time he walked into the room he did nothing but anger and confuse her. He was the last person she needed at the moment.

Her fingers trembled as she tapped Gage's number into her phone. "Come on, come on."

"Hello?"

"Gage?" His voice severed the fragile threads holding her together, and the word came out as a sob.

"Nic? What's wrong?"

She pressed her lips together tightly.

"Are you okay? Where are you?"

"At the hospital."

"What? Why? Are you hurt?"

"It's not me. It's Joe. He's ..."

"I'm on my way. Are you at East General?"

"Yes. The family waiting room in emergency."

"I'll be right there."

She stuck her phone into her pocket and sank onto the couch, hugging her knees to her chest with both arms. *Hurry, Gage.*

Connie still hadn't returned when footsteps pounded down the hallway and Gage burst into the room. Nicole scrambled to her feet and met him halfway across the room. His arms circled her, and he pulled her tightly to him, stroking her hair and whispering in her ear. "It's okay. I'm here." Calm worked its way through her, and she took a deep breath and stepped back. He brushed a strand of hair from her face. "What happened, Nic?"

"It's Joe, he's ..."

"He's what?"

"... dead."

His dark brown eyes widened in shock. "What?"

"He had a heart attack at the diner. I ..." She swallowed the lump in her throat. "I found him."

Pain flickered across his face. Gage pulled her to him again. "Oh, Nic, I'm so sorry."

She rested her head on his chest, the strength of his arms flowing through her.

"Nicole?" She raised her head and stepped back. Connie stood in the doorway of the waiting room. Although lined with sorrow, her face was peaceful. "Do you and Gage want to come and say goodbye?"

Nicole nodded. Gage's hand rested on her back, warm and comforting, as she took Connie's hand. The three of them trudged down the hallway and stopped in front of a closed door. Connie squeezed her fingers. "I'll wait here."

Gage wrapped his arm around Nicole's waist. "Do you want me to come with you?"

"Yes." Her voice shook. "Please."

He pushed open the door and held it so she could go in first. Joe lay on a hospital bed, pale and white beneath the sheet. A sob caught in her throat. It helped to feel Gage's arm around her as they walked toward the bed.

Nicole lifted the hand that lay on top of the sheet. It was cool to the touch, and she held it to her cheek. He'd often brushed the backs of his fingers there. It had always comforted her when she felt sad or completely alone in the world, something that had happened less and less after she had met him and Connie.

"Goodbye, Joe." Her voice broke. "I love you." Gage's arm tightened around her as she set the gnarled hand gently on the sheet.

Gage touched Joe's shoulder. "Thanks for taking care of my girl, Joe. We'll miss you."

Nicole pressed a kiss to the cheek of the gentle face she loved so much before turning to leave.

Connie waited for them out in the hallway. Nicole slid an arm around her shoulders. "Why don't you come home with me for a few days?"

"I'd like that."

The diner looked dark and lonely when they pulled up in front of it. *Not surprising.* Nicole climbed out of the car after Connie. The heart and soul of the place was gone. From the diner and from their lives. How were they supposed to carry on? She took her friend's arm as they climbed the stairs to the apartment above the restaurant. Connie threw a few things into an overnight bag. She paused at the doorway and looked around. A shadow of grief passed over her face as she surveyed the apartment she'd shared with Joe for the last forty years. "I keep expecting him to stick his head out of the bedroom and ask when dinner will be ready."

Nicole's throat ached with still-unshed tears. "Come on. Let's go home. I'll make us some tea."

"Tea would be good." When they reached the door, Connie pressed the light switch. Darkness fell across the tiny apartment. With a small sigh, she pulled the door shut.

They walked together down the stairs and out onto the sidewalk. "Wait." Connie pulled a set of keys from her pocket and unlocked the door to the diner. She reached her hand inside the building. A few seconds later the bright, blinking *Joe's Diner* sign above the door went dark. Nicole's chest constricted until it hurt to take a breath. She'd never seen that light off, night or day. Still, it felt right, somehow, as though the building itself mourned the loss of the one who had brought it life for so many years.

Slipping her arm through Connie's, she held on tight as they slowly walked away.

Chapter Thirty-Three

Nicole closed the door behind the last of the friends who had come by after the funeral to offer their condolences, and more food than she, Gage, and Connie would be able to eat in a month. She turned and leaned against the door, swaying on her feet but filled with an inexplicable peace. The days since Joe's death had been long and dark, but today, surrounded by all the people who had loved him, she and Connie had stood beside his grave and said goodbye. It helped more than she could have imagined to know that the body they lowered into the cold, hard ground wasn't really Joe. That he was in heaven now and would never again know pain or suffering.

Gage came out of the kitchen and walked toward her. She pushed away from the door and went to him. "How are you holding up?" He took hold of her arms and pressed a kiss to her forehead.

Nicole drew in a long, slow breath, taking inventory like someone would after a car crash to assess the amount of damage. Everything hurt, but nothing appeared broken beyond healing. Something she might need to remind herself of in the days to come. "I'll be okay."

"Connie asked me to go to the store for cream, in case anyone else drops by for coffee. Do you need anything?"

"Just for you to get back as soon as possible."

"Done." He kissed her again before stepping around her and heading out of the apartment.

"Nicole?" Connie stood in the living room.

Nicole crossed the room to press Connie's hand between both of hers. "Are you doing okay?"

Her friend nodded as she led Nicole to the couch. "I'm fine. I wanted to talk to you about a few things before I go."

"Go?" Nicole sank down beside her. "You don't have to leave. You know you can stay here as long as you like."

"I know." Connie patted Nicole's knee. "And thank you. It's been wonderful to be here with you the last few days. I haven't felt alone at all, although I know I have to deal with that now. The longer I stay away, the harder it will be. I need to go home in the morning, face the memories, and start learning how to live life on my own."

"You won't be alone," Nicole said. "You know that, right? I'll always be here for you."

Connie's soft white cheeks dimpled as she smiled. "I know that, sweetheart. And Joe knew it too. We never stopped thanking God for bringing you into the diner that day. We knew right away we'd gotten a good worker, and it didn't take us much longer to realize we'd also finally found a daughter."

Tears pricked Nicole's eyes and she blinked them back. "You and Joe were more like parents to me than mine ever were. I don't know what I would have done without you all these years."

"God knew we needed each other, didn't he? And he has ways of bringing people who need each other together. We must have the wisdom and the courage to see those people in front of us and let them into our lives and into our hearts when he does. And not do anything to push them away."

Nicole swallowed. "That can be scary sometimes."

Connie held her hand tightly. "That's why it takes courage. You don't regret loving Joe, do you? Even though it hurts so much to lose him?"

"No. Not for a second." The fog in her head began to clear. It was always a risk to love someone, to let them in. But when that love was real and right, even the pain of loss was worth it. *As long as it is right, and you weren't meant to be with someone else instead.* She pressed a hand to her chest. It was a betrayal to Gage to even let thoughts like that cross her mind. And she wouldn't do that to him. She loved him. He was the one she was meant to be with. Any other thoughts of some man she barely knew were the product of grief and exhaustion. Nothing more.

"Nic?" Connie's soft blue eyes peered intently into hers.

Heat flushed her cheeks. "I'm sorry. I was … thinking about Gage."

"Ah. Such a good man. He really loves you." The words were pointed, and Nicole felt them like a finger pressing into her chest. Were they motivated by what Connie had seen the other day, when she had walked in on her and the detective in the diner?

"I know. I love him too."

Connie squeezed her hand. "Speaking of love, I have something for you."

Nicole's eyes narrowed as Connie let go of her and drew a cream-colored envelope out of the pocket of her sweater. Nicole's name was scrawled across the front of it, and she caught her breath as she recognized Joe's handwriting.

"Joe wrote this a while ago, when he started feeling so poorly, I think. He asked me to give it to you after he was gone." Connie held the letter out. "I'm sorry it's a bit wrinkled. It's been in my purse for months now."

For a few seconds, Nicole couldn't move. A letter from Joe? She struggled to draw in a breath. Slowly she reached out and grasped the envelope with shaking fingers.

"Go ahead. Take your time. I'm going to make us some tea." Connie pushed to her feet with a groan.

Nicole grabbed her arm to help her up. "Okay, Connie. Thanks."

She watched her friend make her way across the living room and through the swinging doors. *I wish Gage was here now.* Nicole lifted her chin. No, this was something she had to do on her own. She swallowed hard and slid her nail under the flap to loosen it. Biting her lip, she pulled out the piece of folded paper inside. She pulled her feet up underneath her on the couch before unfolding the paper. The spidery scrawl brought tears to her eyes, but she blinked them to clear her vision and began to read.

Dearest Nicole,

If you are reading this, then I am already gone. You don't need me to tell you that I am in a better place now, and that you don't have to worry about me any longer. I know you'll miss me, as I will miss you, but we do not grieve without hope, do we, since we know that we will see each other again one day.

Connie and I had so much in this life - love, laughter, joy - but we never did have much in the way of things, which suited us just fine. I did want to leave you one gift though, to do with as you see fit. I want you to have the diner. I talked it over with Connie and she agrees with me. She doesn't want to run it herself, although I'm sure she'll be in there fairly often, walking around serving coffee to anyone who comes in off the street in need of one.

That's why we opened the diner in the first place, darlin'. So there'd be a place people could come, get in out of the cold, and feel, at least for a little while, that they weren't alone in the world. I know you've always held it close to your heart, little girl, but you have a lot of love inside you to give, more even than you know. Open that heart up, look around you, and see all the folks out there that need to feel just a little bit of it. Love and coffee, that combination will take you a long way on a cold night. Believe me, I've received both when I needed them the most, and I'll never forget either.

It will be your decision, of course, whether you want to keep the diner open or if you want to sell it. Either way, I will be watching you, waiting to see where your path in life takes you. Wherever you go, whatever you do, whoever you become, know that I am proud of you, and that you will always be the daughter of my heart.

All my love,
Joe

Tears streamed down Nicole's face. She was vaguely aware of the kitchen doors swinging open and Connie crossing the room toward her, but Nicole couldn't tear her eyes away from the words on the paper still clutched tightly in one hand.

Connie set the tray filled with tea and cookies on the coffee table and sat on the couch beside her. "Are you okay, sweetheart?"

Nicole pressed her eyes shut and drew in a quivering breath. "I think so."

"Here."

When she opened her eyes, Connie held out a tissue. Nicole took it and used it to wipe the tears off her cheeks. "Did you read this?"

Connie shook her head. "Joe wanted you to see it first. Whatever is in there is between you and him. I don't need to know what it says."

Nicole held it out to her. "No, it's okay. I want you to read it."

Connie hesitated then took the letter. Nicole leaned forward and poured the tea, giving her a moment.

When her friend looked up, her eyes shimmered with tears too. "Blessed man."

Nicole handed her a steaming cup of tea. "Yes, he was. I can't take the diner, though. It's too much."

"Of course you can. Joe's known for years he was going to give it to you. That's one of the reasons he kept it going so long. It's always been for you. We discussed it at length, and prayed about it, and it's what we both want."

"But if you don't want to run it, you could sell it, use the money to make sure you have enough to take care of yourself."

"Don't you worry about that. Joe made sure we had enough put aside for me to live on if anything happened to him. And I don't need much. I'll be fine."

Nicole's heart raced. "If I did decide to keep it open, you'd be there to help me, wouldn't you?"

Connie smiled at her, blue eyes warm. "Like Joe said, I'd

pop in from time to time, pour a few cups of coffee. But Nic," her face turned serious. "If you decide to do this, you'll have to stand on your own two feet. You need to do it on your own. I know you can, and so did Joe. That's why he left it to you."

Fear gripped her. Could she do it on her own? Did she even want to? She'd have to be there every day, in the company of a thousand memories and all the strangers that came in off the street. She could never offer them the warmth and compassion that Joe and Connie had always given them. Could she?

Nicole pressed her fingers to her temple, her mind too full of questions and emotions for her to think clearly. "I have no idea what to do."

Connie sipped her tea and set the cup on the saucer. "This is a new idea, and you've had a long week. Give yourself time to think about it. There's no rush. The diner will be there, waiting for you, whenever you make up your mind."

Nicole nodded. It was too late, and she was too tired, to even consider the idea tonight. The diner couldn't stay closed for long though, or all the regulars would find another place to eat.

Sometime in the next few days she'd stop in, check to make sure everything was okay, and try to imagine herself in there running the place alone. Like Connie said, the longer she waited, the harder it would be.

Chapter Thirty-Four

Nicole glanced around the diner. Everything seemed to be in its usual spot, except of course for Joe. When she pushed open the swinging doors to the kitchen, she half expected him to be standing in front of his grill, flipper in hand, like he'd always been. She backed out of the kitchen, letting the doors swing slowly shut after her.

Tamping down her grief, Nicole reached behind the counter and pulled her laptop out of her bag. She needed to stop feeling so much and start doing. The idea that Gage could be involved in criminal activity, while ridiculous, still hung over her like an ominous cloud threatening to burst open at any moment. She couldn't keep living this way.

As the computer booted up, she dropped onto one of the bar stools with a groan. Everything ached. Her heart mostly. Her world seemed to be coming apart around her, and Nicole had the painfully helpless feeling there was little she could do to stop it. Cooperating with Daniel Grey was starting to seem like the only option she had, the only possible way to prove Gage was innocent so the two of them could get on with their lives, maybe even find a measure of peace. They deserved that much, didn't they?

Nicole's jaw tightened. If Detective Grey wanted proof, she'd give it to him. Proof that Gage and Holden were innocent. It was crazy that the police were wasting so much time and energy pursuing the wrong people, while the real perpetrator was likely busy planning another abduction.

Her finger hesitated over the left mouse key. *Come on, Nicole. Get this over with. You know Gage isn't the kidnapper. The whole idea is completely ludicrous.* Still, her hand hovered over the button for a few seconds before she clicked on the search button for the *Toronto Star* newspaper archives. Her search revealed a series of articles on the abductions, and she grabbed a notepad and scribbled down all the dates that children had been taken.

After finishing and clicking on the exit button, she drew in a deep, trembling breath, realizing she had hardly inhaled at all since entering the paper's website. She sat without moving for several minutes, until the thudding in her chest subsided. Then she clicked on the day timer icon at the top of her screen. Maybe if she saw what she and Gage had done on those days, or the days that followed those dates, it might help her to remember if he'd seemed off, or if he hadn't stayed as late as usual, anything that might suggest her instincts about him and his involvement in the disappearances might be wrong. In the absence of that, she'd feel even more strongly that Gage had nothing to do with what was going on with the kids in the city, and Detective Daniel Grey would have to acknowledge that and start looking into other suspects.

She read over her entries for each of the dates that occurred after she and Gage had met, and a couple of days after each one. They hadn't gotten together one of those nights, but that didn't prove anything, did it? From what she'd read, the kids were usually taken in the middle of the night, and he rarely stayed past eleven. The other two nights they'd eaten together, once at a restaurant and once at his place. Had he acted strangely? Appeared distracted? Maybe. Occasionally. Or maybe not. Nicole pressed her palms to both temples, repressing the urge to cry out in frustration. She'd lost all perspective on their time together, now that she was looking back at it through the lens of the detective.

Her palm smacked down on the counter. So what if Gage was occasionally distracted? He was often working on a big case, and it wasn't easy to switch that off, even with her. She had deadlines for school to think about herself, and wasn't always fully present, even when they were together. That didn't mean she was plotting some big crime those evenings, did it?

Stop letting Daniel Grey get into your head.

Nicole coughed into her fist. Her throat had gone paper-dry. Jumping to her feet, she pushed through the doors into the kitchen and grabbed a glass. She filled it almost to the brim at the sink and lifted it to her mouth. Her hands shook so badly that water splashed onto her sweater and she turned and leaned against the island. Gage couldn't have taken those children. He wouldn't have. He loved kids. He would never hurt ... Her head shot up as a memory rocketed through her, of the night Gage told her about his childhood. He'd been so confused about how anyone could hurt an innocent child like that, so frustrated with the abusive parents he saw in the courtroom all the time. Had he found a way to stop some of them from going home and beating up the kids that, as he had said, they were supposed to be protecting?

Nicole bit her lip hard. Detective Grey had said the most likely suspect in the kidnappings was someone who wanted to help those kids, not hurt them. Someone who had been in the same, desperate, brutal situation as a child. Someone who had waited for help for himself and his brother and none had come. She moaned softly. For a few seconds she pressed her eyes tightly shut. Then she pushed herself away from the island.

This is crazy. Nicole returned to the diner and walked around the counter. She pressed a palm to the counter top to steady herself and took another sip of water. It was a coincidence, that's all, that Gage had seemed a little preoccupied the night of the last abduction, and she would prove—

A sharp knock broke the late-night silence of the diner. Nicole whirled around. The glass slipped from her fingers, shattering on the black and white tiles.

Detective Grey stood outside the door. A tsunami of emotions assaulted her at the sight of him. Anger that he had turned her life upside down with his wild accusations, fear that those accusations might actually be true, and a sudden, intense desire to feel his arms around her that only made her angrier. She didn't stop to analyze who the object of that second wave of anger was, but shoved the desire, and as much of the fear and anger as she could, down deep inside of her as she stepped around the mess and strode toward the door. She flipped the lock and yanked it open. "What are you doing here?"

He didn't flinch. If he handled all his investigations the way he'd handled this one, she wasn't surprised that he was used to that type of greeting.

"I need to talk to you. Can I come in?"

Everything in her told her to say no. Somehow, she didn't think that would make him go away. Not for long anyway. Letting out a heavy breath, she moved aside to let him pass.

He stepped over the threshold and looked down at the broken glass. "I didn't mean to startle you. Sorry."

Nicole shrugged and shut the door behind him. "I wasn't expecting anyone to show up here, that's all. We haven't been open for a few days."

"I know. I heard that the owner had died, so I drove by a few times."

Guilt over her cold reception of him doused the anger and fear, at least. "You were checking on the place?"

He shifted from one foot to the other. "I wanted to make sure everything was okay. That's how I knew you were here tonight. I was going by and saw the lights come on."

"Well … thank you."

"It wasn't any trouble. I was sorry to hear about Joe. Were you close to him?"

Nicole swallowed the lump in her throat. "He and Connie were like parents to me."

His face softened. "Then I'm really sorry. I know you haven't seen your own parents for a long time so—"

Her head jerked. "And how would you know that?"

"I …" For the first time since she'd known him, Detective Grey seemed to falter, as though he'd accidentally said more than he intended to.

"You've been investigating me too, haven't you? Why? Do

you still think I know something about this case that I'm not telling you?"

"No, we're covering all the angles, that's all. Looking into the background of everyone who might have something to do with the abductions, or who knows someone who might be involved. It's standard procedure."

"Which is cop talk for 'we can do anything we feel like and there is absolutely nothing you can do about it, so get over it'."

He sighed. "Look, I honestly didn't come here to get into anything with you. Could we start over? Please?"

For the second time, she noticed that exhaustion had drawn dark circles under his eyes. Harassing innocent civilians evidently took a lot out of him. She bit back the sarcasm. "What *did* you come here for?"

"Just to talk." Daniel glanced over at her laptop, still sitting open on the counter.

Nicole followed his gaze. "I was planning out my week. I'm helping Connie sort out all the paperwork, and I don't want to miss any appointments." Had she left the *Toronto Star* website open on the screen? Or her journal? If he saw either, he would know she was entertaining doubts about Gage, which would only make him feel better about the direction he'd taken the investigation. She forced calm into her voice as she walked around him and over to the counter. Hitting the exit button, she snapped the computer closed and turned to face him.

The detective was studying her intently. Her stomach tightened when he took a step toward her.

"Where's the broom?"

Nicole shook her head. "I'll take care of it."

"I don't mind. It was my fault. Is it in the kitchen?"

She hesitated for a moment before giving in. "Yes, behind the door."

"Why don't you sit down? You look a little shaky."

"I'm fine." When he disappeared through the swinging doors, she did sink onto a stool, afraid her knees would give out if she didn't. Nicole waved her hands in front of her cheeks, trying to cool them. When the doors creaked open behind her, she dropped her hands quickly.

"You sure you're okay? You're a little flushed." Detective Grey walked around the counter, a broom in one hand and a dust pan in the other.

"I am a little warm. Must be coming down with something. I should probably head home and rest."

He swept the broken glass into the dustpan, then turned and walked back into the kitchen. Glass clattered into the garbage can. When the door swung open a moment later, he carried two glasses of water that he set on the counter in front of her. "I'm sure you've had a long few days. I won't keep you. I wanted to touch base with you, ask if you've seen or heard anything you'd like to tell me about."

"I told you before, Detective, you are on the wrong trail. Gage and Holden would never be involved in anything like this."

"Are you sure?" He glanced again toward the laptop.

The heat in Nicole's cheeks intensified. "Yes, I'm sure. I—"

The words caught in her throat as he rested a hand on the counter beside her and leaned closer. "So if I booted up your computer and checked the history right now, I wouldn't find anything interesting?"

"You'd need a warrant for that."

"I could have one delivered here in twenty minutes." He reached inside his jacket and pulled out a cell phone.

"Which would be a waste of everyone's time. I told you I was checking my schedule for the week." Her voice shook with nerves and anger. *Please let him only hear the anger.*

"Maybe I'll get one anyway. I have a theory about what you might have been looking up, and I always like to check out my theories. You know, to make sure they're not faulty."

"Go ahead. I have nothing to hide. As long as you realize that while you're standing here talking to me and accomplishing nothing, children are still in danger in this city." Nicole clenched her fists tightly, trying to keep them from shaking.

His piercing blue eyes searched hers. Neither of them moved

for a few seconds, until he dropped the phone into his pocket. "Look, we don't have to fight about this. We both want the same thing, to rule out the possibility that either Gage or Holden is the one taking these children." He sat on the stool beside her, pulling a glass of water toward him and nudging the other one closer to her. "I know you've been through a lot lately, and I really do want to help."

Nicole gritted her teeth at the sudden softness in his voice. The last thing she wanted was to come undone in front of him. She could deal with his pushiness, but not his kindness. "Do you even have a partner?"

Detective Grey stopped with his glass halfway to his mouth. "Yes, of course. She's great. Why?"

"You seem to have the whole good cop, bad cop routine down on your own. I thought maybe you worked alone."

He grinned and sipped from the glass.

"She doesn't know you're here, does she?"

He almost choked on the swallow of water. "Of course she..." Their eyes met, and he let out a breath and set down his drink. "All right, no, she doesn't."

"Does anyone?"

"No."

"Is that normal?"

"It's not protocol. But this investigation is ... unusual."

"Why?" Nicole rubbed her damp palms on her jeans.

"Because I'm starting to wonder if the whole thing is as black and white as I first thought."

"I would guess that it rarely is," Nicole said.

"A month ago I wouldn't have agreed with you, but now I'm not so sure."

She rested her chin on one hand, suddenly curious about the man who had wreaked such havoc in her life. "What made you decide to become a cop?"

He didn't hesitate. "The uniform."

"The uniform?" Nicole couldn't help smiling.

"Yeah, I fell in love with it when I was three. My dad was a cop. Sometimes when he'd been working late, he'd come into my room to say good-night and he'd still have his uniform on. He looked so big and strong to me, like a super-hero, you know? As if nothing in the world could hurt him, or us when he was there. Those were the nights I slept the best. I felt so safe with him in the house protecting us."

Nicole blinked at his use of the word super-hero. The same thought had crossed her mind the day he'd stopped the thief on the street and retrieved her bag.

"That's when I decided to become a cop too, so I could wear the uniform and destroy all the evil in the world and help everyone like he did. I was pretty naïve, I guess. But then, I was three. All the evil in the world lived under my bed and in my closet and fled when my dad walked into the room." Sadness crept into his eyes.

What has he seen in his line of work to destroy that little boy's dreams? Everything in Nicole wanted to reach out and cup his cheek or pull his head down to her shoulder and stroke his hair until the sadness was banished like the monsters under his bed. The rush of tenderness that filled her at the thought of the little, pajama-clad boy, dark hair slicked down from his bath, sitting up in bed and reaching for his father when he walked into the room, almost brought tears to her eyes. She wrapped her fingers around her glass and forced herself to look away.

The only reason she was talking to him was to try to help Gage. While Detective Grey's father was holding him, tucking him into bed and making him feel safe and loved, Gage's dad was yanking him out of his closet and beating him nearly to death. His father had brought evil into the bedroom like a dark cloud swirling around him, instead of driving it away. Gage was the one who needed her, who deserved to have one person in his life stand up and fight for him, not betray him like everyone else had. *God, give me the words. I don't want to get Gage in trouble. I only want to help him.* She swung her gaze back to the detective's.

He was watching her. "What are you thinking about?"

"Gage."

"Ah."

For a second, she glimpsed that little three-year-old boy in the disappointment that flashed across his face. Nicole braced herself against softening. "Would you do something for me?"

"If I can."

"Would you call me Nicole?" She took a deep breath when he didn't answer. "The thing is, I need to trust you."

"You can." Resting an elbow on the counter, he tapped his fist against his mouth for a few seconds, as though contemplating his next words. She waited in silence until he dropped his hand. "You and I go back a ways, you know. We actually met a few months ago."

Her eyes widened. "We did?"

"Yes. My old partner asked me to go with him to give a talk on bike safety at his nephew's school on this side of the city. He bribed me by promising me breakfast at his favorite diner afterwards."

"Joe's."

He nodded. "Gage was in the booth beside us. I had run into him at the police station a few days before that and recognized him when I saw him here. Now that I think about it, if he is the one taking the kids, that would have been an interesting situation for him."

"He's not. But it does happen to him a lot. The diner is a popular place for cops, so he's surrounded by them all the time."

Detective Grey shook his head. "Anyway, I was facing him when you stopped at his table to talk to him. The two of you seemed so close, so happy. I remember thinking how rare that was."

"I thought you looked vaguely familiar when I first saw you on the street that day, but I knew if I had seen you, it was a while ago. You haven't been back since?"

His gaze dropped to his glass. "No. In fact, I didn't even stay long enough to eat that time."

Nicole tilted her head to one side. "Why not?"

When he looked up at her, his cheeks held a tinge of scarlet. "It was the end of a really long shift and I decided I was more tired than hungry."

She studied him for a few seconds before drawing in a quick breath. "You're bed guy."

"Bed guy?" He raised an eyebrow.

"Yeah." Her laughter eased some of the tension that had tightened the muscles in her body. "You're the one who made the comment about your bed being more appealing than anything on the menu, right?"

The detective looked a little nauseated. "You can't seriously remember that."

"I do. I thought you were giving me a lame pick-up line for a second, but then I realized you were way too embarrassed about what you had said for it to have been planned."

"You're right, I was. Still am. I'm not sure I've ever come closer to choking on my own foot than I did that day."

"Is that why you didn't come back?"

He hesitated. "It was more that Joe's is nowhere near where I live. Until recently, I didn't come over to this side of town very often."

"Too bad. We have the best breakfast in the city."

"So I've heard. Maybe I'll actually get a chance to try it some time."

A stab of pain tightened her muscles again. "I don't know if you will. I haven't decided if I'm going to open again."

"You?"

"Yes. Joe left me the place. He said it was up to me whether to sell it or keep it going. I know Connie would love to see me re-open it, but I don't know. There are so many people that only she knew how to …" Nicole lifted a hand, palm up. "I don't know if I can do it, if I even want to do it, without her and Joe." She lowered her hand and swiveled the stool to face him. "But if we've known each other that long, you should definitely call me Nicole. I'd be a lot more comfortable if you did." She tapped her fingers on the counter top. "You told me you were trying to help

Gage and Holden, trying to clear their names."

"Actually, I suggested that you helping me could possibly clear their names. My goal is to find out who took those kids so we can stop them from taking any more." His eyes probed hers. "And for the record, I'm not at all convinced it's Gage doing this. In fact, it makes more sense that it's Holden, since he has access to the Children's Aid files. With Gage's work though, he could also get that kind of information, so we can't rule either of them out yet. I've been reading their files and …"

Nicole started, and his eyes narrowed. "What is it?"

"Gage would hate that. He doesn't like anyone knowing what happened to them."

"It was pretty bad, wasn't it?"

"Yes, it was."

"I'm not saying it's right, but if either Gage or Holden is doing this …" the detective cleared his throat, "I can understand what's motivating them. And I'll promise you one thing. If you help me figure this out, I will do what I can to help them."

"I love Gage, Detective. And Holden. They're both good men. I would never want to do anything to hurt either of them."

"Neither would I." He stared into his glass for a moment before looking up at her. "All right then, Nicole. But you'll have to call me Daniel." He winced slightly, as though he'd crossed a line he knew he had no business crossing.

Nicole wasn't sorry. She needed him over on this side of the line with her.

"You found out something, didn't you?" he said.

How could she do this to Gage? She bit her lip. How could she not? If Gage was involved in this, his life could be in danger. Even if her co-operating with the police resulted in him going to jail for a few years, at least he would still be alive, they could still be together, eventually. She would wait for him. She couldn't sit around doing nothing, not if there was any way she could save him. Nicole still struggled to believe the suspicions the police had about Gage were true, but she was beginning to have suspicions of her own that she didn't know what to do with.

"Nicole?"

She blew out a long breath. "It's nothing really. Except, I did look up all the dates that kids have been taken ..."

"And?"

Her hand shook as she raised her glass to her lips. Some of the water splashed on to the counter. She set the glass down and started to stand. "I'll get a cloth."

He stopped her with a hand on her arm. Tingles of electricity shot across her skin. "Tell me."

Nicole sank down. *Will this help Gage, or hurt him?* She took a deep breath. She had to trust Daniel. And maybe, on some level, she wanted him keeping a close eye on Gage. If he did, he would either quickly find out that he wasn't involved in the abductions, or if Gage was, the detective would be able to stop him before he attempted to kidnap someone else and maybe get hurt or killed in the process. At least Daniel seemed to feel some compassion for Holden and Gage, and he might help them. "I looked up the dates that kids have been abducted since Gage and I started seeing each other and checked them against my day timer. One of those nights he didn't come over, but if I really think about it, the evenings we did spend together, he may have seemed a little preoccupied, as though he had something else on his mind."

Daniel pursed his lips. "Interesting."

"It probably doesn't mean anything. I mean, he's often busy with cases and might have been thinking about what he had to do the next day. That's a much more likely reason for him to be distracted."

"Maybe." Daniel lifted his shoulders. "Better not to discount anything at this point, though."

Nicole contemplated him. "You seem familiar with the Bible. Does that mean you believe in God, Detective?"

He blinked. It wasn't considered a politically correct question, but she didn't really care at this point.

When he spoke, his voice was firm. "Yes. Absolutely. I couldn't do what I do if I didn't know whose hands I was in, and where I would go if I went down on the job. Why, do you?"

"Yes. So does Gage. His faith was his lifeline when he was a kid, helped him survive what he went through, and find peace after he killed his father."

A strange look crossed Daniel's face. It disappeared so quickly she wondered if she had seen it at all.

I have to give him a glimpse of who Gage really is. "It's not only a Sunday thing with him, either. He really lives what he believes and reads the Bible every day."

Daniel leaned closer, his voice gentle in her ear. "So he'd be familiar with verses like, true religion is to take care of widows and orphans and to help them in their time of need. And whatever you do for the least of these, you do for me, wouldn't he, Nicole?"

He'd showered before he came over. His short hair was still slightly damp, curling around his ears, and he smelled of a faint, masculine musk. Nicole wasn't sure if it was his nearness or the words that sent shivers through her body. Either way, she couldn't bring herself to answer.

A sick feeling struck her. She'd made a terrible mistake, asking him to call her by her name. Names narrowed the distance they should have kept between them. The line they had both crossed a few minutes ago had been a protective barrier that had been torn down—that she had torn down—leaving them both vulnerable.

He drew back slightly. "Would you do something for me?"

"If I can."

The corners of his eyes crinkled. "Would you call me the next time Gage seems distracted while the two of you are together?"

"I don't know. I'm ..." she rubbed her forehead hard with her fingers. "... I'm really confused. I love Gage. I don't want to get him in trouble."

"Nicole, you need to know that if you ever suspect he's planning another abduction and you don't tell me, you could be charged with aiding and abetting. And I would really hate to see that happen, because …"

She dropped her hand and looked up. "Because?"

"Because I care about what happens to you. I don't believe you are involved with this in any way, but if people close to you are, you could get caught in the cross-fire. And I …" He reached out a hand toward her and then stopped and pulled back as though he'd suddenly realized what he was doing. "I don't want to see you get hurt."

His eyes met hers and held them. The tough cop façade was gone. The raw vulnerability that had taken its place tightened her chest until she could barely draw a breath.

Neither of them moved for a few seconds, until Daniel leaned in again, closing the space between them. His hand, strong and warm, covered the one she'd rested on the counter between them. All reason and rational thought fled as a thrill of pleasure rippled through her stomach. The desire she'd battled since the day they met overwhelmed her and she surrendered herself to it with a quick intake of breath. Slowly she turned her hand over until her palm pressed against his. His other hand slid behind her head and he pulled her gently toward him.

"Nicole." He whispered her name like a prayer, his warm breath brushing across her lips.

Trembling, she closed her eyes, wanting this, wanting the feel of his mouth on hers, of his hand tangled in her hair.

A soft jingling sound startled her, and her eyes flew open. Heat flared in her cheeks and she jerked back and yanked her hand out from under Daniel's. "I have to get that."

He straightened as she reached over the counter and grabbed her phone. Her hands shook and she nearly dropped it, but managed to grab it and press it to her ear. "Hello?" Her voice was hoarse, and she turned her head to clear her throat.

"Hey princess, are you still at the diner?"

Nicole swallowed hard. "Yes, I'm almost …" She glanced over at Daniel. He had propped both elbows up on the counter and dropped his face into his hands. She looked away quickly. "… Finished here. I'm leaving in a minute."

"Take a cab, okay? It's late."

"Okay." Her throat felt as though she had swallowed a mouthful of sand.

"I brought dinner over. I'll wait to eat until you get here."

"You don't have to. If you need to get home that's fine." If she didn't see him tonight, there was a better chance her emotions would be under control when she did.

"I know I don't. But I want to see you." Gage sounded puzzled and she closed her eyes, hating what was happening to them, what she was doing to them. "Nic, are you okay? You sound upset."

"I'm fine. Being here, remembering Joe. It's been harder than I thought." She'd never intentionally lied to him before, and it made her sick to her stomach. "I'm glad you're going to wait. I … I need to see you. I'll be there soon." She dropped the phone back onto the counter and turned to face Daniel.

He rubbed his face with both hands before dropping them into his lap. The vulnerability in his eyes had faded to weariness. "I take it we're done."

"Yes. We're done. Gage is waiting for me." Nicole crossed her arms over her abdomen, trying to ease the ache that gripped her there.

He nodded. The pain etched around his eyes broke her heart.

"Daniel, I shouldn't have—"

He let out a short, humorless laugh as he got up off the stool. "No, this is all on me. I've always been a by-the-book kind of guy, always. The last few weeks though …" He ran his fingers through his hair. "I've managed to break at least half a dozen rules and most of the code of conduct. If I had any professional integrity left at all, I would march into my boss's office first thing in the morning and take myself off this case. I should have done it the minute I realized you were involved in the investigation."

"You won't though, will you?"

For a long moment he didn't reply then he sighed heavily. "I don't think so. I have to see this through. I want to stop whoever is doing this. And I …" His jaw worked and Nicole bit her lip, waiting for him to finish. "I need to make sure that you're all right." He took a step toward her and stopped. "So will you tell me the next time Gage seems distracted? If he is planning something and we can stop him, you might have saved his life."

"I'll think about it. I don't know what the right thing to do is. I love Gage."

"Yeah. You mentioned that. A few times. Who are you trying to convince, me or yourself?"

She jerked, feeling the question like a stinging slap.

Daniel drew in a long breath. "I'm sorry. I seem to have completely lost the ability to do the right thing. Which means I'd better get out of here right now." He looked out the glass door of the diner. "It's dark. Do you need a ride home?"

"No, that's okay. Gage told me to take a cab."

"Well then, you'd best do that. You do love Gage, you know." A small smile twitched the corners of his lips.

Nicole managed a faint smile in return, grateful that he was trying to get them onto more stable footing.

Bells jangled as he pulled open the door and stepped out into the warm, early-summer night. Nicole locked the door behind him and stood, one hand on the glass, watching until he had disappeared down the street. Then she sank onto a stool and groaned as she covered her face with both hands.

She'd made a lot of mistakes in the last half hour. Now all she could do was pray that one of them hadn't just cost the man she loved everything.

Chapter Thirty-Five

Gage pulled open the door of her apartment as she reached for the knob. "Finally. I thought you would never get home." Grabbing her hand, he pulled her inside and pushed the door shut with his foot. "Come here." He drew her close and pressed his lips to hers.

Nicole held herself back for a few seconds, the image of blue eyes locked on hers still shimmering in her head. Then fury flooded through her, at Daniel, for causing such upheaval in her life, but mostly at herself, for letting it happen. Wrapping her arms around Gage's neck, she deepened their kiss. He stepped toward her, guiding her against the door. His hands moved to the sides of her face. Knees weak, Nicole buried her fingers in his hair, desperate to draw him closer, to convince him—and herself—that he was the only man in the world for her, the only one she wanted to be with.

When he finally pulled away, she was breathless, her cheeks burning. She laid her head on his chest as the room swirled around her. Gage tightened his arms around her and held her close, his breath warming the top of her head. Gradually, her heart rate slowed and she could open her eyes without feeling as though she would drop to the ground if he let her go.

Light glowed in his eyes when Gage stepped back and smiled at her. "Well. That was worth the wait."

Without his arms around her, holding her close, a coolness shivered over her skin. "I'm sorry I was gone so long."

"What were you doing?" He took her hand and led her over to the couch. Red and gold flames flickered behind the glass doors of the wood stove.

Nicole resisted the urge to hold her suddenly ice-cold hands toward the blaze. She turned and pulled her legs up underneath her, facing him. "Checking out everything at the diner. Trying to envision myself there, running the place by myself."

"Could you?"

She thought about it for a moment. "I don't know. There are so many memories there. Every time I open the kitchen door, I expect to see Joe standing at the grill."

Gage took her hands in his, squeezing them tightly. "You don't have to decide right away. You need to take time to deal with Joe's loss before you even consider what you should do with the diner."

"You're right. I can't think about that tonight."

"Good." He kissed her forehead. "All I want you to think about is me. And possibly dinner. Are you hungry?"

She thought about it. With everything that had happened that evening, food had been the last thing on her mind. The confusion that still clouded her thinking, despite her best efforts, dulled her appetite until she wasn't sure she could eat, but Gage had brought dinner and she didn't want to disappoint him. "If you are, I could eat something."

His eyes gleamed in the firelight. "We don't have to eat yet, if there's something you would rather do." He let go of one hand and trailed his fingers along her jaw line.

Her stomach tightened. Gage's mouth followed his fingers, moving lightly over her face and down to her neck. Nicole struggled to breathe. A tiny dart of guilt shot through her, the sense that she was being unfaithful, somehow. *Now* she felt that? *What is the matter with you?* Everything suddenly felt twisted around and backwards. A desperate need to do something to make it right again welled up in her.

She stiffened. Gage lifted his head and met her gaze. "What is it? You look serious. Is everything okay?"

"I am serious." Nicole framed his face with her hands. "I love you, Gage."

A quizzical look drew lines across his forehead. "That sounded a little more like a question than a statement."

"It wasn't. I do love you. I'm trying to find a way to tell you how much."

"You've never had trouble with that before." Gage ran his fingers idly up and down her arms and tilted his head. "Hey, has that guy ever been back to the diner?"

Suddenly weary, Nicole dropped her hands. "He's been in a couple of times. It's a public place, Gage. I can't stop him from eating there."

"Of course not." Something flickered in his eyes that she couldn't quite identify.

A tiny flame of anger re-ignited inside her, but she fought to keep her voice level. "This has nothing to do with him. Why would you even bring it up? Don't you trust me?" *Of course he doesn't trust you. Why should he? No one knows you better than Gage. He must sense that you just lied to him. For at least the second time tonight.*

He searched her face. Like she often did under his intense gaze, Nicole felt completely exposed. She struggled to keep her eyes on his, to not look away. After a few seconds, his face softened. "I'm sorry I asked. Of course, I trust you. In fact ..." he linked his fingers through hers. "I trust you with my life. That's why I want you to share it with me."

She started. "What?"

Gage brought her fingers up to his lips and kissed them. "Marry me, Nic. Please. I love you too, and I desperately want to spend the rest of my life with you."

Her lips parted in surprise. Those were the last words she'd expected to hear tonight. Why now? Did he know, somehow, that she had been with Daniel that evening? Had come close to betraying him by kissing another man? Was this a desperate attempt to hold on to her because he felt her slipping away from him? She pressed her lips together. No, he couldn't. In spite of what he had asked her, the eyes that searched hers were calm and trusting and filled with love. Any lingering doubts lurked inside of her, not him.

What if she said yes? A thrill of happiness leaped inside her chest. Committing herself to Gage would drive the last of those doubts away. Daniel's role in her life would become crystal clear, to both of them. If he was in her life at all, it would be as a co-worker, someone helping her to clear the name of the man she was bound to for life. Together they would prove once and for all that Gage had nothing to do with those missing children. If he did, he wouldn't ask her to marry him, would he? He'd never put her in that kind of danger.

If she married him, she'd have someone. Together they could create the kind of home, the kind of family, she'd always wanted but had never known. Was it possible the life she'd dreamt of since she was a little girl could be within her grasp? Could someone actually care enough about her to make a vow before God to never leave her?

A warm flush of hope flowed through her. Marrying Gage would put to rest all the fear and confusion she'd been wrestling with since Daniel Grey had walked into her life.

Daniel … The happiness faded. Her chest ached at the thought of hurting him, but from what she had seen in his eyes tonight, there was almost no way to avoid that. Nicole lifted her chin. She had never lied to him. He'd known from the beginning that she was with someone, and she had always been honest about the fact that she loved Gage. She'd tell him herself, explain everything, and hope he understood. He'd have to understand.

"Yes."

Gage blinked. "Yes?"

Nicole laughed. "Yes, I'll marry you."

"You thought about it so long, I was starting to worry."

"You took me by surprise, that's all. I'm sorry." Nicole caught his face in her hands and kissed him. Rising up on her knees, she drew him closer, desperately wanting to show him that he was everything to her, all that mattered.

Gage wrapped his arms around her waist and pulled her to him. She ran her fingers through his long, dark hair. The feel of it, soft beneath her fingers, the warmth of his lips on hers, and the pleasure of being held tightly in his arms, drove every other thought from her head for several minutes. The desperate need to take more of him, feel more of him, be closer to him filled her. A faint, far-off warning bell sounded in her head, the distant and unwelcome realization that they were driving hard toward the edges of the boundaries they had set for themselves. It took her several more seconds to summon the strength, but she finally broke off the kiss and rested her forehead on his.

Neither of them spoke until she edged away on the couch and his hands slid from her waist. She reached out and brushed her fingertips across his cheek, and he lifted his eyes, dark and liquid, to hers. A small smile crossed his face. "I think we should get married sooner than later, what do you think?"

"I've always wanted a June wedding. How about this weekend?" Nicole laughed weakly.

His expression sobered. "We could, you know. I looked into getting a license. It takes about twenty minutes."

Twenty minutes. She'd been half-joking when she suggested this weekend, but really, what reason did they have to wait? It wasn't like they had family to notify. Even if her parents did agree to come, she wasn't sure she wanted them there now. Not after so much time had passed. And not when she wanted to focus only on Gage. There was enough going on in her life to threaten that focus already, she didn't need any more distractions. And she didn't need any more time. Lately time had proven itself to be the enemy, systematically attacking and undermining her stable, peaceful life with each passing day. With each visit from Detective Daniel Grey. She'd had enough.

Besides, she loved Gage and wanted to be with him.

Who are you trying to convince?

The words drifted around in her mind for a few seconds, haunting her, before Nicole raised her head and shocked herself—and Gage, from the look on his face—with the words that came out of her mouth. "Let's do it. Let's get married on Saturday."

Chapter Thirty-Six

Daniel pointed his remote in the direction of his car and pushed the lock button. When he heard the confirming beep, he shoved his keys into the pocket of his jacket and strode toward the bank of parking garage elevators beneath the police station.

The number above the elevator door had settled at four and wasn't moving. He bounced impatiently on the balls of his feet. *Calm down, Grey.* He forced himself to stop moving and try to use the time to plan out his strategy for the day, the next step they should take in this investigation. His mind whirled with thoughts of the evening before. Although it was far from evidence—barely even a hunch at this point—it was interesting that Gage might have been preoccupied the evenings preceding an abduction. And even more interesting that Nicole appeared to be opening her mind, even slightly, to the fact that he could be involved.

Nicole. His jaw tightened. The woman infuriated him like no one he had ever met. She knew how to push buttons he didn't even realize he had. Like a little sister.

Except that he didn't think of her as a sister.

With a low groan, Daniel pressed his hands to the wall beside the elevators and banged his head softly against the cold cement. What a mess. He'd never allowed his emotions to interfere with his job before, and he'd picked the worst possible time to do so. He had to get her out of his head. And he would. Not that he had done anything wrong, necessarily. It wasn't like Gage had put a ring on her finger.

Daniel straightened up. The fact that Nicole wasn't married wasn't really the issue. The issue was that she was possibly involved in crimes he was investigating. Or was involved with someone who might be involved. Either way, there were more than enough reasons for him to exercise a little self-control. This was the biggest case of his career and he wouldn't blow it because—

"Grey?"

Daniel drew in a deep, steadying breath before swinging around to face his partner, praying she wouldn't see the angst he was drowning in written all across his face.

He might as well have prayed that she wouldn't notice the sun shining in the sky.

Sharleen's eyes narrowed. "What did you do?"

"What are you talking about?" He shifted around and banged the up button a few times. *Come on. Come on.*

When he turned back, his partner had planted both fists firmly on her hips.

Uh oh.

"Don't pull that innocent act on me, Grey. I've witnessed you messing up often enough to recognize that guilty look when I see it." Tilting her head, she studied his face for a few seconds, and then drew in a sharp breath. "You kissed her."

"No, I didn't."

She raised both eyebrows.

"I didn't kiss her, all right? I … almost kissed her." Daniel frowned. Somehow that distinction had seemed bigger in his head.

Sharleen stared at him for a moment before spinning on her heel and heading into the garage. "Come on."

"Where are we going?"

"Starbucks. We both need something extra tall if we're going to get through today." He couldn't argue with that. He shuffled behind her as she stalked to her burgundy Sonata.

Neither spoke the entire seven minutes it took to get to the coffee shop, which was fine with Daniel. Heat shimmered off his partner, though. He was going to get an earful at some point. Exhaling loudly, he rested his head against the window and shut his eyes. When she pulled into a parking spot and screeched to a stop, he jerked upright. By the time he had undone his seatbelt and climbed out of the car, Sharleen had jumped out and slammed the door behind her.

Daniel shook his head. At least he never had any trouble figuring out what his partner was thinking, or whether or not she was upset. The woman could say more with body language in five minutes than Leo Tolstoy ever had in a novel.

They carried their drinks to a table. Daniel had kind of been hoping for more of the silent treatment, but Sharleen launched into her interrogation before he even had a chance to pull back the tab on his black coffee.

"Tell me exactly what happened."

Daniel sighed. "I did see Nicole Hunter yesterday." He held up one hand. "And before you say anything, I didn't plan it. The diner's been closed since the owner died, and I've been driving by once in a while to check on it. I saw the lights come on last night and went to see who it was. I didn't really think about her being there that late by herself."

"Hmm. If only there was some kind of portable communication device you could carry around in your pocket and use to get in touch with me when something like that happens so I could join you."

Daniel gave her a dark look. "You do realize that sarcasm is the lowest form of humor, don't you? And I didn't want to call you and ask you to come way over to the other side of the city late at night."

"Very thoughtful."

Daniel drew in a deep breath. "Look, I know you don't like it, but it might have been better that I was alone. The last couple of times we've talked, I've gotten the sense that Nicole is starting to question her belief in Gage's innocence. I've been trying to capitalize on that, see if I can get her to commit to letting me know if he does anything unusual. If you'd come with me, we would have been back to square one with building a relationship with her."

"You have a *relationship* with her?"

"Shh." Alarmed at her climbing decibel level, Daniel glanced around the crowded coffee shop. He glared at Sharleen. "Not that kind of relationship, a working one."

"As far as I know there's only one type of working relationship that involves kissing, so do not give me that, Daniel."

"Almost kissing."

"What does that mean anyway? How could you *almost* kiss her?"

Daniel slid off his jacket and hung it on the back of his chair, suddenly feeling very warm. "It means that, while discussing the case…" he emphasized that last part, hoping to drive home the fact that at least at some point he had been on the right track, "…we had a moment. We almost kissed and then her phone rang and we didn't. End of story." He tipped his cup and downed a huge mouthful of the hot liquid. Maybe the burning sensation in his throat would distract him from the pang of that lost moment.

Sharleen shook her head. "Wow. I think that might be the first time you have ever broken a promise to me."

He set his cup down so hard some of the coffee sloshed onto the table. "What are you talking about? I never promised you I wouldn't kiss her, or almost kiss her, or anything to do with kissing, that I can recall. And speaking of which, if we could switch to a topic of conversation that doesn't involve the word *kissing*, that would be really great."

"I'm talking about your promise to be professional. Almost kissing someone you are attempting to get information from for an investigation might not be specifically mentioned in the code of conduct, but I think we both know there is nothing professional about it."

His surge of righteous indignation evaporated. "You're right. I'm sorry."

"Who was on the phone?"

Daniel shut his eyes for a couple of seconds. No wonder he was feeling so warm. He was rapidly descending through Dante's nine rings of hell, each one worse than the last. He opened his eyes and focused on his half-empty cup. "Gage."

"So the subject of a criminal investigation calls as you are about to make out with his girlfriend."

"What is this, tenth grade? We weren't about to make out, we…" He looked up in time to catch her withering glare. "All right, not the point, I know."

"You're in big trouble, Grey. You know that, don't you?"

Daniel started to deny it but realized he didn't have the heart. "I know." He blew out a deep breath as he met her gaze. "Should I take myself off this case?"

"Yes. You definitely should."

He nodded.

"But I don't want you to."

"You don't?"

"No." Sharleen leaned in close to him. "We're so close, Daniel. I can feel it. In spite of one wildly questionable judgment call after another on your part."

"That's a little harsh, don't you …?"

She raised an eyebrow.

Daniel slumped in his chair. "Yeah, okay," he conceded.

"Even so, I firmly believe that somehow you have managed to lead us down the right path here. I know that either Gage or Holden Kelly is involved in these abductions. In fact, if we had the manpower to watch them both 24/7, I'm sure we'd have something concrete on one of them by now. You can't quit. Not when we're so—"

Daniel sucked in a quick breath. As hot as he'd become during this conversation, he suddenly went ice cold.

Sharleen looked alarmed. "What is it?"

"It's them."

"Who?" She started to turn around, but he grabbed her arm.

"Do *not* look. It's Nicole and Gage. They just walked in." For one wild moment he thought about trying to hide, slip out the side exit or into the men's room, but before he could move, Nicole's gaze locked with his. The color drained from her face.

Gage glanced down at her, and then over at him. As Daniel watched, Gage said something to her and Nicole nodded. He spoke again, then put a hand on the small of her back and the two of them walked toward Daniel and his partner. He forced a smile and stood up, wondering, as he did, if Dante had been wrong and there actually were more than nine levels of hell. It felt like he'd suffered through at least a dozen in the last few minutes.

"Ms. Hunter." Daniel held out a hand and she shook it briefly. Her fingers were as cold as he felt, down to his core. "Good to see you."

"You too." Her voice was strained, but she managed a weak smile as she turned to Gage. "I think you've met my boyfriend, Gage Kelly. Gage, you remember Daniel Grey?"

Unlike Nicole's and his, Gage's smile was genuine, warm and friendly. He grasped Daniel's hand firmly. "Fiancé, actually."

"Really." Daniel's gaze flicked to Nicole's, but she didn't meet his eyes. He returned his attention to Gage. "I hadn't heard. Congratulations."

"Thank you." Gage released his hand. "Yes, we have met, down at the police station. Haven't we, Detective?"

Daniel swallowed hard, hoping to ease the tightness in his throat. "That's right. And this is my partner, Sharleen Roberts."

"Good to meet you." Gage greeted her before swinging his gaze back to Daniel's. "I hear you've become a regular at Joe's."

"I've been there a few times, yes. Best breakfast in the city."

"That's true. It is. Or was. I guess you'll have to find a new place to go now, since they've shut down for a while."

"Yeah, I guess I will."

"Might be just as well. It's easy to get stuck in a rut, revisiting the same old place. Sometimes it's good to try something new, get a fresh perspective."

"You're probably right." Daniel didn't miss the fact that the warmth in Gage's smile had faded. Or that the dark eyes that were riveted on his had hardened to steel.

Nicole rested a hand on his arm. "Gage, we should go."

He covered her hand with his and smiled at her. "Yes, we should." Gage looked at him. "The wedding is this Saturday so, as you can imagine, we've got a long list of things to do today to get ready. Good to meet you, Detectives."

Daniel nodded his head woodenly. *Saturday? That's the day after tomorrow.* He sank onto the chair, his legs trembling. Once, as a rookie cop, he'd foolishly chased a suspect into a dark alley without any backup and been jumped by the guy and two of his buddies. Before he could draw his weapon, the two buddies had grabbed his arms so the suspect could drive a fist deep into his gut. The deep, shocking pain had driven him to his knees, gasping for a breath he never thought would come. He felt exactly the same way now.

Concentrating on inhaling slowly and evenly to combat the dizziness, he watched the two of them until they had walked out the door with their drinks. Nicole didn't look back. *What is going on here? I saw her last night and she didn't mention—*

"Grey?" Sharleen touched his hand.

Daniel gave his head a shake and attempted to focus on her concerned face. "What?"

"Are you okay?"

He tried to force a smile, but apparently he'd reached his limit of faking it for the day. "Of course. Why?"

"Don't even try it. You look like a shell-shocked soldier returning from battle." She pursed her lips. "Did that change everything? Should you take yourself off this case after all, do you think?"

Daniel considered the question for a moment. The ball of ice that had settled in his stomach began to melt as a rush of hot anger poured through him. He straightened up, his thoughts suddenly clear. "No way. I'm going to see this through. Gage Kelly just threw down the gauntlet. Maybe that was only about Nicole, I don't know. But there's no chance he is scaring me off."

"Off the case, you mean."

He met his partner's gaze. "What?"

"You're saying that he's not going to scare you off of continuing with this investigation. I'm assuming he does have you appropriately terrorized at the idea of pursuing anything further with the woman he is going to marry in two days. Right?"

The three seconds he waited to reply had his partner's eyebrows starting to rise again, but when he spoke, Daniel's voice was firm. "Yes. Absolutely. From now on, I will be completely professional. I promise."

"You won't go and see her alone again?"

"Of course not."

She didn't look entirely convinced, but Sharleen nodded. "Good. Then let's go wrap this thing up."

She didn't say them, but he heard the words as clearly as if she had. *Before you make any more questionable errors in judgment that blow this case for both of us once and for all.*

Chapter Thirty-Seven

"Daniel?"

He spun around at the sound of her voice. Nicole stepped out of the shadows of his building. She stopped on the sidewalk in front of him, twisting her hands together as though uncertain how he would react to seeing her.

Daniel wasn't too certain himself. "How did you know where I lived?"

The corners of her mouth lifted slightly. "411?"

He raised an eyebrow.

"Okay, I followed you from work. It wasn't that hard. You didn't take any evasive measures at all. And you probably should, you know. I mean, I could be some drug dealer recently sprung from prison coming back for revenge."

"Why?"

A tiny v appeared between her eyes. "Because I was angry that you put me away?"

In spite of himself, he laughed. "The fact that you've been watching way too many CSI episodes aside, I mean why did you follow me?" His smile faded. "Why are you here, Nicole? Shouldn't you be out deciding on china patterns or interviewing DJ's or something?" He tried to keep the anger that was twisting through his gut out of his voice, but he was hurting too much to put a lot of effort into it.

Nicole winced. "I … I'm sorry you had to find out that way. I was going to tell you myself."

"The wedding's in two days. How were you planning to tell me, on a postcard from Bermuda? 'Having a great time – so glad you're not here.' Something like that?" It took everything he had to keep his voice low and even.

She glanced around the deserted street. "Could we go inside?"

"That's not a good idea."

"I know."

Daniel stared at her for a moment then, with a deep sigh, he turned and shoved his key into the lock. Pulling open the heavy glass door, he swept his arm in front of him. "After you."

Nicole walked past him and through the doorway. He closed his eyes for a few seconds as the scent of apple blossoms floated past him. Really? Did she have to smell like that tonight? His gaze darted up to the sky. *You're going to have to help me here. Please.* Pushing away his apprehension, he followed her into the building.

Neither of them spoke on the stairs, or in the hallway leading to his apartment. Once inside, he pushed the door shut behind them, strode across the room, and tossed his jacket onto a kitchen chair. He hesitated, then pulled off his badge and dropped it on the table before turning to face her. "Would you like a drink?"

"That would really be a bad idea."

"I know." His jaw tightened. "But we should have wine or champagne or something. I could make a toast to the bride-to-be. Celebrate this momentous occasion. What do you think?"

"Don't do that. Please."

His anger dissipated at the pleading in her voice and, with it, the energy he had hoped would carry him through this conversation. Completely drained, he lifted a hand and pointed toward the living area. "I'm sorry. I'll behave. Do you want to sit down?"

She nodded and sank onto his black leather couch. Her loose hair drifted around her shoulders. When she looked up at him, the soft light of the lamp he had left on reflected in the gold flecks in her green eyes.

Daniel swallowed hard and lowered himself onto the chair across from her, clutching both arm rests. "Does Gage know you're here?"

Nicole shook her head. "No. He wouldn't be very happy if

he did."

"My partner wouldn't be either."

"She doesn't want you talking to me?"

"Not alone. She has some crazy idea that I have been less than professional around you."

She smiled faintly. "Was that the discussion at Starbucks this morning?"

"Yes." Daniel winced. "That was what is known in the business as an official kick in the butt. Not entirely undeserved, either." He tightened his grip on the arm rests. "The punch to the gut I got from Gage might have been though."

"I'm sorry. I really was going to tell you myself. This has all happened so suddenly. He only asked me last night."

"Yeah, about that. Why are you rushing into this? Don't you think it would be a good idea to wait until we know for sure if Gage is involved in these kidnappings before you commit yourself to him for the rest of your life?"

"Until he's arrested or gets himself killed, you mean?" Her voice held a tinge of bitterness. "Because that's the only way you would know for sure, isn't it?" Nicole leaned forward and clasped her hands together as if beseeching him to listen to her. "If Gage is the one you're looking for, then if we are married, he'd be risking a lot more by breaking the law. He'd have a lot more to lose. I don't think he would take any other children. This could all be over."

She was too close. All of his senses were on overload, except for touch, the one he most desperately wanted to use at the moment. Daniel stood up and moved away, toward the window, where he could think more clearly. Crossing both arms over his chest, he turned to face her. "Over? How can you say that? Even if no more children are taken, there are still six of them missing, still out there only God knows where. And evidence could surface any time, even years from now, linking Gage to even one of those kids and then he'd be in prison for the rest of his life."

Her face paled in the soft light. Clearly she hadn't considered that possibility. Rising to her feet, she paced the room for a moment before stopping in front of him. She looked dazed and confused, like a child who had just been slapped and didn't understand why.

A stab of pain shot across his abdomen. He had to get through to her somehow. Reaching out, he cupped her shoulders lightly, resisting the urge to tighten his hold and shake her to force her to listen to him. "All I'm asking is that you wait a bit, a few weeks, until we know for sure. Most likely it will turn out not to be Gage, and then you can marry him without this hanging over your head."

She bit her lip. "I can't. I've given this a lot of thought, and it has to be now. As soon as possible."

"Why?" His eyes searched hers. What he saw sent hope surging through him. "Nicole." Daniel lifted his hands from her shoulders to her face. "Don't marry him."

"You're only asking me that because you think I'm going to get caught in the middle of something, that I'll get hurt. But Gage would never let that happen."

"I am worried that you will get caught in the middle of something. And I'm terrified that you will get hurt. But that's not why I'm asking."

Her skin was warm beneath his fingers, her eyes wide and soft. He couldn't do it anymore. Every promise he'd ever made to anyone, including himself, was suddenly meaningless. All that mattered was her. And this moment. And this one last chance he had to hold on to them both. His mouth sought out hers. Her lips parted, and she leaned against him, giving herself, taking from him. With a low moan, Daniel slid his hand to the back of her head, her hair soft and silky around his fingers. Wrapping his other arm around her, he pulled her closer. It wasn't until he tasted warm salt on his tongue that reality came crashing in around him.

Still, it took everything he had in him to pull back. To wipe the tears off her face with his fingers. For a few seconds, she clasped his fingers in hers. Her eyes, filled with pain, met and held his.

Then she dropped her gaze and let go of his hands, and he knew he'd lost.

"I'm so sorry, Daniel. I never meant to hurt you." Another tear slid down her cheek, but he didn't touch her this time. "If things had been different when we met, if I hadn't been with Gage …"

He nodded. "I know."

Daniel closed his eyes as she turned away. He listened as she crossed the room, walking out of his life. The doorknob creaked and his eyes flew open. "Nicole."

She turned to face him.

Daniel went to her. He brushed away a strand of hair from her forehead and rested his knuckles on her flushed cheek for a few seconds, before dropping his hand and stepping back. "Be careful. Please."

She nodded and went out into the hall. He stood in the doorway until the sound of her echoing footsteps on the stairs faded.

Then he stumbled inside again and closed the door tightly behind him.

Daniel stood in the middle of the room, head spinning. Now what? He took a step toward the door and stopped. He couldn't think where to go, what to do. The only thing he wanted to do— go after Nicole and do everything in his power to persuade her not to marry another man—was the one thing he couldn't.

Daniel forced himself to turn and start for the kitchen. A soft rapping on the door froze him in place. *Nicole.* Had she changed her mind? He spun around and crossed the space between him and the entryway in four strides. Grasping the knob, he yanked open the door.

Becca stood in the hallway. For a few seconds, Daniel gaped at her. Like eyes trying to adjust after coming in out of bright sunlight, his mind struggled to make the leap from expecting Nicole to seeing his sister in front of him. "What are you doing here?"

A slight frown crinkled her forehead. "You invited me, remember?" She held up a pizza box. "Austin dropped me off on his way to work because you said to come over and we'd watch the Jays game together."

Daniel gave his head a small shake. It didn't help. "Of course, sorry." He stepped back. "Come on in."

Becca inclined her head back down the hallway. "I saw a woman in the stairwell. She looked like she was crying." She ran a hand over her rounded belly. "I didn't think I should run down the stairs after her, but maybe you should go see if she's okay?"

Daniel repressed a sigh. He took the box from his sister and grasped her elbow lightly to direct her into his apartment. "I can't go after her. I'm the reason she's crying." He closed the door behind them. "And why are you climbing four flights of stairs anyway? You're two months away from giving birth." He tossed the pizza box onto the coffee table.

It was a feeble attempt to divert her attention away from Nicole. As expected, it worked about as well as a grandfather clock that hadn't been wound in a decade. Becca's eyes were wide as she stared at him. "*You're* the reason she's crying? Why? What did you do? And who is she, anyway?"

Daniel held up both hands in a T shape. "Bec. Time out. Please." His legs refused to hold him up any longer and he sank down on the couch.

His sister rounded the coffee table. She held her stomach with one hand and braced herself on the back of the couch with the other as she eased herself down beside him. For a moment neither of them spoke then she drew in a sharp breath. "She's that waitress, isn't she?"

Daniel ran a hand over his eyes. The last thing he felt like doing was talking about Nicole. He dropped his hand into his lap. "She's the one I told you about, yes."

"What happened between the two of you?"

"Nothing, really. I mean, there was chemistry there. I've seen her a few times since, and I definitely felt it and I know she did too. But whatever there might have been between us is over now. She came here tonight to say goodbye."

"But she obviously has feelings for you too or she wouldn't be so upset. Are you sure her goodbye was final?"

Daniel let out a short, humorless laugh. "Pretty sure, yeah. Remember the guy I told you she was with that day in the diner?"

Becca nodded.

"She's marrying him the day after tomorrow."

His sister slumped into the couch. "No."

"I'm afraid so. I found out about the engagement this morning. She came over to try and explain to me why she is marrying him so quickly. From the look in her eyes, I gathered it might actually have something to do with me. That gave me enough hope to try and talk her out of it, but I wasn't able to." He lifted both hands. "So that's that."

"I'm sorry."

He shook his head. "I totally brought this on myself. I knew the first day I met her she was involved with someone else and I still let myself fall for her. That wasn't only stupid, it was highly unethical. Possibly even sinful." The aroma of hot cheese and processed meat wafting from the box in front of him, normally one of his favorite smells, was turning his stomach.

"Does he know about you?"

"I'm pretty sure he does, or that he suspects something, anyway. He's the one who told me this morning that the two of them were engaged, and he clearly enjoyed doing it."

Her eyes grew stormy. "I don't like him. He sounds horrible."

You have no idea how true that might be. Daniel shrugged. "I don't blame him. If I had a girlfriend, certainly if she was a fiancée, and I thought someone might be moving in on her, I'd probably act the same way."

"Still, I feel like I'm to blame for all this. If I hadn't pushed you so hard to find someone, maybe you wouldn't have even noticed her that day in the diner and all of this could have been avoided."

Daniel mulled that over. "First of all, what I felt that day, and all the times I saw Nicole after that, had nothing to do with you or anything you said or did. Something just sparked between the two of us. I felt the connection the moment I saw her. It happens sometimes. Not often, certainly not to me, but it does, and never for any rational or explainable reason. And secondly, if I could do it all over again, I wouldn't change a thing."

"You wouldn't?"

"No. I always thought the old 'better to have loved and lost' line was just cheesy drivel, but for the first time in my life, I think there might actually be something to it."

"Wait." Becca straightened up and gripped his arm. "Are you saying you love this woman?"

Daniel blew out a breath. "I'm saying that I wouldn't give up a moment that I had with her, even now, tonight, when it hurts to take a breath. Even though I hope and pray the sharp edge of that will fade, eventually, I wouldn't trade the time I had with her for anything."

"Wow." Becca squeezed his arm. "She must really be something."

"She is. But the lesson I learned from all this, you'll be happy to hear, is that I might be more ready to settle down than I'd thought. If Nicole hadn't already been involved with someone else, I could easily have seen myself spending the rest of my life with her."

His sister's face lit up. Daniel lifted a hand. "Don't even think about it. I need time to get over this. But I will. And when I do, I promise you I'll keep both my heart and my mind open to the possibility of meeting someone else, okay?"

"Okay. And I promise not to push you on it again before you're ready." She let go of him and lifted the lid of the pizza box. "Are you hungry?"

A cloud of garlic-laden steam curled toward him and Daniel breathed it in. He wasn't sure if he could keep anything down, but since Becca had gone to the trouble of bringing it over … Daniel reached for a piece and lifted it out of the box. "I don't think I've had anything to eat or drink since Sharleen and I got coffee at Starbucks this morning, so this smells pretty good." Had it really only been that morning? It felt as though a lifetime had passed since Gage and Nicole had come through the door of the coffee shop.

He switched on the TV and found the ball game. His sister kept the conversation light and didn't bring up the subject of him and Nicole again, which Daniel deeply appreciated. She even managed to make him laugh a couple of times, which he hadn't expected to do again for a while. When the game ended and their team had won, he nudged his sister in the shoulder. "Thanks."

"For what?" Her eyelids were heavy and she sounded drowsy. Good thing he was driving her home.

"For being here tonight. I'm not sure what I would have done with myself if you hadn't come over."

"I'm glad I did. I had a lot of fun." She yawned and pressed her palm to her mouth.

Daniel chuckled. "Looks like it." He stood and reached for his sister's hands to pull her to her feet. "I had fun too, which a couple of hours ago I wouldn't have thought was possible."

She met his gaze, her blue eyes sad. "This will pass, you know."

"I know." He slid an arm around her shoulders to guide her toward the door. Except that he didn't know. *God, please let her be right.* Because, at the moment, it felt as though the deep, almost unbearable ache in his chest had lodged itself there for good.

Chapter Thirty-Eight

Rogue sighed as he walked into the reception area outside of Natalya's office and the secretary rose to her feet and held up one hand.

"She's expecting me, Lydia."

"I know that, sir." Her tone was frosty. "I'll check and see if she's ready to see you."

He gritted his teeth and crossed his arms over his chest as she sat down again and picked up the phone. "He's here."

The pause was interminable. No doubt the receptionist was drawing it out longer than necessary, trying to bait him. He had no idea what he'd done to get on her bad side, but he wasn't going to rise to it. This time.

"Very well, I'll send him in." She replaced the phone and nodded curtly in the direction of the door.

"Thank you." The exaggerated politeness was beneath him, but it made him feel a little better anyway.

He pushed open the door and walked into the cool, quiet office. As usual, Natalya sat at her desk, watching him silently as he shut the door and crossed the room.

Rogue sank onto the chair in front of her. "I want out."

Natalya pressed her palms together and rested her chin on her fingertips, regarding him coolly. She didn't speak for a full five seconds, during which he reflected, with a grudging admiration, that no one in the world could speak more loudly with silence than she could.

When she did talk, her voice was ice cold. "As you may recall, Kelly, when you agreed to join us, you committed to helping us as long as we needed you."

"I know, but things have changed."

"What things?"

"I'm getting married."

"Congratulations."

"Tomorrow."

"Ah." She tapped her fingertips together a few times. "That could be problematic. Is it possible to delay that?"

"No. Not without arousing her suspicions. And things are becoming too hot around here anyway. A police detective has been talking to her."

"About you?"

Gage shifted in his chair. "I don't know. She hasn't said so. She claims he's nothing more than a customer where she works. But she's been acting strange lately, distant. I thought it was because she was grieving the loss of someone close to her, but now I'm not so sure."

"You're worried about this man, aren't you?"

"Of course I am. He's a cop."

"I don't mean as a cop."

Gage dropped his gaze to the hands clasped on her desk.

"Is that why you are marrying her so quickly?"

His head shot up. "Of course not. I love her, and I want to start my life with her as soon as possible. And if it's all right with you, I'd rather not do it from behind bars."

Natalya nodded slowly. "I hope Nicole Hunter realizes what a fortunate woman she is."

Heat surged through him. "How do you know her name?"

She didn't answer, just leveled that implacable stare across her desk that he was pretty sure was capable of seeing right inside him.

Probably didn't need her intelligence team to tell her about Nicole. No doubt she read it straight from my mind. "Is there anyone out there that doesn't know every little secret in my life?" He couldn't keep the bitterness out of his voice.

A small smile played around her lips. "I'm sure there are a few. Your fiancée, for one."

That one stung like the sharp tip of a knife and he flinched.

The smile faded. "I apologize. That was uncalled for, especially as you have proven your loyalty to us by keeping all of this a secret as we asked. I'm sure it has been difficult for you, not being able to share this part of your life with the woman you love." She studied him for a moment before drawing in a deep breath. "It takes a lot of courage to feel things as deeply as you do, Kelly. I admire you for that." She straightened in her chair. "That aside, I am going to hold you to your commitment. We have one more mission planned and then, as it happens, we are leaving anyway."

"Leaving?" His heartbeat quickened. This really could all be over.

"Yes. We don't usually stay this long in any one city, but things have gone well, and we have extended our time in Toronto, trying to help as many children as possible. Now, however, as you so eloquently put it, things are getting hot around here and it is time for us to move on." Natalya pursed her lips as she studied him. "You should know, Kelly, the board is very pleased with what you have done for us, and for the children. You have been all they ... all *we* had hoped for and more. You are a genuine hero. I hope you understand that."

She picked up a folder from her desk. "Unfortunately, you will have to remain an unsung one, but we, and you, at least, will know what you have done."

"I still think the risk is too high to do another mission. The police could be watching me and ..."

He broke off when her gaze hardened. "What is it?"

"This is not optional. The child we are going after is in one of the worst situations we've seen yet. It's only a matter of time before his father kills him." Natalya flipped open the file and turned it toward him, but Gage refused to look down.

"His name is—"

He held up one hand. "Do *not* tell me."

"Matthew Gibson."

Gage sagged against the back of his chair. Matthew Gibson was a tiny four-year-old with curly blond hair and blue eyes. His mother had died of cancer when he was two, but in spite of that, and the fact that his father vented his frustrations against the world on him on a daily basis, the little guy still managed a sweet smile whenever Gage saw him. It was one of his most heart-breaking cases, one that he knew Children's Aid was frustrated about too, but the father had a connection to someone high up and they didn't seem to be able to touch him.

Exhaling loudly, Gage shook his head. "That was a dirty ploy."

"I know." The platinum in her eyes softened slightly. "One more mission, Kelly, and then you will be a free man. The instructions will be delivered to you in the usual way, on the day of the operation."

"Which is?"

"Monday."

Gage stood up and pressed both palms to her desk, leaning in close to her. "That's two days after I get married."

Natalya didn't blink. "It was supposed to be Sunday," she said calmly. "Consider that your wedding present."

They stared at each other for a few seconds until, with a heavy sigh, he pushed up from the desk. "Fine. One more. And deliver the instructions to Nicole's apartment. I take it you don't need me to tell you where that is."

She nodded. "Incidentally, I don't believe Detective Daniel Grey will be a threat at this point. Not to the mission, anyway."

Another direct hit. Gage gritted his teeth. He was getting a little tired of wearing the bull's-eye for the target practice she seemed in the mood for today. "How do you know that?"

"Although he has been to see your fiancée several times in the course of his investigation, the chief suspect, as far as the police are concerned, is still Holden, since he is the one who works at Children's Aid. Which is exactly what we hoped would happen when we chose you."

Gage stiffened. "I don't appreciate you using my brother as a decoy."

"We both know your brother would do anything for you. If

you asked for his help, he would give it to you without question. That's all he is doing now, if unknowingly, by turning police attention away from you long enough for you to complete this final assignment. If and when he is questioned, he won't know anything. It won't take them long to realize he is not involved and let him go."

"But they can make his life difficult in the meantime."

Her smile was cool. "Holden has survived much worse than this. Do not underestimate his strength. He will be fine. And by the time they realize they are on the wrong trail, we will be gone. And there will be nothing to link you with any of the abductions either. We've been doing this a long time and are very good at covering our tracks, I assure you."

"I'm counting on that." Gage turned and headed for the door.

"Wait."

He stopped and faced her. Natalya pushed back her chair and rose from her desk. Her high heels clicked on the marble floor as she crossed the room and stopped in front of him. The faint spicy scent of exotic perfume wafted from her, and he swallowed hard as she took both of his hands in hers. "It has been a pleasure working with you, Gage." She moved closer and pressed her full red lips—as soft and warm as her eyes were hard and cold—to his briefly before stepping back. "As I said before, you are an extraordinary man. I truly wish you and Nicole every happiness."

For the first time since he had known her, the slate-gray eyes swirled with emotion. His throat tightened, but he managed a smile as she let him go.

Gage felt her gaze on him but didn't turn back as he headed out of her office and pulled the heavy wooden door shut behind him for the last time.

Chapter Thirty-Nine

Sharleen was waiting in his office when Daniel arrived. She leaned against the wall, arms crossed in front of her.

"I don't want to talk about it." He slipped off his jacket and hung it up on the hook by his office door.

"Grey."

"Sharleen. Please. I'm begging you."

"Look, I'm not asking about her, I'm asking about you. You look terrible. Are you eating? Sleeping? Thinking about the wedding tomorrow?"

He shot her a look. "I thought you weren't asking about her."

"I wanted to see if I could slip one by you."

"Nice try." Daniel dropped down onto his desk chair and scrubbed his face with both hands before lifting his head to meet her gaze. "Okay, I know you're concerned. So here goes." He held up his fingers and ticked off the answers to her questions. "Yes, I've been eating. Hot Pockets and Pop Tarts three times a day. And yes, I've been sleeping, usually in front of the TV after Jimmy Fallon. And no, I still don't want to talk about it. Satisfied?"

She didn't answer.

"I'm kidding. I haul myself off the couch after Fallon and crawl into bed every night." He looked at her pointedly. "Alone."

A sympathetic look crossed her face. "Aw, not *almost* sleeping with anyone these days?"

"Oh, that's hilarious. Kick a man while he's down, why don't you?" Daniel pointed a finger at her. "And I don't think that those of you who have it all figured out should make fun of us poor slobs that don't." He leaned back in his chair and folded his arms behind his head. "How do you do it anyway, you and Tom? You met this great guy, created a fabulous life together. You make it look so easy."

"Don't kid yourself. No one has it all together. And it's never easy." Her face grew serious. "But it did help that, when I met him, he wasn't in love with someone else, and he wasn't involved with a possible suspect in a major criminal investigation."

Daniel dropped his arms and laughed. "Ah, the secret to a successful relationship. That would have been good information to have a few months ago."

Sharleen's face softened. "You're going to be okay, Grey."

He waved a hand through the air. "Of course. Next female person of interest that comes along, I'll forget Nicole Hunter ever existed."

She smiled. "Yeah, okay."

"Although," he continued, "since you so stealthily snuck the question into the conversation, I will tell you that yes, I have been thinking about the wedding. Way too much, in fact. Now what I would like to do is move on with my life. The best way I know to do that is to get back to work and get something done. I don't want to think about what happened with Nicole. Or what she will be doing tomorrow. And I definitely don't want to talk about it."

His partner studied him for a moment. "Okay. What do you want to do then?"

"Drive my fist through a wall. Kick someone's teeth in, maybe."

"Remind me to stay out of your way today."

"Stay out of my way today. Please." Daniel grinned at her before swinging around to face his computer.

"Anyone's teeth in particular you'd like to kick in?"

He threw her a look over his shoulder.

Sharleen pushed away from the wall. "All right, but let's do it the legal way, shall we? Let's get something on Gage Kelly and bring him in."

"That's the plan." He pulled his keyboard closer to him as Sharleen leaned over his shoulder. "Okay, I thought about this a lot last night." He shot her a sideways glance. "Before I went to sleep. I think we should get files on every child abduction in the United States in the last five or six years, see if any other reported cases fit the pattern. We're looking for kids taken right out of their beds at night, which is unusual."

Sharleen nodded. "And kids who all have a file with Children's Aid—extreme cases of abuse that no one has been able to do anything about, for whatever reason. Not to mention an abductor that, as far as we know, isn't known to the family, which is also unusual. And don't forget, there's more than one person involved here. Besides the front man, whom we've been focussing on, there are at least two others – the driver and the person in the back seat of the car."

"All of which adds up to some pretty unique crimes. I know we checked the Canadian database for any similar patterns and came up with nothing, but let's check the American one now, see if we can find anything."

"Good idea. If these guys have operated in any major cities in the States in the past few years, it should be fairly easy to pinpoint when and where."

"Okay, let's look at the last six years. I'll take the first three, you take the rest."

Sharleen straightened up. "I'm on it." She rested a hand on his shoulder and waited until he looked up. "You know I'm here for you, right? Any time you need to talk."

"Thanks. But I'm pretty much done talking. Now I need to do something."

"All right, if you're sure. I'll be in my office if you need me."

"Okay."

She stopped in the doorway and turned around. "It's good to have you back, Grey."

"Yeah, I guess I was pretty gone there for a while, wasn't I? Sorry about that."

Sharleen shrugged. "Hey, we can't choose who we fall—"

He threw a hand up in the air. "Don't say it. Do not say those words."

"Would they be wrong?"

He blew out his breath. "Maybe not. But they'd make all of it a little too real."

She gave him a sad smile as she left his office. Daniel turned in his chair and started typing away at the computer, refusing to let his mind wander anywhere but to the task at hand.

It took most of the rest of the day, but by three p.m., he'd compiled a list. Grabbing the print-out from the computer, he jumped to his feet and headed across the hall.

Sharleen spun her chair around. "Any luck?"

Daniel stepped into the room and pulled the plastic chair up to her desk. "Yeah. Look at this. Boston, May to July—three kids taken. Chicago, September to October—two kids taken. New York City, April to June—four kids. Denver, September to November—two kids. Los Angeles, March to April—two kids, and Detroit, October—three kids. All taken out of their beds at night, all disappeared without a trace. Did you get anything?"

Sharleen ran a finger down the screen. "Similar stats: Seattle, Baltimore, Washington D.C., Houston. One to three months in each place, two to four kids taken each time."

"So, all American cities until now, but they've obviously moved up here." Daniel studied the monitor, doing some quick calculations. "That makes something like thirty kids gone without a trace, with no one ever caught or charged with their disappearances, few leads, fewer witnesses, pretty much nothing." Daniel's head felt suddenly heavy and he rested it on one hand and looked over at his partner. "Shar, I don't think we're dealing with a few amateurs here. This thing is starting to feel huge. I mean, both Gage and Holden have been in Toronto their whole lives, so if either of them is the one taking the kids here, that means they must use locals wherever they are. And setting up an operation like this in all those cities, operating that efficiently, and then leaving town without a trace? That can only mean one thing."

Sharleen looked at him and they both spoke at the same time. "Big money."

Daniel nodded. "And power. I'm guessing there are people involved here that are incredibly well-connected, possibly politically, backing an organization that is highly organized and even more highly funded." For a few seconds he had trouble drawing a breath. "Let's put a report together for the DS. He should be notifying the P.D.'s in every major city in Canada that these guys could be coming there next. He should also recommend they work with Children's Aid. These are extreme cases. There can't be too many in each city. They can at least try to predict who they might go after."

Daniel leaned forward and studied the screen.

"What are you thinking?"

"That the Toronto situation is a bit different from those others."

"More time here, you mean?"

"Yeah, closer to six months. And more kids taken. I wonder why they're sticking around so long."

"Maybe they're not. Maybe they're done."

"Yeah, maybe." Daniel clasped his hands behind his head, trying to put all the pieces together. "But *if* Gage is involved with this, and *if* his warning yesterday had more to do with our investigation than with Nicole, then maybe they're not done yet."

"That's a lot of ifs and maybes."

"I know, but if I'm right ..." he grinned at Sharleen, "... then the question is why. I mean, their intel is obviously sophisticated. The only reason they failed the one time is because of an alarm in the house that no one could have known about. If they're that good, they must know that we're watching Holden and Gage pretty closely. And if that's true, then there are only two reasons that they would even consider making another attempt. Either we're so far off the mark that they're not even worried about us, or there's a child somewhere in this city in such an extremely abusive situation that they're willing to risk getting caught. And although it's not out of the question, let's assume for the moment that we're not that far off the mark ..."

Daniel lowered his hands and stood up, grabbing his suit

jacket from the hook by the door and slipping it on. "Are you okay with putting that report together?"

"Sure." Sharleen's eyes narrowed. "But where are you going?"

"Nowhere near Nicole, don't worry. I'm heading to the DS's office to demand a warrant to open up some CAS files. And I'm going to tell him I want it yesterday."

Chapter Forty

Gage could hardly breathe. Every time he looked at Nicole, his wife, the air was sucked from his lungs. She was so beautiful. And his.

The ceremony had been brief and simple. Their pastor had been free, even on such short notice, to marry them, and the service was held in a small room behind the sanctuary. Connie had stood up with Nicole, and Holden had been at Gage's side. There hadn't been time to invite anyone else, but it hadn't mattered. There could have been three hundred people in the pews and he still would have only seen one.

Afterwards they'd all gone out for dinner. The restaurant he and Nicole had chosen was one of their favorites. They served the best Italian food in the city, and the décor was so authentic Gage always half-expected to see a gondolier waiting to take them for a ride down the canal when they stepped out the door. Tonight he barely noticed the surroundings. His empty plate was a testament to the fact that he'd eaten, although he couldn't remember taking a bite. His eyes strayed constantly over to the woman he'd pledged to spend the rest of his life with—something he'd always thought would terrify him into paralysis. Instead, all it did was make him smile. Especially now, when his work with the organization was nearly done and he could dare to hope that his life might go on for many more years.

Gage's chest squeezed. He hated that he'd had to keep that from Nicole, that he was entering their marriage with a secret. But it was one he could never share with her, not without putting her in danger, or forcing her into an ethical dilemma he couldn't bear to watch her struggle with. All he could do was look forward, to their future together, and vow to never keep anything from her again.

Nicole had pulled her blonde hair up today and soft wisps fell around her face. Her green eyes shone and sparkled like the sun playing on the sea. He wanted nothing more at the moment than to pull her into his arms and kiss her. Speaking of which ... Gage looked at his watch.

When he lifted his head, Nicole was watching him, an amused glint in her eyes. Their softness told him she was thinking the same thing he was. As good as it was to be with family and friends, neither of them could wait to be alone.

It was Holden who saved them. He'd always been sensitive to his brother's moods, and Gage had never appreciated that fact more than he did when Holden looked at his own watch and pushed back his chair. "I think I'm going to head out. I have an early morning tomorrow, and I'm pretty sure Gage and Nicole are anxious to go as well." Laughter broke out around the table, but the party broke up fast after that. In spite of the pink tinge that appeared on her cheeks, Nicole didn't seem to mind. She winked at him before she slipped her arms into the coat he held for her, which didn't ease Gage's desire to be on their way one bit.

The anxiety hit him in the car. Everything had happened so fast that he hadn't really had time to think about the honeymoon. Nicole had never seen him without a shirt on. He was careful about that. The red welts the buckle of his dad's belt had left across his back had barely faded over the years. Other than the doctor who had examined them the night their parents died, Holden was the only one who had ever seen them, and his back was the same so it wasn't a big deal. Now, though ... Gage suppressed a shudder at the thought of anyone else seeing them, even Nicole. They revealed too much—pain, humiliation, fear, shame. Baring his back meant baring his soul. *Not sure I'm ready to do that, even to my wife.*

His hand shook slightly as he signed into the hotel and followed her to the room. Gage's breath caught when Nicole dropped onto her back on the king-sized bed, arms splayed like a snow angel on the thick, soft duvet. Desire rose up in him, a rush of heat that weakened his knees and tightened his stomach muscles. He swallowed hard and sank on to the chair by the desk.

Nicole sat up. Her playful grin faded as she studied him. "Everything okay?"

"Sure. Why?" His voice sounded strained in his ears.

"You look a little ... anxious."

He forced a smile. "Of course not. It's been a perfect day."

"It has, hasn't it? The ceremony was beautiful, and it was nice to only have the people we care about the most in the world there to witness it." She pushed herself off the bed and started toward him.

His chest constricted.

"Gage." Lowering herself on to his lap, she pressed her lips to his neck. "We're married."

Everything in him wanted to wrap his arms around her and hold her close, but he kept his hands at his sides.

Nicole moved her lips to his ear and whispered, "And we're alone."

He swallowed hard.

Her fingers found the top button on his shirt and she undid it and nuzzled the curve of his neck.

When she was halfway down his shirt, Gage gave up with a low groan. Bringing his arms around her, he pulled her close, breathing in the soft floral scent of the curls that brushed against his cheek. He reached behind her for the zipper of her dress and drew it down.

Nicole stood up and slipped the gown over her shoulders, letting it drift to the floor. "Come." Holding out both arms, she invited him to join her.

A single lamp beside the bed cast a soft glow around the room. If he could turn it off ... Gage grasped both her hands and rose to his feet on legs he wasn't sure would support him.

A small smile turned up the corners of her mouth as she backed toward the bed and sank down on it. He sat down beside her and ran a hand over the soft, creamy skin of one shoulder before pressing his mouth to it. Beneath his lips a shiver rippled through her.

She undid the last few buttons on his shirt and began to push it off.

"Wait." Gage reached for the switch on the lamp. Before he could press it, her hands cupped his shoulders.

"Don't, please. I want to see you."

The sigh escaped his lips before he could stop it. Her hands still on his shoulders, Nicole turned him to face her. "What is it?"

"Nothing. I just …" His eyes met hers. He had no words to explain to her, to make her understand how hard it was for him to even think about anyone seeing what his father had done to him. If she saw it, she would see *him*. And she would realize what a mistake she had made, marrying someone like him. A lump rose in his throat. He didn't deserve—

"Is it your back?"

He looked away from the eyes penetrating far too deeply inside of him.

"Let me see."

Gage shook his head.

"Please." Slowly, Nicole slid her hands to the collar of his shirt. Panic rose up in him as she pushed it over his shoulders.

Fine. Let her see if she wants to so badly. He lifted his arms from the bed so she could pull off the shirt and toss it onto a chair beside the bed. Nicole kissed him on the forehead. Her lips trailed across his cheek and neck as she moved slowly around to kneel behind him.

He was shaking.

Her warm hands rested on his upper arms for a few seconds. Gage held his breath, forcing himself to stay, to not bolt from the room. *God, help me.*

Her fingers passed over his shoulder blades and he drew in a sharp breath. When her soft lips pressed between them, his throat tightened. He closed his eyes as she continued down his back, covering every inch with her mouth or her hands.

When she was finished, Nicole pulled him down beside her on the bed and raised herself up on one elbow. The tips of her fingers danced lightly over his chest. A soft glow lit her eyes and he was drawn into them, mesmerized by the dancing gold flecks. Her full, pink mouth curved into a smile as she leaned toward him. "You are the most courageous and beautiful man I've ever known." The words were whispered, but they echoed through his whole body, pouring warmth and light into the dry, empty spaces carved out with fists and belts and angry words. Tears filled his eyes as he rose up and covered her body with his. She lay back and wrapped her arms around his neck, drawing his mouth to hers.

All the lies he'd been told in his life, about who he was and how little he was worth, were shattered by the few whispered words of truth. The fingers that caressed him, that drew him close to her, were warm and healing, like soothing oil poured over the scars on his skin and the scars on his soul.

All those years and thousands of dollars spent on therapy, as much as they had helped him, hadn't accomplished what the last few minutes had.

All he'd ever really needed was his wife.

Chapter Forty-One

Daniel knocked lightly and pushed open the door of his dad's room in the retirement home. "Hey, Pop." He glanced at the television set. *Hockey Night in Canada—what else?*

His dad glanced up from his La-Z-Boy chair. "Hey, Son!" Reaching out, he grasped Daniel's hand tightly in his. "Good to see you."

Daniel tried not to wince. His dad's heart may have weakened over the years, but his grip of steel never had. After a few seconds, his father took pity on him and let him go with a laugh. "Still got it, don't I?"

"Yeah, Pop. You still got it." Daniel smiled and sank down on the couch, his hand throbbing slightly. "Got any chips? Soda?"

His dad shot him a dirty look. "Smart mouth. You know they don't let me have any of the good stuff in here." His face turned hopeful. "Unless you smuggled in some contraband for me?"

Daniel laughed and pulled a bag of peanut M and M's out of his jacket pocket. "For an old cop, you sure don't have much respect for the law around here."

His dad clapped his hands together and reached for the bag. "For a young cop, neither do you. Thank goodness." He grinned and popped a couple of candies into his mouth.

Daniel tried to focus on the game, but his mind kept straying to thoughts of Nicole. The wedding was probably over. With such little lead time, it had to have been pretty small and informal. Which made sense, since neither she nor Gage had any family around other than Holden. So she was married to someone else now. He glanced at his watch. And it was her wedding night, so most likely she was ..." Daniel slammed the door shut on that thought, not wanting to go there, even for a second. His chest ached until it hurt to take a breath.

"Everything okay, Son?"

He snapped back to the present. "Is it over?"

"Yeah. A nail-biter, as always. Sadly, the Pens held on to beat the Senators 3-2. Tied up the series." His dad pointed the remote at the TV and clicked it off. "Where did you go?"

Daniel ran his fingers through his hair. "Nowhere. I'm tired, I guess. It's been a long week."

Pop tilted his head and studied him. "Don't kid a kidder, Danny-boy. Something's bothering you. Might as well tell me— you know I'll get a confession out of you one way or another."

It was true. Daniel had heard countless stories over the years from his dad's policeman buddies about what a tough interrogator he had been, and he believed every word. Daniel blew out a long breath and rested his head against the back of the couch. "It's this case I'm working on."

"I doubt that."

He lifted his head and stared at his dad. "What do you mean?"

"I mean, you have heartache written all over your face. I know you're working that big case, and I'm sure that's part of it, but the thing that's weighing down on you like the load on a pack mule has to do with a woman. Don't even try to deny it."

Defeated, Daniel laid his head back again. His dad may have been pushing eighty, but he was still as sharp as he'd ever been. He didn't miss a thing. When he was a kid, Daniel had hated that, and he wasn't sure he liked it any more now. Not tonight, anyway. "Shouldn't you be getting dementia one of these days? That would make my life a lot easier."

Pop barked out a laugh. "The only thing that will make your life easier at the moment is spilling your guts. I'll know if you're hiding something."

"You always did." Daniel blew out a long breath then sat up and faced his dad. "Okay fine, there was a woman."

His dad raised a thick, bushy eyebrow. "Was?"

"Yeah. She got married today."

"Ah." A flicker of pain shot across his father's face. "So the woman you love is in the arms of another man tonight. That hurts, Son. I know. I've been there myself."

His head jerked. "Whoa. Slow down for a second," Daniel sputtered. "First of all, I never said I loved her, and secondly, what? Are you saying Mom spent the night with another man?"

His dad chuckled. "No, no, not your mom. My first love, Eleanor Russell." The dreamy look that came over his dad's face was almost more than Daniel could process.

"You had a first love? Other than Mom? How come I'm only hearing about this now?"

"I don't tell you everything, you know."

"And yet you never let Becca and me get away with keeping one little thing from you."

"Father's prerogative. When you have kids of your own, you'll understand."

The ache in Daniel's chest intensified.

His dad exhaled loudly. "That one hit a sore spot, didn't it? Still sticking to your story that you don't love this woman?"

Daniel didn't answer.

"That's what I thought. So, you're facing a long, dark night of the soul, aren't you?"

"Between that and you throwing out the fact that you loved another woman before Mom, yeah, I guess I am. Are you going to tell me about it?"

"There are a couple of blankets at the foot of the couch there, toss me one, would ya? And take one for yourself. Might as well make ourselves comfortable."

Daniel handed his dad a blue knit blanket and pulled the other—a worn white one with big yellow sunflowers on it, his mother's old favorite—over himself. A pang of grief shot through him. His mother always knew how to make him feel better when some girl had broken his heart. The extent to which it had been trampled this time may have been beyond the healing power even of her homemade peanut butter cookies, but he still sure would have loved to have seen her tonight and felt her comforting arms around him.

"So, Eleanor. We were high school sweethearts. We met the first day of ninth grade and dated all through high school. By the middle of our senior year, we had started planning our wedding, and we got officially engaged the day of our graduation."

Daniel's eyes widened. "You were *engaged* to this woman?"

"Briefly, yes. That summer I went out to B.C. to plant trees. The plan was I would make a pile of money, and then come home, we'd get married, and I'd start at the Academy. Well, things took their usual course. Eleanor wrote me almost every day at first, and then the letters started to come fewer and further between. The last one, in late August, was a Dear John. She was breaking off our engagement to run away with Tommy Wilkinson."

The look on his dad's face when he said the name, like he'd breathed in some foul odor, made Daniel laugh, easing the tension in his chest slightly. "Let me guess. Tall, dark, handsome, captain of your high school football team?"

"Baseball, actually. And blonde. Otherwise you've got it pretty much right. I didn't have time to fly back from B.C. before they up and married, which was probably for the best. I might have rammed my fist down his throat, or worse, if I'd come home and seen them together."

"Yeah. I get that. Today I told Sharleen I'd really like to kick the groom's teeth in."

His dad chuckled. "Anyway, their wedding night was definitely a long, dark night of the soul for me. There've been others, of course. Kind of hard to live on this planet for very long without facing a few of them, especially in our line of work."

"Oh yeah?" Daniel yawned and reached for a pillow to stick behind his head. "Tell me about them. Unless you're tired. I don't want to wear you out, old man."

His dad waved a hand at him. "Old man," he said scornfully. "I'm not so old I can't take you, you know."

"Yeah, I know. You'd take me or break a hip trying, wouldn't you?"

"In a heartbeat." His dad's eyes lit up.

Daniel grinned at him affectionately. His dad had never been one to back down from a fight. Although he *had* let Eleanor Russell run away with another man. He sighed. Maybe the smartest fighters were the ones who knew when the battle was lost before it was fought and who bowed out gracefully. *Good thing for me.* If Dad hadn't let his first love go and ended up marrying his mom, Daniel might never have been born.

He sighed. Tonight that idea was kind of appealing.

Pop was talking again, telling another story about a rough night he'd once had at work. Daniel tried to focus, but his unruly thoughts continued to float off in their own directions, oblivious to his attempts to control them. Suddenly some of the words his dad was saying caught his attention. "What was that? What did you say about those boys?"

"Yeah, bad case. Two young boys, brothers. When my partner and I got there, the house looked like a war zone. Their mother was lying on the kitchen floor dead. Upstairs, we found the father, who had been stabbed and killed with a jackknife, and two of the most traumatized little kids I'd ever come across. One of them had been knocked out cold by his dad and left in a pool of blood. The other had been nearly choked to death." His dad stopped and shook his head. "I'll never forget those two little guys. Even bleeding and barely conscious, the older one crawled over to his little brother and put his arms around him, and the two of them sat there together, rocking back and forth, staring up at us with these big, dark eyes. When we came over to talk to them, the big brother attempted to fight us off, trying to protect the little one. Fought like a tiger, he did, even with blood dripping down his face."

His dad's features softened as he remembered. "It took both of us to calm him enough so the paramedics could take a look at him. Even then, he wouldn't take his eyes off his brother, and he wouldn't let us take him away. He became hysterical until we let the younger one go with him in the ambulance. Never saw anything like it before or since."

Daniel could barely draw a breath. He hadn't even bothered checking to see who the officers on the scene were, he'd been so distracted when he realized both Gage and Holden's profiles fit his theory. So his dad had been the one to go in and find them? Of the hundreds of cops in Toronto at the time, what were the chances of that? And what he'd said about Gage being so heroic, well, that was definitely not what Daniel wanted to hear tonight. He pressed his fingers against both temples, trying to push back a surging headache.

"Son?"

The concern in his dad's voice brought Daniel's head up quickly. "I'm okay. It's just …" He dropped his hands into his lap with a sigh. "I know that guy."

"What guy?"

"The older brother. Gage Kelly, right?"

His dad frowned in concentration. "Kelly. Yeah, that was it. How on earth do you know him?"

The look he gave his dad was one of pure misery. His dad studied him for a moment before his eyes widened. "No. It couldn't be. He's the one your girl married today?"

Daniel swallowed hard. "She's not my girl, obviously, but yeah, he's the one."

"Well, I'll be. He survived. I mean, I knew he lived, but I couldn't imagine what his life would be like. I heard he and his brother went into the system, but then I lost track of them. Kind of figured they'd end up on the wrong side of the law or something, but if he got married to a girl good enough for you, he must have turned out all right. Although …"

"What?"

"You didn't say how you knew him. Or her, for that matter. Anything to do with that big investigation of yours?"

Daniel grimaced. "You know I can't talk about that."

"Yeah, I know, but you did answer my question. Hmm. Interesting."

"How so?"

"Just … interesting. You'll tell me when it all breaks, right?

As soon as you're able to discuss it?"

"Sure, Pop. So you know, they both turned out okay. Gage is a crown attorney and Holden is a child services worker." Exhaustion suddenly pressed down on Daniel so hard he could barely lift his head. He started to push back the blanket. "I think I better head home." He yawned again.

His dad stopped him with a firm grip on his arm. "Why don't you stay?"

The thought hadn't occurred to him, but suddenly there was nothing in the world Daniel wanted more. Pop understood what he was going through, had even been there himself, and Daniel needed a little empathy right now. What he didn't need was to go home to an empty apartment. To walk through the living room, past the spot where, only two nights ago, he and Nicole had … He nodded. "Sure, I'll stay. If I won't bother you."

"Not at all. You comfortable there?"

"Yeah, fine."

His dad switched off the light. Daniel stretched out on the couch and pulled the blanket over himself, listening to the rhythmic ticking of the clock that had hung on the kitchen wall of the home he'd grown up in. As exhausted as he felt, he couldn't close his eyes. When he did, all he saw was Nicole, smiling at him, green eyes glowing, blonde hair drifting around her shoulders. Which was funny since, other than that day in front of her building, Nicole had never really looked at him that way when they were together. More often than not she'd been angry, her eyes glittering slits of emerald. Then later, she'd mostly been confused and in pain.

The La-Z-Boy creaked as his dad shifted in the chair.

Daniel winced. He'd never meant to cause her any of those feelings. What an idiot he had been to let things go as far as they had. He'd never for—

A strong hand settled on his shoulder. Daniel started, then relaxed back on the couch, a smile turning up the corners of his mouth. He may have wanted his mother when he was heartbroken or sick, but when he'd had a nightmare as a kid, it was his dad he called out for. Pop would search all around the room, under the bed and in the closet, until Daniel was assured that the monsters were gone. Then, to convince him they wouldn't return for him, his dad would pull up a chair beside the bed and rest a hand on his shoulder until Daniel went to sleep. He hadn't thought about that for years, but the sense of being safe—of being loved and cared for and not alone—that his dad's hand on his shoulder always filled him with came rushing back to him now.

With the weight of that comforting hand pushing all other thoughts out of his head, for tonight at least, Daniel closed his eyes and drifted off to sleep.

Chapter Forty-Two

Nicole's uneasiness had started out by wrapping itself around her shoulders like a scratchy wool shawl. By dinnertime it had become more like a noose, heavy around her throat and threatening to cut off her oxygen supply.

With their wedding happening so quickly, Gage hadn't been able to schedule time off work yet, although he promised he would soon. They'd spent all day Sunday locked in their hotel room but had to return home early Monday, so Gage could go to work. He'd called her from the office to say that he wanted to see her tonight so he would be coming home to eat, but only for a couple of hours. He needed to get back to meet with his team so they could go over a case they were working on.

Her stomach twisted into knots as she pulled items for a salad out of the fridge. Gage wouldn't be considering anything illegal, would he? Not two days after they had gotten married. Not when he had so much more to lose now. Nicole kicked the refrigerator door closed and set the vegetables on the counter. Of course he wouldn't. The man was a lawyer, and he had a case to work on. He was going to work late some nights. She couldn't let herself get so worked up every single time.

The apartment door opened, and she took a deep breath to settle her nerves before Gage came into the kitchen. When he pushed through the French doors, she managed a smile. He dropped his briefcase right inside the door, strode across the room, and grabbed her around the waist. Pulling her to him, he kissed her soundly. The feel of his strong arms around her pushed back her fears and she relaxed into the embrace.

When he finally let her go, a grin crossed his face. "Hi."

"Hi." Nicole reached up and pushed back the unruly curl that always fell across his forehead.

Gage caught her hand and lifted her palm to his lips. "I love coming home to my wife."

"Are you hungry?"

"Starving." He leaned in and kissed her again. "I could use some food too."

Warmth flooded her cheeks as she laughed.

Gage pressed his lips to her forehead and stepped back. "Do you mind if I have a quick shower before we eat?"

"Sure. I'll make the salad. Dinner should be ready when you get out."

"Sounds good." Gage started to push open the door then swung around to face her. "By the way, I'm expecting a packet of legal documents to be delivered here that I need tonight. If they come while I'm in the shower, would you mind signing for them?"

Heaviness settled in her stomach, but she met his gaze and smiled. "Sure."

"Thanks. Oh, and they're confidential, so don't open them, okay? That would get me in big trouble at work."

"Of course not." Nicole stood and watched the French doors swinging back and forth behind her husband until they slowed and stopped moving. Her hands felt weighted down as she turned to the counter and pulled a knife out of the block. Maybe it had been a mistake, marrying Gage so quickly. As much as she loved having him come home to her, she couldn't deal with this dread that snaked through her chest at any hint he might be doing something that would mean he might never come home again.

When the doorbell rang, the knife slipped from her fingers and clattered to the floor. *Calm down. You are being ridiculous.* After drying her hands on a towel, she headed into the living room and pulled open the door.

"Delivery for Gage Kelly?" A young man in a brown UPS uniform greeted her.

"I'm his wife. I'll sign for it." Nicole took the stylus he offered and wrote her name on the line at the bottom of the screen. "Thanks."

He nodded and turned away. She kept her gaze on him as he headed for the elevator, but he didn't look back. Biting her lip, she shut the door behind him. Nicole carried the delivery into the kitchen and set it on the counter. She picked up the knife from the floor and tossed it into the sink, then grabbed another one and returned to making her salad. Every few seconds, she found herself stealing a glance at the large yellow business envelope. Finally, she set the knife down on the cutting board with a thump. She listened carefully until she could make out the sound of water running in the shower, before edging around the counter to stand in front of the envelope.

Father, show me what to do. Nicole reached out a trembling hand and turned it over. Her breath caught. It wasn't sealed. She could take a quick look inside and Gage would never know. *Don't do it, Nicole.* The papers inside were almost certainly what he claimed they were, legal documents pertaining to the case he was working on. What if she tore the envelope, or left some other sign that she had opened it up? Even if she didn't, she would know that she had broken the law and, more importantly, his trust, by not keeping them confidential. Nicole set the envelope down on the counter quickly.

But what if they're not what he says? What if they had something to do with the abductions? He was working late tonight. It was possible that the envelope in front of her contained information that she could use to stop him from doing whatever he was planning to do, keep him from getting arrested or even killed. Nicole clenched her jaw. She would do anything, even break the law and betray his trust, if there was a chance she could protect him by doing so.

She drew in a deep, quivering breath as she snatched up the envelope, lifted the flap, and stretched the opening out far enough that she could read the first page. After a few sentences, she let out her breath in a rush of relief. They were what Gage claimed, documents filled with legal jargon. She didn't grasp most of it but understood enough to see that it was information about a case.

A door closed in the hallway, and Nicole jumped. She slid the flap down inside and dropped the envelope onto the counter.

Her heart still pounding, Nicole rounded the counter and picked up the knife again, chastising herself for her inability to let go of the suspicions she still harbored against her husband, without any kind of proof. Her teeth clenched. Why did Daniel Grey ever have to come and see her and plant these crazy doubts in her head? When the police did arrest the right man, she was going straight to him to let him know exactly what she thought of him, his shoddy detective work, and his careless disregard for the mental health and well-being of innocent people and the ones who loved them.

She brought the knife down hard on the cutting board. *Enough, Nicole. If you really want to be happy with Gage, you have to let these doubts go.* On the other hand, she could be placing them both in danger by letting her guard down and not watching for the signs that might lead her to the truth. She sighed. If only the police could track down the real perpetrator. All she knew for sure at the moment was that she couldn't live with this uncertainty much longer. Either she would drive a wedge between her and Gage because she couldn't give herself to him completely, or she would drive a permanent wedge between fantasy and reality and lose her mind. Sooner or later something would have to give.

I could ask him. Nicole grabbed a carrot and set it on the cutting board. *I'm his wife. I have a right to know if he is involved with something that might rip us apart forever.* Gripping the knife tightly, she started to chop, the blade thumping loudly against the board with every swipe.

Gage walked into the kitchen, his hair damp from his shower. "Good, they got here." He picked up his briefcase and set it on the table. After clicking it open, he grabbed the envelope off the counter and tossed it inside, then snapped the lid shut and set it on the floor.

Nicole concentrated on chopping the carrot.

"Everything okay, Nic?"

"Yeah, fine. Sorry." She started to cut again, more softly this time. Gage opened the cupboard and took down some dishes, but she felt his eyes on her for several more seconds. She held her breath until he closed the cupboard door and walked over to the table.

"Ah!" The sharp blade sliced into her left index finger. "Shoot." She grabbed for the paper towels and fumbled with them for a moment before the roll slipped to the floor.

"Here." Her husband rounded the counter and scooped the roll up from the floor. "Let me see." He tore off a couple of sheets and held out his hand for hers.

Terrified the fragile restraints holding her together would snap if he touched her, Nicole quickly turned to the sink and smacked on the tap. The cold water stung but she was glad for the pain. "I'm fine."

"Hey." Gage took her by the shoulders and turned her around. When she stubbornly refused to meet his gaze, afraid of what he might see on her face if she did, he lifted her chin with his fingers. Confusion and concern filled his eyes. "You're not fine. Let me take care of you, okay?"

The noose around her neck loosened slightly and she took a shaky breath. "Okay."

Gage reached for her hand and used the paper towel to gently wipe off the blood still dripping from the gash. After winding another one around her finger, he wrapped his hand around it and held it tight. "Better?"

"Better." Nicole gave him a weak smile. "I guess I wasn't paying attention."

His eyes searched hers. "You've been distracted since I got home. What is it?"

"It's nothing."

He shook his head. "Don't. Please. Don't pretend there's nothing bothering you when clearly there is."

Her shoulders slumped, and she leaned against the counter. Gage moved with her, his fingers still holding hers tightly. "What is it, princess?"

A stab of pain shot through her.

"Oh, baby. Come here." His voice was tender, and when he cupped the back of her head with his free hand and drew her to his chest, all the anxiety she'd been plagued with the last few weeks pushed down on her until she sagged against him, pressing her face into his soft black sweater.

After a few moments, Nicole reluctantly raised her head. A tentative smile crossed Gage's lips as he smoothed the hair away from her face and kissed her forehead. "Wait," he said. He pulled the drawer beside her open and grabbed a Band-Aid out of the box, wrapping it gently around her still-throbbing finger. He held the finger up to his mouth and kissed it. "All better."

She nodded. Gage cupped her face in his hands. "Now tell me what's bothering you."

"It's just ..." She couldn't put it into words, this dark feeling that had hovered around her for weeks now. "Gage, you wouldn't do anything that would ..."

"That would what?"

"Destroy what we have. Would you?"

The eyes searching hers hardened. "I don't know what you think I'm doing, Nicole, but at this moment, I'm holding everything I've ever wanted in my hands. Why would I do anything to put that—or you—at risk?"

Which doesn't answer my question. She tried to draw comfort from the fingers pressed against her skin, but they had gone as hard as his eyes.

His jaw tightened, as though he could read the uncertainty on her face. Or hear it in her silence. "He's gotten into your head, hasn't he?"

She frowned. "I don't know what you're talking—"

He dropped his hands. "That cop. Grey. He's planted doubts about me in your mind and now you don't know which of us to believe." His voice rose. "Don't try to deny it, Nic, I can see it in your eyes." He shot out an arm and swiped the cutting board and knife onto the floor. Carrots scattered across the tiles. Nicole gasped.

Gage pressed his fingers to his temples. "I can't stop seeing it, you and him in the diner that night. I know you said there was nothing between you, but that's a lie. I saw the way he looked at you in Starbucks last week."

His eyes had gone dark and wild, the way they had the night he had grabbed her wrist and ordered her out of his apartment. Nicole's chest tightened until she could barely draw a breath. Would it always be like this? Would Daniel continue to be a specter in the background of their marriage, overshadowing their lives? Even if Gage could move past seeing them together, they might encounter other situations in the future that sent him spiraling out of control. What if he got sucked deeper and deeper into the black hole until the day she could no longer bring him back?

Heat roared through her. No. She wouldn't let that happen. She couldn't. She grabbed his face and forced him to look at her. "Listen to me. Maybe there was something, but it's over now. I chose you. In front of God and witnesses, I chose you. And I will always choose you. As long as we are both drawing breath on this planet, I will choose you. Every day. Every minute. You never have to doubt that. Never."

The eyes that met hers still churned, but Nicole refused to look away. Gradually, calm crept into them, and the tightness in her chest eased. Gage lowered his forehead to rest on hers. "You're right. I'm sorry. I love you so much, it scares me sometimes."

Me too. "I love you too."

They stood like that for a moment, until he lifted his head. "I told you once that I would fight for us, and I will. Always. You have to trust me, Nic. Please tell me you can do that."

Nicole shoved back her apprehension as she let him go and stepped back. "I do trust you."

"Good. Then everything is going to be okay. I … I know it."

Had he been about to promise? A chill worked its way through her at the thought that he couldn't bring himself to say that word. Nicole lifted her chin. *Enough.* She'd told Gage she trusted him, and she did. She had to. She had nothing left to cling to but that. "I wish you didn't have to go back to work."

He rubbed his hands up and down her arms, as though he felt the cold that shivered through her. "So do I, but this is a big case, probably the biggest one I've handled so far. I really want to be prepared so nothing goes wrong."

"I know it's silly. But I was looking forward to spending time with you tonight."

"It's not silly. I would have loved that too. The good news is that this should be my last late night for a while. I told them I have to cut my hours a bit, and the all-night work sessions, now that we're married. I also told them I need to take time off next week for our honeymoon."

"Really?"

"Yeah. Since the diner's closed, you can get away for a few days, right?"

Nicole's thoughts whirled. What did that mean, Gage wanting to go away? That he wasn't involved in the abductions so he didn't have to stay in the city, or that he was and he wanted to lay low for a while, get out of the country, especially now that he knew Daniel had been talking to her? She straightened her shoulders, deathly tired of trying to analyze every little thing he said and did. "Yes. Absolutely."

"Good. Then why don't you think about where you'd like to go?" Gage said. "My vote is someplace tropical, although, as long as we're together, I don't really care where we are."

"Me neither."

Gage studied her. "So you're okay with me going to the office tonight?"

"I guess so, if it means we can go away soon," Nicole said. "Are you working with someone else on this?"

"Yes. Bob, Louise, and Brad."

"You could meet here instead. It would be more comfortable," she offered.

"Too comfortable. And way too distracting, for me anyway. We'll get done a lot faster if we're at the office where we have everything we need."

Tears pricked her eyes, but she blinked them back.

"Nic." His hands stilled, and he gripped her arms lightly. "I'm sorry I'm not one of those stuffy big-firm lawyers. I could have given you so much more."

She shook her head. "You're all I need. If you were one of those guys I would never see you, and no amount of money is worth that."

"I'm glad you think so. Having you in my life makes all of this worthwhile." He let go of her and bent down to retrieve the cutting board. After tossing the knife and pieces of carrot onto it, he stood and set it on the counter.

All of what? She couldn't stop the thought from flitting through her mind, until Gage pulled her to him and pressed his lips softly to hers. When he lifted his head, Nicole glanced down at the stove. "Dinner's getting cold."

His grin was wicked. "Let it. We can heat it up later." His mouth covered hers again, not as soft this time, but firm, demanding.

A deep urgency rose up in Nicole, as strong as the desire that rocketed through her system. As tired as she was of analyzing his motives, she was even more tired of feeling helpless, confused, and uncertain about what to do next. For too long now she had felt like a branch carried along on rushing water. A few weeks ago, a fork in the river had risen up before her and she'd been torn in two, not sure which direction to take. Now that she had made her decision, it was time to stop being swept along by forces out of her control.

Nicole took her husband's hand and led him down the hall to their room.

Chapter Forty-Three

Nicole bolted up in bed and glanced over at her alarm clock. 10:45 p.m. Her heart pounded wildly, and she rubbed her palm over her chest. "Gage?" He wasn't there. He must have slipped out after she'd fallen asleep. Throwing back the covers, she swung her legs over the side of the bed.

Her fingers shook so badly she couldn't button her shirt. Frustrated, she tore it off, flung it on the floor, and grabbed a sweater from the closet, pulling it over her head before stumbling down the hall to the kitchen. The food she'd prepared earlier was gone from the top of the stove. She yanked open the door of the fridge and stared at the containers Gage had stored their dinner in, debating about whether or not she could keep it down if she tried to eat. After deciding she couldn't, she shut the door again and sank onto a kitchen chair.

Ever since she and Gage had met, she'd played tug of war with their relationship. From the beginning, part of her had pushed him away and part of her had grasped hold of him tightly, trying to keep him from leaving. Nicole propped her elbows on the table and lowered her face into her hands. *Father, help me. I have no idea where my husband is or what he is doing. All I know is that I can't fight to hold on to him anymore. I'm too tired. I'm giving Gage to you. He's yours, not mine. I'm sorry I forgot that for a while. Please help me to remember that, whatever happens, you are with me.* She lifted her head. *You are with me, right?* The words were a silent, desperate plea.

No sound broke the silence in the room, but she felt the *Always* deep in her soul, and peace flooded through her. *Thank you.*

A revelation struck her. Nicole blinked at the force of it, at the belated understanding that God was the only one who could promise to never leave her. Trying to force another human being to make a vow that only God could make was like trying to hold a ray of sunshine in her fingers. Without realizing it, she'd been chasing after sunbeams for most of her life.

It was time to stop, to lift her face to the brightness and warmth and revel in them, instead of living in dread of the moment they would give way to the darkness that might someday follow.

So what should she do now? Call Daniel? What was the use of that? If Gage was at work, she'd be calling Daniel for no reason, and if he wasn't, she had no idea where to tell the police to look for him. She exhaled loudly and pushed to her feet. *I have to get out of here, or I'll drive myself crazy listening to the clock ticking and ticking and ticking.* She strode to the door, pulled on her running shoes, and grabbed a jacket and her car keys. The apartment door slammed behind her as she fled out of the building and headed to the parking lot.

For over an hour she drove aimlessly. When she changed lanes and was startled by a loud, indignant honk from the blue Forester she'd inadvertently cut off, she pulled over to the curb and put the car into park. It took her a few seconds to realize that she had stopped a block away from the police station. Somehow that didn't surprise her. On some level, she knew she had been heading this way all evening. Or maybe for weeks now. For a few seconds more, she hesitated then, sighing deeply, she pushed open the door and climbed out of her car.

Chapter Forty-Four

"Excuse me, I'm looking for Detective Grey?" Nicole clasped both hands together tightly to keep them from trembling.

The receptionist tilted her head to one side. "Do you have an appointment?"

"No."

The woman's eyes narrowed as she studied her. She reached for the phone receiver and punched in several numbers. "Sharleen? Can you come down to reception? There's someone here to see Daniel."

She listened for a moment. "One minute, I'll ask her." Holding one hand over the receiver, she raised her eyebrows. "Your name?"

"Nicole Kelly."

The woman nodded and relayed the information. "Okay, thanks." She replaced the receiver and looked up at Nicole. "Detective Roberts is coming. She's Detective Grey's partner."

"Thank you." Nicole's throat ached, and she absently rubbed her neck with one hand. Her nerves were stretched so tightly that she jumped when the door to the office opened.

"Mrs. Kelly?"

It was the woman Daniel had been with at Starbucks. Nicole took the proffered hand in her ice-cold one and shook it. "I was hoping to speak with Detective Grey."

The woman released her and nodded toward the door. "He slipped out for a few minutes. Why don't you come to his office and wait? I know he'll want to see you."

Nicole followed Daniel's partner through the office until Detective Roberts stopped at the opening to a cubicle. "Go on in and sit down. He shouldn't be long. I'm across the hall if you need anything."

Nicole managed a weak smile. "Thank you."

The detective nodded and disappeared out the door. Nicole sank down on the hard plastic chair in the corner and looked around the tiny space. The room was neat and sparse. A single photograph sat in a frame on a shelf above the computer. Too agitated to sit, Nicole stood up and walked over to see it better. A sweet-looking woman, soft, dark-brown curls framing a gentle face and smile, stood to one side of Daniel, her arm around his waist. A beautiful woman with sapphire eyes and long, dark hair splashing down around her shoulders stood on the other side of him. Probably Daniel's mother and sister.

The one who dominated the photo though, was a tall, powerfully-built man whose silver hair clearly belied his strength. It was easy to see where Daniel got his height and looks from, and to catch a glimpse of the man he would someday be.

She looked away quickly. Her gaze dropped to the one item out of place on the desk, a single piece of paper lying beside the keyboard. Nicole started to read it then straightened up with a jerk. *What are you doing?* She had taken one step back when the words on a yellow sticky note on the paper caught her eye.

Daniel, I found this in a pile of papers to be filed. Anything to do with Gage or Holden Kelly, do you think? Dot

Cold chills shivered up and down her spine as Nicole glanced behind her at the door. Biting her lip, she lifted up the sticky note with one trembling finger and read the words underneath. It appeared to be the transcript of a conversation between a police dispatcher and a concerned citizen. A note across the top reported the date and time of call, 8:30 p.m., March 15th. Nicole caught her breath. Almost four months earlier, shortly after she had met Gage. She took a deep breath and read on. An anonymous caller had phoned in with details about a conversation he had overheard in a coffee shop and thought was strange. The caller had only caught a few sentences, but each word drove into Nicole's chest like the tip of a dagger.

Woman: Everything's ready. Every day we delay means these children wait longer for someone to come and help them.

Man: I understand.

Note: The caller's cell phone went off at this point and he missed the next few minutes of conversation. After completing his call, he picked up on the end of the exchange.

Woman: You can't tell anyone about this.

Man: Of course not.

Woman: Not even your brother.

Man: If you read my file then you know my brother has had to live with the fact that he killed our father all his life. I'd never ask him to keep another secret.

Woman: I trust you. That's why I want you for this. I hope you'll help us. I really believe that you are the one to save these children.

Note: According to the caller, the man left at this point. The woman watched him go and sat for a minute more, before getting up and leaving herself.

End of report.

Nicole pressed a hand to her chest, trying to draw in a breath as she stumbled backward and sank onto the chair by the door. She dug her elbows into her knees and rested her forehead in her hands, trying to comprehend what she had read. It was true, then. The police had been right to come after her family. Not Gage, though. Holden. Relief rushed through her, dissolving the tension in her muscles. After a few seconds, fresh pain tightened them again and she pushed to her feet. She had to see Holden, had to hear from his own lips what he had done and why he had done it. If she let him know that the police suspected him, maybe he would turn himself in before someone got hurt, before any more children disappeared. Somehow, she and Gage would help him through this.

Nicole stepped to the doorway and peered up and down the hall in both directions. Seeing no one, she fled the office, ignoring the receptionist who called after her in surprise as she flew out the door and ran for her car.

Nicole stopped at the end of the walkway as Holden's front door opened and a woman with long, reddish-brown hair came out onto the porch. Holden moved into the doorway behind her. Neither of them noticed Nicole as he took the woman's face in his hands and kissed her. Nicole glanced back at her car. Should she go? Hope they didn't see her and realize she had caught them in an intimate moment? Nicole hadn't even realized Holden was seeing someone. Did Gage know? More importantly, did the woman on the porch know what Holden had gotten himself into? If not, Nicole couldn't be the one to tell her. She'd have to talk to Holden later.

She took a step in the direction of her car, but Holden's voice stopped her. "Nicole?"

Cheeks warm, Nicole turned back to face them. "I'm sorry. I didn't realize you had company. I can come back."

The woman walked to the edge of the porch, a friendly smile on her face. "No, it's fine. I was about to leave."

Holden gestured for Nicole to come to the house. When she walked up the stairs, he slid an arm around the shoulders of the woman. "Nic, this is Christina Lang. We work together. Chris, my sister-in-law, Nicole Kelly."

Chris shook her hand warmly. "Good to meet you finally, Nicole. Holden's told me so much about you and Gage."

Really? He's told us absolutely nothing about you. She forced a smile. "Nice to meet you too."

Christina touched Holden's arm. "I should go."

"Okay. I'll call you tomorrow."

"All right." She smiled at him as she started for the stairs. "Goodbye, Nicole."

Nicole lifted a hand.

Holden watched the woman until she had climbed behind the wheel of the red car Nicole hadn't even noticed was parked in his driveway. After she had pulled out onto the street, Holden propped a shoulder against the post at the top of the porch and looked at Nicole. "Christina and I have been seeing each other for a few weeks now. And no, I haven't told Gage yet. He's been a little busy, but I was going to tell him the next time I saw him."

Nicole pressed her hands together, palms sweaty. The last thing she felt like doing at the moment was discussing Holden's love life. "Does she know about you?" Her voice quavered, and she pressed her lips together to keep them from trembling.

Holden pushed away from the post. "Does she know what about me?"

"Does she know what you're involved in? What you've been doing the last four months?"

Deep lines furrowed across his forehead. "I think you better come inside." Grasping her elbow, he directed her to the door and into the house.

Nicole followed him into the living room and, when he gestured to an armchair, sank down onto it, her legs trembling.

Holden sat down on the couch across from her. "Where's Gage?"

"He's working."

"This late?" Holden glanced down at his watch. "Must have a big case coming up."

Nicole checked her watch too. After midnight. "I didn't realize it was so late. I'm sorry to come by without calling."

Holden waved away her apology. "Don't be silly. You're family. You never have to call." He clasped his hands between his knees and leaned forward. "I would like to know what you meant by what you said on the porch, though. What do you think I'm involved in?"

Nicole bit her lip. Where should she even begin? "Holden, if something was going on with you, I mean, if you were in trouble, you'd tell me or Gage, wouldn't you?"

"I guess." He drew the words out, as if he was trying to understand what she wasn't saying to him. "Do you think I'm in some kind of trouble?"

"That's what I'm trying to find out. I don't know if Gage

ever told you this, but the night he called you Luke, we talked about the deaths of your parents. About the night he killed your father."

He jerked as though an electric shock had jolted through his system. "Nic, I don't have any idea where you are going with this, but Gage didn't kill our father. I did."

Her eyes widened. "What?"

"Our dad was out of control that night. He had already killed my mom when he came upstairs after us. As usual, he was gunning for Gage. We were in the closet and he ..." Holden swallowed hard, "... he hauled Gage out and punched him in the face. Gage fell back against the bed and was knocked unconscious."

Nicole nodded. She clasped her hands so tightly that her knuckles turned white. "He told me that much. But what happened then?"

"Dad was trying to kill him. He was about to kick him in the head with his boot when I ran out of the closet and slashed his arm with Gage's jackknife. He turned on me then and grabbed me around the neck. I thought I was going to die. From what he told me later, Gage was in and out of consciousness. He could see what was happening, but he couldn't do anything about it." Two wine glasses sat on the table in front of him. Holden picked one up and drained the last few drops before setting down the glass with shaking fingers.

"Anyway, I was close to losing consciousness too. Everything started to go black, and then I managed to kick my dad, really hard, and he dropped me. I felt around for the jackknife and picked it up." Holden stopped and took a deep breath, clearly trying to push back the feelings of terror and horror he'd felt that night.

Nicole reached out and laid a hand on his arm. He didn't seem to notice, just pushed on with his story as if he needed to get it over with as quickly as possible. "When I picked it up, Gage groaned, and my dad spun around and started back toward him. I ran after him and drove the jackknife into the back of his

neck and he crashed to the ground. I didn't mean to kill him, I ..."
His voice broke. "I was trying to stop him from hurting Gage any
more."

Oh God, no. No. It's Gage. Gage is doing this. A thick fog
swirled through her head, but Nicole forced herself to listen to
her brother-in-law.

"Gage was still unconscious, and I thought he was dead too.
He didn't come around until the police arrived. When they did, he
told them that he had killed our dad. He whispered to me that the
police would arrest me if I told them the truth, so I let him tell the
story that way. We didn't understand then that kids didn't go to
jail. Years later, when I started working for Children's Aid, I read
my whole file, and it turns out the police didn't believe us
anyway, that they knew I was the one who killed him." He let out
a humorless laugh. "We hadn't thought the story out too well.
Like I said, Gage was clinging to consciousness when they
arrived, and from the extent of his injuries they knew he couldn't
have been the one to do it. The official police report in our file is
much closer to what actually happened than the statement they
took from us. We didn't even use our real names, called ourselves
Ben and Luke, like somehow that would help us."

Nicole's body had gone cold and clammy, as if life was
ebbing out of it. "Why wouldn't he tell me the truth?"

Holden covered her hand with his. "Did he actually come out
and say that he was the one who killed him?"

She scrunched up her face, trying to claw through her fear
and confusion enough to remember. "No, he didn't. He got so
upset, telling me about it, that I told him not to finish the story.
We never talked about it again. I guess I assumed that it was him.
He didn't make it sound like you were the one who had done it."

"Maybe he's lived with that story for so long he's actually
started to believe it. Or maybe he's still trying to protect me,
trying to keep anyone else from knowing the truth. Most likely
though ..."

"What?"

"I think it's always bothered Gage, a lot, that he wasn't able to save me that night, or our mom. That she died, and I easily could have while he was unconscious. There wasn't anything he could have done, but he's always felt like there should have been, you know?" Holden squeezed her fingers. "What is this all about, Nic?"

She pulled her hand out from under his and stood up. She tried to force a smile, but her lips quivered, and she couldn't quite manage it. "You know what? It's nothing. Now that I know what really happened, I realize I've made a big mistake."

He stood too and studied her face for a moment. "So you're okay?"

"Yes, I'm fine. Tired. I haven't been sleeping well for a while now."

"Do you want me to drive you home?" Holden followed her as she crossed the living room and went into the hallway.

"No, of course not. I'm okay to drive." Nicole grasped the handle and pulled the door open. "Gage will finish soon and I should be there when he gets home." She turned back and gripped his arm. "I'm really sorry to have dredged all that up for you. It can't be easy to talk about."

"Don't worry about it. Drive carefully, okay? And get some rest."

"I will." Her hand slid from his arm as she turned and made her way across the porch and down the stairs, clinging to the railing so her legs wouldn't collapse beneath her. Somehow she made it to the end of the walk and around to the other side of her car.

Nicole tugged the car keys from the pocket of her jeans and was fumbling to find the unlock button on the remote when her brother-in-law came after her.

Holden took her by the arms and turned her around to face him. "What is going on, Nic? Did something happen with you and Gage?"

"Yes. No." She shook her head, trying to clear it so she could think straight.

His dark eyes, so much like Gage's that she almost groaned

in pain, searched hers. "Is he actually at work?"

Nicole choked back a sob. "I don't know."

Holden's hands moved up and down her arms, as though willing her to calm down. "You have to give me something here, Nicole. Is my brother okay?"

She pressed her eyes shut for a few seconds, and then took a deep, shuddering breath. "I think Gage might be involved in something. Something dangerous."

His eyes narrowed. "What?"

She knew he wouldn't believe her next words. She couldn't believe them herself, although she finally understood they were the truth. "You know those kids that have gone missing the last few months?"

He nodded.

"Gage is the one taking them."

Holden started to laugh but broke off when his eyes met hers. He stepped back, his face uncomprehending, as if she'd spoken in a foreign language.

Nicole slumped against the car and waited.

After several seconds, he stepped closer to her, his jaw tight. "That's insane. Gage would never be involved in anything like that."

"I didn't believe it either, at first. A detective from Toronto Police Services, Daniel Grey, came to see me a few weeks ago. He told me the police suspected either you or Gage of taking those kids."

His head jerked. "Me? Why?"

"All of the kids were in extremely abusive situations. They believed that the kidnapper was doing it to save the kids, and they figured that it must be someone who had been in that kind of situation himself for him to be willing to take that great a risk. He'd also have to have access to CAS files so he'd know which kids were in the most danger. You and Gage fit the profile."

Holden rubbed his temples with the fingers of both hands as though he was trying to absorb way too much information at one time. Then he dropped his arms and lifted his head. "When you came here, you thought it was me, didn't you? What changed your mind?"

"I went to see Daniel Grey at the police station tonight, to tell him I thought Gage might be contemplating another abduction. I ..." she swiped at a tear that had slid down her cheek. "... I didn't want to get Gage in trouble. I was trying to stop him before he got hurt."

"And what happened?"

"Daniel wasn't there, but they let me wait in his office. I saw a note there, the record of a conversation between the abductor and the person who hired him to take the kids. She told him she believed he was the one to save those children, and asked him not to tell anyone about this, even his brother. He replied that his brother had lived with the fact that he killed his father all his life and he'd never ask him to keep another secret." Hysteria crept into her voice and she stopped and drew in a shuddering breath.

"Because I believed Gage was the one who stabbed your dad, I thought it was you. Then I got here and you told me you had done it, so I knew I was wrong. That it was Gage after all."

Holden studied her for a moment then pulled a cell phone out of his shirt pocket. "Let's start by calling him at work. Most likely he will be there and all of this will turn out to be nothing." He held out the phone to her.

Nicole didn't move.

"What is it?"

"What if he isn't there?"

"Then we'll deal with that. Together. Let's rule out the most likely scenario first though, okay?" Holden reached for her hand and closed her numb fingers around the phone. "Call him."

Nicole drew in a deep breath. At least she wasn't alone now. She had God's promise that He would always be with her, and, whatever happened, Holden would help her get through it too. And he was right, Gage would likely answer, and they could all go home and laugh about this. She tried to type in the numbers, but her fingers shook so badly she kept hitting the wrong ones. Holden covered her hands with his for a moment, to still them, then took the phone and punched in the number. Silently, he handed it to her. Nicole pressed the phone to her ear. *Please God, let him answer. Please, please.* Her heart sank when another male voice came over the line.

"Crown attorney's office, this is Robert."

"Bob? It's Nicole. Could I speak to Gage?" Her voice cracked, and she cleared her throat.

There was a slight pause before he spoke again. "Sorry Nicole, Gage isn't here. He left a few hours ago." He sounded puzzled.

"Oh sorry, I thought he was working late tonight. I must have misunderstood. I'll try his cell."

"If he does come in, I'll tell him you're looking for him, okay?"

She pressed the off button without replying and handed the phone back to her brother-in-law. "He's not there Holden. He's going after another child. But I don't know where he is, and I don't know how to stop him." The words ended almost in a wail, and she covered her face with both hands.

Holden grasped her arms again. "Nicole, listen to me."

She looked up at him.

"I still think this is crazy, but we need to try and find Gage, make sure he's okay. All right?"

Nicole nodded.

"On the off chance that all of this is true, he might have gotten instructions about where to go and when. Do you know if he got a phone call today? A text, anything like that?"

"UPS delivered an envelope to the door for him. But he told me they were legal documents. I looked inside to make sure and that is what they looked like."

"Did you see anything on them that might have been a message? A name or address? Anything?"

"I glanced at them quickly. I don't remember …"

His fingers tightened around her arms. "Think, Nic, please. Can you remember anything at all?"

She squeezed her eyes shut, desperately trying to see the top paper again in her mind. "There was a name. The people versus Gordon or Gilbert, something like that." Her eyes flew open. "Gibson. It said Gibson."

Holden's face paled in the light of the streetlamp above them. "Matthew Gibson?"

Her eyes widened. "Yes, that's it. You know who that is?"

He let go of her arms. "Give me the keys. I know exactly where Gage is."

Chapter Forty-Five

Daniel leaned back in his chair and took a bite of the doughnut, hoping the sugar hit would help wake him up and clear the fog in his brain. Sleep would be better, but he couldn't bring himself to go home yet. Not until he was exhausted enough to stumble in and go right to bed without thinking about anything … or anyone.

Sharleen had told him earlier that the team watching Holden's house last night had seen a woman come by around 8:30 and leave at 11.

"Do we know who she is?" Daniel had asked.

"They're still analyzing the footage, but no ID yet. All they gave me was…" She'd spun around in her chair and grabbed a piece of paper from her desk. "… Hot. Long, reddish-brown hair. Longer legs."

"Helpful," Daniel had said, drily. "Let me know if they manage to come up with an actual name, okay?"

The papers he'd printed off after he'd gotten the warrant to access CAS files sat in a pile on his desk. He hadn't dared use Holden's password again—he'd been lucky to get away with it the one time. With a sigh, he reached for another one and scanned it. Reading about kids in his city that were in the most horrific situations imaginable was not his idea of a good time. His stomach roiled as he worked his way through the pile, reading story after story of hospital visits, injuries, violence, and lies. He was ready to fling the whole lot across the room when the front legs of his chair hit the floor with a clang.

A picture was attached to the top of a pile of reports with a red paper clip. The face of Matthew Gibson, dark bruises on his cheeks and chest, stared up at him. Daniel fought a surge of nausea. He'd been called to Matthew's house several times. His mother was dead, and his father was a real piece of work. Arrogant and charming, he could spin tale after tale of the ways his tiny son had found to hurt himself, speaking so smoothly and eloquently it was almost impossible not to get sucked in, to start to believe every word coming out of his lying mouth. Although they almost always took him in anyway, the charges never stuck. Daniel had stopped being shocked when he heard that Matthew Gibson was back at home with his father, but he had never stopped feeling sick and frustrated at the news.

He drummed his fingers on the desk, frowning in concentration. All of the stories were horrible, but Matthew's had to be the worst. If any situation could entice the kidnapper to risk everything by going into one more home, it could be this one. He'd take Matthew's file in to his boss first thing in the morning and tell him his suspicions. Maybe they could put a team out there to watch the Gibson place too. The problem was it could be days or even weeks before something happened, and even then it was merely a hunch that this child was the next target. And the DS had made it pretty clear how much he loved acting on a hunch. Still, it wouldn't hurt to ask.

Holden would certainly know about Matthew's case. If Holden was the one passing on information, no doubt he'd have sent this file to whoever was behind the child abductions. And it did make more sense that it would be him. Especially since he'd inferred that whoever was taking the kids wasn't doing it with any intent to harm them. Daniel wished he'd had a chance to push him further on that, but they'd been interrupted at that point by—

His head snapped up. The redhead with the legs. He knew who she was. The woman who had stuck her head in the door and asked Holden about going for coffee. What was her name? Daniel made a fist and tapped it against his forehead. *Think, Grey.* Chris. It was Chris something. He'd have to check the list of social workers and see how many women named Chris or Christine worked at CAS. What had he done with that list? Was it still on his desk?

Daniel lifted the reports and a loose piece of paper slid across the surface of his desk. He reached for it and scanned the words quickly. Drawing in a sharp breath, he jumped to his feet. "Shar!"

She swiveled in her chair to face him when he stepped into her office. "Yeah?"

"It's Gage."

Her dark eyes widened. "What? How do you know?"

"This transcript. Did you see it?"

"No." She craned her neck to look around him. "Is Nicole gone?"

"Gone?" Her name still hit him like a slug to the jaw.

"Yeah, she came in half an hour ago while you were out. I told her she could wait for you in your office. Didn't you see her?"

"No. She wasn't here when I got back. Why didn't she wait for …" A chill moved through him. "Oh man. She saw this. She'll think Holden is the one taking the kids."

Sharleen lifted both hands. "Why would she think that, and how do you know it's not?"

"She hasn't read Gage's file. She mentioned to me when I was talking to her at the diner Wednesday night that Gage had killed his father. I'm not sure where she got that idea though, because according to the police report, it was Holden. And this transcript quotes the abductor as saying his brother killed his dad. I'll bet she's gone to confront Holden about this."

Sharleen folded her hands. "If we know it's Gage, should we bring him in?"

Daniel shook his head. "I don't think we have enough to hold him yet. I've been going over those CAS files, and I have a hunch I know who they might be going for next."

"Who?"

"Matthew Gibson."

Her features hardened. "That makes sense. I've often wanted to go in there and grab that kid myself, take him somewhere safe."

"Me too."

Her eyebrows rose.

"What?" Daniel asked.

"Whatever happened to, 'there's no room for vigilante justice in this country'?"

"I still believe that." Even in his own ears the words lacked conviction. "Okay, it's been a little difficult to stay so hard-lined since I put a face to this guy. I mean, Gage Kelly isn't my favorite person on the planet right now, but I am prepared to admit that might be more of a personal opinion than a professional one. I do know that what he's doing isn't right, but at least he has the courage to stand up for what he believes. And to put action behind it, even though he's risking everything to do it. That's a pretty rare thing these days. Do not quote me on this or I'll deny ever saying it, but you kind of have to admire a person like that, don't you?"

She smirked. "So what you're saying is that we can expect a little less black and white and a lot more gray from Grey now?"

Daniel rolled his eyes. "Very clever. How many years have you been saving that one? Must have been driving you crazy." He snapped his fingers. "Speaking of being driven crazy, I think I figured out who the redhead is who's been visiting Holden. Do you have your list of social workers handy?"

Sharleen pulled out her bottom desk drawer and grabbed a piece of paper. She held it out to Daniel. "You think she's with CAS?"

"Yes. The day I was there talking to Holden a redhead came in and reminded him they were going for coffee. It was pretty clear there was something going on between them. I should have thought of her when you first mentioned it." He set the sheet on the desk and ran his finger down it. Two people named Chris were listed on the page. Daniel slid to the edge of his seat. "Can you look up a Chris Washington and a Chris Lang on LinkedIn or Facebook? See if there's a picture?"

Sharleen typed for a minute. "Chris Washington is a guy. Let's try Lang." She typed again then turned the screen toward him. Daniel nodded. "That's her. Christina Lang. They must still be together. Find out what you can on her and maybe we can go see her tomorrow."

A soft buzzing sound caught his ear. "Is that your phone?"

Sharleen, still focused on the screen, waved a finger at the silent device on her desk. "Not mine. Must be yours."

Daniel patted his jacket pockets but couldn't feel the device. "Must have left it in my office. Hold on." He jumped up and strode across the hallway to his cubicle. Scooping up the phone from beside his computer, he tapped the screen as he crossed over to Sharleen's office. Four texts, the first from one of the female cops who'd been assigned to keep an eye on Gage, two from the guys who'd been sent over to stake out Holden's place, and one from Steve Simons, the IT guy. Daniel's heart rate picked up. Was this it? Was something finally happening? "Shar, I think something's going on."

She swung around in her chair. "What?"

Daniel stabbed at his phone, opening up the one from Steve. He scanned it. By the time he'd finished, his pulse was pounding. He looked up and met Sharleen's eyes. "They got Stiller. Somewhere in Turkey. Sounds like he's open to a plea bargain. Shar, this could be it. They're already assembling a team to go in. By morning we could bring down this entire organization." *And stop them from saving all those kids who are still in danger.* Daniel batted away the thought. Whatever their motivation, these people were still breaking the law. There had to be a better way.

He hit the button to read the most recent text. "Morales says a blonde woman pulled up in front of Holden's a few minutes ago." He nodded. "Must be Nicole." She'd be devastated when Holden told her the truth. Should he go over there? At least now maybe she'd be more willing to talk to him. Although, if she did know something, she couldn't be forced to testify against Gage, since he was now her husband.

That thought brought another stab of pain, but Daniel ignored it as he scrolled to the next message. "And a redhead left Holden's as Nicole was arriving. That would be Christina Lang."

Daniel hit the last text and noted the time. The one from Gage's tail had come in fifteen minutes ago. Had he been talking to Sharleen that long? Daniel quickly scanned the message. "Jackson saw Gage coming out of his apartment and followed him for ten blocks, then lost him when he drove through a red light and they had to stop for a truck that didn't stop when they put their lights on. By the time they got through the intersection, Gage had disappeared into the side streets." Daniel flung a hand in the air. "How could they lose him? Do they have any idea what's at stake here?"

"It happens. Especially if the person figures out they're being followed."

Daniel looked up. "And if he did, and purposely ditched them, that could only mean one thing—he was going somewhere he didn't want to be followed." Frustration was twisting his stomach into knots, but Daniel forced a deep breath. Getting worked up wasn't going to help him think clearly. He sent a quick message back asking if anything had changed in the last fifteen minutes then shoved the phone into his pocket. "I'll lose my mind if we stay here another minute. Let's—" His cell phone vibrated, a phone call this time, and he yanked it out of his pocket and pressed it to his ear. "Grey."

"Daniel?"

"Nicole?" His chest clenched at the distress in her voice. "What is it?"

"It's Gage. He's ..."

"What?"

"I think he's going after another child."

Daniel glanced over at Sharleen and jerked his head toward the door. She followed him down the hall. "When?"

Nicole didn't answer. Still holding the phone to his ear, Daniel passed his cubicle and broke into a jog. The silence stretched out for several seconds. She was in a car. Tires squealed as the vehicle rounded a corner. He and Sharleen reached the elevators and Daniel stabbed the down button with his thumb a few times.

"When, Nicole?"

She drew in a deep breath. "Now. Holden is with me. He thinks Gage is going after someone named Matthew Gibson."

The heavy beige doors slid open and they hurried inside. "Nicole, listen to me." Daniel spoke urgently, willing her to hear him and do what he asked. "We're called to that place all the time." The doors opened and they raced for his car. "The guy who lives there is extremely dangerous and likely armed. Do *not* go there. Do you hear me?" He yanked his car keys out of his jacket pocket and unlocked the door with the remote. Sharleen jumped into the passenger seat as he slid behind the wheel and slammed the door. His chest constricting, Daniel started the car and squealed out of his parking spot.

Nicole didn't answer.

"Nicole!"

The line went dead.

Daniel slammed the phone against the steering wheel before tossing the device to Sharleen. "Text Jackson again and tell them to meet us at the Gibson place. We'll need back-up." He shoved his foot down on the accelerator, breathing a prayer with every breath that they would get to Matthew Gibson's house in time.

Chapter Forty-Six

Gage crept around the corner of a wooden house covered in peeling yellow paint, then stopped, his back against the wall. For several seconds he held his breath, waiting to make sure that the information he'd been given about this mission was correct and no dogs or sensor lights existed on the property. Nothing moved in the backyard. A sliver of moon cast a pale glimmer of light over the trees and bushes, reflecting off the drops of moisture in the thin mist that draped like gauze over the tips of the thick grass.

Releasing a long, slow breath, Gage stepped away from the wall and looked up at the second-floor window that was his target. A small crack appeared between the window pane and the sill in the dim light. He mentally ran through the list of possible tools. They had supplied him with numerous high-tech gadgets, several of which he'd used on other missions. He studied the window again and nodded. This time he was going old school. With a grimace, he slipped a black backpack from his shoulder and set it on the ground. He crouched in front of it and rummaged in the front pocket for a moment before pulling out a screwdriver.

A rickety metal ladder hung on the outside wall of the shed in the backyard. Gage crossed the yard toward it, moving silently from bush to bush. When he reached the shed, he lifted the ladder carefully from its rusty hooks and made his way slowly across the lawn to the house. After propping the ladder against the wall, he stood on the bottom rung and bounced lightly, hoping the decrepit thing would hold both his weight and, on the way back down, the child's. Clutching the flat-head screwdriver in one hand, he gripped the sides of the ladder and started up.

When he was at eye level with the window, he balanced

himself carefully against the rungs and reached around the side of the ladder. The thin edge of the screwdriver slid easily beneath the window pane and he pushed down hard on the handle. Bits of rotted wood gave way beneath the metal. He raised the glass a couple of inches, then set the screwdriver down on the sill and slid the palms of his hands beneath the window. The wood creaked but moved up a foot. Gage held his breath. Nothing moved inside the house, and after several seconds he gave the window another shove. It opened enough for him to swing a leg over the pane.

He ducked under the window frame and pulled himself inside, dropping lightly to the floor. For thirty seconds he stayed in a crouched position, waiting for the pounding in his chest to subside. As his eyes adjusted to the dark, he could make out the shape of the child beneath the blankets.

Slowly, he stood and took a tentative step toward him, feeling carefully for any loose floor boards that might creak beneath his weight. At the bed, he stood for a moment, watching Matthew Gibson's thin shoulders rise and fall beneath the sheet. His heart squeezed. Taking a deep breath, he reached into his jacket pocket and pulled out a needle. With a quick, practiced movement, he released the air from the syringe and slid the sharp tip into the boy's arm. Matthew moaned a little in his sleep and turned over onto his side. Gage held his breath, afraid to move. After a few seconds, the child's breathing deepened and evened out, and Gage leaned down and scooped him up. Matthew's eyes didn't open, but he murmured under his breath, and Gage pressed the little face to his black sweater and turned toward the window.

He had almost reached it when the child, his eyes still closed, muttered something and flung out an arm. The small fist landed squarely on Gage's jaw. Startled, he stumbled forward a step, bracing himself with a shoulder against the window frame.

The screwdriver he'd set on the sill rolled toward the opening. Gage grasped Matthew tightly with one arm and grabbed for the tool with his free hand. His fingers closed around empty air. The screwdriver dropped from the sill and disappeared from sight, clattering against three of the metal rungs before hitting the ground below with a soft thud.

Gage froze.

Chapter Forty-Seven

"Hurry, Holden."

"I'm going as fast as I can. Getting us both killed won't help Gage." He gripped the steering wheel tightly as streetlights whipped past the car windows in a stream of white.

Nicole's heart beat frantically, the blood pounding in her ears, and she forced herself to breathe slowly and deeply. It wouldn't help Gage if she passed out before they got there either. "Who is Matthew Gibson?" She shifted in her seat to face Holden.

A shadow crossed his face. "Horrible case. He's a sweet little kid whose mother died a couple of years ago and whose dad cannot seem to keep from taking out his pain and frustration on him. We get called there all the time, and we've removed Matthew from the house a few times, but somehow he keeps getting released into his dad's *care*." His laugh was bitter. "Cases like those are the reason I think about quitting this job every other week. It's unbelievably frustrating to see something like that happening and not be able to do anything about it."

Nicole nodded slowly. "Maybe that's how they were able to talk Gage into working with them, by offering him the chance to finally do something about all the kids he sees and didn't think he could help."

"Yeah, I guess I kind of get it. I might have done the same thing, given the opportunity." He looked sideways at her. "Did you say the guy who came to see you was named Grey?"

"Yes. Daniel Grey." His name shot a pang of sadness through her. "Why?"

"He came to see me once at Children's Aid, looking for information on a guy they suspected of abducting those kids. Not

Gage though, someone else. Obviously the investigation took a different turn after that." He slammed a hand down on the steering wheel. "I really hope nothing I did or said got them thinking about Gage." He stared out the window for a few seconds, forehead wrinkled, as though trying to remember everything he'd mentioned to Daniel. "Anyway, he looked a bit familiar, and the name rang a bell, but I wasn't sure why. Nothing recent though. Like I heard it a long time ago."

"He told me his dad was a cop too. Could it have been him?"

Holden thought for a moment then drew in a sharp breath. "That's what it is. His dad came to the house that night. He was the one who found Gage and me."

"You're kidding." Nicole shook her head at the way her life and Daniel's continued to interweave.

Holden reached over and grabbed her hand. "We're two minutes away. Are you ready?"

"No."

He offered her a grim smile. "Me neither."

The sickening lurch in her stomach had nothing to do with the speed they were traveling, but Nicole reached for the door handle anyway, and held on tightly as Holden pressed his foot down on the accelerator.

Gage glanced toward the open window. The thud of feet hitting the floor in a bedroom down the hall told him what he already knew—he didn't have time to get out that way. Holding the child in his arms tightly against his chest, he leaped for the door. He was halfway down the stairs when footsteps thundered down the hall behind him and a man's voice yelled at him to stop.

Gage jumped the last three steps and sprinted across the main floor. He shifted the boy to his left arm so he could flick the lock on the front door and fling it open. As soon as he stepped outside, he waved wildly toward the vehicle parked halfway down the block. Headlights flickered on, and a dark-colored car sped toward him. In the distance, the eerie wail of a police siren broke the silence of the mist-shrouded neighborhood. The car slowed to a crawl in front of the house. The loud creak of the screen door being flung open behind him sent adrenaline coursing through Gage. The back door of the vehicle flew open. He tossed the boy into the arms that reached out for him and pounded on the roof. The door slammed shut and the car accelerated away from the curb.

Down the street, an unmarked police car, red and blue lights flashing through the windshield, flew over a crest in the road and squealed to a stop. A second vehicle pulled up right behind it. Gage started to turn toward them, and then he heard it, the unmistakable metal sliding against metal clang clang of a 12-gauge shotgun being pumped. He grabbed for the Glock pistol he had jammed in the back of his jeans and spun around, but before he could lift the weapon to fire, a deafening crack split the night air. A weight slammed into his chest. Gage stumbled off of the curb behind him and fell onto his back on the cold, hard cement.

Nicole. He didn't feel any pain, except for the sharp stab of grief that impaled his heart at the thought of the life they would never have together.

"Gage!"

From somewhere far away, he heard her scream. Fog swirled around him. Strength ebbed from his body with the blood seeping through his sweater, thick and warm. Gage lifted his head slightly off the pavement and turned toward the sound.

In the dim light of a street lamp, Daniel grabbed Nicole around the waist and pulled her to the ground. Relief flowed through Gage. *She's safe.* Holden skirted Daniel and Nicole and bolted toward him. The clang clang of the racking shotgun slashed through the night air again. *No. Stay back.* Gage tried to call to his brother, but he couldn't force sound up past the heavy weight in his chest.

Now we're not just brothers, we're blood brothers. That's even better, stronger. It means we'll always be together, and we'll always keep each other safe.

Gritting his teeth, Gage summoned the dying embers of strength left inside him. He gripped his gun in both hands, raised it, and fired at the irate father who had swung his weapon toward Holden.

The man staggered backwards on the porch and fell against a chair, sending it crashing onto its side. The shotgun flew end over end down the porch stairs and clattered on the sidewalk below.

Gage collapsed back onto the street.

"Grey! Call it in. I'll contain the shooter." Sharleen sprinted toward the house, both hands on the gun she held up beside her head.

Daniel went back to their vehicle and flung open the door. Gripping the top of the door with one hand, he reached inside the vehicle and grabbed the radio receiver.

"Control."

"This is 42. We're on the scene of a child abduction. Two civilians down. Request ambulances and back-up." He gave the address. "Another vehicle has left the scene with the child, a four-year-old male. Black sedan, license beginning with H2N. Last seen heading ..." Daniel glanced down the street where the vehicle had disappeared over a hill, heading east against a backdrop of dark sky penetrated only by hazy stars and the orange glow of city lights. In a few short hours, the sun, in a blatant affront to every person at this scene, would begin its relentless rise, parting that same stretch of sky with fingers of red and gold.

His gaze shifted to Nicole, bent over the still body of her husband. The picture his dad had painted of ten-year-old Gage, dripping with blood and fighting to protect his brother, flashed through his mind, followed by a glimpse of Matthew Gibson as he had last seen him, covered in bruises and doing his best to muster a smile. Daniel drew in a deep breath. "... west."

He tossed the receiver onto his seat and shoved the door

shut. Another police car and an ambulance roared in behind Nicole's car, sirens wailing. The red flashing lights reflected off the hazy fog, giving the neighborhood an otherworldly feel. Daniel pointed to where Sharleen crouched beside the man lying on the front porch then headed for Nicole.

Chapter Forty-Eight

The back of his head scraping against concrete, Gage turned to watch Nicole, her blonde hair streaming out behind her as she ran toward him.

Holden reached him first and dropped down beside him. It helped Gage to know his brother was there, to feel his strong fingers clutch Gage's and pull them to his chest. To have the scars on their palms pressed together, warm, damp blood mingling between their clasped hands once again. It gave him the strength to keep his gaze steadily on the woman he would always love as she drew close.

Images drifted through his mind like a movie in slow motion. He saw her in the diner that night, clutching the small gold cross between her fingers. The look on her face as she studied him the day her parents hadn't shown up, wanting to believe it when he told her he loved her for the first time. A faint smile turned up the corners of his mouth when he remembered the joy that flooded her face when she finally accepted the truth.

Those pictures faded as a vision of her lying beside him on their wedding night shimmered in the air before him. Her freckles glowed in the lamplight that caught the gold flecks in her eyes as she trailed her fingers over his chest and told him he was the most courageous man she had ever known. He clung to that apparition, lifting his hand slightly into the air, reaching for her, desperate to touch her, to feel her soft, warm flesh beneath his fingers one more time.

The images faded as a terrible cold moved through him, beginning down deep in his core and spreading all through his body. He blinked away the fog as Nicole fell to her knees at his other side. He kept his eyes fastened on her as she flickered and dimmed, as her trembling hand grasped his and held it tight, as he heard his name on her lips one last time, and as—thank God—a faint light of understanding glimmered in the green eyes he loved.

Then everything went dark.

Chapter Forty-Nine

Daniel turned off the engine of his car and sat, gripping the wheel and bracing himself for what lay ahead. For once, Sharleen was silent beside him, giving him time. When he felt fortified enough to get out of the vehicle, he drew in a long breath, released his hold on the wheel, and pushed open the door. He closed it quietly behind him and rounded the front of the car. His legs were weak, and he leaned against the hood.

His partner came around to stand beside him. The two of them gazed down the hill of lush grass, spread out before them like a calm sea. At the bottom of the slope, beneath a towering maple tree, a small group of people had gathered. Dressed in somber colors, they huddled together in front of a closed coffin. Behind the simple wooden box, a hole in the ground gaped black and empty. A shudder gripped Daniel and he crossed his arms over his chest.

Sharleen nudged him. "You okay?" Even her quiet whisper seemed a desecration of this sacred moment.

Daniel had no idea how to answer that. After a few seconds, he lifted his shoulders. "I will be. It's not me I'm worried about." His eyes sought Nicole out. She wore a simple black dress and had pulled her blonde hair up into a loose bun. Even from a distance she appeared to be shivering, although that was likely less about the unseasonably cool July morning and more about the circumstances. Connie stood to her right, clutching a small beige purse. Holden flanked Nicole on the left, his arm around her waist. *She's not alone.* The thought brought Daniel scant comfort, but he prayed it would help her get through the endless days and nights ahead.

A man stood at the foot of the coffin, holding a book. Daniel couldn't hear what he said, but he didn't envy him the task of commending the soul to God of a person who'd been gunned down in the streets, sacrificing himself to save a child. Hopefully the preacher would have more success reconciling those two truths than Daniel had achieved.

"What are you going to do?"

His partner's whispered words tore through him like an agonized scream. Did she mean in this moment or with his future? The distinction was irrelevant. He was incapable of thinking beyond the scene playing out before him. He clawed through the darkness pressing on him to find the answer. "I'm going to talk to the DS this afternoon about the night Gage …" He stopped and cleared his throat. "The night of the last abduction."

She tensed. "What are you going to tell him?"

"The truth. That I sent everyone in the wrong direction."

"Could have been a mistake, in the chaos of the moment."

He met her gaze. "It wasn't."

"You might be done."

"I know." Although he supposed he would care, at some point, today he couldn't bring himself to. "That will be up to internal affairs."

Sharleen released a long, slow breath. "I don't want to lose my partner."

Too late for that. I'm already lost. He uncrossed his arms and slid one around her shoulders. "I know. I'm sorry."

She rested her head on his chest. "Don't be. You did what you had to do."

Daniel studied the flower-draped coffin. Was the man beside it saying the same thing about Gage? That was the only way to begin to comprehend what Nicole's husband had done. Whether it had been his conscience, or his past, or his belief in a God who stood with the vulnerable and hurting—likely all three—Gage had done what he'd been compelled to do, in spite of the potentially astronomical cost.

For a few brief seconds, at the scene that night, Daniel had managed to fully grasp that. And to do what he had to do in response. As steep a penalty as he would face, gazing down at the people gathered around Gage's grave, shoulders bowed beneath their loss, Daniel couldn't bring himself to regret that decision. It gave the people who'd taken Matthew the time they'd needed. As before, the vehicle had disappeared without a trace. Gage's death had not been for nothing. Matthew Gibson was safe. Daniel hoped and prayed that knowledge would bring Nicole at least a small measure of peace.

"What about Nicole?"

He looked down at Sharleen. "What about her?"

"Will you try and see her?"

Daniel's attention shifted back to the grieving widow. "I don't know. Not for a while, anyway." The timing had been wrong for him and Nicole from the start. Would it ever be right? Only God knew.

He transferred his weight from one foot to the other. He hadn't been entirely truthful with his partner. He *would* see Nicole. From a distance. As compelled as he had been to help Matthew Gibson escape, he was equally driven to watch out for Nicole, to make sure she was okay. If he couldn't be with her, he could at least keep an eye on her. For his own peace of mind, he had to know how she was doing. And if she ever needed him, he'd be more than happy to slip into Good Samaritan mode and be there for her.

A movement at the bottom of the hill caught his attention. Daniel's chest clenched as Nicole stepped forward and rested a hand on Gage's coffin, her shoulders shaking. He forced himself not to look away, although the sight ripped out his heart. The futility of his plans struck him. He'd do what he could, assuming he wasn't behind bars, but for now, at least, Daniel had to let her go. Nicole was in God's hands. So was Matthew Gibson.

And so was he.

Chapter Fifty

Nicole stood for a long time on the first step of the diner. Snow drifted down from the pewter January sky. Icy flakes landed on her head and shoulders and slid down her neck, but she ignored the tingling chill. Her eyes remained focused on the dark sign hanging above the door. She could barely make out the letters in the dim glow of the street lamp down the block. Joe's.

She pressed her eyes shut as two tears slipped beneath the lids and trickled down her cheeks. Their warmth on her cold skin roused her and she shook her head, sending snowflakes swirling around her to the sidewalk. She opened her eyes and drew in a slow, deep breath as she pulled the set of keys from the pocket of the long black wool coat she wore. *Father, help me. Give me strength. I can't do this without you.* Her fingers shook, but she managed to slide the key into the hole. The lock slid across with a soft click, and she turned the handle and pushed open the door. The jangle of bells greeted her, bringing a sad smile flitting across her face.

Nicole reached around the doorframe and felt for the light switch. With a heavy sigh, she flipped the switch and moved back outside to watch.

The sign above the door flickered and hummed before all the letters lit up. Nicole nodded slowly and stepped back into the diner. When the door closed behind her, she took hold of the sign bouncing lightly against the glass and turned it to *Open*. She slid off her coat and hung it on the hook behind the door.

The employees she'd hired and trained arrived a few minutes later, laughing and talking loudly to each other. Customers gradually filtered in, most offering their condolences on Joe's passing and telling her how happy they were that she had opened the diner again. As they shared with her their favorite memories of Joe, and of this place that he and Connie had created, a gradual warmth seeped through her, thawing the cold ache of loss in her chest. The familiar noises coming from the kitchen—the sizzle of a basket of home fries lowered into a vat of hot grease, the clanging of silverware pulled from the racks, the clinking of mugs and glasses—although they clutched at her chest, felt right, somehow. Brought life back into this place.

Connie came downstairs in time for the morning rush. She grabbed a pot of coffee and worked the room, refilling cups, hugging old friends, and comforting everyone who expressed sorrow over Joe's loss. Across the crowded room, Nicole caught a glimpse of her laughing as she tucked a stray curl into her hairnet. The familiar gesture tugged at Nicole's heart. Yes, the diner was hers to run now, but Connie would be nearby if Nicole needed her. *I can do this.* She grabbed the two plates loaded with fried eggs and ham that the new cook slid through the window from the kitchen and headed for her table.

As the sky lightened, more and more of the old customers streamed through the door, filling the red vinyl benches. Nicole ran all morning, carrying trays loaded with bacon and eggs and sausages. As noon approached, she passed by the kitchen with a load of dirty plates. She bit her lip when the aroma of frying burgers drifted out above the swinging doors, then she pushed back her shoulders and carried the dishes over to the gray bin behind the counter.

Bells tinkled. Nicole was in the middle of taking an order from a crowded table, but she glanced over. A woman with long reddish hair stepped into the diner. *Christina.* Nicole's breath caught when Holden followed her in, his round glasses fogging as they hit the warm air. He tugged them off and their eyes met. Holden waved a gloved hand. Nicole pointed to an empty booth with her pen. He nodded and rested his hand on the small of Christina's back to guide her across the room.

Nicole finished taking the order. She clipped it to the line hanging across the top of the opening between the diner and the kitchen before making her way to the booth. When she reached it, Holden rose to kiss her on the cheek. He gestured to the packed room as he sat. "This is incredible."

"I know. It's been a little crazy. Good, though."

"You must be exhausted." Concern swam in his dark eyes as he studied her.

She shoved a strand of hair behind her ear. "I haven't had time to think about it, to be honest. I'm sure it will hit me at some point." The light above the table glinted off something and Nicole's eyes widened. "Christina!" She grabbed the woman's left hand and lifted it to examine the ring on her finger. "It's gorgeous." She shifted her attention to Gage's brother.

Holden looked a little sheepish. "Yeah, sorry Nic. We got engaged a few days ago. I was going to call you, but Christina suggested we come in today and tell you in person."

"I'm glad you did. I'm happy for you both."

Christina squeezed Nicole's hand. "Thank you. We're happy too."

Nicole let her go and contemplated her brother-in-law as she pulled out her notepad to take their order. Holden had struggled since Gage's death. For a while he'd floundered in the dark hole that had so often sucked him and his brother down into its depths. Christina had never given up on him, and between God, her, and his psychiatrist, he'd managed to break free. Deep lines grooved his forehead and he was thinner than he'd been six months ago, but the light had returned to his eyes, more so today than Nicole had seen in a long time.

She kept an eye on them as she waited on other tables and cleared away dishes. The two rarely took their eyes off each other as they ate. As crowded as the room was, they could have been the only two people in it. The tension in Nicole's shoulder muscles eased. He would be okay.

When they'd finished and paid the bill, Holden pulled Nicole in for a hug. "Take care of yourself, all right?"

She nodded. "I will."

Christina hugged her too. "Come to Holden's for dinner your

next day off?"

"I'd love to."

"Good." The warmth in her voice was genuine and Nicole smiled. She'd been so busy the last few years, between school and work and Gage, she hadn't had time to invest in making friends. It appeared as though God had brought one into her life at the moment she needed her the most. "Holden will wait on us so you can sit and put your feet up for a change." Christina winked at him.

Holden held Christina's coat for her as she slid her arms into the sleeves. "I can do that." He whispered something in her ear and she laughed, her cheeks pink.

The ache that accompanied Nicole every moment, that had burrowed itself between her lungs like another organ in her body, deepened a little. Would she ever know that kind of love again?

Nicole gazed after them as they maneuvered between chairs and disappeared out the door. A man at another table lifted a finger and she tugged the notepad from her pocket and went to calculate his bill.

By the time the supper crowd had thinned out, every muscle in Nicole's body ached. She groaned and dropped onto a stool, propped her elbow on the counter, and rested her head on one hand. Connie had headed to her apartment around three for a nap. If they were going to stay this busy, she would definitely need to hire another waitress or two. Maybe she could ask—

The door opened behind her with a loud jangle of bells. Nicole whirled around as a blast of frigid air blew into the diner. A rumpled fedora poked around the edge of the door and was quickly removed and pressed to the chest of the older man that followed it inside, wariness and hope flitting across his weathered face. "Are you open, then, ma'am?"

Nicole hesitated, then jumped to her feet and strode across the diner to grasp the handle of the door and open it wide. "Yes. We're open. Come on in."

Three other men, their clothes worn and grimy, trudged through the door after the first. The last one stopped and closed his eyes. As Nicole shut the door behind him, he took a long, slow breath. When his eyes opened, a look of pure pleasure had settled on his face. "Ah, I've missed that aroma." He patted Nicole's arm. "It smells like home."

She glanced down, expecting revulsion. Instead, an overwhelming desire to warm up the fingers that the intense cold had gnarled and twisted filled her. A revelation slowly wove its way into her consciousness, the thought that Connie and Joe had shared a secret wisdom she hadn't been privy to or had refused to acknowledge. Nicole covered the man's hand briefly with her own before nodding in the direction of the booth in the corner. "Why don't you go make yourself comfortable? I'll get you all cups of coffee. The burgers are on the house tonight, opening day special."

"Thank you, ma'am." His blue eyes twinkled as he dipped his chin to his chest.

Nicole watched him until he slid into the booth with the others. She glanced at the clock above the door. 8:02. *Right on time*. The corners of her mouth turned up as she headed to the counter to grab the coffee. Gripping the steaming pot tightly in one hand, she made her way to the back of the diner. The red glow from the stoplight on the street corner reflected rose against the glass and she stopped for a moment to gaze out the big front window. Her hand rubbed small circles over her rounded belly as she watched the cars passing by, sending mounds of slush shooting toward the curb.

As she started to turn away, something caught her eye and she looked back quickly. Daniel leaned against the lamppost down the street, his gaze fixed on the window where she stood.

Their eyes locked and for a moment, she couldn't move. Then a smile crept across her face and she raised a hand.

Daniel lifted his hand in response. A soft light fell from the lamp above him, casting a golden circle onto the glistening snow below. In its warm glow, she caught his answering smile, and the heaviness that had settled down deep inside of her six months ago—the night Gage died—lightened a little.

With a slight nod, Nicole tore herself away and walked over to the table in the corner. Bracing herself with a hand on the shoulder of the man who had come in last, she leaned in and filled all the cups with hot coffee. When she passed by the window again and glanced out, Daniel was gone.

For a few seconds Nicole stared out at the empty sidewalk, sadness flowing through her for all that might have been.

Then her hand moved to her stomach and, whispering a prayer of thanks for all that was, she went to get dinner for the boys.

Author Note

Dear Readers,

I wish I could tell you how this story came to be. I have fellow author friends who see fodder for their characters and their books in everything that happens around them. I don't look at the world that way. My stories are birthed somewhere deep inside of me. Or, to be more accurate, they are planted deep inside me by someone outside of and much greater than me. This story, like all others I have written, came to me as a gift.

At the core of *Vigilant* are two questions: As a believer, how far would you go to obey the command in God's Word to take care of the vulnerable or, in the words of King David, the weak, fatherless, poor, oppressed, and needy? And, if all legal channels have been exhausted and the least of these—especially children without a voice or the ability to defend themselves—are in need or in danger, at what point does civil disobedience become an option?

I don't have answers for you. In *Vigilant*, I propose one scenario, but I leave it to followers of Jesus Christ to decide, between themselves and God, what they might do if offered an opportunity, as Gage was, to risk everything to fight for those unable to fight for themselves.

When I ask myself how I might respond under those circumstances, the only words I can imagine saying are those that came to Gage: *Lord, I have no idea what to do. Show me.*

And I trust that, should such an occasion arise, He will.

Sara

I would love to connect with you further. You can find me at the following places:

Blog: www.saradavison.org;

Twitter: @sarajdavison;

Facebook: @authorsaradavison;

Instagram: www.instagram.com/davisonsara/

Discussion Questions

1. It has been said that grief is the price we pay for love. Have you ever guarded your heart as closely as Nicole does when she meets Gage? Why did you feel the need to do so? Did you end up taking a chance anyway? What happened?

2. Have you ever felt abandoned by someone you loved and trusted, like Nicole was by her parents? How did you deal with that? Were you able to find healing and, if so, how?

3. Think of the relationships of couples you know. What can you learn from the unhealthy relationships you have witnessed, and what lessons have you gleaned by watching a couple in a strong, happy relationship like Joe and Connie's? What would you say are the top five characteristics of a healthy relationship?

4. Can you think of anyone you know, or who you have seen, who is vulnerable and in need of someone to speak up for them? How might you be able to help? What would you have to risk or sacrifice in order to help them? Are you willing to do that? Why or why not?

5. Is there ever a situation in which a believer would be justified in carrying out civil disobedience like Gage does? Are there any Scripture verses that might justify this? Can you think of any Biblical or historical examples of people following God's law or their own moral code rather than human laws? Do you believe they were right or wrong? What happened to them?

6. How do you feel about love triangles in fiction? What do you like or not like about them? Do you believe that in real life it is possible to have strong, romantic feelings for more than one person? Has this ever happened to you? How did you resolve the issue?

7. Have you ever gone through the grief of losing someone you loved? How did you deal with that loss? What helped and didn't help you as you traveled that journey? How would you advise someone who wants to help someone else who is grieving? What should they say or not say, or do or not do?

8. Do you or does anyone you know suffer from PTSD? What helps you to deal with the trauma of your past? How can others help you as you work to find hope and healing in your life?

9. Nicole struggles with whether or not to work with the police to stop Gage from breaking the law. Have you ever found yourself in a situation where you wrestled with turning someone in to the authorities—including a teacher or a parent—in order to help that person? What did you decide? How did the situation turn out?

10. A dark night of the soul has been defined as a time of such great sadness and despair that all hope seems lost. However, it has also been said that such an experience heralds a time of change and transformation, a turning point in someone's life. Is that what happened with Daniel? Have you ever experienced this in your own life?

Now, a Sneak Peek at Book Two
of The Night Guardians Series

Guarded

Chapter One

God, help me. I can't lose him too.

Nicole Kelly choked back an overwhelming panic and forced herself to stop running, to turn in a slow circle and scan the park. Jordan had to be here. She had seen him ten minutes earlier and it wasn't like him to wander off.

"Jordan!" Heads swiveled toward her. Nicole forced a tight smile, suddenly aware that the fear in her voice was causing concern on the faces of the other parents at the park. One young mother yanked on the hand of her toddler who had been playing beside her in the sandbox, pulling him onto her lap. He responded to the interruption of his digging with an indignant holler and struggled to free himself from the arms that had tightened around his waist.

Nicole drew in a long, slow breath. Terrorizing young families wasn't going to help Jordan. She forced herself to start walking in the direction she had last seen him, over by the swings. Beyond the playground area, a small hill rose up that she couldn't see over from her vantage point. Her son was likely there, in the grassy section that widened into an open field. Her six-year-old had always been fascinated by the people playing football and throwing Frisbees to each other, and had probably become so distracted that he had forgotten to check in with her.

Nicole climbed the small slope on trembling legs and cleared the top. Holding the side of her hand to her forehead to block out the bright October sunshine, she let her eyes adjust. When they did, she could make out her son's orange jacket and Toronto Blue Jays baseball cap and her chest clenched. He wasn't alone. A man was crouched in front of him on the walkway that wound around the edge of the field, his back to her. The two of them appeared to be deep in discussion.

Anger rose in Nicole's chest, competing with the fear as she started down the hill toward them, almost at a run. When she was close enough that she wouldn't have to scream, she called out, "Jordan!"

The man in front of him rose and turned. Nicole stopped abruptly, the breath that had become ragged over the last few minutes suddenly catching in her throat. "Daniel."

A slow smile crossed his face as he lightly touched the back of her son and the two of them walked toward her. "Nicole."

For a few seconds she couldn't speak. His dark hair was a little longer than she remembered, and ruffled from the wind, but his eyes were as blue and piercing as she always pictured them whenever she thought of him. Judging from the jeans and long-sleeved navy T-shirt, he was off-duty. Or maybe he wasn't even a cop anymore. It had been a long time since she'd seen him. A lot could have changed.

Daniel contemplated her for a moment, then let out a small laugh and stepped around her son to reach out to her. Nicole hesitated before sliding her hand into his and letting the strength of the fingers that closed around hers draw out the last of the fear.

He searched her face. "You're shaking. Are you okay?"

Nicole pulled her hand away. She had no idea whether the trembling was a remnant of her fear over not knowing where her son was, or from being in Daniel's presence again after so much time. "I thought something might have happened to Jordan." She wrapped an arm around her son and pulled him to her side. "He doesn't usually go off without me, so when I couldn't find him, I kind of panicked."

Jordan kicked at a pile of leaves on the pathway. "Sorry, Mom."

"It's okay. Now."

"I found him over by the skate park. He was pretty interested in what those kids were doing. I think you might have to invest in a board one of these days." Daniel grinned.

"A skateboard? I'm still trying to get up the nerve to let him ride his bike on the sidewalk. I'm not quite ready for anything with wheels that actually leave the ground." She tilted her head. "Did you know he was my son?"

"Yeah." A sheepish look crossed Daniel's face. "I've seen the two of you in the park a few times since I've been back."

"Back?" The word clanged around a sudden emptiness in her chest. She hadn't seen him since the night she caught a glimpse of him standing outside the diner watching her. Still, for seven years the thought that he was close by had comforted her as she'd mourned the loss of her husband, given birth to Gage's son, and raised him on her own. The idea that Daniel hadn't been there after all left her feeling irrationally bereft.

"Yeah, I left town for a while."

"Where did you go?"

"London."

Her eyes widened. "England?"

Daniel chuckled. "Not quite. London, Ontario. Couldn't be that far from … my family."

So only a couple of hours away. Somehow that didn't feel much better. And what had he been about to say? "What were you doing there?"

"Two buddies of mine and I decided to try our hand at the private eye game."

"And?"

"It went well, actually. The business took off. They're still at it, but a while ago Toronto Police Services offered me my old detective job, and Sharleen talked me into accepting. We're partners again."

"So you've been back for …?"

"Six months."

And you haven't called. Nicole shook her head. Of course he hadn't called. Why would he? The last time they'd spoken, she'd broken his heart by choosing Gage over him. She was lucky he was even speaking to her now, when they'd accidentally bumped into each other in the park. Or maybe not accidentally? "So you've been watching us since you've been back?"

His cheeks colored slightly. "I prefer looking out for you, but yeah, I guess I have, off and on."

"How did you stay out of sight?"

He offered her an indignant look that was so clearly feigned she had to press her lips together to keep from laughing. "Might I remind you that I am a professional detective? I can blend into any surroundings so well that, unless I chose to reveal myself, you would never know I was there."

"Clearly. So why haven't you talked to us before now?"

He sobered. "I wanted to give you time."

Her smile faded. "Daniel, it's been almost seven years."

"Six years and ten months. Believe me, I know." The sadness in his voice tugged at Nicole's heart. Neither of them spoke for several seconds, until she glanced at her watch. "I should get Jordan home. He has a friend coming over in a few minutes."

"Okay if I walk with you?"

Nicole nodded. "Sure."

They turned and headed in the direction of Nicole's condo, at the far end of the park and across the street. Jordan pulled away from her grasp and ran ahead of them.

"Stop at the corner, Jord," Nicole called out after him.

"I will."

She shook her head as her son veered off the path, chasing a squirrel until it disappeared up a tree before making a wide running arc in the direction of the sidewalk, his arms out to the sides like an airplane.

"He's a great kid."

"Thanks. I think so." Nicole tore her eyes from Jordan and looked up at him. "You really are a great detective. Except for the night I re-opened the diner, I haven't seen you once."

"Well, I've seen you. And you're a great mother."

Warmth flooded her chest. "Thank you. That means a lot. So what made you finally show yourself?"

"I saw Jordan alone and figured you'd be worried, so I thought I'd bring him to you."

"What made you think I'd be worried?"

Daniel looked down at her and smiled.

Nicole stopped walking.

He stopped too and turned to face her.

"I guess I don't usually let him get too far away, do I?"

"Not from what I've seen. Not that that's necessarily a bad thing. It's wise to be careful."

"But you think I'm too careful."

"I didn't say that." Daniel lifted both hands in the air. "I'm not a parent. I'm not about to give advice. I can imagine there are lots of things for a mother to worry about, especially when she's raising her child …"

"Alone?"

He sighed. "Yeah."

Nicole turned and started walking again and Daniel fell into step beside her.

"I know I can be over-protective. It's just that Jordan's all I have left of …"

"Gage. I know. I really do understand that, Nicole. And it's okay for you to talk about him with me."

The muscles across her shoulders relaxed. "Are you happy to be back with police services?"

"Sure. It's where I always wanted to be, working the super-hero thing, on a perpetual mission to rid the world of evil."

"Oh yeah, I always think of you when I see the bat signal in the sky at night."

Daniel laughed. "I wish. I'd love to have some of the toys he gets to play with. And the black cape is pretty cool."

Nicole bit her lip. She hadn't realized until she saw him again how much she'd missed him. They came to the edge of the park. Jordan stood waiting for them on the corner. "Well, I'm glad you finally came out of hiding. It's good to see you."

"Again, I prefer 'surreptitiously observing' to hiding, but thank you. It's good to see you again too. Up close, I mean, not from behind a bush or while peering around a corner wearing a disguise."

Nicole giggled. "What kinds of disguises did you wear?"

"Oh you know, I like to keep it simple. Sometimes it was a moustache and thick glasses combination. Other days I'd wear my blond wig and brown contacts. The best was the nun's habit, though. That was even better than my old police uniform to make everyone straighten up and behave themselves."

Nicole burst out laughing.

"What's so funny, Mom?" Jordan trotted over and stood at her side, looking back and forth between them.

"Detective Grey was telling me about some of his undercover work."

Jordan swung around to look at Daniel. "Undercover work? That's cool. Do you have a gun?"

"Jordan!"

Daniel smiled. "That's okay." He crouched down in front of Jordan again. "I do carry a gun when I'm working, but not when I'm off-duty, like I am now."

"Can I see it sometime?"

"If it's okay with your mom. Maybe the two of you could come over for dinner one night and I can show you."

"Can we, Mom?"

With both of them looking at her expectantly, Nicole didn't have the heart to say no. "Sure, Jord."

Daniel pushed to his feet. "How about Thursday?"

"That would work. Tuesday and Thursday are my nights off from the diner." She looked at him and wrinkled her nose. "Which I guess you already know."

He shrugged. "You do keep a pretty regular schedule."

"I have to. Between running the diner and being a single mom, it makes things easier if I know what's coming."

"I can see that. Of course, sometimes surprises are good. They keep life interesting."

"They do that." Nicole lost herself in the blue eyes that probed hers. An insistent tugging on her sleeve finally got her attention and she looked down.

"Alex is coming. We have to go."

"Right, okay." Nicole took a deep breath as she held out a hand toward her son.

"Mom, I'm six. I don't have to hold your hand anymore. I can cross with the lights."

Nicole could feel Daniel's eyes on her. She exhaled loudly and dropped her arm. "Okay, fine. But don't run." She watched him until he reached the other side of the street and jogged to Alex and his mother before she shifted her attention to Daniel.

"I guess I better go too."

He nodded. "See you Thursday? Six o'clock? I kept my apartment here, so I'm at the same place."

Her stomach twisted. The place she'd last seen him, where she'd kissed him goodbye. How would it feel to walk into his home again? "Sounds good." She started for the crosswalk then paused. "Daniel?"

"Yeah?"

"Thanks for watching out for us."

"You're welcome. It's been fun. I'm kind of going to miss the skulking, actually."

Nicole grinned. But as she crossed the street after her son, the grin faded, and she pressed a hand to her abdomen. What had she done? Agreed to open up the Pandora's Box she'd shut the lid firmly on a long time ago? Not very smart. Surprises were all well and good, but there was a fine line between life getting interesting and life spiraling out of control.

A line she'd crossed seven years earlier and had no desire to go anywhere near again.